A PATRIOT'S DREAM

DREAM

THE RESTORATION

KENT THOMPSON

ISBN: 9781088186398

Printed in the United States of America

This book was produced and published in partnership with Ballast Books, LLC.

www.ballastbooks.com

We love to partner with new authors and bring their books to life. For more information, please email info@ballastbooks.com.

TABLE OF CONTENTS

Cast of Characters. i

Prologue: Deadwood, South Dakota. v

Chapter 1: Mogen Compound – The Black Hills of South Dakota
– Present Day 1

Chapter 2: China Lake Naval Testing Range August 29, 2002. T-4
HALO – Black Dragon – Initial Manned Test 9

Chapter 3: Mogen Compound – The Black Hills of South Dakota .15

Chapter 4: Arlington, Texas. 19

Chapter 5: NSA Fort – High Performance Computing Center 2
– Meade, Maryland 29

Chapter 6: The Black Hills – South Dakota 33

Chapter 7: Rapid City Regional Airport – South Dakota. 39

Chapter 8: Mogen Compound – The Black Hills of South Dakota .45

Chapter 9: Rapid City, South Dakota 51

Chapter 10: NSA Fort – High Performance Computing Center 2
– Meade, Maryland 57

Chapter 11: Undisclosed Location – Dallas, Texas 63

Chapter 12: Justine Residence – Arlington, Texas 67

Chapter 13: Mogen Compound – The Black Hills of South Dakota .73

Chapter 14: NSA Fort – High Performance Computing Center 2
– Meade, Maryland 83

Chapter 15: Mogen Compound – The Black Hills of South Dakota. . .87

Chapter 16: Mogen Compound – The Black Hills of South Dakota . .93

Chapter 17: CIA Headquarters – Langley, Virginia 105

Chapter 18: Northwest Wyoming Coal Mine – Outside of
Gillette, Wyoming. 107

Chapter 19: Arlington, Texas 109

Chapter 20: Lockheed Martin "The Lighthouse" – Suffolk, Virginia . 111

Chapter 21: Mogen Compound – The Black Hills of South
Dakota 115

Chapter 22: NSA Fort – High Performance Computing Center 2
– Meade, Maryland 123

Chapter 23: Colonel Allan North Residence – Dallas, Texas 127

Chapter 24: Mogen Compound – The Black Hills of South
Dakota 133

Chapter 25: Justine Residence – Arlington, Texas 143

Chapter 26: Springhill Suites – Moore, Oklahoma. 147

Chapter 27: Justine Residence – Arlington, Texas 151

Chapter 28: Lowery's Restaurant – Arlington, Texas. 155

Chapter 29: Justine Residence – Arlington, Texas 161

Chapter 30: Mogen Compound – The Black Hills of South
Dakota 163

TABLE OF CONTENTS

Cast of Characters. i

Prologue: Deadwood, South Dakota. v

Chapter 1: Mogen Compound – The Black Hills of South Dakota
        – Present Day 1

Chapter 2: China Lake Naval Testing Range August 29, 2002. T-4
        HALO – Black Dragon – Initial Manned Test 9

Chapter 3: Mogen Compound – The Black Hills of South Dakota .15

Chapter 4: Arlington, Texas. .19

Chapter 5: NSA Fort – High Performance Computing Center 2
        – Meade, Maryland. 29

Chapter 6: The Black Hills – South Dakota 33

Chapter 7: Rapid City Regional Airport – South Dakota. 39

Chapter 8: Mogen Compound – The Black Hills of South Dakota .45

Chapter 9: Rapid City, South Dakota 51

Chapter 10: NSA Fort – High Performance Computing Center 2
        – Meade, Maryland 57

Chapter 11: Undisclosed Location – Dallas, Texas 63

Chapter 12: Justine Residence – Arlington, Texas 67

Chapter 13: Mogen Compound – The Black Hills of South Dakota .73

Chapter 14: NSA Fort – High Performance Computing Center 2
– Meade, Maryland 83

Chapter 15: Mogen Compound – The Black Hills of South Dakota. . . 87

Chapter 16: Mogen Compound – The Black Hills of South Dakota . . 93

Chapter 17: CIA Headquarters – Langley, Virginia 105

Chapter 18: Northwest Wyoming Coal Mine – Outside of
Gillette, Wyoming 107

Chapter 19: Arlington, Texas 109

Chapter 20: Lockheed Martin "The Lighthouse" – Suffolk, Virginia . 111

Chapter 21: Mogen Compound – The Black Hills of South
Dakota 115

Chapter 22: NSA Fort – High Performance Computing Center 2
– Meade, Maryland 123

Chapter 23: Colonel Allan North Residence – Dallas, Texas 127

Chapter 24: Mogen Compound – The Black Hills of South
Dakota 133

Chapter 25: Justine Residence – Arlington, Texas 143

Chapter 26: Springhill Suites – Moore, Oklahoma. 147

Chapter 27: Justine Residence – Arlington, Texas 151

Chapter 28: Lowery's Restaurant – Arlington, Texas. 155

Chapter 29: Justine Residence – Arlington, Texas 161

Chapter 30: Mogen Compound – The Black Hills of South
Dakota 163

Chapter 31: The #10 Saloon – Deadwood, South Dakota 171

Chapter 32: NSA Fort – High Performance Computing Center 2
– Meade, Maryland 177

Chapter 33: Rolling Hills Country Club – Arlington, Texas 179

Chapter 34: Mogen Compound – The Black Hills of South
Dakota – Late Saturday Afternoon 183

Chapter 35: Just Outside of Ellsworth Air Force Base
– Rapid City, South Dakota 195

Chapter 36: Ellsworth Air Force Base – Rapid City, South Dakota . . 201

Chapter 37: Outside the Mogen Compound and Rapid City,
South Dakota 211

Chapter 38: Ellsworth Air Force Base Tarmac – Rapid City,
South Dakota 213

Chapter 39: Minot Air Force Base – North Dakota 217

Chapter 40: NSA Fort – High Performance Computing Center 2
– Meade, Maryland 221

Chapter 41: FedEx #1 B-1B Bomber Nearing Drop Zone for CIA
Headquarters – Langley, Virginia 225

Chapter 42: CIA Underground Satellite Operations Center
Outside Washington, D.C. 237

Chapter 43: Mogen Compound – The Black Hills of South
Dakota 243

Chapter 44: Home of Retired Master Sergeant Jack Ellis
– Rapid City, South Dakota 247

Chapter 45: Mogen Daughters – Texas 251

Chapter 46: CIA Underground Satellite Operations Center
Outside Washington, D.C. 263

Chapter 47: Minot Air Force Base – North Dakota 265

Chapter 48: Mogen Compound – The Black Hills of South Dakota . 267

Chapter 49: CIA Underground Satellite Operations Center
Outside Washington, D.C. 271

Chapter 50: Minot Air Force Base – North Dakota 273

Chapter 51: CIA Underground Satellite Operations Center
Outside Washington, D.C. 277

Chapter 52: Minot Air Force Base – North Dakota 281

Chapter 53 287

Chapter 54 297

Chapter 55 299

Chapter 56: CIA Underground Satellite Operations Center
Outside Washington, D.C. 303

Chapter 57: Lake Mary Road – Mogollon Rim – Central Arizona. . 307

Chapter 58: Minot Air Force Base – North Dakota 313

Chapter 59 315

Chapter 60 319

Chapter 61: Lake Mary Road – Mogollon Rim – Central Arizona. . 327

Chapter 62 : Creech Air Force Base – Command Center – Nevada . 351

Epilogue: Capital of the Western Southern Alliance of States
– Arlington, Texas 365

Acknowledgments 371

CAST OF CHARACTERS

John Mogen	Main character (militia colonel); sixty years old
Jaylynn Mogen	Wife to John Mogen; fifty-eight years old
Kayla Lynn Mogen	Younger daughter of John Mogen; twenty-eight years old
Jessica Jo (Jesse) Mogen Tryon	Older daughter of John Mogen; thirty years old
Dave Tryon	Married to Jessica Jo, son-in-law to John Mogen
Libby Tryon	Daughter of Jessica and Dave, niece of John Mogen; seven years old
Caleb Tryon	Son of Jessica and Dave, nephew of John Mogen; ten years old
Carl Justine	Brother of Jaylynn, brother-in-law to John Mogen, uncle to Kayla Lynn and Jessica Jo; Retired Air Force colonel
Mary Ann Justine	Wife to Carl Justine
Arlington Colonels' Club Members	Allan North – Retired Army colonel; West Point
	Bill Musgrave – Retired Marine colonel
	Carl Justine – Retired Air Force colonel
	Torger (Torg) Vigdahl – Retired Navy captain; Annapolis
	Chris Kendall – Navy commander – SEAL logistics, NSA

NSA Connections	Samuel (Houston) Hudson – Node supervisor
	Gloria Baker – Research/data collection
	Luke Anderson – Domestic connections lead
	Henry (Bulldog) McLaughlin – New researcher; Retired captain
CIA Connections	Nathan Parkinson – Luke Anderson's contact
John Mogen's Team	Steve Lunquist – Pastor to John and Jaylynn; wife is Susan; Rapid City, South Dakota
	Jack Ellis – Sponsor (AA) for John Mogen – Mentor
	Jason Wilder – Communications; owner of IT business; retired Air Force Special Forces staff sergeant
	Jason Wilder's Team – Protectors
	Daniel Rodriguez – Air Force Special Forces
	Eric Thompson – Former SEAL
	Mark Buckley – Air Force Pararescuer, former Special Ops
	Matthew Van Sharrel – Former SEAL
	Truen Walsh – Air Force Special Forces, overwatch, high cover
	Zachariah Overgaard – Former Marine sniper
RED Cell – Black OPS Group	Bob Richards – Colonel – Commander of Minot AFB – Old friend of Carl Justine
	Jim Henry – Commander – Special Forces – Ellsworth AFB
Politicians	Paul Carbajal – U.S. Senate, Texas
	Ted Gosnor – U.S. House, Arizona

FBI Agents	Molly O'Keefe – Field office supervisor in Rapid City, South Dakota
	Agent Jefferies – Senior agent based in Rapid City, South Dakota
	Agent Backtow – Junior agent based in Rapid City, South Dakota
Creech: Drone Pilots	Gomez, Lewis, Roden, Kappel
TV Interviewers	Pete Heidleman, Lea Gabella, Greg Kellerman

FBI Agents	Molly O'Keefe – Field office supervisor in Rapid City, South Dakota
	Agent Jefferies – Senior agent based in Rapid City, South Dakota
	Agent Backtow – Junior agent based in Rapid City, South Dakota
Creech: Drone Pilots	Gomez, Lewis, Roden, Kappel
TV Interviewers	Pete Heidleman, Lea Gabella, Greg Kellerman

DEADWOOD, SOUTH DAKOTA

TWO YEARS BEFORE RETIREMENT

John and Jaylynn Mogen were sitting in the Black Hills Real Estate office on Main Street in Deadwood, South Dakota. They lived in Houston, Texas, and for the last two years, they had spent all their summer vacation time in the Black Hills of South Dakota looking around for a place to retire. However, this trip was different. It was a serious "find that place" kind of trip. Their ideal location would be at least five miles out of the main downtown area, and it had to be at least twenty acres of land with a good building site. They wanted a year-round stream, some large rock outcroppings, and John's trees. He had to have pines and aspens if at all possible. They didn't want flat land. They had had enough of that in Texas. John had grown up in a small town in northeastern Wyoming just sixteen miles from the South Dakota border, and he had always loved the Hills.

The realtor laid out several printouts of available properties. One of them caught John's eye. The price was higher than they'd budgeted, but he was fixated on this property. It was part of a ranch that was being subdivided into mostly twenty-acre parcels, except this one was one hundred acres. It had an old ranch house that was barely livable and a newer barn with living quarters above and stalls for horses below.

The realtor noticed John had picked up the ad more than a few times. "I know it's more than you want to pay," he said, "but it has it all—everything you're looking for. I thought we could take a look at it. It just might be a possibility. The property has two wells with great gallons per minute (GPM) numbers." As John and Jaylynn continued to look over the listing, the realtor continued. "I'm not one who tries to steer my clients to a specific property, so take your time and look at the five in front of you. Let me know which ones you would like to drive out to and in what order. I'll give you time to look over them, and then I'll set up the appointments with the owners. How about we start out in the morning as early as you would like?"

John and Jaylynn proceeded to pore over the listings sitting on the desk before them. They'd been looking on their own, but evidently, this subdivided ranch had just hit the market. They saw two parcels on the ranch they wanted to look at—one being the one-hundred-acre parcel. The pictures looked amazing.

After stepping out into the waiting room for ten minutes to check his phone messages, giving them time to consider their choices, the realtor returned to his office. By then, John and Jaylynn had developed a plan. "Mark, we want to see this one-hundred-acre parcel first. How soon can we take a look?"

The realtor was a little surprised they wanted to check out that parcel since he had thrown it in knowing it was a stretch for the maximum amount they wanted to pay. "Let me make a call, and we can find out."

Mark pulled out his cell phone and dialed a number. John and Jaylynn could tell from the realtor's side of the conversation that they might get out there this afternoon.

"Okay, guys," said Mark enthusiastically after ending the call. "They already have a multi-list lock on the gate, so we can head out right now if you're up to it. We won't be able to get inside the buildings, but we can peek in."

John and Jaylynn stood on a huge granite rock outcropping looking over the property as Mark worked to get a handle on the property lines. The pair couldn't stop smiling. They would have to compromise some on the house they planned to build, but this was it. They didn't have to look any more. When Mark drove up in his SUV, he said he had a handle on the property lines, and he could show them. As they drove around the site, they became more and more excited.

John wanted to get this locked in now. "Mark, we would like you to get an offer ready for us to sign by tomorrow if you can? We want to start with an offer of 75K less than the list."

The realtor was a little taken aback. Hesitating, he stated back to them, "Okay, you two. You want this property without looking at any more—is that what you are saying? If so, I'll get busy and see what we can do. We should be able to get an offer in by tomorrow, no problem."

John thought he'd made himself very clear. "Yes, Mark. We know what we want, and this is it—let's move on it!"

ONE YEAR FROM RETIREMENT

John and Jaylynn had been working with a log home company out of Idaho ever since they had purchased the property a year ago. As they headed south on Highway 385, they caught up with a truck with Idaho plates hauling a load of some beautiful logs. They followed the truck until it turned off on the road that took them to their property. As it pulled into their gate, Jaylynn squealed about how immense and gorgeous the logs were.

It was early March in the Black Hills. The sun was shining off the five inches of snow that had fallen the night before. It was already up to forty degrees, and the snow had started to melt. The weather in South Dakota this time of year, especially around Deadwood, was a crapshoot for sure. However, this day was spectacular!

They couldn't believe how many tarps the contractor had just removed so they could start stacking the log walls. The foundation with a partial basement was completed, and they had the first course of logs set. It was amazing to see their dream coming to fruition!

John was anxious to get this completed before their retirement next year. He and Jaylynn had felt the need to get out of the city and move to a place away from what they sensed was the coming chaos. As Christians, they believed a time of testing was on the horizon. John was deep into what had been a lifelong study of the republic and how the forces he knew were evil were attempting to destroy it. He didn't know what to do. He and Jaylynn were escaping to South Dakota, but the path the country was on was causing him to lose sleep at night.

The design of the house in the Hills and the last big offshore platform project he was in charge of was coming to an end. Maybe he could find peace in the Black Hills. All the stock options he had taken advantage of and all the money he and Jaylynn had worked hard to invest had paid off. Their dream of retirement was at hand. Maybe—just maybe—John Mogen, the engineer, the project manager, could finally relax. Jaylynn, a geophysicist who had been consulting by evaluating seismic data for other companies, was ready to call it a career also.

A slight breeze came up, and John could hear the wind in the pines and smell their distinctive scent. Snow drifted out of the branches and sparkled in the sunlight as it floated by. The trees took on a special color of green against the white snow. The contractor was showing the progress they had made and asking questions to a distracted John, who was in awe of the beauty God had created. He felt at home here. He and Jaylynn were so ready to begin this life—so ready. No more summers in Houston.

Just hang on for one more year, he told himself.

As they drove away, their emotions were a mixture of elation and wonder at God's creation and excitement to be moving in by this time next year! Jaylynn would have that wraparound porch she always wanted, and they would sit and watch the great Black Hills sunsets with the dogs at their feet and the wind whispering in the pines, telling them they were finally home. Dreams can come true. They were blessed beyond measure!

John still felt that they were somehow escaping something that would eventually catch up with everyone in the United States, no matter where they escaped to. But they were ready. He had his '68 Ford F-100 4WD. They already had one year of emergency food supply. The solar array and battery backup were ordered, as was the wind generator. The three one-thousand-gallon propane tanks as well as the propane-powered generator were purchased. They had water wells that they would add solar power to. They did still need to install a water holding tank. The few head of cattle and chickens would come after they got settled.

John had been proactive his entire career. It just didn't sit right with him to complacently wait for the worst-case scenario to hit this country he loved. Yes, their dreams were coming true, but he was still troubled—troubled to the deepest part of his soul. What could one man do though? What could one man do?

Jaylynn glanced over at John and sensed his melancholy. She softly reminded him, "One more year, John—one more year."

CHAPTER 1

MOGEN COMPOUND — THE BLACK HILLS OF SOUTH DAKOTA — PRESENT DAY

As John sat staring at his computer screen, a sudden sadness enveloped him. He was looking at the red state-blue state map of the United States. The sadness was the realization that his country was, at least in his mind, irrevocably broken in two. The progressives or human secularists or whatever you wanted to call them had won. The founding fathers, who had pledged their lives, fortunes, and sacred honor and had made that "leap" into a constitutional republic, had to be spinning in their graves at about fifteen thousand revolutions per minute!

As he watched the sunrise break over his beloved Black Hills, the six-foot-two, 230-pound man began to cry at his desk. The country, the republic he had held so dear, was being systematically destroyed—dismantled by the progressives who worshipped government instead of God and wanted elitist control over individual freedom.

John literally jumped in his chair when Jaylynn's hands grabbed his shoulders. She was seldom—if ever—up this early. Comforting him with her words, she said in a soothing tone, "I know, John—I know."

If you have been married—I mean, really married as in the two shall become one flesh—you know that you develop senses that work outside the normal list of five. Jaylynn had awakened with a start as if something

1

wasn't right with her universe, and she'd somehow understood that John needed her. Not a general "I need you in my life" need but an anxious and immediate need for her presence at his side. As soon as she saw what was on his screen, she recognized why she was required.

John got up from the computer and turned to hold her. Other than his dark brown hair and linebacker build, he resembled the country singer George Strait and had been mistaken for him often. John, the man in her arms, was not one to sit and cry at his computer—this was serious. "I think I am going to take a walk with the dogs," John finally said as he released his embrace that had gone on for much longer than their normal body-against-body greeting.

"First, I need to show you another map...the map that displays the most religious states." As she sat down at the computer, Jaylynn actually felt wetness on some of the keys, which made her even more upset about what was troubling John this morning.

John saw the pattern immediately, and it only heightened his realization that it was definitely two separate countries now. Unfortunately, he saw no way to stitch it back together short of a religious revival of epic proportions. As Jaylynn looked up at him, he questioned, "What in the world can anybody do to turn this around? This has been going their direction for over one hundred years, and now they have control."

Jaylynn's green eyes flashed as she spoke. "John, you are Christian man. We both know that God is in control, and we best not forget that! The question is: What is God leading us to do about it?"

Jaylynn's correction hit John hard, and he knew she was right, of course, but his frustration about this country and where it had been taken was consuming him. How could a couple of just retired engineers living in the shadow of the Black Hills help turn the country back to the Constitution and, more importantly, back to God?

"John, snap out of it and think about what you did when you were in charge of that offshore building project. You developed a plan—a design. You put a team together, then you executed the plan step by step!" Jaylynn was waiting for a response, and John knew it.

"Okay, Jay, okay. But this is just a little different."

Jaylynn tensed up a little more. "John, if you are looking at it as a problem to solve, don't make it rocket science. Just write down an outline of what needs to be done so you can figure out the first step and get going. Sitting at your computer and staring at a screen is not helping!"

Now, John's intense expression shifted as a smile brightened his face. "I love you, Jay."

Jaylynn grinned back. "I love you too. Just do something because you scare me when you act like this. Write a book or something for heaven's sake! But right now, I'm getting dressed, and we are going for a walk with the dogs."

John's smile grew wider still. "You have never seen what this place looks like in the early morning. You will love it!"

"Shut up and get the dogs ready—and stop being mean to me."

John was laughing a little too loudly when he walked away to get the dogs. "Sadie, Lilly, are you ready? Walk?" The two yellow labs heard the magic word and were at the ready.

"So, John, what's your plan?" She always did this—she always pushed him when he wanted to just go to his nothing box for a while.

John was going to put on the dogs' leashes but decided to just let them run on their own and try to keep track of them.

"Stop it," he said as if that was going to end it.

Jaylynn had grown up in Texas. Not just in Texas but on a ranch in Texas. She was as tough as she was beautiful. Jaylynn Justine was five feet and nine inches tall with vibrant green eyes that captured everyone's attention when they first met her. Her silver hair, olive skin, and perfectly symmetrical face with model looks made her the queen of every rodeo she was in. Years in the sun were etched in her face but somehow did not detract from her beauty. If a woman ever looked like she belonged on a horse, it was Jaylynn.

Although she had just turned fifty-eight, she did not have an ounce of fat on her body, and she was stronger than you could ever imagine. When she jumped on John without notice and locked her legs around him, he might as well have been in the grasp of a giant boa constrictor. Even though John outweighed her by one hundred pounds, he literally had to take her to ground to get away—if he felt like it. When she did put on a dress and throw on some makeup, she could hush a room full of people. Her green eyes flashed as bright as her smile. She was every bit a woman but also every bit his equal intellectually, even though she was an aggie. She thought she was his match physically. Okay, he lost at tennis but always reminded her that he was bigger than her and could hold her down and lick her face.

The first and last time she challenged him to really do this, he didn't hesitate, and it caught her off guard. She was quickly on her back on the floor screaming. John went from licking to nibbling her neck, and then things got a tad more physical. Since that first time, she had continued with the ritual by ambushing him from behind, nipping his neck, and whispering, "So, you think you can hold me down and lick my face? It's nothing but foreplay, John, and like it!"

Thirty-five years of wrestling and still going strong. Other couples were amazed at how John and Jaylynn had never stopped playing.

"Jay, you know what we've allowed our country to become? It keeps me up at night." They were now walking on the path up behind their home surrounded by huge pines.

Jay's reply was a quick counterpunch. "John, the question is still the same—what is your plan...what is *our* plan?" John noticed the change in pronoun immediately. "We are divided by geography—sort of. By those who desire to follow the supreme law of the land and those who don't. By those of us who believe in God and the divine providence that created and protects this nation and those who believe the state is god. And, finally, by those who believe our rights are God-given and not allowed by the state. It's clear by the maps that the west, or at least the Mountain West, and the south are of a specific bent and need to do something to restore the Constitution or separate."

John was a little stunned by how Jay had articulated the problem and solutions.

"I am from Texas, so I say we separate!" Jay announced.

John smiled at her. "You're out of your mind."

Jaylynn was into this now. "I am not out of my mind. We need some sort of alliance of states."

"Some sort of alliance of states from the west and the south—like a Western and Southern Alliance?"

"Yes, John, the WSA."

"Oh, God, another acronym…I feel like I'm back at work in the oil business!" John replied, but Jay was undeterred.

"We just need to figure out how to do this."

Suddenly, John remembered that the Civil War had killed more Americans than any war the United States had been involved in. An estimated 620,000 soldiers had died. "Yes, Jay, we just need to figure out how to do this as the Christian people we are. How many people need to die in a civil bloodbath to get this done?" As they reached the edge of the meadow where the creek wandered into it, the dogs took off and headed for the creek as usual. Jaylynn was still incessant.

Jay was into this big time. "A coup, John—a bloodless coup like the progressives have pulled off."

John had thought about that and, yes, there were those who were already working on restoring the republic, but wouldn't it take generations to accomplish? "We don't have one hundred years to do this, Jay!" John complained.

"Okay, John. Let's plan a really *fast* bloodless coup."

John smiled again. "You *are* completely out of your mind!"

Jay reminded him that he had already said that to her. "John, you're writing a book, remember? Just do some research and see if there's a way to pull it off."

"You're killing me, Jay!" That was John's way of saying back it down a little.

"John, just call Carl. He's a retired Air Force colonel for heaven's sake. Maybe he can think of something." John was mortified at the thought of calling Jay's brother and asking something like that. As usual, Jay could tell what he was thinking just by his expression. "John," she sighed, "Carl won't mind. He's of the same mindset on the state of the country, and besides, wasn't he involved in some advanced weapons systems he couldn't even talk about?" The Mogen's had nearly completed their walk, the house was in sight. The dogs sprinted ahead since they knew a treat was waiting for them when they got back to the house.

"And still can't, Jay. Even though he's retired, he still has an obligation to maintain security about things still classified," John reminded her.

Jay was getting frustrated with John. He was letting this consume him without doing anything about it. At least the writing could give him a Walter Mitty daydream kind of satisfaction about the whole thing and also be an outlet for his angst!

"Okay, I'll call him," she said, "but you're going to talk to him. And then, you are going to sit down and start writing our way out of the mess this country is in." Little did she know that this particular morning would alter their retirement plan more than she could have imagined.

John's reply was only, "Where are the dogs? Where on earth are those dogs? SADIE! LILLY!"

John had convinced his Texas-born wife that they needed to retire to the Black Hills of South Dakota. She'd fallen in love with the area as soon as she saw it. The winters would be hell, but the rest of the year and the natural beauty of the area made it all worth it.

Their dreams had been realized when they'd first laid eyes on their one hundred acres. It had a year-round creek, a seventy-five-GPM domestic well with the sweetest water you could imagine, and trees—the beautiful Ponderosa pines and aspen that John loved so much. There was an old homestead that was still habitable on the land. A newer barn built with reclaimed wood, large enough for living quarters on the upper level, stood close by. When they'd traveled to the compound during the build, they'd stayed in the two-bedroom loft. It housed a full kitchen, a bathroom, and a wood stove.

The land also had the old original bunkhouse with some "upgraded" WWII metal bunks. It could sleep eight if some more mattresses were thrown on the empty bunks. There was an old wood stove in the middle of the large open room, which might stay above freezing in winter if some of the obvious cracks in the walls were plugged. Jaylynn wanted to tear it down, but John had refused. It was history. It had no bathroom, but it did have an outhouse next to it that Jaylynn had refused to even look in!

They'd moved into their log home last year, just before winter had set in, so this was their first spring in the Hills. The design of their home had been a collaboration between the two of them, finishing up at 3,700 square feet with four bedrooms, each with their own bathroom, and a great room to die for. It opened into the kitchen—straight out of the Pinterest posting Jaylynn had taped onto her bathroom mirror a couple of years ago.

They would sit on the second-floor deck off the master bedroom in the morning and have coffee. Then, they'd watch sunsets on the wrap-around porch in the evening. It was a lot of hard work, but their retirement dreams had been fulfilled. They were blessed beyond measure. Jaylynn would plant her garden in the one-hundred-by-thirty-foot area they had enclosed with an eight-foot-high fence to keep the elk out. They had all they needed.

CHAPTER 2

CHINA LAKE NAVAL TESTING RANGE
AUGUST 29, 2002.
T-4 HALO – BLACK DRAGON
– INITIAL MANNED TEST

The weighmaster came on the radio and declared, "Captain, we are loaded and ready to take off."

Captain Carl Justine was nervous about this test flight. He and Sam, the pilots, were just the Air Force delivery boys, but he still felt an extra responsibility since this was the first manned test. They'd had their security clearances upped just to look at the damn thing and the specs they needed to help the weighmaster figure things out. This was not their normal low-altitude parachute extraction but rather a high-altitude pushout. As they went through the engine startup of their C-130 Hercules Cargo aircraft, the Navy SEALs were simultaneously going through the preflight on their *Black Dragon* sitting in the cargo bay. Flimsy—just flimsy—was all Carl could think to describe the little black submarine sitting in the cargo hold of his aircraft.

Carl was snapped back to reality as the lieutenant sitting in the copilot seat started through the preflight check. With all four turbines whining and brakes squeaking, they turned onto the runway for their takeoff run.

The naval officer in charge of this test flight had them in a hold while he communicated with the Navy SEALS and the contractors responsible for the device in the back. They finally got the call.

"HERC, are you guys ready for takeoff?"

Carl was used to dumb questions (as was everyone in the military) and had gotten over giving snarky responses. "Affirmative, Test Control," he replied in his serious pilot voice.

"Cleared for takeoff. Climb out per specifications in the test manual, sir."

Carl was trying not to laugh and guessed the control voice had to be that of a nineteen-year-old. "Affirmative," is all he said as the prop pitch changed and dug into the air as the C-130 headed down the runway.

At test altitude, when they were ready to make the run, Carl asked for the weight of the object in the back again. The weighmaster replied, "3,100 pounds plus 381 pounds of frog legs, sir. Less of a jolt than a Humvee release, sir."

"Sergeant, comms are being monitored and recorded, so I think you meant 'Frogmen,' right?"

"Ahhhh yes, Captain. I meant to say Frogmen—sorry, sir."

Carl knew what the sergeant was doing but felt he needed to correct him for the record, although the sergeant might still get his ass kicked depending on what mood the SEALs were in today.

"Sir, we will be at the drop zone in thirty minutes."

Carl turned to his copilot and replied, "Thanks, Sam. I also have confirmation that the recovery team is in position offshore."

It seemed like a lifetime had passed before Test Control relayed the order to commence with the drop on their mark. The weighmaster replied in the affirmative while Carl and Sam prepared for the change of weight and center of gravity as the load left the aircraft.

Carl made the final call. "Altitude and attitude correct. Airspeed correct. Sergeant, make the drop."

An affirmative came from the cargo bay, and ten seconds later, they felt the aircraft jump in the air a little as the weight left the bay. The Pacific

Ocean below them seemed extra blue today, and the Catalina Islands really popped.

"Sam, make the right turn and make sure to execute it according to the manual. The cameras need to track based on that turn and airspeed." Carl knew Sam had all the procedures down but was still talking for the test log.

Sergeant Castillo, who was the smart-ass weighmaster in the back, sounded a little less routine as his comms broke in. "Sir, we have a problem. The drag chute deployed, but one of the main temporary wings stayed in while the other three deployed."

Carl knew what this meant. "How bad is it, Sergeant?" he asked, hoping for an answer that might be a surprise.

"Sir, they are in a hell of a spin! One of the SEALs released and was hit by one of the wings, and now that wing is broken and flapping. He's free-falling, sir. Looks unconscious. I'm quickly losing sight of them, sir."

It was Carl's responsibility to quickly make the call. "May Day, May Day, package has malfunctioned. Track and recover. Track and recover." Even though he knew Test Control was hearing this, he had to make sure they realized the problem was a serious malfunction. The other SEAL had to detach or die!

"Son of a bitch! Can't get detached—too much centrifugal force! Knife—knife, cut the section that is material. Cut it—cut it." As the SEAL remained safely tethered to the mini submarine, the centrifugal force caused a near blackout and would not let him unhook, but he never stopped fighting to get free. He summoned all the strength he had to get his knife and cut the safety belt.

Luckily, he was thrown clear before being hit by a spinning wing. He quickly went into skydive mode, and as soon as he was in stable flight, he did a 360-degree turn to look for his teammate. No luck. He did another 360-degree turn on the vertical plane and spotted his buddy below him. From there, he went into a falcon dive at full speed, reaching him at five thousand feet and realizing he was unconscious. The only thing to do was deploy his buddy's chute and then follow with his own. As the chutes popped, the spinning mini submarine overhead shot past them, no less than a hundred feet to the left.

The SEAL took a deep breath and then emitted a long string of profanity that would be recorded as part of the test log for posterity. He cussed the Navy, he cussed the contractors, and then he questioned his own sanity. Everyone on the channel understood and did not interfere.

One thing that defines SEALs is their ability to stay in the fight, and he'd done that along with saving his buddy. Another characteristic of SEALs is their uncanny ability to remain calm under fire—in very stressful situations. Because of this, his tirade ended quickly, and he immediately started giving a detailed account of what had happened and the condition of his buddy—as much as he could discern. He did this while concentrating on steering his chute to land as close to his buddy as possible, double-checking that his wrist GPS was giving coordinates for recovery so medical assistance could happen fast. He knew Seahawks were standing by and would be airborne soon—if they weren't already. He was hoping his buddy would not drown before he got to him. He didn't know if the rigid inflatable boats (RIBS) were close.

Carl and Sam were ordered to return to China Lake and unload all remnants of classified hardware, contract personnel, and Navy personnel. Since fuel was not an issue, they were then instructed to return to Vandenberg Air Force Base. There, they would be debriefed by naval personnel from Naval Air Station Point Mugu the following day. They were also reminded that the stop at China Lake was not to be discussed. At least they knew that both SEALs were still alive based on the last radio transmission they'd heard, but they would never know if the one who had been hit by the wing would make it through his parachute landing or what the extent of his injuries would be if he lived.

Carl never enjoyed his crossovers into the black world, especially when they came down like this. It was usually pick up, fly, drop, and return or continue to another base. No knowledge—no concerns. This one was different—this one made him want to move up to a major rank and get out of flying except maybe to give check rides and help with training.

He would never forget the SEALs who had attempted to ride a mini sub with temporary stealth wings. If all had gone according to plan, they would have proceeded with a very low-altitude parachute opening and dropped into the ocean slow enough to just kiss the water. After 9/11, there was this crazy push to apply stealth technology to everything the Department of Defense (DoD) could think of. This was one of those hare-brained ideas that got people hurt. Carl was mad but at least had time to cool off as he drove home to Santa Maria.

As Carl opened the front door, his wife, Mary Ann, asked how his day had gone and if he had flown, which was their customary greeting. He grabbed her and held her a little tighter than normal as he said, "I flew with Sam today, and I think nobody got killed."

Mary Ann broke the embrace and held him at arm's length so she could look into his eyes. She knew him and recognized something about today was different. She had gotten used to him saying he had flown and the flight had been good. She hated when he added *and no one got killed*, but today, he had changed it a little. "Why did you say you don't think anyone got killed?"

Carl hadn't even realized he had changed his usual line. "I can't talk about it. I just can't talk about it—secret stuff."

Mary Ann absolutely hated it when this happened, but at the same time, she knew it was for her safety as much as his and their country's. She still despised not being privy to knowledge that was affecting her husband, but she stepped back into his arms and said, "I think it's time to become a major and fly a desk."

Wow, what a smart lady he had married. The next year, Carl would be a major but would still be flying. Only this time, it would be in the Middle East supporting the invasion of Afghanistan.

CHAPTER 3

MOGEN COMPOUND — THE BLACK HILLS OF SOUTH DAKOTA

"Carl, how are you and Mary Ann?"

"We're fine, Jay—because we live in Texas. When are you and John moving back down here?" Carl and Jaylynn had had this same conversation ever since she and John had retired to South Dakota. "I really don't want to hear that my sister has been found frozen to death in a snowbank!" Carl just had to keep giving her a bad time about not living in Texas, knowing she and John loved the Black Hills too much to ever leave. "What's up, big sister? Do you want to talk to Mary Ann?"

Jaylynn took Carl's ribbing, knowing he meant "older" when he said "big." She ignored the little brat and got straight to the purpose of her call. "Carl—John is extremely upset and is consumed with the appalling state our country is in. He really needs to talk to you."

Carl was taken aback by what the call was about. "If I had my way, Texas would be seceding right now. Let me talk to John." Carl knew that John was a student of U.S. history and of the U.S. Constitution, so this was important to both of them. Unbeknownst to John, Carl had been consumed with what to do about the situation as well.

When John got on the line, he hesitantly started talking. "Hi, Carl. This is a little silly, but I have decided to write a book about how to restore our republic before we lose it completely, and I have a theory about how to do it that I want to run by you if you don't mind?"

Carl was all ears. "What's your strategy?"

John jumped right in. "A constitutional restoration coup is my thought, Carl. We just need a big stick, or sticks, in the right place, and then we can clean house and start over with a separate alliance of states that will become the new republic that actually follows the United States Constitution." There was a pause. Carl had vapor locked. "Carl, are you there?"

"Yes, I'm here," Carl replied cautiously. "But slow down a minute, cowboy, and tell me what your big stick would be in this scenario."

Realizing he had Carl's interest at least, John continued. "Nuclear devices set in six or seven liberal cities on the coasts and maybe Chicago with handlers for the devices and failsafe systems to protect them or a detonation will occur."

"Last time I went to church with you two, you seemed like the true Christian my sister married for God's sake!" Carl said with a bit of sarcasm in his voice. "And how, pray tell, are you going to acquire these devices, put them in place, and then protect them as your big stick?"

"That's why I called you, Carl—so you could tell me how this could be done." Carl was silent again. "Geez, Carl, I'm talking about writing a book. Are you okay? Remember that 620,000 soldiers died in combat during the Civil War. I have a real concern we are at the beginning of a second civil war, which would kill a lot more people, and I believe my idea would prevent that."

"Let me call you back in an hour, John," was Carl's only response.

John wasn't quite sure why Carl seemed so shaken about him asking for ideas to write his book. "Okay, Carl. Thanks. Remember, we are just talking about writing a book here. Fiction, Carl. Fiction." As the call ended a few minutes later, thoughts of what he had just heard swirled in his head.

Mary Ann was gazing straight at Carl who looked like he was a thousand miles away and deep in thought. Carl's head snapped around and their eyes met as Mary Ann spoke. "Is everything alright? Are John and Jay okay? Did something happen to their kids? You look like you have the weight of the world on your shoulders or something worse. Please talk to me, Carl! ... That's it—I'm calling Jaylynn."

Carl seemed to calm himself. "Don't call Jaylynn. John has decided to write a book about taking our country back from the crazies in Washington. He just wants some ideas about how to do it peacefully."

Mary Ann and Carl had discussed this and the fact that it might take generations to accomplish. She asked, "And how does he want to start this takeback exactly?"

"Nuclear devices placed in cities around the country," Carl answered in a doubtful tone.

"I thought you said he wants to do it peacefully for heaven's sake!" Mary Ann was now as upset as Carl seemed to be.

Carl reminded her as John had reminded him, "He's writing a book—just a book of fiction. A catharsis for John if you will."

Carl had an ache in his stomach, and his mind was about to overload. Every synapse was firing as things went swirling through his mind. *My God, this is what they had all been on the lookout for—"THEE PATRIOT"* patriot—and it had come from the most unexpected source. How could he even consider what John and Jaylynn would go through if he even thought of involving them—much less Mary Ann, who knew absolutely nothing about it?

Carl recalled John's mantra when they would talk about the miserable state of the country. "Exciting times, Carl. For such a time as this, we were put upon this earth. It is our time and God's time." He would say this with a confidence of faith that made Carl feel like he had lost his mustard seed. John's faith seemed gigantic, and his own faith was maybe the size of an electron right now.

Carl's integrity was colliding with his love for his sister and her husband, and he didn't know how to make the call to set up the meeting, but he found himself on his cell phone. "Allan, this is Carl. We need to set up a golf game... We may have a new player."

Retired Army Colonel Allan North was the guy who had originally gotten the colonels' foursome started. The four were like-minded. All had been forced to retire, and they all knew it was because of how vocal they had been about the state of the military and things that had been coming out of Washington that made no sense. The rule of law was being ignored, which was a most dangerous thing. Decisions were being made that were so ridiculous that the people who were making the pronouncements were either complete idiots or they knew what they were doing and it was the most nefarious plan ever being pulled off on the American people. The officers left in the military would do anything they were told without question in spite of their oath to the Constitution of the United States.

The colonels' golf group knew they could only discuss things away from all electronic devices that might catch anything they were saying. Mary Ann had questioned Carl about why none of them carried their cell phones during their rounds after she had tried to contact him. Carl had matter-of-factly stated it was so that the National Security Agency (NSA) wouldn't be able to get access to their conversations.

"Sure, Carl," Mary Ann had replied. "I'm sure that NSA is interested in the conversations of four old bulls out munching on those disgusting cigars and looking for their balls."

"Very funny, Mary Ann—very funny!" Carl had responded. He'd been relieved she didn't buy his reasoning at all and didn't bother to ask a follow-up question because he had told her the truth and gotten away with it.

CHAPTER 4

ARLINGTON, TEXAS

Colonel North understood the coded message Carl had just sent him and was eager to hear about the new golfer that might fit right into their group. "I'll get us a tee time for tomorrow as early as I can, Carl. Let me call the club."

"Thanks, Allan. Just text me the tee time." Carl's stomach was really in a bind now.

Carl remembered he'd told John he would get back to him within the hour. So, he sent John a text letting him know that he needed at least twenty-four hours to do some research on the question. John responded by thanking Carl and reminding him not to stress out about a book he probably wouldn't even get started on anyway.

Carl was so anxious the next day as the club were tying their golf shoes and preparing their equipment that Colonel Allan North took notice. "Geez, Carl," he said. "You're not getting married—we're just playing a round of golf for God's sake!"

"We've been looking for the right civilian to be our figurehead in all this, and now my brother-in-law calls me out of the blue with a plan that could make it happen. So, yes, I am a little jumpy."

"Okay, Carl, quiet down. We aren't on the course yet, and you know the rules! Are you talking about the brother-in-law that retired from the oil business... You mean, Jim?" Allan asked.

"His name is John, and he was in the oil business, but now and he's writing a... I'll wait 'til we get on the course."

Carl was deep in thought. The report of the first tee ball sounded like a shot, and he physically jumped back into the reality of the situation. How could he approach John with this—how could he tell Jaylynn that it would be alright?

"Carl—wake up, for God's sake. It's your turn. Let's go!" said Colonel Bill Musgrave who had been forced out of the Marine Corps when he'd refused to allow his men to go through transgender sensitivity training. His refusal had been long and laced with expletives only known to a few of the most accomplished swearers.

Bill's propensity to swear while being a faithful churchgoer and a professed Christian was a paradox he didn't seem to understand or give a rat's butt about. The other three in the group had actually had a meeting about Bill and decided to acquiesce to his flaw because of his actions since his retirement—mentoring young Marines returning home with post-traumatic stress disorder (PTSD) and even allowing some to stay in his home for a time. He made himself available twenty-four hours a day to take their phone calls and find counseling for these young men. They were all sinners after all. Carl still attempted correction, but Bill was Bill, and he would die that way. Even so, Carl had had Bill on his prayer list to correct this shortcoming for at least ten years.

The Arlington Colonels' Club always sat on a lone picnic table that was about one hundred feet off the club's restaurant deck. It sat under a huge red oak tree, and after their round of golf, they would have their lunch in the shade of that oak. Of course, they would blame Carl for the bombing run every time an acorn hit the table.

The wait staff was not unhappy about the walk to this table but instead had a rotation schedule printed out in the kitchen just to be sure they all got their chance to serve the colonels. The tips received were legendary, and the arguments between staff ended when this schedule was posted every Wednesday.

Today was not the Arlington Colonels' Club's usual day to play, so the argument began as soon as the round ended. In fact, the club pro had to actually intervene and appoint the server taking care of the deck to also take care of the colonels.

The group waited until their lunch order had been taken and the server had left to get another pitcher of sweet tea to discuss Carl's possible candidate.

Taking a serious tone, Allan North said, "Okay, Carl, tell us who you have in mind for a possible patriot leader." Allan knew who Carl was referring to but decided to let him make the case as if he weren't aware of the person being recommended.

"Okay, men. I have a brother-in-law whom I think I have talked about—the guy who was in the oil business. John Mogen. He called me last night to ask about how to get nukes into several large cities so they could be used as a *big stick* to execute a coup—a bloodless coup—and take our government back. This is the plotline in a book he is writing."

The looks on the faces of the other three expressed bewilderment, enlightenment, and excitement all mixed together. Torger Vigdahl, who was a retired Navy captain, came to his senses first and said, "Carl—this is your sister's husband, so do we even want to consider this?"

The table erupted instantly with conversation to the point that Allan had to do something he very seldom did. The others heard the knock of his ring on the table over the noise of the conversation, and quiet ensued.

"Why don't you stick that ring up your ass so far it glows in your right eye at night!" Bill certainly had a way with words but still understood the respect the ring engendered whether he liked it or not. Bill had not gone to an academy, and neither had Carl, but the other two had. Allan had attended West Point, and Torger had gone to Annapolis.

Allan smiled at Bill, who already regretted his comment, and reminded everyone that time was of the essence since a conservative Supreme Court Justice had been assassinated in their state, and the country's God-given rights were at stake—the republic was at stake. Then, he asked, "Carl, can you tell us about John?"

Carl's mind filled with years of stories and experiences about his brother-in-law, and he realized very quickly John was perfect for their assignment. His head was spinning with thoughts he had to get under control.

"John is a retired petroleum engineer who ended up heading up some huge offshore platform development projects. He just recently retired and lives in South Dakota with my sister, Jaylynn. They have been married for almost thirty-five years. They have two children, both daughters. John looks the part, and he stays in shape by running and lifting weights. He was a linebacker in college and still looks like he could put on the pads and hurt a running back! When John has a three-day beard and an axe in his hand, he looks like he was sent by central casting. In his forties, he had issues with alcohol, but he has been clean and sober for at least twenty years. His passion is the United States Constitution and the Federalist Papers. John can discuss and/or argue this with anyone, including college professors. He's tough physically and mentally, and most importantly, he understands that this country is out of options, especially since we can no longer expect a fair election that has not been tampered with. The book he is starting to write presents one audacious strategy that we have actually discussed, sketched out a plan for...and dismissed."

Carl was a little shocked by what he had just said about his brother-in-law. He had always liked John but had never realized how he had underestimated him and his abilities. John had always treated his sister with love and respect, even through the challenges with alcohol. His love for Jaylynn had caused him to never take another drink. John wasn't perfect, but he was a Christian man that got up every morning and tried to do the right thing, just like Carl did.

Colonel Allan North broke the silence. "Carl, we all know you understand that this is your sister's husband and they and the rest of their family will be in danger if we bring him into this."

"I understand that more than you could ever know," replied Carl. "But I trust John with my life and know he has the will to do what is necessary. He has a poster on the wall above his desk that talks about pledging lives, fortunes, and sacred honor to secure our God-given rights. The more I think about it, the more I know he is our guy!" Carl's heart and respiration rates were both elevated now. He felt like he did when flying through hostile airspace when he got to captain the C-130 they called Spooky. The chills were going up and down his spine and occasionally meeting in the middle.

Carl almost jumped out of his skin when the server asked, "More sweet tea anyone?" He wondered how long she had been behind him and what she had heard. However, he suddenly realized a facial expression from one of the others at the table was letting him know she had just walked up.

When she was halfway back to the deck, Allan began again. "Okay, gentlemen. This is not the first time a possible candidate for our militia colonel has been put forward, but this one feels different. Let's go ahead and query our contacts on their possible readiness of this plan. Do we have the people? The parts? Equipment? Remember, no phone calls, no emails or texts, only face to face in a secured location. Carl, what is the closest base to where John and Jaylynn live?"

"Ellsworth AFB," replied Carl. There was a noticeable gasp at the table.

Allan continued, "Torger will visit the harbor. Bill..."

At that point, Bill broke in. "Yes, Allan, I'll head to Sonora Pass in the morning. What are you going to do other than give us orders, Allan?"

Allan smiled at Bill and answered, "I'm going to see if I can buy ten of the biggest Caterpillars I can find—are D-12s the biggest? In the meantime, Carl, you need to touch base with Ski in procurement and find out what progress she has made in securing ordnance."

"What is our code name going to be? Any ideas, Carl?"

Carl immediately had a code name. "John has always had the dream of being a cowboy, and now he and Jaylynn ride almost every day and plan to actually buy a few steers this year. He hasn't quite figured out how to keep his hat on yet, but he is working on it. Let's call it 'Cowboy Up'!"

Torger Vigdahl was a man of the sea and the city and didn't have a clue what Carl was talking about, even though he lived in Texas. "What exactly does 'Cowboy Up' mean, Carl?"

Carl laughed when he realized that if you hadn't been raised in the country you might not know the term. "Well, Torg, it means to make a determined effort to overcome a formidable obstacle. If you get bucked off, you get back on and ride that horse, no matter what. You know, in the SEAL creed, it says, 'Never give up,' and we are 'never out of the fight.' It's that kind of thing."

"Got it," said Torger. "I like it. Plus, it means nothing to anyone in particular and won't trigger NSA geeks."

Torger and Bill excused themselves as they got up from the table. The sense of urgency was palatable, and they just had to get going. Allan was staring at Carl, and Carl knew what he was thinking. "I'm sure he is someone we can trust, Allan."

Allan responded, "This plan is back on the table. Once this plan 'has a go,' there's no backing out. We have to go big, and we have to go fast. They won't be ready for it, and we need a code word or phrase from John that only Jaylynn will understand and know it's from John and no one else." All nodded their heads in agreement.

"What on earth are you going to do with Caterpillars, Allan?" Carl queried.

"Ten Caterpillars—ten really *big* Caterpillars. Hannibal's elephants, Carl, Hannibal's elephants. Size and surprise, Carl, size and surprise!"

Carl still didn't get it, but he knew Allan had taught military tactics at West Point, so he would wait for Allan to reveal what he was doing. "How are you going to pay for these, Allan?"

"I have a connection—a black hole connection. You know the black ops money that has no restrictions on it. Remember, Carl, those who want to restore this republic within our military are not a small number. The biggest challenge is to keep it quiet until we can execute it. I assume you will be flying to South Dakota?"

"I'll be landing in Rapid City tomorrow if I can get a flight." Carl spoke as he and Allan got up and began walking toward the parking lot. For a moment, they stared at each other with a knowing look that they both understood. As they shook hands, they knew this was it and they had to move fast but run quietly through the forest. One snap of a twig, and they could all be compromised. They knew the four of them had been watched and listened to since they had retired. John was another story, and they needed to keep him off the radar as long as possible.

"See what John has done so far—what he has searched for on the computer when you get there?"

As if Carl had to be told this, but Allan had to say it anyway. "I'll find out as soon as I get there, Allan."

Carl's hands were sweating as he called to make flight reservations. Mary Ann was taken aback by his insistence that they needed to travel to South Dakota so he could talk to John face to face about his book.

Likewise, Jaylynn looked a little puzzled as she ended her own phone call. John had overheard her say, "Okay, Mary Ann. We'll pick you up at the airport in Rapid City at 10:30 in the morning." She started to talk before John could get his question out. "Carl and Mary Ann are flying up tomorrow and need us to pick them up at the airport. He wants to talk about your book in person."

John was already feeling some regret about getting Carl involved in this whole thing, so he resolved to get something accomplished in the research department for this book before Carl called back. He hoped to have an intelligent conversation about how to get some nukes into cities without detection or at least have them in place so fast that nothing could be done about it. He was thinking about parachuting down nukes with retired Navy SEALs or retired Air Force Pararescue guys out of Commentative Air Force bombers from WWII that were showcased at local air shows. Earlier, he had typed in a search for something the Navy SEALs might have to get their little subs in the water. The search he'd put in was "*dragon rider SEAL subs parachute.*" He'd thought of dragon rider from the movies he had watched with his grandson.

"Good Lord, Jay, they don't have to fly up for this! This isn't a classified operation. It's just an idea for a book! I need to call them back and tell them it isn't that big a deal and they shouldn't spend money on plane tickets."

"John, Mary Ann said Carl needed to talk to you as soon as possible. She also said Carl doesn't want you to do any research on the internet about how to pull this thing off. Don't you think that seems a little strange?"

John got loud now and said again, "We are talking about writing a book here, not actually pulling off a coup! What is everybody so uptight about?"

Jaylynn just stared at him with that look she got when she had some sort of epiphany. "John, what if Carl is involved in something we don't know about and what you are doing might jeopardize that?" Jaylynn had a sparkle in her eye now. "He has a lot of connections and has said out loud that we are very close to needing to take up arms to save the republic!"

"Jaylynn, you need to stop the wild speculation right now. I don't know why Carl feels the need to come up here on short notice, but I am not going to let my imagination run rampant. I already did some searching on the internet before you told me not to do it, but I can explain it as research for the book and nothing else."

Jaylynn was in a state of excitement now and, of course, did not listen to John's rant about wild speculation. "John, we have to tell Carl exactly what you searched and why. Let's sit down at your computer, and I'll write down the search history for Carl so we can show him what you have done."

By this time, John had had enough. "I'm going to saddle the horses, and we're going to ride to the top of the ridge. You need some uncontaminated air in your lungs so you can start thinking straight!"

"I'm right behind you as soon as I get these websites written down."

John's hands gently began to massage her shoulders. Bending forward, he started kissing her neck and nibbling her earlobe as he breathed a little deeper and exhaled into her ear. Boy, did he know how to distract her! When he slid his hands down to start the underarm tickling, she grabbed his wrists and put his hands under her arms to cover her breasts.

She squealed with delight as he lifted her out of the chair. Her body was covered with goosebumps and was reacting in that way she couldn't control. The man knew how to absolutely divert her and prime her at the same time.

She said in a breathless voice, "Okay, cowboy, hang on." They could ride the horses a little later.

CHAPTER 5

NSA FORT — HIGH PERFORMANCE COMPUTING CENTER 2 — MEADE, MARYLAND

"**S**ir, I know this is boring, but we have to review the significant possible data hits that Brady reported on." Retired Captain Henry "Bulldog" McLaughlin had been removed from any combat role and promoted to intelligence officer of his Marine battalion. He was one of those intuitive geniuses who couldn't just put two and two together but could connect five, seven, nine, and twenty-two if they related in any way. In fact, he recalled every name he'd heard in Afghanistan. Henry loved to make the puzzle pieces fit as he looked for possible or real family connections. If the name had been on any of the lists of Taliban he had seen, he'd remember it.

"Bulldog, this is the job you signed up for, so pay attention!" His handler in the shadows was watching him closely.

Henry had only been on the job for three months and was already losing focus. He thought back on his eight years in the Corps with longing. He missed being in the mix of it all, and now all he did was read about it.

"Remember, Bulldog, that every so often, we find the needle in that haystack, and they come from the facts the data mining machines have gathered."

Three months had passed, and he had not found one thing to follow up on or sink his teeth into as his nickname implied. "Okay, Gloria, put the search hits up on the screens so we can discuss them." Henry was hoping against all hope that this report might have something of interest since it was the last report of the day. Gloria, the NSA lead tech, broke the silence as all the hits started showing up on the screens.

Google searches: "*Navy SEAL mini submarine high altitude low opening launch system*" plus "*dragon rider, seal subs, parachute*"

Code name: "**Dragon Rider**"

Actual project: U.S. Navy—**Black Dragon**—Testing 2002—stealth strap-on technology, C-130 launch platform

Top secret – no public release or leaks reported

Naval project test failure: one injury – Navy SEAL, broken leg, broken collarbone, and skull fracture

Project status shows: more testing TBD

Henry was not impressed. It looked like a WAG (wild ass guess) from someone and nothing more. "What information do we have on the searcher?" he asked, knowing the information would be coming up. Gloria was ready to put up the next screen but was expecting some questions about the Black Dragon project. "Okay, here is the searcher information."

John Phillip Mogen: Deadwood, South Dakota. Retired oil production engineer. Specialized in offshore projects. University of Wyoming graduate.

Attends Tea Party meetings monthly. Challenges Facebook friends when the U.S. Constitution is involved.

Heritage Foundation member. Contributor to Hillsdale College.

Married to **Jaylynn Justine**, San Antonio, Texas. Geophysicist – Texas A&M graduate.

Data hit: Jaylynn's brother – retired Air Force Colonel **Carl Justine – NSA watch. 1177351AFR**

Data hit: Captain Carl Justine flew the C-130 during the test of the **Black Dragon** device in 2002.

Okay, now, this was piquing Bulldog's interest. It may all be a series of coincidences, but the connections were intriguing to say the least. John Mogen evidently knew the colonel, but did he know the correct name of the device that was tested, or was it just a guess? Was Colonel Justine still maintaining his oath of secrecy into retirement? The Bulldog's nose was twitching now, just like it did when he put things together in the field!

"Gloria, why the watch on Colonel Justine?" Henry was anxious for the answer. Gloria pulled up the information Bulldog requested.

NSA Watch 1177351AFR: During his interview for promotion to lieutenant general, he was asked if he had any issues carrying out orders without reservation or questioned such orders. He replied, "Yes."

"Gloria, is that it? That's why he is on the watch list?"

Gloria knew it was a rhetorical question. "Sir, I can get you the transcript of the interview when I get Air Force approval."

"Henry, let's back this thing down a little." His handler spoke from the shadows. "We can pick this up in the morning. Gloria will get the transcript of his lieutenant general promotion interview and run a current activity search on Colonel Justine."

"But, sir, I would like to…"

"No, Henry. I can tell you might think there is some meat on this bone, but nothing here says 'threat,' and there is nothing urgent enough to pursue at this moment. Let's shut this down for tonight. We only have a one-word match on this black project name and two guys who maybe have a problem with our government or Armed Forces right now, and that's all. Good night, everyone!"

Henry felt like a hound dog that had been called off in the middle of a mountain lion hunt. Maybe it was a trail that would lead to absolutely nothing, but Henry's gut said otherwise, and he trusted his gut since it had kept him alive more than once while he was downrange. As he walked out of the area, he looked up at his handler, who had been helping him learn for two months, and shook his head in disgust.

After Henry had scanned out of the area for the night, Sam Hudson, Gloria's supervisor, walked down toward her workstation. "Gloria, Henry's two months with our node is complete, so let's get him set up for his next training evolution starting tomorrow."

Gloria reminded Sam that it was a couple of days short of two months, so Henry could finish out the week with them and then make the move. However, Sam gave Gloria a look that didn't leave doubt about what he was conveying.

Gloria broke the silence. "Sam, this is a little strange, and I'm not understanding the why of this move?" She had become Sam's work wife a few years back and could read him as well as anybody. As a result, she knew this attitude was so out of character for him.

"Gloria," Sam said in a tone she did not hear often, "I was Captain Justine's copilot on that test flight for the Black Dragon project. He's my friend, and I want to follow this personally."

"Sam, that is absolutely against protocol, and you know it. You could get into big trouble on this because you are letting your personal feelings get in the way. You have always been completely professional as long as we have worked together, and this is a little scary for me!"

"Gloria, just make the transfer to the Foreign side—Middle East Division, effective tomorrow, and let Henry know by email now." Sam was adamant about this, and Gloria understood that this was an order she would execute ASAP.

"Sam, I should report this. You know I won't, but I'll have to keep track of what you are doing. You know that, right?"

Gloria was nervous as she waited for Sam's reply. Rubbing his chin, he looked lost in thought but finally said, "See you in the morning, Gloria."

Prompt as ever, she made the arrangements for Henry's transfer and sent him an email. This was not sitting well with her, and Sam knew it. All this would probably end up being a big nothing burger anyway, but she felt compelled to follow up. As Gloria's night shift relief sat down next to her, she showed her the connections concerning the search for "Dragon Rider" that had turned up the "Black Dragon" hit and asked if she could put a location and movements watch on retired Colonel Carl Justine.

CHAPTER 6

THE BLACK HILLS — SOUTH DAKOTA

As John Mogen headed out of Rapid City on Highway 44 and started up into the Hills, Carl really did understand why John and Jaylynn had retired here. However, it was springtime, and the remnants of a seriously snowy winter hid in the trees. That was why Carl just couldn't bring himself to relocate to the Hills.

As they turned onto Highway 385 and headed north toward Deadwood, Jaylynn spotted a herd of about thirty elk on the west side of the road and called out to get the others' attention. "Look—what a beautiful sight!"

Mary Ann could not contain her excitement as they passed the herd. She gently touched Carl on the shoulder, and he turned to look at her.

"I know what you're thinking, but you need to remember all the snow pictures Jaylynn sent us just a couple of months ago." Carl knew Mary Ann was getting tired of the heat in Arlington, but why go to the other extreme? Nonetheless, he had to admit to himself that the Black Hills did have some of the most picturesque scenery in the entire country.

"We could buy a summer cabin in the Hills?"

Carl just smiled as Mary Ann and Jaylynn nodded at each other.

After arriving back at the Mogen compound, Jaylynn and Mary Ann headed to the kitchen to make some lunch for the four of them.

"Why don't you guys get out of the house for a little while?" Jaylynn was hoping Carl would succumb to the smell of the ponderosas and find himself mesmerized by the aspen leaves. "This place is calling you, Carl!"

"You're not helping, Jaylynn!" her brother retorted.

"I am helping Mary Ann's cause, big brother."

"We're going to ignore you both and go outside," John chuckled as he headed out of the room with Carl in tow.

The latter gave John a serious look as they approached the front door. "We need to leave our phones in the house."

John paused, stunned by the serious expression he had gotten from Carl when he'd made the request—it was more like an order than a suggestion.

"Let's head down to the creek," Carl suggested in a calmer tone.

Dropping their phones on the side table as they exited the house, John replied, "Sounds good."

As they reached the creek and sat down on the two Adirondack chairs placed by the bank, John didn't know whether he should be excited or apprehensive about the impending discussion. He felt a mixture of both emotions as he waited for Carl to speak.

"John, have you done any research online for this book you're writing yet?"

John hadn't expected the discussion to start like this. If anything, he'd expected Carl to ask what he needed to know about possible scenarios and some trick hardware that he might not be aware of. So, John had to think a moment before responding. "Well, I wasn't anticipating that question, so I need to ponder it a little. We can look at the search history when we get back inside just to be sure my memory is solid. I think Jay wrote out a list."

Carl agreed that they would do that when they got back in. Then, John started listing off what he remembered of his search history.

"I know I looked up the Commemorative Air Force, Ellsworth Air Force Base, Dyess Air Force Base, and the Oathtakers sites. I did a stab in the dark search for how to deliver and soft land some unknown device. I put in something like a Navy mini sub the SEALs could ride down from a high altitude and then open a black chute and soft land. I would think the SEALs would have mini subs, but I don't know how they would deploy them. I called it Dragon Rider, I think?" John stopped short because Carl was staring at him a little wide-eyed and quickly stood up, knocking his chair over in his haste.

Agitatedly pacing the area, Carl whispered, "Holy crap. HoLY crap. Holy crap. John, how did you come up with a search like that?"

"I'm pretty good at stinky rabbits, Carl—it was just a stinky rabbit!"

"Holy crap—holy crap," Carl kept repeating.

"Carl, would you please say something other than holy crap!" John was becoming concerned about his brother-in-law's reaction, so he grabbed on to what had become one of his mantras. "I am just writing a book for God's sake. What's wrong with that? You made us leave our phones in the house, and now you are freaking out about a Google search—what's up? I feel like I'm in the middle of a Vince Flynn novel!"

Carl took a deep breath, righted his chair, and sat back down. "John, what I'm about to say stays here at this creek. It cannot be discussed anywhere but out of listening range of any electronic device of any kind and only with me. No phones, TVs, anything! Do you understand?"

"Geez, Carl, ever since I mentioned I wanted to write this book, people have been really overreacting, and I just don't understand. So, why is this such a big deal? Let me in the door!"

After John finished, there was a long pause as if Carl were carefully choosing what to tell him. Finally, he spoke in a soft but firm voice. "I'm part of a group we call the Arlington Colonels' Club. There are four of us. We all go to the same church in Dallas—that's how we met. You know I'm retired Air Force, right? Allan North is retired Army. Bill Musgrave is a retired Marine, and Torger Vigdahl is a retired Navy captain. Torg was assigned to Special Forces, SEAL Team Six, and at the end of his career, he was involved in the training detachment (TRADET) that took care of advanced Navy SEAL training. The club started after we figured out we each had a genuine commitment to help others, especially returning vets.

We do some things individually and others as a group. Then, we started playing golf together once a week and, yes, we also pray together."

John had no idea where Carl was going with all this but held his questions as his brother-in-law continued.

"We have made a lot of friends and have a lot of contacts in all branches of the service. We don't like what is happening to our republic and have been discussing ways to effect a course correction. We have been considering the idea of a military coup, although it will take current and former military involvement to make that happen. What we have been looking for is a civilian patriot to lead the…lead the cause if you will. To be the face of change we want to happen. That change is a return to the Constitution—the rule of law—and to destroy the deep state once and for all, even if it takes a full change out of our supposed servants in elected positions, including the Supreme Court."

Now it was John's turn to be not just pensive but speechless. Carl took advantage of his silence to forge on with his explanation.

"The reason for my holy craps was…I was a pilot on the C-130 that was the mother ship for a test program for a SEAL mini submarine with bolt-on and plug-in wing systems. After being deployed, we could control the flight of the mini sub from high altitude and deploy a black chute to soft land the sub into the water—not on land. The wings could be quickly detached. The code name for this system was Black Dragon. The test was a failure, and I don't know if the project was continued or dropped. Sorry, but I was shocked that your search—the rabbit you pulled out of your ass—was so close to the real project."

Now John's heartrate was running in overdrive, and he was doing his best to control his breathing. This was so out of left field; he was having trouble processing all that Carl had just dropped on him.

Noting John's rigid form and uncertain expression, Carl sighed and got straight to the point. "John, I—I know you're my brother-in-law, and I love you and Jaylynn, so believe me, it's with a lot of hesitation… Putting all that aside, I have real confidence in your abilities to plan, organize, and lead. I'm telling you that I think you are that guy—that guy to lead the restoration of our republic."

My God, Carl was serious about this! John's stomach was getting upset the more he thought about it. In fact, he realized he was feeling lightheaded.

"I didn't know what to do except come straight out with it, and I know it is a lot to…" Carl was abruptly interrupted by a raised voice from the house.

"Lunch! Come on, you guys—lunch is ready." Jay's call literally caused John to jump and Carl to stop mid-sentence.

"We'll talk more later," Carl said rather calmly.

Before they could head inside, John's other mantra came out of his mouth. "You are completely out of your mind, Carl! Out of your ever-loving mind! What is TRADET anyway?"

"The girls will have to be in on this too," Carl added. "Oh, and TRADET is training detachment."

Looking shell-shocked, John whispered, "Please let me get my mind around what you told me before you even talk to Jay."

Carl nodded in understanding. Then, as they reached the house, he quickly added, "No more searches until we get you encryption."

Mary Ann caught Carl just as he stepped inside and said, "Sam Hudson called and would like you to call him back when you get a chance."

CHAPTER 7

RAPID CITY REGIONAL AIRPORT — SOUTH DAKOTA

As they headed to the end of the security check line at Rapid City Regional Airport, Carl grabbed John's arm and whispered, "I'll understand if you can't do this. I've lost sleep about this whole thing, but we need a decision either way so we can move forward with or without you. I know we will be putting the ladies we love in harm's way—I get it. Just remember that pledge you have above your computer. I love you and Jaylynn."

"I know you do, Carl, and we love you and Mary Ann. I'll let you know within twenty-four hours if I'm with you or not."

Lives, fortunes, and sacred honor. John thought to himself. He knew it might be that time.

As they all hugged, Jaylynn noticed the look between John and Carl. Something was different. She didn't know why or how she knew, but as her brother and sister-in-law headed through security, her senses went on high alert.

"Y'all come and see us!" Mary Ann yelled as they headed through Clear check. Carl hated this shortcut through security but had yielded to her pressure after she had gotten patted down twice in a row. He thought, *What the heck? The eyes of Texas are on all of us anyway!*

After getting through airport security and realizing they had an hour before their flight boarded, Carl decided to call Sam Hudson back. A good six inches taller than Carl, Sam had gone through a couple of wives while they had been in the Air Force together. The incorrigible ladies' man had blond hair and blue eyes, and his chiseled chin had a scar from childhood that ran from the top right to the bottom right. The stitch marks were faded but still visible. Sam would have covered it with a beard if he could ever grow a decent one. He had always been a chick magnet, and that didn't help him stay married. He was built like a basketball player but had acquired a little more muscle as he'd matured.

Sam and Carl had always stayed in great shape. They had spent a lot of hours in the air together until Sam had gotten a left seat in the C-130 and ended up flying C-141s. He'd then made a rare switch to B-1B bombers to stave off the boredom. They hadn't talked in almost a year but still had a close relationship. There was no doubt they could pick up right where they'd left off as good friends can do.

Sam was prompt to answer the call. "Carl—how are you? How are things in the Black Hills?"

Carl was a little perturbed that Sam had obviously been using his spook sources to know where he was—but why? "Hi, Sam. I suppose you know where I am right now, you turkey?"

Sam laughed. "I see your flight doesn't leave for another fifty-five minutes."

Carl was becoming truly upset now. "You're such an asshole. What's with the surveillance? Is there someone in this terminal watching me?" He was nervously looking around, and Mary Ann, sitting beside him, was questioning why he had just called his friend an asshole.

"No, Carl, we don't need boots on the ground to keep tabs on someone." Sam was surprised Carl didn't know this.

"The NSA is not supposed to spy on Americans, are they, Sam?" Carl got to his feet and paced to a quieter area.

Sam laughed and replied, "Carl, I needed to talk to you about a data hit—a data connection on you and your brother-in-law, John Mogen. So, as your asshole friend, I'm trying to head things off—off the record. I'm on an encrypted phone."

"I'm not!" Carl responded, furrowing his eyebrows in concern as his mind raced. Had he blown the whole operation? What on earth could have been the data connection Sam was talking about? He and Sam had talked about the state of the union, but he had never talked to him about what the Colonels' Club was up to. Sam worked for the NSA for God's sake! How could Carl possibly trust Sam with any of this? "Okay, Sam, talk to me," he said in a more subdued tone.

"Carl, do you remember the HALO test for the Navy SEAL mini submarine we did back in '02?"

Carl's heart rate rapidly increased, and he took a deep breath while covering the mic on his phone. "Yes, Sam, I remember. I still don't know if that SEAL who got hit with the deployable wing ever lived."

Sam hesitated a moment, deciding whether to divulge anything specific to Carl. *Oh hell, I'm on an untraceable phone*, he thought. Shaking off his hesitation, he continued. "Carl, this is classified. Yes, the SEAL did survive, and the project underwent several unmanned tests before we tried it again as a manned test. Carl, Black Dragon has been used several times by the SEALs and has been highly successful. Anyway, the data connection we got was an internet search your brother-in-law did that got everything about the project right except he searched 'Dragon Rider,' which was only one word off."

Carl was so relieved that he started to laugh, which also put Sam at ease because he could tell the laugh was sincere. "Sam, John is a patriot and is very upset about the state of our union, just as I'm sure you are. He is so distracted by the state of our country that my sister encouraged him to write a book about how to get our republic to course correct back to the Constitution and away from progressivism. She was hoping that might quell his angst so he can enjoy his retirement and not dwell on things he can't do a lot about. His search was a WAG—a stinky rabbit. He called me because he needed some professional advice and really wanted to know how much of the military would rise up and defend the

Constitution as they had pledged to do or blindly follow orders up to and including firing on civilians if needed. So, Mary Ann and I decided a visit would be nice and took the trip up to chat in person. Like I said, he's just writing a book."

Sam had just one more issue to raise. "The other question that came up was why you booked a flight for the next day. That must have cost you three times the normal amount. Why the urgency, Carl?"

Carl happily responded, "I guess your team didn't dig deep enough, Sam. We used mileage points to get a very good price. Check it out if you want."

A sarcastic note in his voice, Sam replied, "You fly all over the world to build up points to visit South Dakota? I just had to ask to make sure we didn't have a nefarious plot in the works."

Carl quipped back just as sarcastically. "Is this how you treat all your friends, Sam?"

By now, Sam was a little frustrated by Carl's attitude, but he understood where he was coming from. "Hey, Carl, I am your friend. I'm just trying to stop this nonsense cold. I don't want some CIA dinks showing up at your door."

"Sorry, Sam. I really do appreciate what you're doing. I just find it hard to believe you've become one of the shadows and rights violators we both hated a few years back." Carl was letting his true feelings show, which was probably not smart. "Anyway, thank you for calling me to get the facts before someone released the hounds for no reason."

"Hey, Carl, I'll be in Texas this fall and will stop in to see you and Mary Ann." Sam was from San Antonio and came to visit family at least twice a year but had missed last year since his family had come to D.C. instead.

"It will be good to see you," Carl said with a smile.

"Likewise. Say hi to Mary Ann and take care of yourself, you old bull!"

"Oh, I will, and we'll see who can hike farther faster when you get here," Carl challenged. As the call ended, he let out a big sigh. "We have to really get our comms off the grid *now*," he mumbled to himself.

After the initial comments, Carl had wandered away from his wife since he hadn't been sure what Sam was calling about. As he returned to her side, she asked, "What did Sam want?"

"Oh, he apologized for not getting to Dallas to see us last year, but he plans to be there in the fall and will stop in to see us." Carl just couldn't let Mary Ann know what was happening quite yet—especially if John said no. Besides, it could be months before anything happened. For now, that information could wait.

As their plane took off and headed south toward Dallas, he was feeling the need to apologize to John for dumping this on him so quickly. Already, he was regretting that he had even brought up John's name to the Colonels' Club. What had he been thinking?

He had prayed about it for hours and still had no clear indication from God. He was asking for something to make it clear that this was the right thing to do—that John was the right man for the job. The internet search John had done was so close to the real project he and Sam had flown—how could that be coincidence? Was that the sign? How could Sam have been the one at the NSA to see the data connections? How would Jaylynn respond if John said yes? Oh God, had John told her? Carl hadn't told him not to...

As Mary Ann put her hand on Carl's arm, he stiffened and quickly turned his head toward her. "What's on your mind? You are a million miles away. Is everything okay with you and John? You seemed to be having some very serious conversations." Always the loving wife, she was worried about Carl. She knew him better than anyone, and his behavior had changed in the last few days.

"Everything is fine with John. We were just having a significant discussion about how to get our republic back on track." Carl needed to bring the woman he loved more than anything on earth into the circle soon— very soon. *Come on, John—decide to be the chosen one: our militia colonel.*

CHAPTER 8

MOGEN COMPOUND – THE BLACK HILLS OF SOUTH DAKOTA

Keeping a secret from Jaylynn was unacceptable, and John was being tugged to fill her in on what was going on, even though he was still reeling from what Carl had asked him to do. The more important question: Was God telling him to do this? How could he determine the right path on his own? He just knew it was time to tell Jaylynn what was going on and the reason Carl and Mary Ann had made such a quick trip to see them.

He started to speak, but Jaylynn broke the silence first. "John, I have a funny feeling that you and my brother are into something that you are keeping from Mary Ann and me. I saw the look you and Carl gave each other at the airport. Promise me you'll tell me if I need to know what you two might be stepping into. It seems to be more serious than background material for a book?" As they drove away from the airport, John carefully pondered how to start. "Well, I'm waiting, John. Since you didn't dismiss my rantings as crazy, give me the scoop. What is going on?"

John started in a very businesslike tone that Jaylynn recognized as his serious voice. "Jay, Carl came up because some things in my life and his life have aligned either by coincidence or maybe in a God-directed way that has me scared. Believe it or not, I was just getting ready to tell you when you asked me about it. Your 'spidey' senses are working well today.

So, let me lay this out for you, okay? Carl belongs to something called the Arlington Colonels' Club that consists of three retired colonels and one retired naval captain."

Jaylynn broke in. "Why a Navy captain and not... Wait—do they have colonels in the Navy?"

John patiently and respectfully schooled her on the naval ranks and how the Navy captain rank was equivalent to colonel in the other services. "Anyway," John continued, "These colonels, including Carl, all have the same bent, and it's the very same thing I believe. They're certain that we have to do something to restore our republic. They have contacts spread throughout all the services and some additional connections that might make it possible to pull my scenario off."

After hearing this, Jaylynn started moving closer to freakout mode, which wasn't one of her positive traits. The questions came in rapid-fire succession. "Oh my God, John, do you hear what you are saying? Are you talking about bringing your book to life—real life? Carl is out of his mind—bless his heart. Why did he need to fly in immediately and talk to you about this? Does he want you to stop writing the book or what? Is this Colonels' Club scheme and your book what you mean by things 'lining up in your lives'? This is so dangerous even talking about it, John— geez. Is that why you two went for a hike before lunch? Does Mary Ann know about this?"

"Jaylynn—take a breath!" John exclaimed. "Carl and I, along with three other men, have the same idea, and it might be possible to pull it off."

"Holy crap! HoLY crap!" yelled Jaylynn.

John actually started laughing at her exclamation since it was the same reaction Carl had had.

Jaylynn instantly became heated. How could he be laughing at a time like this? "What is so funny, John? This is not a time to be laughing! You had better not be messing with me!"

"Easy, easy, Jay. Catch your breath and listen to me for a minute and please don't interrupt. I'm sorry I laughed, but your brother said holy crap the same way you did when we were talking. It must be a family trait."

"Yes, John. My mom says it a lot." Jaylynn couldn't keep quiet to save her life right now.

"Please, Jay, stop interrupting! I'm not messing with you!" John felt the blow on his right arm just as he finished his last word. Jay had not hit him that hard in forever. "Okay, Jay, that's it. I'm not saying any more until we get home. I have to drive! So, don't hit me anymore."

"Does Mary Ann know about this?" Jaylynn was just a little out of control, and for some reason, the thought of Jay being on his side made John feel good—almost relieved somehow. "John—does Mary Ann know about this? Does she?"

"Not that I know of, but I'm sure Carl will be filling her in as soon as they get home," John explained, trying to give Jay some comfort.

"Did Carl tell you that, or are you just trying to make me feel better?" Jay quizzed. The tone in her voice had changed enough that it made him turn to look at her. To his surprise, there were tears streaming down her face. His tough ranch girl who seldom cried had lost it. John had to finish what he was saying now before he lost it too.

"Jay, Carl didn't tell me to keep this in confidence, so I'm operating on the unverified assumption that I am allowed to tell you and he is going to fill Mary Ann in. It's terrifying to think, but we just might be the ones to restore our republic as a true Christian nation, even if we have to split the country. We can ask the question 'Why us?' till the cows come home or take a real look at the possibilities."

Jaylynn was still composing herself when John dropped the next bombshell on her.

"Carl was sent up here to talk to me for a very specific reason." He inhaled a calming breath and resumed. "And that was to ask if I would… could be the face of this restoration of the republic? I don't know exactly what it would entail and what my involvement would be, but regardless, it'll be extremely dangerous for us. I told him I would give him an answer in twenty-four hours."

John was ready for another smack on his right arm but instead felt a gentle hand, a lovingly soft touch that he had felt so many times before. He wasn't sure what it meant but was glad for the 180-degree shift in her emotions.

Jaylynn took a deep breath and slowly exhaled before continuing. She decided to put on her geophysicist hat and analyze what had been said. She had to protect that terrified little girl who was screaming inside. "First, I was going to say that you being in a federal prison for the rest of our lives was not in our retirement plan, but now I realize you getting killed definitely was not a part of our plan either."

John felt the wetness from her tears on his right arm as they turned off Highway 385 and headed toward home. Two people still madly in love with each other after thirty-five years were facing an impossible decision. Should they go for it? Was this something they would or could get behind? Did they have what was needed to follow through with this life-saving plan for the United States, or should he just write his book and wonder what might have been, especially if the colonels went ahead with their plan without him? He and Jaylynn could be part of the renewal of their beloved republic or could just sit on the sidelines, afraid to get into the game when called upon.

John broke the moment by saying, "I'll call Pastor Steve when we get in the house. I'd like to talk to him about this."

Jaylynn nodded. "Are we still going on that sunset ride you promised me this evening? We sure need it, and I think the horses would enjoy it too!" Her mind was spinning out of control, and she was trying to catch up with the mass of thoughts as they flew by. Her first thought was to fly to Dallas and put an end to the crazy ideas Carl was putting into her husband's head. The next piece she landed on was that she needed to stand by John, whatever he decided to do, no matter what, and if he got killed, she would die with him—oh God!

Every evening, she and John would sit on their porch and watch the Black Hills sunset. At some point, one of them would inevitably say, "It just doesn't get any better!" They had prepared for years and made all the right moves to have the retirement they had dreamed of, and it had become their reality. Was she willing to give up their dreams for a dangerous and iffy—at best—shot at turning their country around? This was way more than just a little inconvenience.

Jaylynn's mind flashed on the little sign that hung above John's computer. *"WE MUTUALLY PLEDGE OUR LIVES, FORTUNES, AND SACRED HONOR..."* Why did that have to pop into her mind? This tough Texas ranch girl was just plain scared, and she could count on one hand the times she had been really afraid. Let's see...her wedding day, the first time she went into labor, and the time she had to make a decision about John's drinking and the pledge she made to herself to leave him if their intervention didn't work. But was this new quest asking too much of her? What they had dreamed of and finally achieved could all be gone if they became part of this plan.

As they rode the ridgeline above their house and watched the Black Hills sunset from the back of their horses, Jaylynn took in the smell of the ponderosa pines as well as the smell of her horse and leather. The aspen trees shimmered as their new leaves quaked.

Eventually, she was startled out of her thoughts when John spoke. "It just doesn't get any better than this."

Tears rolled down her cheeks as she realized what they had to do even if it meant losing it all. Did John feel the same? *We must be out of our minds.* "You are right, honey—it just doesn't get any better."

CHAPTER 9

RAPID CITY, SOUTH DAKOTA

"**S**teve, we need to talk." There was an urgency in John's voice that Steve sensed immediately.

"Susan is out of town at a women's conference, so how about breakfast in the morning at the Millbrook's Cafe?" Steve was eager to eat someone else's cooking other than his own.

"Sounds good, Steve. Jaylynn is coming, so can we make it 0800 instead of our usual 0700?"

"No problem," Steve responded. "Is something wrong? Are you two okay?"

John hesitated, looking for the right words. "We have what I guess you would call an opportunity to discuss with you because it has some—ahhhh—some negative consequences if things don't go right."

Steve was intrigued but had learned to let things be until the person was face to face with him. He needed to be able to read the expressions on their face and also their body language. "Okay, see you two in the morning!"

Disconnecting the call, John turned to his wife. "Okay, Jay, we have a breakfast date with Pastor Steve in the morning."

Jay was quick with the question John knew was coming. "How early and where?" Likewise, John was quick with the answers she was looking for: 0800 at Millbrook's. She was extremely pleased it wasn't earlier but complained anyway. "0800—*ugh*, okay, but what time do I have to be ready?"

"0730."

"*UGH*," was Jay's whiny response.

Steve and his wife, Susan, had become friends with John and Jaylynn shortly after the Mogens had moved to the Hills. John had helped get a response team together for the church and was one of Steve's accountability partners. John had been in AA for twenty years, and for him, TMI did not exist. One of his favorite things to remind people about was the phrase "no secrets in your life." So, Steve was happy that John and Jaylynn would contact him for feedback on their endeavor.

The next morning, Steve arrived early at the restaurant and took a seat in the corner booth facing the front doors. John always insisted they sit in that booth whenever possible so he could see the entire restaurant. The pastor stood up as the Mogens approached the table. Jaylynn looked wonderful as usual but had a slight sleep-deprived look in her green eyes. Small talk ensued as they ordered breakfast. John's prayer was longer than normal. It included a plea for a sign—for direction in an important life decision.

John looked around the restaurant to see who was there, noting that no one was sitting close enough to overhear what was going to be discussed. Satisfied, he started speaking. "Steve, I've decided to write a book about how we might get our country back on track, back to the model of limited government the founders intended. I've been so distracted by what's been going on with Congress that Jaylynn suggested I do something to deal with my angst about the situation—thus, a book."

Steve was a little confused about how writing a book could have negative consequences other than people not liking the book? Despite his uncertainty, he waited patiently as John continued.

"The book will be...let's say a blueprint on how to take back our republic in a very short time. A coup that would involve a few very big sticks to force Washington to respond quickly. The big sticks would be weapons of mass destruction (WMDs) placed in a few cities throughout the country to force change. Jay talked me into calling her brother, who is a retired Air Force colonel, to ask hypothetically how to do this. Well, he flew to South Dakota the next day and told me in no uncertain terms that this very initiative was in the works for real and just needed a civilian to be the face of the movement. He asked me to be that face...a militia colonel if you will. This would be a nonviolent coup if we can pull it off. A lot of people could die if something goes wrong. My plan is to create a Christian coalition of states called the WSA, which stands for the Western Southern Alliance of States, so that we can maintain our Christian values without federal interference."

Steve had stopped eating his pancakes, but his mouth had stayed in the open position since he had heard the words that this might be a real possibility. WMD—did he say nukes? Completely speechless, Steve simply looked at John in stunned silence.

John knew he had to get this out while they had a quiet corner to talk without ears within hearing distance. Luckily, although Steve was in shock, he was able to respond. "My stars, John! You're saying this is a real possibility—I mean, a real-life thing? The possibility of a threat to set off nukes in American cities—really? Did I hear you correctly?"

"Let's keep our voices down, Steve—especially when we're talking about WMDs."

"Holy cow. Holy cow!" Steve was still shell-shocked and needed to process what had been said. John looked at Jay, who was giggling about the 'holy cow' exclamation that had come out of Steve's mouth.

Still overwhelmed, Steve rubbed his shaved head as if to feel hair that had been gone for years. "I need some time to process this and do some praying before I can even respond. I mean, I want this country to turn around just as much as you do, and I'd also love to see a huge revival in this country. I know we Christians are quickly becoming a remnant in the U.S., and we seemed to be in the way of the progressives. But good grief, John—I need to go pray and ponder this."

John finally spoke again. "I know how you feel—and I know this initially causes a fight-or-flight response. It's scary and exciting at the same time. I'm sorry about this, but I'm about to raise your blood pressure another twenty points." John hesitated just a moment before moving on. "So, if I say yes to this, we'll need a chaplain. Now, let's finish breakfast. These blueberry pancakes are delicious!"

"Uff da! How can you talk about the pancakes at a time like this? Are you playing a joke on me? I know how you are—tell me this is a joke." Steve was upset, and Norwegian pastors just don't get upset. It was simply not in their genes.

"Steve," John reiterated, "this is very real and will happen with or without us being involved! Are you okay, Steve? Take a big breath. Breathe!"

Steve looked at Jaylynn and just shook his head. He just could not believe what he was hearing. So, Jaylynn started to speak in a soothing tone. "Steve, this is just as hard for us to assimilate as it is for you. I'm not sure why, but my brother needs an answer from us by tonight. I don't have to remind you, but I will anyway—please keep this in the highest confidence."

Steve looked in disbelief at Jaylynn. "I don't know how or why we have been caught up in this or whether it is of Satan or of the Lord. Maybe it's our time, but I need to do some praying and listening for a whisper from God. Are you going to be involved in this with John also?"

Jaylynn responded in a way that surprised all three of them. "Steve, I'll be all in if John says yes. I'm not sure what my involvement will be, but a female militia captain would give the movement credibility."

John's head quickly snapped in her direction as he regarded her with a combination of surprise, pride, and fear. What a strange mixture of emotions!

"Okay, you two, I'll contact you after I get my head right on this thing. It's not something pastors get training on. Why couldn't you have a simple marital problem for heaven's sake?"

John and Jay hugged Steve a little tighter than they probably should have as they said goodbye. Then, they left the restaurant quickly. As they reached the pickup, John turned to his wife. "I'm not sure we should be talking to others without consulting Carl?" John's answer to his own question would be more important than either one of them could imagine. "If we are going to do this, we have to have people we can trust and confide in, and we have to be able to discern who is trustworthy—who we can trust with our lives. So, Jay... You want to be a militia captain, huh?"

As Pastor Steve drove toward his office, his mind went flying back to last Sunday's sermon. He remembered talking about the inconvenient callings we get from the Holy Spirit that can interfere with our daily life and, for that matter, our entire life path. Sometimes we end up thinking more about what we didn't do instead of our sins that we did commit. Instead of praying, why were his thoughts bringing up that sermon? Was he being challenged for a very inconvenient calling? A calling that could cost him dearly, both privately and publicly, not to mention his career as a pastor.

At that moment, a Bible verse from 1 Samuel popped into his head: "And David had success in all his undertakings for the Lord was with him." Steve wasn't sure if this verse was supposed to be pertinent to his situation. They were talking about nuclear devices for God's sake. Yes, David was a warrior king and, yes, he had killed tens of thousands of warriors, but come on.

Before Steve could continue his argument with God, another verse darted in—1 Chronicles 12:32: "of the sons of Issachar who had an understanding of the times, to know what Israel ought to do, their chiefs were two hundred; and all their brethren were at their command."

"Okay," he said out loud, "these were men who had committed to fight with King David. The only thing that was unique in the verse was that they, 'had an understanding of the times, to know what Israel ought to do.'"

Steve didn't know why these verses had come to him, but as soon as he got to the church, before even getting out of his car, he sent a text to John with the Bible addresses of the two verses—no explanation, just the verses—and hoped they would mean something more to John and Jaylynn. The thought of being the chaplain for a militia that would look like a terrorist organization was a little out there. In fact, it sounded crazy town! *Think, Steve. Pray, Steve.*

CHAPTER 10

NSA FORT – HIGH PERFORMANCE COMPUTING CENTER 2 – MEADE, MARYLAND

"**G**ood morning, Sam." Gloria was anxious to talk to him again about the Colonel Justine hit and the untimely personnel move he had made concerning Henry McLaughlin.

"Good morning, Gloria. You look great this morning!" Sam exclaimed as he put on his headset.

"Sam, I put a watch on Carl Justine's movements. and he did something a little strange. He booked two plane tickets to Rapid City for him and his wife. He was met at the airport by his sister and her husband, John Mogen. A very quick trip that must have been expensive on such short notice. Why would he do that?"

Sam needed to cut this off now. "Carl's brother-in-law is a fledgling writer, I believe, and that is what the trip was about."

Gloria just knew it. "You talked to Colonel Justine, didn't you, Sam? What are you thinking?"

"Gloria, keep your voice down. He's a personal friend, and I will not let this go on any longer. Go ahead and check to see how he paid for those tickets. Then, maybe I'll listen. He's a patriot! He has served in combat, and I'll not have him hounded by us! I do want to know this though... How do you know he was met by his sister and brother-in-law?"

"I searched John Mogen on social media and got a photo of him and his wife. Then, I accessed the Rapid City Regional Airport security camera records and found the footage. Next, I did facial recognition on him and your friend Carl!" Gloria had never seen Sam pull something like this. "Sam you're being completely unprofessional with this information. You do know that, don't you?"

"I'm not asking you to take the watch off his movements, am I?" Sam responded rather tersely.

Gloria was good at her job—very good. She was a real believer and follower of rules—as legalistic as they came. She accessed the airline records within seconds and found the information on the Justines' airline tickets. It turned out they had used mileage points and picked up some very cheap round trip flights between Dallas and Rapid City. Gloria's face got a little warm out of embarrassment, but she was going to stay on this to protect Sam, if nothing else.

As soon as Gloria settled back to work, she received a phone call.

"Gloria, it's Henry McLaughlin. I just wanted to call and thank you for all the help you gave me on how to put that puzzle together."

Gloria was surprised to hear from him because he seemed like the type who just moved on. "Thanks, Henry. Always glad to help someone who has a real interest in learning as fast as they can."

"I'm still a little confused about being moved over to Foreign on a Wednesday night. The Foreign division folks said it was very unusual. Was Sam not happy with me or something? I had a gut feeling about Colonel Justine and his brother-in-law, so I did some checking, and the Colonel made what seemed like a quick unexpected trip to South Dakota. Sound fishy to you?"

"Well, Henry..." Gloria had this. "John Mogen is writing a book and wanted to get some information from the colonel. The airline tickets were very economical because they used mileage points, so there seems to be nothing there. Might as well drop it, Henry. I still have a watch on the colonel's movements, and you should be working Foreign threats anyway!"

There was still something nagging at Henry about this, but he couldn't zero in on it yet. For the moment, he would let it go. "Okay, Gloria. I just have one more thing to give you, and I'll leave this alone. I found some connections to Colonel Justine in Arlington, Texas. Something called the 'Arlington Colonels' Club.' It has three colonels and a Navy captain as members, and they have popped up in some charity and veteran sites as donors and volunteers. Colonel Justine is a member. The thing about this is the other members all seem to have been retired when their answers during a promotion interview were 'counter to command-level standards,' whatever that means?"

Gloria was a little surprised to hear that Henry had gotten to this level of detail in his searching. "Well, that's interesting, Henry. But the problem we have is…it isn't a good enough reason to move forward in the investigation. Unless you have uncovered something else that makes you believe this leads to anything that might be a threat?" Gloria was still in teaching mode with Henry.

"Not at this time, but okay, I'll back off on this. However, if you need help on anything, I hope you'll give me an assignment, and I'll follow up on it."

Sam was sitting in his office, pondering the Mogen situation, when he received a phone call from his boss in Domestic Intelligence, Luke Anderson, who asked him to pop into his office ASAP. "Sam," he said curtly when Sam made his way over to him. "Sit down. We need to talk." Luke was in official mode. "I just got off the phone with Gloria, and she was concerned about a violation of protocol over a former colleague of yours."

Sam could feel his blood pressure rising as he thought to himself, *Gloria, you just have to follow the rules all the time, bitch!* He was incensed at what he considered a betrayal by her.

Sam unapologetically responded. "Yes, Luke, I went outside the lines on this one at my discretion because, years ago, I sat next to this man in the cockpit, and I would take a bullet for him. I let my emotions and friendship get in the way of my professionalism, but I didn't stop Gloria from pursuing any hits and will not stop any follow-up."

"Did you call Colonel Justine, Sam?" quizzed Luke.

"Yes, I did, and I found out it was simply research for a book his brother-in-law is writing that caused the hit. You know how often that happens and how those invariably become rabbit holes that create unnecessary surveillance on individuals. Then, we just waste resources chasing nonsense. I'm glad I was able to get to the bottom of it efficiently in this case."

Sam was surprised by how unguarded his response was, and Luke was stunned at his colleague's candor as well. "Thanks for your honesty, Sam. You and I have put in a lot of time and effort into defusing threats, and I don't take that lightly. But in the future, I'm still going to assign anything that comes across my desk concerning Colonel Justine to a different handler, and Gloria will report to that handler moving forward. You will not be privy to anything about this situation in the future." Luke took a deep breath and continued without hesitation. "Now, are you aware of a group called the Arlington Colonels' Club?"

"No, I'm not," Sam responded.

"Okay, Sam. Moving forward, you don't call your old friend, and I want you to stay out of this. Is that understood?" Luke's boss voice came through loud and clear, but he did have a slight smirk on his face.

How did they know I made that call? This was another one of those times when Sam wished he had never walked away from being a pilot. But he had a new wife, a new beginning, and wanted to become someone she could be proud of. He wanted to get it right that time. He would also have to live with the fault of his second short-lived marriage. He had transitioned from cargo to bombers and was a B-1B pilot when he retired. Oh God, nothing could replace being back in the cockpit of a Bone (B-1B bomber) and throttle up for takeoff. Very few men understood the feeling of that much power pushing them back into their seat—nothing like it. He missed it now more than ever.

As he headed back to his workspace, Sam mumbled to himself, "Oh well. You had better settle down and walk the line before you end up suspended."

As he walked past Gloria's cubicle, she questioned if everything was all right.

Sam just couldn't resist. "I have been terminated and have to immediately leave the building. A detail will be coming by to box up my personal things and escort me out!"

"Sam—SAM!" Gloria shouted in disbelief.

He just kept walking and broke into a laugh when he reached his space. *I'm quite the asshole this morning,* he thought to himself. He had been doing this for seven years now, and maybe it was time for a change of scenery. He was sad that Gloria couldn't get out of her safe little box built of rules and regulations and be more of a person than a robot, though a very good-looking robot, he had to admit. She never thought to question what they were doing, how they were doing some things, and why they were doing them. This made Sam just a tad bit nervous. How many more who worked for the NSA were of her ilk? Fortunately, Luke was the best and did only what he absolutely had to do in any cases concerning discipline, which made him the ideal boss—for Sam at least.

Meanwhile, Gloria was frantically knocking on Luke's glass door as he was talking on the phone. She had a look on her face that only came when an imminent threat crossed the screens, so he ended the call promptly and motioned her in.

"Luke, Luke… I had no idea you were going to fire Sam! I didn't want that. He just—he just wasn't following protocol!"

"Whoa, Gloria, whoa. What are you talking about?"

Gloria looked bewildered. "Sam…Sam said you terminated him and he had to leave the building! Did you really fire him?"

Luke was trying hard not to smile. "Gloria, he's just messing with you. I didn't fire him, and besides, I don't even have the power to do that! He's teasing you—probably as payback."

"But Luke, I heard…" Gloria was wounded that Sam would joke about such a serious thing. Her emotions were firing quickly from anger to shame and back again.

"Gloria," Luke interrupted, "you did the right thing. He had to be held accountable for his actions, but all I did was remove him from being included on anything about Colonel Justine...period."

For the first time that Luke had ever seen, Gloria lost her composure. "Now I *want* you to go fire him for being a complete asshole!" she literally yelled as she turned and stormed out of his office.

CHAPTER 11

UNDISCLOSED LOCATION – DALLAS, TEXAS

Retired Navy Captain Torger Vigdahl went outside to make the call. His close friend, Commander Chris Kendall, was still active and in charge of logistics for Naval Special Warfare Command. Chris was an Oathtaker, as was Torg, and they had a code talking ability that was absolutely incredible. No one listening in would even know what they were discussing outside the surface conversation. They had used this technique to speak in person about certain scenarios that might occur, and now it was time to test their ability to discuss it over the phone because time was of the essence.

"Torg! How the heck are you? And how is that beautiful wife of yours?" Chris hadn't spoken to him in months, and it was great to hear his voice. Torg was the only SEAL officer who had bested him in physical testing and was as tough as they came.

"I'm doing great, and so is Pam. Golf doesn't quite make an enduring workout, so I'm hitting the gym four times a week. I'm so ready to go downrange right now! Oh, by the way, we found another golfer to join our group."

Chris picked up on the code talking right away. He was surprised at how quickly Torg had launched into it. "Well, I'm really glad to hear you're staying in shape. Don't be surprised when I can still best you in that pull-up competition. I know the time is right—I can sure feel it!"

Torg asked, "Are you at Coronado or Pearl right now?"

"I'm in Pearl working on how to keep my ammo dry, and I think I have it all figured out. I can walk on water and wear a halo at the same time if I need to."

Torg was laughing. "Navy SEALs, forever the humble ones, huh! What if your halo fell off and hit the ground—could you keep it from breaking?"

Chris had to stop and ponder how he was going to respond to Torg's last question. He knew Torg was asking if they could soft land a Black Dragon mini submersible—but why? Chris wasn't sure whether Torg would get what he said next. "I'll ask my old friend Martin that question, Torg."

Torg understood that Chris needed to check with Lockheed Martin on his inquiry, and they wouldn't ask why because one just didn't ask when black projects were involved.

"How many of your precious halos could you break figuring this out—five maybe?"

Chris was a little concerned at how specific Torg had become and hoped the code was still vague enough. He was struggling to come up with something to say next.

Torg didn't give him a chance. "I have a riddle for you, Chris. If I have five Bones, all with halos, can they all go to heaven?"

Torg was taking a chance Chris would understand the question without knowing about the possibility of delivering the mini subs with B-1Bs somehow and then soft landing them.

Chris was absolutely stunned by what Torg had just said. At his wits' end, he realized he had to stop this conversation now. "Torg," he said in an official sounding voice. "I have to go—got a message coming in on a secure line. I'll get back to you. Meanwhile, I will work on that riddle—it's a tough one!"

With the call disconnected, Chris sat pondering the conversation. "Did Torg mean dogs going to heaven—I mean, all dogs go to heaven?"

Chris continued muttering to himself. "Did he mean Salty Dogs? Did he mean Navy SEALs? Bone… Bone… Oh God, is he talking about B-1B bombers? Launching the stealth Black Dragons out of B-1B bombers? Five bombers and five subs. He wants to soft land the subs—but where? Why five? That is half the mini sub fleet! Okay, okay…settle down, Chris. This is so very serious. Torg is asking me to get five HALO stealth mini subs ready to deploy from B-1B bombers and soft land to avoid damage to the subs. I think that's it? Wow! How on earth can we do this? I've got to get in contact with him on something encrypted. I'm not even sure if I have this right. For all I know, Torg may be out of his mind?"

If someone had walked by Chris at this very moment, they probably would have assumed he was losing it—and he was. Chris's unending mumbling continued. "Wait—wait, he said they had another golfer join the group. How did I miss that? Did we really find our civilian to be the front man of our plan? Wow!"

Chris recognized there was one thing he could do to move this plan along. He'd have to contact the engineer at Lockheed Martin and get the particulars on what it would take to get one of the Dragons to soft land on land and not in the water. An extra parachute? Wind could affect the landing with that much chute. Weather would be critical. To prevent damage to the subs, they could fit a Kevlar skid to the bottom of each one. This was still a risky way to land the mini subs. He had to get to work on this ASAP!

CHAPTER 12

JUSTINE RESIDENCE — ARLINGTON, TEXAS

"**C**arl!" Mary Ann shouted. "Jason Wilder is here to see you!"

Carl was outside on the back patio and quickly came into the house to greet Jason. "Mary Ann, Jason is a retired Air Force staff sergeant that I worked with quite a bit before I retired. Jason owns his own communications business now and deals with radios, phones, and computers. A division of his company provides IT and personal security. He is the best comms man I've ever worked with."

"Thanks for the compliment, Colonel! But I'm only worthy of your praise because of all the fantastic people working alongside me."

"Would you like something to drink, Jason—maybe some sweet tea?" Mary Ann offered, shooting Carl an inquisitive look. Her questions would have to wait until after Jason left, but she was determined to get her answers!

"That would be great, Mrs. Justine. Thanks so much."

Moments later, Mary Ann handed each of them a large glass of sweet tea.

After murmuring a word of thanks to his wife, Carl turned to Jason. "Let's go out on the patio, Jason, and I think you should leave your phone in the house for now."

Jason immediately understood what Carl was saying. He took both of his phones out of his pockets and set them on the kitchen table before they headed out to the patio. Once outside, Carl directed him to the sitting area that was on the far side of the pool about fifty feet from the house. Two chairs were arranged around a small patio table.

Inside, Mary Ann stood by the sliding glass door as she observed the two. She couldn't believe this; Carl was having another secretive conversation out of her earshot. What was going on? She'd had about enough of being shut out of these discussions. She did have a college degree, after all, and hadn't just fallen off the turnip truck! It was time to get to the bottom of all these private chats her husband was having, and she was going to do that just as soon as this Jason was gone.

Meanwhile, Carl jumped right to the point as soon as he and Jason had taken their seats outside. "It might be a *go* in the next day or two, so we need to get the encrypted phones ready. I'll get you a list of the warriors that I know about at this point so we can get those phones distributed. Everything has to be offline from now on."

Jason hadn't heard that commanding tone come out of Carl's mouth since he'd retired. He'd always had that fighting attitude that you did not question—both authoritative and adamant at the same time.

Jason couldn't contain his excitement! "Colonel, I'm so ready for this. I have twenty phones equipped to go and can acquire additional units and get them up and ready within hours, if need be. I have two friends who are former snipers who are ready to drop whatever they are doing and join the cause for as long as it takes!" Jason barely took a breath as he continued. "I've been to the range with them multiple times, and they are good—I mean one thousand yards good, sir! I also have my trusted crew that are in my company, all vets and all Special Forces.

"Okay, Jason, it's time to drop the 'sir' and 'Colonel' and just call me Carl, okay? And I hope we don't need snipers at this time."

"Yes, sir—whoops, sorry, sir... I mean... Dropping the 'sir' is going to be harder than I thought. Okay, Carl—it's so weird to call you, Carl." Jason smiled sheepishly.

"That's okay. I understand how military protocol can be burned into people's brains. From now on, we're all just patriots who happen to also be warriors—got it?"

"Yes, Carl," Jason responded with a little more confidence now.

"Now, Jason, I'm glad you've been looking for other patriots to stand beside us, but we have to be absolutely sure of the loyalty of each one you contact. They have to be trustworthy to protect us and our cause. What branches are you pulling from, and when can I meet them? We already have some former Navy SEALs ready to move as soon as we give the go, and as you know, we also have a few former and current Air Force special ops guys ready. We're pretty flush in the sniper department also."

Carl was a little uneasy about bringing in all these wildcards, but he told himself he had to have faith in Jason. He had to believe in the patriots, or this would never work.

Jason could see that Carl was getting more tense the longer he talked. "These guys are former Marines, Carl. They have had serious time downrange in Iraq, and one continued on to become a sniper instructor. Both are disheartened about what is happening to our country, and the best part is they are both Texans, born and bred."

Carl took a deep breath and let go of his anxiety. He marveled at the mix of military Jason was putting together. Former Navy SEALs, former and current Air Force Special Forces, a force tougher and more superior in their training than the general public realized. Then, add into the mix former Marines—that was the knockout punch they needed. They might have to keep them from killing each other while waiting for the go signal!

"Okay, Jason, I'm giving my okay, but patriots or not, we still need their names so we can run a background check on them."

Jason pulled out his small notebook and began to write as he spoke. "I've already done some checking on them myself, anticipating we might need them. Here are their names and addresses. I drink and pray with these guys, Carl—I believe in them."

"Okay, Jason, I believe in you more than you can imagine and absolutely trust your instinct. Thank you for being all in on this project."

Carl really did believe in Jason. He wasn't just a comms guy; he was former Air Force Special Forces and had served in some hazardous places doing forward command-and-control assignments. Carl was smart in a geeky kind of way but as tough as they came physically and mentally.

Jason took a deep breath before responding. "Carl, all of us actually sit down and discuss the Constitution. They have kept up with me in our discussions from the beginning, and one of them has even been studying the Federalist Papers. They are educated warriors, Carl—educated!"

"Okay, okay, you sold me, but they will be your responsibility—you know that?"

"Yes, sir—damn it! Yes, Carl, I know."

As they walked back to the house, Carl provided Jason with John Mogen's information and handed him ten thousand dollars in one-hundred-dollar bills.

"Are you ready for a road trip, Jason? Ready to camp out in the Black Hills again?"

"I am so ready, Carl—so ready!" Jason responded excitedly. Carl and Jason shook hands, and the latter headed out the Justines' front door.

When Carl turned around, Mary Ann was right there staring at him with her arms crossed, waiting for what had better be a good explanation of what the heck was going on!

"Alright, Mary Ann—alright! Stop with the look. I'm sorry. Sit down, and I'll give you the whole story. You know how you and I have been in agreement about how the rule of law has been ignored and how we wish Texas could just leave the union and become its own country again? You also know all the guys in the Colonels' Club and recognize they feel the same way. Well, we—ah... We have been working on a little bit of a bigger plan than just Texas. We've been at work on a way to restore the rule of law...to restore the Constitution—the republic. We now have the players and pieces pretty much ready to go. What we didn't have up until recently was the civilian to be the face of our...I guess you could call it a coup."

Mary Ann's eyes bugged out at that, and Carl realized he needed to keep explaining before she got the wrong idea. "Now, don't spin out when I tell you that the book John is writing is literally the script for one of our scenarios. He came up with this independently from us. I was in shock even though I saw it as a sign that John was our guy—our civilian face. Believe me when I tell you that this is not my idea. It had to come from a higher source, or I would never even have considered involving my sister's husband in this plan."

Mary Ann was definitely spiraling on this new information. Her mind was spinning with all that could happen and not with a desirable ending. What was he thinking using family in this plan? Wasn't it enough that Carl was involved? "Carl, you were telling me the truth when you said you left your cell phones in your lockers because the NSA might listen in—is that right?"

"Yes, sweetheart. I told you the truth, and you made a crude joke out of it, but that was okay. I was relieved you didn't buy it. Now it's time to move forward on this project because the second civil war has already begun, and in our hearts, we know this… You know, don't you, sweetheart? We have to do something besides pray and go to Tea Party meetings. We have a chance to turn our country around—to keep it from running straight off a cliff at one hundred miles an hour! Congress is an absolute disaster. It has become a complete failure, and we need to clear the slate and get people—get servants of the people—in place. Patriots who know and believe in the Constitution and will follow it! Fedzilla has to be brought down now!"

Carl took a cleansing breath; he was relieved that he had finally told Mary Ann everything.

"Carl, I don't even know what to say to you! Are you telling me you and all your colonel buddies and… and…" Mary Ann couldn't grasp the enormity of the whole project. "You want your sister's husband to be what? What is he going to be? How will this end? Are all of you going to end up in prison or, worse yet, dead? All of you *dead*? Good God in

71

heaven, how can you bring us into this? How can you destroy our lives like this? *Why us?*"

Mary Ann couldn't hold back the tears now—they were streaming down her cheeks. All the emotions mixed together; the anger and fear were consuming her.

Carl couldn't handle it when she cried. He turned, walked outside, and looked heavenward with his own tears rolling down his face. He knew Mary Ann felt betrayed and terrified. At that second, he started praying for his wife, for himself, for Jaylynn and John, and for all the others the Colonels' Club was drawing into this plan—but most of all for reassurance that he was doing what God wanted. Was this God's will? Maybe he should just run from this—or maybe God was asking him to run toward it? Would Mary Ann come around and stand by his side or completely retreat from him?

CHAPTER 13

MOGEN COMPOUND — THE BLACK HILLS OF SOUTH DAKOTA

John Mogen heard the ding notifying him that a text had come in on his phone as he and Jaylynn were driving home from their breakfast with Pastor Steve. After entering the house, he sat down in his recliner while Jaylynn heated water for tea. With a sigh, he picked up his phone and scrolled to the new message. Taking a deep breath, John prayed for direction for the days ahead. What words of wisdom did Steve have for them?

As John stared at the text, looking at the two Bible verses Pastor Steve had sent him, he leaned over, grabbed the notebook and pen he always kept on the table next to him, and wrote down the Bible references. Then, he grabbed up his Bible and started to look them up.

A little while later, Jay came into the room, her tea in her hand, ready to sit down next to John in her own recliner. "So, what kind of insight did the pastor have for us? I hope he didn't say we are out of our minds?" It was very hard not to hear the sarcasm in her voice.

"Well, all I have in front of me is a text with two Bible verse references. The first one is First Samuel 18:14, and it says, '*And David had success in all his undertakings for the Lord was with him.*'"

"That's it? That's the whole verse?" Jay asked.

"Yes, that's the entire verse. No explanation—just the verse. But I believe I recognize what it's saying. I just don't know how we're supposed to know if it's God's will. How are we supposed to know that? We know it can't be just a coincidence that my book and what Carl's club wants is lining up so closely. Is that a clear go-ahead from God?" John could see the wheels turning in Jay's head…and knew another question was coming his way.

"John, how did Pastor Steve come up with these verses so fast? Given when the text came in—we were still on the road. How long does it take him to get to his office from Millbrook's restaurant? He didn't have much, if any, time to study. I think I'm going to give him a call right now to ask him about this."

John turned to the second verse. Meanwhile, Jay's phone was already at her ear as she waited for Steve to answer.

Steve wasn't surprised how quickly the call had come from the Mogens. "Hi, Jay. I assume you are calling about the verses I sent to John. Do you two need any clarification on why I just sent those?"

"Steve, I just put you on speaker so John can listen also," Jay informed him as she hit the button on her phone.

Steve was actually excited to explain how God had put the verses in his head as soon as he'd started driving away after having breakfast with them. After all, it seemed significant because he didn't recall having memorized these specific verses in the past.

"How was it that you came up with the two verses you sent us so quickly, Steve?" Jay queried.

Steve was eager to tell them how God was involved. Taking a deep breath, he began to fill them in on his revelation. "Well, as I pulled away from the restaurant, I began silently praying to God for some guidance for you and John, and instantly, those two verses came to me. Totally a God thing, I'm sure! However, I'm still researching the verses so I can try to give you some additional insight into how they relate to your circumstances. I'm especially thrilled how quickly God gave them to me and how they truly fit the situation."

"HoLY crap!" Jaylynn couldn't help herself.

"Jay!" John admonished with a smile in his tone. "That's not exactly the response Pastor would expect to hear from us."

They could hear Steve laughing at the other end. "Oh, and by the way, Colonel Mogen, I can't accept your offer to be the chaplain of the militia you are commanding. By the way, what is the name of the militia?" Steve had completely forgotten about secrecy in his excitement.

John replied as deftly as he could under the circumstances. "Very funny, Steve—very funny. Let's talk about this another time. You do understand, Steve?"

Steve realized what he had done and wished he could take it all back. They now had to talk in code. He had blown it badly and was embarrassed. He carefully retreated by saying, "I understand, John. I guess you need to get to the place in the book where my character comes in. I'm humbled that you want your chaplain character in this book to be modeled after me, but I just don't think it's a good idea."

John was not happy about this and was now regretting even confiding in Steve. "Thanks for the Bible verses. We'll see you Sunday," he said quickly. "Have a good rest of the week."

Steve had to let John know why he was declining to be a part of this whole scheme and spoke up before John could hang up. "By the way, John, I am rereading a book by Dietrich Bonhoeffer called *The Cost of Discipleship*. Let me read you something that Bonhoeffer says about evil."

There was a short pause. John could hear the rustling of pages in the background as he waited for Steve to speak.

After a moment, the pastor continued with the quote. "Bonhoeffer says, 'The only way to overcome evil is to let it run its course, so that it does not find the resistance it is looking for. Resistance merely creates further evil and adds fuel to the flames. Evil becomes powerless when it finds no opposing object, no resistance, but instead is willingly borne and suffered. Evil meets an opponent for which it is not a match.'" Steve took a breath and kept going. "John, I agree with Bonhoeffer. We need to pray—just pray for change."

John was frustrated by Steve's approach. "You know that Bonhoeffer was hanged for being part of a plot to kill Hitler, right? You know that if Hitler's evil had been allowed to run its course, every Jew in Europe and maybe the world would have been exterminated? Do you really think that's what God would have allowed to happen? All those men who fought in World War II for God and country—not just that but for the world—were wrong? Bonhoeffer changed—he got it. He lived his faith by defying—by personally joining the fight against evil. You are wrong to sit on the sidelines—just wrong. You are going to miss your Bonhoeffer moment, Steve." With that, John promptly hung up. Then, he turned and looked at Jaylynn.

Jaylynn was mortified. "John, I'm so sorry for not being able to control myself and making that call. I really put Pastor Steve on the spot. I am not used to being—to being…covert I guess."

John looked at her lovingly while shaking his head. "Covert is one thing you have never been, that's for sure. You are as *overt* as anyone I have ever known. That is why I fell in love with you, Jay. You tend to be spontaneous, while I'm the planner. You have a math brain and a wild heart—a very rare combination. I sure don't know what's in store for us in the next year or month—or, for that matter, the next hour with things moving so fast. What I do know is you saved me from what I envisioned as an engineer's life—boring and predictable. Do you remember that first time we met? I actually saw your cross necklace before I looked into your incredible green eyes. At that moment, I thought I was going to drown in them— no, I *wanted* to drown in them! A Christian woman who was strikingly beautiful. And you know what you said to me, Jay?"

Jaylynn just had to jump in at that point. "I said, 'A cowboy, huh?' I saw that University of Wyoming logo on your shirt. And then I asked you if you even knew how to ride a horse. You said, 'I'm a cowboy, aren't I?' I will never forget the look on your face when you asked me if I could ride, and I said that I had grown up on a cattle ranch and had a room full of trophies for barrel racing—so yeah, I can ride. I swear your face still gets red when I tell people what you asked me about barrel racers."

John smiled and reminded her, as he did every time they talked about that first meeting, "Yes, I do recall what I said. I asked you if it was true a barrel racer could crush a man with their thighs. And your reply—from a Christian woman, no less—was…"

Jaylynn promptly took over the telling of the story. "My reply was, 'Yes.' I don't know what came over me that day!" Jaylynn was shaking her head with a genuine smile breaking through. "I wouldn't normally have been so bold to say that to a man I had just met, but it came out so fast. I was looking up at you. I don't know…I guess it embarrassed me."

John was surprised at what Jaylynn was saying. This wasn't how the retelling normally went. Her words had changed. She had never told him this before. They both knew their connection had been immediate, but that first exchange had been so deeply sexual, it was breathtaking. The friends with them at the time had just kept looking back and forth between the two of them until John's buddy had blurted out, "Wow, man—wow!"

Jaylynn teased John as she tried to pull him out of his recliner. "Come on. Let's just see if what I said is true, John. Let's see if a barrel racer can pop a man's head like a grape!"

John loved it. He loved the playful side that showed up at unexpected times in their day. "Careful, Jay, you're going to break the recliner. Jay! Jay!"

That's how their marriage was. Lightning could strike at any time. Jay screamed as the recliner went over backwards.

After the dust had settled and they had their clothes back on, Jaylynn resumed the conversation. "Now, what was it we were talking about?"

John reminded her that they had one more Bible verse to look at. "Okay, the second verse—stop giggling, Jay! The second verse is from First Chronicles 12:32. How did we even get sidetracked that bad?"

"You started it, John," Jaylynn reminded him as she pointed her finger at him and continually declared, "You! You! You!"

"Can we pause this for another time, Jay?" John loved it when she let loose, but now they had to get back to business. The timeline on this whole project was moving quickly—too quickly. So, John continued by reading the Bible verse: *"of the sons of Issachar who had understanding of the times, to know what Israel ought to do, their chiefs were two hundred; and all their brethren were at their command."*

John and Jaylynn sat there looking at each other in bewilderment at how this verse fit in. Shaking his head, he said to his wife, "I'm really going to have to do some research on this verse." He was in a quandary about this one.

The couple sat in the swing on their front porch with both dogs at their feet and the Hills ablaze with a spectacular sunset. They continued to pray together about what to tell Carl until nothing but the illumination from the solar landscape lights was left. Still, all John could think about was the numbers. How many people could die if things went south? If fewer than 620,000 died, would that justify it? As long as they kept the number lower than the first Civil War, would that please God?

John was comforted by Jaylynn's hand on his arm until she prayed, "Lord, be with us both as we try to restore a place for your kingdom here on earth so it can thrive. Let this be a bloodless undertaking if you can and do not spare our lives if that is what is required for success. Let it be your will, Lord—your will."

Before this all got dropped in his lap, John was pretty sure it would have taken a logging chain and a D8 Cat to pull him into a plan like this, but now, with reluctant understanding, he believed it was time. Someone had to do this. He would be the one to answer the tap on the shoulder.

With a look of authority and calmness, John quietly turned to Jaylynn and whispered the words he said he would live by if the time came. "Okay—we pledge our lives, fortunes, and sacred honor to the cause of freedom." Talking to himself more than his wife, he continued. "Now it's all in—no turning back." John was working hard to convince himself that they had made the right decision.

"Jay," John pleaded, "we have to be careful how we communicate and who we communicate with until this thing is over. We can't just make calls like we did to Pastor Steve. It just can't happen. Now that we've made the right decision, I feel like all the eyes of Texas are upon us! I need to put a call in to Carl."

As John reached for his phone, it started ringing. Sure enough, it was Carl.

"Hi, John. I'm just calling to let you know Mary Ann and I were just praying about you two."

After Carl's greeting, John's first question was, "Is Mary Ann in the know and all in for our trip to Alaska?"

Carl got it immediately and responded, "She was surprised that the trip was almost all planned without her, but she has warmed up to the idea."

"Just wanted you to know that Jay and I have also been praying. We are all in, Carl. Whatever it takes to make it happen. Jay wants to be part of the planning—a major part." John finally took a long, deep breath. He had no illusions about what they were committing to.

Carl responded by saying, "Great to hear it, John! The kids don't know yet, so let's not discuss it with any of them until things are set, okay?"

"We may have mentioned it to one of the kids, but they will keep it in confidence," John said sheepishly. *Oh, God, what had they done?*

Carl was as cool as they came under fire, but he had to get a handle on himself quickly. "Okay, John. One of my kids will be in your area very soon and will stop by for a visit. He might stay a few days. He has some presents from us we forgot to bring when we flew up. Take care of him, will you?"

John responded quickly. "Sure. We will be looking for him."

As he spoke, Carl was getting a signal from Mary Ann. "Okay, okay. Are you on speaker, John? Is Jay listening?"

"She's right next to me, so I'll put it on speaker. Just a sec, Carl."

"No problem. Mary Ann wants to say something to both of you."

They could tell Mary Ann was crying but trying to stop as she said, "I love both of you and—and I'm sorry we got you into this!" That is all Mary Ann could get out before succumbing to more tears.

Jay responded, trying to comfort her. "Mary Ann, you know us—we are up for anything. I might even get in a helicopter this time. No wimping out. Anyway, life is an adventure, right?"

Carl came back on. "Thanks, Jay—Mary Ann needed to hear that from you. We'll be in touch. Call us after our kid shows up with the presents. Got it?"

In the background, Mary Ann yelled, "We love you two!"

"We love both of you. Good night and don't feel bad about any of it, Mary Ann!" Jay replied.

Carl ended the conversation by commenting, "Hope you are making some progress on your book. You should have a few chapters written by now?"

"I'm all over it, Carl—making good progress."

"I'm impressed, John," said Jaylynn, turning to her husband as he disconnected from the call. "At first, I didn't know what the heck you were talking about. How did you learn to talk in code like that? Carl picked up on it right away—wow. But what I don't get is which kid is coming and why he didn't mention a name. I would like to know if it's our nephew or one of our nieces at least."

John rolled his eyes as he said, "First of all, I learned to talk in code this morning when talking to Pastor Steve who totally blew it when he called me 'Colonel' and then used the word 'militia.' Secondly, none of their kids are coming. Carl was talking about someone he is sending to get us set up. He said not to call them back until after he delivered the presents, which probably means he is sending an encrypted way to communicate. I just hope we haven't blown it already. We can't be talking about this at all around our phones or TVs—any device that might be picking up voice!"

Jaylynn's mouth was wide open. "John, you just said all that with your phone in your hand. And who is this *kid* he is sending, and how will we know he is from Carl?"

John put his right index finger over his lips. Then, setting their phones on the deck rail, he took her by the hand, which he noticed was damp and shaking. Together, they headed for the barn. It was time to feed the horses and take a moment for a deep breath.

"Jay," he confessed shaking his head as they walked, "I'm getting so paranoid in all this chaos. We are so not used to all this, and we have to assume we're being listened to—maybe even being watched—day and night, anywhere we happen to be! Think 1984 only more high tech! New rule: We talk in the barn or in the pines behind the house—that's all. And I'm sure Carl will have a way for us to know who this kid is when he or she shows up. You and I have to realize that from this time forward, our lives may never be the same."

Jay and John stood in the barn, each realizing it would be harder than they imagined to move forward with this plan, and they saw that in each other's eyes. Hers were welling up with tears at the same time as John's. They embraced and cried in each other's arms.

What's next? they wondered. *And how will we accomplish all that needs to be completed?* They would have to act and think differently until the plan for the restoration of their beloved republic was carried out. Either they would both be in prison, be dead to this world and with the Lord, or be part of the hoped for outcome—a restored nation! Thank the Lord they were not alone.

CHAPTER 14

NSA FORT — HIGH PERFORMANCE COMPUTING CENTER 2 — MEADE, MARYLAND

Sam was nervous when he saw Gloria and Henry (who was supposed to be working Foreign Division) head for Luke's office and then close the door behind them. Henry had arrived at the node, walked by Sam without so much as a hello, and continued over to Gloria's station, then whispered something to her. Almost immediately, she had gotten up, and they had entered Luke's office together. There had been no attempt to hide what they were doing from Sam. He had been taken out of the loop with anything concerning Carl Justine or John Mogen, and Gloria had barely spoken to him since he had smoked her about being fired.

As the door closed behind Henry and Gloria, Luke said his hello and inquired, "So, what's the concern you two have about Colonel Justine and his...his...?"

"His brother-in-law," Gloria finished Luke's thought and continued. "Henry has a feeling about this whole thing that he can't shake, so I have been doing some further follow-up on it. I thought this was all about this brother-in-law writing a book. Do I have that right?"

Luke nodded, acknowledging Gloria's assumption. But he had a gut feeling that Gloria was being overzealous about this, especially since she seemed to be humoring a newbie and maybe—just maybe—was still upset with Sam.

Gloria went on. "Well, I asked for some additional phone records from the Bumblehive in Utah, and I got two more word hits for John Mogen. As you know, I have continued to add to his red flag list, and we now have a transcript from a call to a Steve Lunquist. This Steve addressed John as a colonel of a militia. Mogen's reply seemed to be a tad bit strained, and he seemed to be trying to send a message to this Steve guy not to use those words."

Luke was skeptical of the importance of the conversation. He hated the fact that these transcripts didn't let him hear the tone of voice of either party. "Okay," he said. "Let me see the context of the conversation." Viewing the transcript, Luke took in the lines that were highlighted in yellow, which captured the part that had Gloria and Henry suspicious. "Do you have at least three sentences before and after this?" Luke questioned. "I'd really like to see more of this exchange if there is more."

Gloria excused herself and hurried back to her desk, picked up the requested information with the entire conversation on it, and returned to Luke's office. Reading on, Luke got to the part about Steve thanking John for modeling a character after him in his book. He stared up at both of them. "Okay, you two. You did read the part about this guy being a model for a character in this Mogen guy's book, right?"

Gloria spluttered, "Yes, but—"

Luke cut her off. "Henry, report back to Foreign, and Gloria, you stay here for a minute." After Henry had left, Luke reflected on Gloria. She was good at what she did, but he was questioning whether her judgment had been clouded by this Colonel Justine thing like Sam's had been. He decided not to scold, just redirect. "Gloria, what is your gut telling you about this? Tell me you aren't using Henry to get back at Sam somehow. Just because Sam has done something out of character—unprofessional, that is—don't go down that path with him. Get over it, don't wait for an apology from him, and remember you still report to him except on this tracking. I respect your work ethic and abilities, so what is the deal here?"

Gloria was not deterred. "Luke, I know how it looks. This one has bothered me from the moment Sam relieved Henry and then called his friend, Carl. I don't suspect Sam of anything, but I'm looking at the behavior of the subjects on this. I think they are quick on their feet and go into code talking when it's needed."

Luke was still skeptical about the whole scenario, but that was part of his job. "Okay, Gloria. Stop including Henry on this and get Char to help you follow up on this investigation. Do you have any idea what these guys might be up to? Is John Mogen former military? Is this other guy military? We need some hard facts to move forward. Get on it!"

Gloria knew Luke was right. They couldn't just go on something that was little more than a feeling. With a quiet sigh, Gloria responded to his question. "John Mogen is a retired engineer who spent a lot of his career in the oil business as a project manager on offshore oil projects. He grew up in Wyoming and graduated from the University of Wyoming with a degree in petroleum engineering. The other guy, Steve Lunquist, was an architect but made a career change when he was in his thirties and is now a Lutheran pastor. Neither one of them have any known criminal past or associations, other than the Tea Party, that would raise a red flag."

Luke raised an eyebrow.

Shuffling her feet, Gloria spoke before Luke could voice his concerns. "I know, I know, Luke—you need something more. Give me one more week on this, and if I find nothing, I'll drop it altogether."

Luke smiled and replied, "Agreed. These guys just don't fit any terrorist profile. One more week in this rabbit hole, and that's it!"

Gloria was frustrated as she turned to leave his office. "Okay, Luke—thanks for the week," she grudgingly responded.

As soon as she reached her workstation, she began typing in additional requests for all phone records for John Mogen and Carl Justine for the last month. Utah Data Center should have all of it for Carl at least since he was already on a watch list. She also made a mental note to check in with her NSA contact about John Mogen's internet activities and phone conversations to see if anything new had popped up. She needed something more than her gut feeling, so she would just keep digging.

CHAPTER 15

MOGEN COMPOUND – THE BLACK HILLS OF SOUTH DAKOTA

Jay walked into their bedroom, looking for John to remind him tonight was his regular Monday evening AA meeting. She shouldn't have worried; he was already changed and ready to go. He had faithfully attended meetings since his intervention when he was in his forties. He had not taken a drink since then. He got it. He knew he had to stay involved and understood that he didn't have to feel out of control or that he had a weak faith in God. He had helped others in the program but had yet to start sponsoring anyone here in South Dakota. He still received calls from some of the guys he had sponsored in Houston but had told them after his move to South Dakota they really needed to find someone local.

On his way out the door, John kissed Jaylynn goodbye and headed to Sturgis since he had found that meeting had his kind of sick, twisted freaks in attendance. He hadn't talked to his sponsor since Carl had revealed the plan, and because of that, he was in the middle of a moral dilemma about what or if to tell him.

"Coach Jack!" John smiled as he thought about the fact that this moral predicament should not exist in his life.

"No secrets" was one of Jack's mantras, and he meant it. When John had first met Jack, he'd known right away this former Army drill instructor and old football coach, as well as old linebacker like himself, was the sponsor he needed. No nonsense, all black and white, and by God, do not lie to him. When John had met with Jack after asking him to be his sponsor, Jack had told him in no uncertain terms that absolute honesty was a requirement, and if he found out he had been lied to, he would show up at John's doorstep to personally kick his ass. Jack had been eighty years old at the time and probably couldn't do it, but he had still made his point, and John truly believed Jack would follow up with his threat if he messed up.

The second rule Jack had was that if he called John, then John had better take the call. The way Jack had put it was, "I don't care if you are screwing your wife. You had better stop and take my call! Do you understand? If your cell rings, you had better pick it up and look at that screen. If my name is there…!"

John had responded with, "Yes, sir," which had been a huge mistake.

Jack had yelled at John, saying, "I am not an officer, son. Do not call me 'sir.' It's Sergeant—I mean, Jack!" Then, Jack had smiled, realizing he had just time traveled back fifty years to the Fort Benning, Georgia, parade ground.

Jack had already agreed to become his sponsor when John had first heard him speak. He had an amazing story of redemption, and in spite of his large and growly demeanor, he loved the Lord and his fellow human beings. Jack, like John, had become a real student of the Bible and the U.S. Constitution. Jaylynn thought he was actually a big teddy bear but didn't hesitate to be as tough as he needed to be.

John had realized he needed a new sponsor when he'd moved to the Black Hills, and he and Jack had hit it off from the start. At that point, Jack had become another surrogate father to him, even though they had only known each other a short time. With all this in mind, John knew he had to tell Jack what was going on and had no doubt it would be held in the strictest confidence. He knew he needed Jack's support during this entire situation, and although he had made a commitment to Carl, his resolve was vacillating.

After the AA meeting, John and Jack went out for their normal fare of pie and coffee. As they were getting seated, John popped up and excused himself so he could put his phone in his truck. It was a quick trip, and he was back in a couple of minutes. As usual, they had picked out their favorite table in the back with a full view of the entire restaurant and no other people around them.

Jack immediately asked John why he had gone back to his truck.

"I had to put my phone away because people might be monitoring all my calls."

"That sounds more than a bit paranoid to me, son," Jack said a little sarcastically.

"You'll understand when I tell you what I'm involved in." John was speaking in a tone that Jack hadn't heard from him before.

This got Jack's full attention. "Should I turn my phone off?" he asked a little nervously.

"It does no good to turn your phone off, Jack. They can still listen in," John pointed out in a low voice.

"John, who the hell are you talking about? The CIA? The NSA?"

"Both of them—maybe more agencies. They have what is called artificial intelligence, which looks for certain words or phrases that lock their computer on to you and report it."

Jack grimaced. "Geez, John. What on earth are you involved in?" He was all ears now!

Now, it was Jack's turn to take his phone to his truck. After he returned, John quietly proceeded to tell him the whole scenario from the time he had studied the online maps of the U.S. that had revealed to him a completely divided country to the second he had said yes to being the colonel of the militia—the face of the constitutional restoration coup.

Jack stayed surprisingly silent during John's explanation. In fact, when John had concluded, Jack continued to sit quietly while rubbing his chin. The silence was deafening for a time, but when Jack spoke, all he could say was, "Wow! Logistics and personnel and a whole lot of moving parts to get this done. What are your odds, John?"

John hadn't even thought about the probabilities. "Well, Jack, the only likelihood I really know about is the one that tells me we have a 100 percent chance of losing our country if we don't do something mighty quick. I know it's a complicated plan, but if we can just go big and go fast, this will work." John sounded like he was trying to convince himself more than Jack.

"I don't see how you can do this without anyone finding out—without a rat sneaking into your tent and spying on you. It does sound like the Colonels' Club must have connections with other Oathtakers—I'm one myself—who can help. How do you keep this big of a secret? You have to know who you're going to war with. You need to have warriors on your side—warriors who are loyal and understand the times we are living in. Like those who threw in with King David in First Chronicles chapter… twelve I think."

"Holy crap, Jack! Wait, wait, it's in my wallet. I wrote it down!" After fumbling for a moment, John pulled out the slip of paper. "Okay, First Chronicles 12:32. Is that it? Is that what you are talking about?" John was losing it. How could Jack know this? Could this just be a big coincidence? God sure had a sense of humor if it was.

"Hold on just a sec, John. That sounds about right. I'm looking it up," Jack replied as he searched for the small Bible he always carried with him.

"Okay, let's see… It says, 'of the sons of Issachar who had an understanding of the times, to know what Israel ought to do.'"

John sat back in his seat in amazement. "Let me give you the background story on this. When I shared all this with our pastor, two Bible verses came to him before he even opened his Bible, and he gave me the references. Jack, this is one of the verses. Wow—just wow!"

The hair was standing up on Jack's arms as he said, "John, it took me a long time to understand that life is not a series of random events and amazing coincidences. Things are orchestrated by God, and He talks to us if we just take the time to listen. I spent a lot of my life railing against the will of God to no avail, and because of that, I had too much heartache and misery. It took me two years and five or six wagon falls to get through step five. If you ask me, this sure sounds like a message from God! I say, find those sons of Issachar to go to war with you. To me, it sounds like you already have found them. Am I right in my thinking?" Without waiting for a response, he asked, "Now, what is the second scripture?"

John glanced at the piece of paper in his hand again and read, "First Samuel 18:14."

"Ah yes," Jack whispered. "*...and David was successful in all his endeavors because the Lord was with him.*"

They sat in silence, both lost in their own thoughts, until Jack looked at John and proclaimed, "I'm here to help you in any way I can, Colonel Mogen. I will be honored to be one of your sons of Issachar."

John didn't even realize he had been holding his breath until that moment. As he exhaled, his appreciation for the support of his friend and mentor grew tenfold. "Thanks, Jack. You just gave me some incredible help in getting this right in my head!"

CHAPTER 16

MOGEN COMPOUND – THE BLACK HILLS OF SOUTH DAKOTA

The next morning, John and Jaylynn saddled up the horses and set out on their morning ride. Jaylynn had that look in her eye that she had when she wanted a challenge. So, John gave his horse a beg and took off as fast as he could, knowing she would catch up to him and Jake.

This time, he had gotten a good jump on Jay and her horse, Buttercup. Even though Buttercup had balked at first, she was digging her hooves in now—with dirt flying—and hitting her stride. Of course, John's hat came flying off as he looked back to see Jaylynn low in the saddle and driving hard. Jay caught him fifty feet from the crooked arm pine, which was their set finish line.

After the race was over, John trotted up next to his wife, but Jay was preoccupied with looking at something in the sky, which caused John to do the same. When John spotted it, he immediately pulled out his .45 Long Colt Ruger revolver and was taking aim just as it disappeared over the top of the tall pines. Although both of their horses were pretty much bomb proof and had been trained to handle gunshots, the buzz from the drone was something they had never experienced, and Jake was dancing.

"Really, John?" Jay said, laughing. "You were going to shoot that little thing out of the sky with your .45?"

John wasn't laughing as he replied, "I have to find out where that came from and who it belongs to! And I am not paranoid!"

Jay had mercifully forgotten about their commitment to the audacious and most likely suicidal plan for constitutional restoration. But as the reality of the situation came into focus, her heart rate quickly soared. "Probably just one of the neighbors," Jay said, trying to calm herself just as much as John.

"Going forward, I'm going to have my shotgun ready so I can do some drone skeet shooting if I get another chance!" The tension and anger in his voice were thick.

Trotting up to the barn as they finished their ride, both were surprised to see the car belonging to their daughter Kayla parked in the half-circle drive of their log home. The look that they gave each other conveyed that neither of them had known their daughter was coming. She had obviously driven all the way up from Austin, but why—and why unannounced?

"Looks like we might be in for some daughter drama," groused John.

Jaylynn gave John the *look*. "Maybe she just needs some family time. It's a lot of stress planning a wedding! Now, promise me you won't talk politics with her. Please? I just want a normal, no-drama visit."

"Go see what she is up to, and I'll put the horses up." John's response was tepid at best as he turned and led both horses toward the barn. He loved his daughter, but...

Kayla Lynn was twenty-eight years old and living with her fiancé, Trevor. She was hopelessly addicted to the liberal Kool-Aid that was served on a daily basis in the city of Austin. She and John had, at best, a strained relationship that was exacerbated by Kayla and Trevor living together before marriage and Kayla's refusal to attend church anymore.

Kayla was a taller version of Jaylynn. Standing at six feet tall, she had the same glowing olive skin as her mother that would tan when touched by the sun. Her auburn hair was just a little redder than Jaylynn's had been before her silver had taken over. Kayla's clear green eyes were as remarkable as her mom's. One would think they were looking into the depths of her soul, they were so vibrant. She also had been a rodeo queen like her mother back in the day, and Kayla commanded the attention of every male when she entered a room. She had that one-in-100,000 shape—a Barbie doll shape—that had warped many a young girl's mind when they looked in the mirror. Kayla's ample breasts, small waist, and curved butt gave her that beauty queen figure.

She'd refused to enter any pageants but had warmed to a modeling career at one time because the money had appealed to her. The first and only modeling agency she and her mother had visited had blown it with Kayla almost immediately. They'd measured her body and mumbled about her height. Then, they'd measured her face—again muttering all the while. "Eyes a couple of millimeters wide, chin a little shallow, length between bottom of nose and top lip a little long. Let's see… Hmmm, we can get a few teeth pulled to get the face narrower."

As the little flaws in measurements and the idea of pulling perfectly good teeth were being discussed, Kayla had gotten up and walked out of the office. The assistant in charge of the interview had dashed after her, calling, "We haven't talked about your photo shoot to get your portfolio together!"

Without a backward glance, Kayla had kept walking out of the building and then climbed into the Mogen SUV. That was Kayla. If you upset her—especially if you talked about her as if she weren't there—you would lose her. As the car had pulled out of its parking space, the woman had pleaded with Kayla to roll down the window to no avail. There would be several phone calls from the agency, but Kayla had already moved on. She had later been approached by a fitness magazine representative who had encountered her at the gym, but Kayla had refused to do any photo shoots with them also.

After entering the house, Kayla had gone upstairs and was quickly taking up residence in her usual room when Jaylynn caught up with her. As Kayla's eyes met her mom's, Jay knew it wasn't good. Kayla's bottom lip quiver immediately gave her emotions away, as it had since she was a small girl. The tears came so quickly that Jay didn't even say a thing but just wrapped her arms around her daughter.

When Kayla's crying finally subsided to some extent, Jay broke the silence. "Is the wedding off?"

The sobbing quickly ramped up again as Kayla nodded her head against her mom's shoulder. Jay continued to hold her daughter, but as time went on, Kayla pulled away, more calm and in control even though she continued to bite nervously on her bottom lip.

"Mom, I need some time to get my nest built in the bedroom and bathroom. Then, I'll be down to talk."

Jaylynn understood that Kayla needed a little time to regain her composure, just as she had when she was little. As always, she would do that by performing small mundane but necessary tasks.

"I'll be downstairs, honey. Just come down when you feel like it. Did you drive all night?" Kayla nodded in the affirmative. "Fine, you get some sleep," Jaylynn said as she turned to leave. "And we might see you around lunchtime? Your eyes look more than a little red." Jay wanted to give Kayla a speech about the dangers of all-night driving in an agitated, emotional, and distracted state but held back. Kayla was here—safe in their home—and that was the most important thing.

"Where is my little girl?" John asked, walking through the front door.

As Jaylynn descended the stairs, she answered her husband. "She is up in the south guest room and needs some sleep, so let's leave her be until she gets some rest and comes down. She said she drove all night, and she's overtired, not to mention an emotional wreck."

"It's that Trevor, isn't it? I don't trust that kid. I've never had a good feeling about him!" John snapped as he paced at the bottom of the stairs.

"All I know is the wedding is off for now, but I don't know why. She'll tell us when she comes down, I'm sure. It will be our time to listen, John. You hear me? Emphasis on 'listen.' Do not bad mouth her fiancé or act relieved about it—just listen!" Jaylynn said sternly.

"I understand. She really must be hurting. I truly don't like that she drove all night—and I surely don't..."

John was cut off mid-sentence by his wife. "John, do not bring that up with her! She is here safe, and that is all that matters!"

"Geez, okay, Jay..."

John jumped as the doorbell rang. Actually, it played the national anthem. Jaylynn started laughing at John's reaction, and he gave her a look as he went to answer the door. He glanced at the loaded M&P .40 in a holster attached to the log wall just inside the front door and was tempted to grab it before he answered but decided to leave it in its holster.

When he opened the door, there stood a young man standing slightly taller than John at about six-foot-four. He had reddish brown hair, a squarish jaw with at least a two-day beard, and blue-gray eyes that were purely alive. He was built like John—an old linebacker—only a bigger, more fit version. He filled up the whole doorway with his wide shoulders and looked more like a guy who had just completed a Special Forces mission than the geek tech John was expecting Carl to send.

When the pair shook hands, John felt like his hand had been put into a vice. He had to up his grip pressure quickly to offset the young man's strength.

"Jason Wilder, sir. Are you John Mogen? Colonel—I mean, Carl Justine sent me. I'm your comms man for this mission." John had known that Carl had someone coming but was so shocked by the young man's presence in front of him that he forgot their protocol.

"Come in, Jason. Welcome to Pine Creek Ranch. This my wife, Jaylynn," John said, still marveling at this young man who looked nothing like a technical geek whatsoever.

"Sir, I think we need to start using some verification protocol from now on. A phrase, I believe, has been agreed upon?" Jason queried.

John's face got red as he realized this kid in front of him could have been sent by anybody. "Sorry, Jason. Cowboy up—that's it, cowboy up," John responded sheepishly.

"Thank you, sir. Now, let me get my bag of gear out of the car so we can get started. By the way, sorry about the drone," Jason said apologetically. "I was just getting a good look at the property for a possible base camp for the detail that's coming in tomorrow. We need to set up perimeter security. Thanks for not shooting the darn thing down—it's one of the expensive ones."

That got Jaylynn laughing again. John scowled at her as he and Jason headed outdoors to the custom four-wheel drive pickup with a camper shell that Jason had obviously arrived in. They had more than one bag to offload, and he realized getting the comms bags into the house might become a problem.

"Our daughter Kayla showed up this morning out of the blue, so I think we need to put you and the equipment up in the apartment over the barn for now. I'm sure this will be a little more complicated since she is here," John explained.

"I know she is here, Colonel. She's a very beautiful woman—takes after her mother. She's very smart as well. Though, politically, she is out in progressive land. How do you handle that?" Jason wondered.

"Not well," John admitted, shaking his head. "Not well at all. It's as if all reason goes out the door with her when it comes to politics and the Constitution. And it doesn't help that she works for a liberal state senator in Austin and is engaged to a guy who works for Dell!"

John contemplated whether he should correct Jason for calling him 'Colonel' but decided to let it go. Then, as the thought ebbed, he glanced over at his wife to see her sending optical daggers across the room at him for divulging such personal family information to a man they had just met.

"How did you know she's here, and how do you know what she looks like?" John questioned.

"We have access—or can gain access—to things like Facebook and Twitter accounts. We know who she works for and where she works, who she is engaged to, where she went to school, where she lives, what kind of car she drives, even what she ate for dinner last night."

"Really? What she ate for dinner?" Jaylynn questioned.

"No, I was just kidding about dinner, but we have to know a lot of this data just in case... I'll just say..." He hesitated briefly before plunging forward. "...if others attempt to use your daughters or your son-in law or your grandchildren as leverage against you and your wife. We already have our guys assigned to them," Jason said casually.

John could see that Jaylynn's countenance had changed considerably. Now, she was fighting back tears. The realization that they and their kids and grandbabies were going to be put in mortal danger had hit Jaylynn like a semi-truck going eighty miles an hour. She could barely breathe.

"Jason, what exactly is your background?" John asked.

"Well, sir, I am former Air Force Special Forces Command—Pararescue. My group is—*was*—forward targeting and communications for air operations as well as rescue operations oversight. We could be anywhere in the world, dropping out of a C-130 or C-17 with equipment to set up full satellite comms and radar on the hilltop of our choice, within two hours. Although people probably wouldn't believe it, we were right up with the Navy SEALs in physical and mental abilities. I still train five days a week, and now I own my own IT security business. We provide systems and personal security for businesses and affluent clients in the Houston area mostly."

John and Jaylynn exchanged startled glances, more than a little impressed by this young man standing before them.

Unaware of the couple's reactions, Jason forged ahead with his explanation. "Five more of my guys will be arriving tomorrow to set up security here at the ranch. They are self-contained and will be camping back in the trees out of sight. Two are former Air Force Special Forces, two are former Navy SEALs, and one is a former Marine sniper. You'll meet them tomorrow. They will be guarding you and your family with their lives."

As they moved into the great room, John had to sit down. His mind was reeling with all that Jason had just said. He'd known Carl was sending some people, but now his stomach was really churning. If they had one breach or just said one thing to the wrong person, they would be toast. He was already regretting talking to Pastor Steve, and then he'd opened his mouth to his AA sponsor about what was being planned as well. This had better happen fast—it just had to because he was feeling a little nauseous like he had before every football game he'd played in. It was the reaction he had before going into battle. God in heaven, why did he ever agree do this? Should he contact Carl now and call a timeout on this whole thing?

At that moment, Jaylynn's arms came around him from behind, and he knew he had to do this for her and his grandkids.

"Sir—sir, are you okay?" Jason asked.

John was suddenly snapped back into the moment. "Yes, Jason, I'm okay—just a little reality check," he muttered. Then, he glanced back at Jaylynn with a resolve that gave her some much-needed reassurance.

"Okay, sir, let's get started with the encrypted phones for you and your wife. But first I need to ask…does your family—your daughter Kayla—know about this whole thing?" Jason inquired.

"No, just Jay and I know. I did share with two trusted friends. Our pastor and my AA sponsor, both of whom I trust completely," John admitted a little sheepishly.

"Not good, sir—not good. I will need names, addresses, and contact info for both of them please."

John nodded and then wrote down the info for Jason. After that was taken care of, the three of them went through the complete communications plan, the security plan for the ranch, and an emergency evacuation plan. Jason also requested that John and Jaylynn carry a weapon with them until the completion of the restoration.

Jason also noted to himself, as he looked John directly in his eyes, that he would try to remember to call him John instead of Colonel but might slip. He then asked the couple for a password or phrase that only the two of them would recognize to help them verify whether someone was working with or sent by him, his men, or Colonel Justine.

John and Jaylynn looked at each other, pondering the question. Then, a big smile came across John's face. Jaylynn was still preoccupied with the task, and she wondered what John had come up with.

"Meet me in Cairo in three days!" John said with some excitement in his voice. It was code talk he and Jay had used when they were first married and in the presence of family or coworkers. It meant "I love you," which he had been embarrassed to say out loud at the time, but they could utter this phrase and know it was between just the two of them. It made their love fresh and exciting. Even though he had gotten over the embarrassment a long time ago, he and Jay would never forget it—never.

"Okay, I have no idea what that means, so that's a good one. Now, you need to come up with a backup in case that one gets compromised or we decide to change it up."

"Gig 'em!" Jaylynn yelled out with exuberance.

With a furrowed brow, Jason asked her to say it again. So, Jaylynn repeated it and even spelled it for him.

"Ma'am, that one is a little hard to understand. I thought you said 'git 'em.' It needs to be cleaner—something that would not be misunderstood. Maybe you have something else? But if you don't mind me asking, ma'am, what is that anyway?" Jason was clueless.

Jaylynn was a little red-faced but mad and a tad embarrassed. "Aren't you from Texas, son? Don't you know about Texas A&M and the Aggies?"

Jason was a little shocked by her reaction. "Okay, ma'am, we will use it as the backup—didn't mean to offend."

John's laughter was just a little too loud, and Jaylynn smacked him on the shoulder so hard that Jason started to chuckle also.

"It's going to be fun working with you two—I can tell that! Now, let's talk about my cover story. This is your long-awaited housewarming present from Carl and Mary Ann, so that's why I'm here. I have an eighty-inch smart TV in the truck and some other electronic goodies for your house. The smart TV has been changed up so it cannot listen to you or watch you. I will also need to scan the house for any listening devices just as a precaution."

"That's wonderful to know, but I think we need to get you settled in the barn apartment before Kayla comes down. Then, you can get started on what you have to do. We should have some lunch ready by the time you're unpacked."

Kayla had just gotten up minutes before and had wandered out to the loft railing. She had brushed her hair a little but was standing at the railing in panties and a cropped top with no bra in sight. As John and Jason headed for the door, they disappeared from Kayla's view, never noticing her standing above them on the landing.

Still in the great room, Jaylynn spotted Kayla from where she was standing and just couldn't resist the mischievous thought that came into her head. Before she knew it, the words came out. "Well, good morning, Kayla. Are you ready for some lunch there, sunshine?"

John and Jason followed Jay's gaze, but they had to step out from under the loft and turn around to see Kayla above them. As the men came into view, Kayla's eyes met Jason's, and time suddenly stood still in the Mogen house. Had this guy just come to life off the cover of one of her mom's romance novels? Was this woman with the most beautiful tanned and toned Barbie doll legs, deep green eyes, and long auburn hair real?

Kayla had completely forgotten what she had on—that is, what she didn't have on—and was staring at this hunk standing next to her dad. Her body was reacting to this guy she had never even spoken to—*oh my God!*

John broke the silence. "This is Jason. Jason…Kayla. Nice panties, Kayla, but you might want to get some pants on before you come down for lunch!" John snickered and shook his head.

Kayla's face turned bright red at that instant, and she turned and ran to the back of the loft. Then, she grabbed a quilt from her mom's quilt rack and draped it around herself before heading back to the rail for another look at the man who had taken her breath away.

But John and Jason were already heading out the door. As they exited the house, Kayla overheard Jason say, "Thanks, Colonel—I mean, John."

As Kayla quickly walked back to her room, reality struck about what she had heard, and she began to wonder who this guy was. What was he doing here, and why had he called her dad 'Colonel'? As she stepped into the shower, she couldn't make the smile on her face go away. The exchange of a gaze with a man had never—*never*—had that kind of an effect on her physically and emotionally. Wow—just wow!

As Jason walked to the barn apartment, he kept reminding himself that Kayla was John Mogen's daughter. She was a raving liberal progressive, and he had to concentrate on his task at hand. He had to get the

Mogen ranch secure. He had to keep Colonel Mogen out of any traps—communication or otherwise—that might endanger the mission. And he had to teach Colonel Mogen how to be a commander. Jason just had to concede that Kayla was a fine physical specimen—*my God, she was fine!* He also had to keep his buddies from seeing her, or it would become a huge distraction from the job they had to concentrate on.

As John was showing Jason the details of the upstairs space, he noticed Jason was looking at everything—truly at and in everything.

"How far to the ground if I exit this window onto the roof and need to jump to the ground, John?"

"Twelve feet—maybe a little less because of the overhang. There is another thing I need to show you, Jason." As they walked over to the back of the main room, John continued. "This closet's back wall actually has a storage space behind a concealed door. Then, there is a second door that leads out to the balcony. We can walk through it to get in or out of the apartment."

Jason checked out the storage and secret egress. "Awesome, John. Thanks for showing me this. Very well hidden!"

"I'll leave you to get settled in. When you are ready, wander back over to the house for lunch—it should be ready by then, and my daughter should be fully dressed!" John stated slyly. He had seen the wide-eyed look on Jason's face when he'd laid eyes on Kayla. John could only wish she would be attracted to someone like Jason—oh well.

As John was leaving the apartment, Jason dropped a paperback book onto the small dining table in the kitchen. John glanced at it as he was walking by and stopped dead in his tracks. The title on the cover was *Sons of Issachar for the 21ˢᵗ Century* by Bill Lewis. Goosebumps erupted all over his body, and he quickly turned and asked, "How did you come across this book? Is it any good?"

"Well, all of us working with you are Christians, and we are all Oathtakers, but we call ourselves 'The Sons of Issachar' because we have an understanding of the times and know what America needs to do."

The only words out of John's mouth were, "First Chronicles 12:32."

John and Jason just stared at one another, and then a huge smile broke out on John's face because now God was not just affirming but hitting him over the head with a heavenly rock! He reached down, picked up the book, and opened it to the dedication page. At the end of the dedication, it read, *"May the Lord raise us all up as Sons of Issachar for the 21st century."*

John quickly turned away from Jason as he made his way toward the apartment door. "See you in a few for lunch," he reminded him as he headed out of the barn. The tears betrayed him, but no one could see. He was a colonel of the...what? They didn't even have a name for the militia. He was a colonel and had to show strength and resolve and wasn't about to cry in front of a former Special Forces kid.

John would soon come to understand just how important this kid would be to him and his family.

CHAPTER 17

CIA HEADQUARTERS – LANGLEY, VIRGINIA

"**S**ir, Luke Anderson over at NSA needs to talk to you—line 2," Nathan Parkinson's aide said as he popped his head into Nathan's office. Nathan had the job of assigning agents within the U.S. to check out possible domestic threats from foreign nationals. The invisible line was being crossed with U.S. citizens at a higher frequency. Nathan was the person who decided whether the FBI needed to be brought in. This protocol violation was becoming routine.

Gloria had had John Mogen's computer hacked and had shared with Luke the outline for the novel. Luke had carefully reread everything about the Arlington Colonels' Club, especially Carl Justine and his retired engineer brother-in-law, without discussing it with Gloria Baker or Sam Hudson. At this point, Luke's gut told him to at least take a "boots-on-the-ground" look at the situation.

Nathan hesitated just a moment before he picked up his phone. "Luke, how are you? I'm guessing this isn't just a call to find out how I am?" he snarkily questioned.

"It's nice to talk to you too, Nathan. So, how is your son doing in football? I bet his moves are something else by now?"

"Okay, Luke, sorry about the smart-ass comment when I answered. Guy is doing great. He has been working with a strength coach this past year. He stands at six-foot-two and weighs in at 220 now." After touching base with Luke about his wife, Nathan changed the focus back to the reason for Luke's call. "So, what is it you're calling about?"

"I'm emailing you a file concerning the Arlington Colonels' Club and a retired engineer, who is the brother-in-law of one of the club members. The colonels on this list are being watched because of the nature of their retirements. Colonel Carl Justine is retired Air Force and, as you will see, made a quick and, I believe, unplanned trip to see his brother-in-law and sister. All the contact information on the colonels and this John Mogen is included, of course. Mogen's IP address and cell phone numbers for him and his wife are also included. I need you to review all the info and let me know if my gut is still giving me good vibes or if it's all coincidence and I'm reading too much into this."

"I need a couple of days to review all this data. I've got requests coming out my ass right now, but I'll get back to you as soon as I can."

"Okay, Nathan," Luke said softly. "I know my hunch isn't as big a priority for you, especially if you have foreigners to work on." Luke felt a little queasy about taking an agent's time away from other investigations for his gut feeling, but at least he could put this to bed if nothing was afoot.

CHAPTER 18

NORTHWEST WYOMING COAL MINE – OUTSIDE OF GILLETTE, WYOMING

"**Y**ou are looking for the D11Ts with the remote operation option, right?" quizzed Mr. Knutson.

The young man from Waco Excavating Co., who looked to be no more than thirty years old, replied, "Yes, we are. I'm so sorry you are shutting down, by the way."

Knutson shrugged his shoulders and calmly said, "That's how it goes in the mineral extraction business—boom or bust. Hopefully, some other company will buy the coal mine. I truly wish someone would build a power generation plant right next to us. That would solve the problem and makes the most sense! Now, back to the business at hand. Do you know how much these used D11Ts cost, son? We have five of them, and I assume you are looking at just one machine to buy?"

"No, sir, we're interested in all five. I've looked at them on the website, and I would like to offer you 750K."

"You are talking per machine, right?" Knutson responded, a little more than surprised.

"Yes, sir, that's per machine. I know you have them listed at 850K per unit, but I'm asking for a discount because I'm buying all five," the young man stated flatly.

Knutson stared at him and responded by saying, "Son, you're telling me you have 3,750,000 dollars to spend on these five machines? Really?"

The young man opened the manila folder he was holding and handed Mr. Knutson a certified check for 3,750,000 dollars from a bank in Waco. "Of course, we'll wait till you get the funds in hand before we take possession of the machines. Also, we'll be transporting them to a yard in Rapid City, one at a time, before we haul them down to Texas."

Mr. Knutson was impressed with the professional manner of this young man. "Well, by golly, son, you are definitely not a 'lookie-loo.' I'll call the home office and run this by the powers that be, but I am going to give you a 'yes' right now since I'm making the calls on site. Let's go pull the files on the machines so I can get the serial numbers to put on the temporary receipt for you."

"Thanks, Mr. Knutson. Let me give you the information on the trucking company that'll be moving the machines to Rapid City until we can set up the convoy to take them all to Texas."

Knutson's call to his home office was short and sweet. The company was in desperate need of the cash right now. They had tried to hang on a bit too long, hoping to get other contracts before they called it quits.

Three days later, a special rig with a lowboy specifically designed to carry the big Cats, weighing over 200,000 pounds, pulled into the mine yard to pick up the first D11T. The special permits had been secured, and all the Cats would be in the Rapid City yard Colonel North had rented through a dummy corporation that had been set up within the week.

CHAPTER 19

ARLINGTON, TEXAS

Colonel Allan North took a deep breath when he got the call telling him to meet the young man who had secured the Cats. This young man had been under his command in Iraq and had really been struggling since his return. Even though Allan hadn't personally known him in Iraq, he was encouraged that the young man had sought out the PTSD program after his return. He was honored to have been asked to become his mentor, which had grown into a friendship as he'd helped the young man function with his PTSD in a positive way. Now, he was a mentor for other returning soldiers as well as a suicide intervention specialist.

"Colonel, I received word that we've got the service dogs for all five of our vets on the waiting list. They should arrive within the week," the young man said with anticipation in his voice.

This is what it is all about, thought Colonel North as he sat at his office desk. He had trusted this young man not only with the vets' dogs but with a lot of money and a lot of logistical maneuvering to get those machines they needed purchased and moved to the yard in Rapid City. The young man and his buddies had the training that was needed to remotely operate those Cats.

"Well done, Billy—well done! Let me know when the dogs and vets are all trained up as teams!" Colonel North replied with satisfaction. This piece of the puzzle was way ahead of schedule.

CHAPTER 20

LOCKHEED MARTIN "THE LIGHTHOUSE" — SUFFOLK, VIRGINIA

Jackson Trumbull had just arrived at his desk and begun checking his cell phone for any calls he had missed. He'd been in an area of the research facility that was off limits to any personal technology, so he'd left his cell in his desk drawer.

Right away, he saw he had missed a call from Naval Commander Chris Kendall. Jackson was always happy to talk with Chris. He was always running things by him that no one else in Research came up with. Even though Research had some talented engineers—the best and the brightest—they had never been downrange and lacked that "I wish I had this" kind of thinking that can only come from field situations.

Chris's cell began to ring, and as he picked it up from the corner of his desk, he saw the incoming call was from Jackson. "Jackson—thanks for getting back to me!" he said with exuberance.

"Always good to talk with you, Chris. It's never boring, and the concepts you bring to me are like fresh blood transfusions for those of us who are supposed to be innovators. Do I need to go to a secure room and call you back on a different line? Are we talking a classification level here?"

"Well, the B-1B patent for the dropdown gun swivel is on my computer right now, and it is evidently in the public domain. I have an off-the-wall application for it that I'd like to run past you."

"I will call you back on your encrypted number," Jackson said, as Chris had piqued his curiosity. "But first, I have to get access to *the room.*"

Three hours later, Chris's encrypted line rang. It was Jackson, who had finally secured access to the shielded communication room. "Okay, Chris, we are good to talk classified now. Whatcha got for me?" Jackson queried.

Chris inhaled deeply and started in. "Well, I know you were and are still deeply involved in the development of the Black Dragon mini subs, and we push them out of C-130s currently. If we wanted to get subs somewhere faster, like in the belly of a B-1B bomber, could we do that using the dropdown gun turret Boeing has designed? What I mean is, drop it down with the riders on top, then deploy the stealth wing assemblies and let it drop?"

Chris drew another breath and continued. "The other thing we need to develop is a new chute design that will let the subs kiss the water instead of plunging in. What we have now is hurting my guys and doing some damage to the subs. Do you know what the minimum airspeed of the Bone is? I can't find that info in the public domain."

Jackson sat there in amazement as his mind opened up to all the concepts Chris had laid out before him. Of course, no one at the Lighthouse had considered anything like this. They had been given a briefing by Boeing engineers about the bomb bay gun dropdown turret apparatus and had then been challenged to come up with ideas for additional applications for the turret. They had recommended the use of rail guns and lasers for the apparatus, and a Boeing engineer had responded that it was actually designed for that since the B-1B could outrun traditional ballistics and shoot itself off course. Even now, Boeing was working on the additional auxiliary power needed to operate lasers and rail guns and was developing the targeting algorithms required.

"Jackson, did I lose you? Are you there?" Chris asked.

"I'm here, Chris. Geez, my mind is going like crazy. We were briefed on that dropdown gun turret by Boeing and were asked to come up with applications for it. You know how justifying a project can be. It all helps to keep the money flowing. I actually have all the specs on the Boeing design. I calculated for them that if you could slow the B-1Bs to minimum speed through a turn, they could still use the Vulcan mini gun cannons safely. I'll do some additional calculations to see if the subs can hold together with the stealth wings deployed at the bomber's minimum speed with the wings full forward and trimmed for slowest level flight. The bomber's speed is slower than most would believe."

Chris could hear Jackson's mouse clicking away in the background.

"Let's see…the latest I have on the chutes—hang on." More clicking could be heard. "Okay, here we go. The new chute design has been sent to the manufacturer already. It will allow the subs to kiss the water. They have actually been redesigned to hit the ground without causing damage to the subs by equipping them with skids on the bottom to keep the sub upright. The only problem I can see you might have with the new design is if you encounter high winds. Looks like if you do have high wind gusts when landing, you can get lifted back up into the air with the bigger chutes. The SEAL riders will have to time the chute release carefully if they encounter these conditions. But at least they will be landing in water since a ground landing is not intended, of course. I just have a couple of additional pieces to figure out. The first one is how to get the gun swivel arms to hook onto the four pop-out knobs that are used to crane lift the subs. The other one is, will the sub's detachable wings hold together at the B-1B's minimum speed? I'll get back to you with the answers to your questions, but right now, my next step is to convert this into a proposal so I can get it approved. I'll need that approval to move forward on your project." Jackson took a deep, cleansing breath, which only brought more ideas swimming into his head.

"Thanks, Jackson. It's great to hear that the new chutes are being made already. I know that some things usually take more time than I like them to, so I'll wait patiently for that approval. Since you will be spending hours working on this for me, let me remind you that evil doesn't wait—it acts, it moves, and it destroys," Chris responded in code.

Chris knew Jackson would be back on the project as soon as they got off the phone. He would still do the proposal for the higher-ups, but Jackson would make it happen personally. When Chris had said he would wait patiently, he'd meant the opposite, and Jackson knew it. Chris needed to eventually meet with Jackson and see if he was actually an Oathtaker or what.

His mind was spinning as he pondered whether Boeing had even built any of these dropdown gun swivels—or would they have to use C-130s and do pushouts? Was the high-speed range of the B-1Bs that important, or were they trying to do something crazy for no good reason?

CHAPTER 21

MOGEN COMPOUND – THE BLACK HILLS OF SOUTH DAKOTA

Jaylynn was just finishing up the turkey and ham sandwiches when Jason came in from the barn. At the same time, Kayla was descending the stairs from the loft.

Jason was wearing a light blue T-shirt with an image of a SR-71 Blackbird on it. It fit like a second skin, and there was no question he worked out regularly, as his biceps could attest to that fact. His outfit also included a pair of dark blue tactical pants, and on his right hip, he carried a concealed handgun that he wasn't too careful about keeping covered. Dark gray hiking boots finished off his outfit.

Kayla had carefully picked out some olive-green yoga pants and a tan tank top that was cut low to show her sports bra and significant cleavage while her white running shoes looked brand new. Kayla did not make direct eye contact with Jason until she reached the last stair. She was extremely worried she might take a misstep in his presence. When she finally looked up and their eyes met, she was simply in awe of this male specimen standing in front of her. A fleeting thought crossed her mind that there must be something wrong with him, for he seemed too good to be true.

As she continued toward the kitchen, Jason kept reminding himself he was on a mission, and he could not get distracted. But damn, she was so tall and so fit and—he betrayed his attraction for her by glancing toward her chest as she approached. Kayla noticed his glimpse, smiled at him, and was happy to see that he was a genuine male that she could distract.

John's voice interrupted the surreal moment as he stated, "Join up and let's ask a blessing before we start."

At that very moment, Kayla had been getting ready to shake hands and reintroduce herself to Jason, but that abruptly turned into holding his hand as her father offered the blessing. His hand engulfed her own, and his grip was firm, though he embraced her hand in a gentle manner. Kayla felt like a thirteen-year-old airhead who was holding hands with the boy she had had her eye on for the entire school year. Her thoughts were on anything but the prayer her father was offering. *Okay, Kayla,* she thought, *control your breathing—control the situation.*

At the end of the prayer, she and Jason squeezed each other's hands, but the release was enticingly slow as if both of them knew the other wanted to extend the contact a little longer than appropriate for the situation. Kayla's face was flushed—her body was responding again, and she felt out of control. Besides, she just knew that everyone else in the room could guess what was filling her thoughts at that moment.

As Kayla's hand left Jason's wanting more, he looked at her left hand. Long, slender, feminine fingers, tan with an obvious white band where a ring had been.

Early the next morning, Kayla dressed in her customary running gear as she took off for her morning run. She had stayed at her parents' one-hundred-acre property a few times before and knew the route her father had laid out for a running path. It had some challenging hills and beautiful pines that made it an amazing cross-country journey.

As Kayla crested the first hill, she saw someone running a quarter mile ahead of her. She was pretty sure it was Jason by his size and hair color, so she decided to kick it up and catch up with him. She had researched his name on the internet last night and found out he owned his own company and had a degree in electrical engineering. He wasn't just a "TV guy" like her dad had said. His company provided security for computer systems, home or business security, and bodyguards as needed. He was a decorated former Air Force Special Forces guy. Definitely not just a "TV guy."

Jason was far enough ahead that he had disappeared over the next hill, and Kayla was really pushing to catch up to him. She had misjudged how fast he was going and thought she would have been closer by the time she crested that next rise. But as Kayla topped the hill, Jason was nowhere in sight. She stopped in a stand of pines to catch her breath and lost it just as quickly as a hand touched her shoulder from behind.

"I have pepper spray," she said teasingly. She knew it was Jason.

"I have a gun," he quipped. "Are you following me?"

She turned and looked up at him, which was unusual since she was six feet tall. "I did a little research on you last night. You aren't just helping my dad hang TVs, are you?"

Jason knew he couldn't reveal his true mission here, especially since she did not share his and her dad's political bent. "I used to work with your Uncle Carl in the Air Force, and he knew how hard I've been working at my business. I told him I needed to get away and smell some pine trees, and he suggested I come up here to help your dad with his new house and to install some state-of-the-art audio/visual and security systems. A smart house that is almost impossible to hack. So, I'm bringing up some of my guys to help out. They will be camping out on the other side of the creek later this week. Anyway, how long do you plan to be here?" he queried.

Ignoring his last question, Kayla responded by asking, "Are you like my dad and mom? Are you one of those conservatives who thinks the Constitution still works and the founders were wonderful even though they owned slaves?"

Jason answered without hesitation. "Yes, I am one of those conservatives, and I'm also a Christian like your mom and dad. I believe you were also raised in the faith, weren't you? I sense you are speaking out of ignorance of the history of our founders and the Constitution. So, I won't be discussing any of this with you until you read a particular book. I found it very useful—it's titled *The 5000 Year Leap.* It's all about how our nation came to be. Seems to me, if we would have just followed the Constitution, we wouldn't be in the mess we are in now."

With that said, Jason took off running, and Kayla stood there realizing that her political beliefs had again completely alienated a man she was attracted to. She concluded she might as well get on back to Austin, find a like-minded man to fall in love with, and forget about her ex-fiancé and this Jason Wilder guy, who had just turned her off with his politics and beliefs.

As she took off at a quick pace, she could still feel the touch of his hand as it had rested on her shoulder. Why couldn't she shake the effect it had on her? She had gone from wanting to pull him behind some pines and drop her pants to despising him for his screwed-up worldview in a matter of seconds. How dare he call her ignorant?

Good God Almighty, he was such a hunk, and for a moment, she thought about trying to catch up to him (knowing she probably couldn't) and making him listen to her point of view. Then, she realized that was why she was up here in South Dakota. She had completely alienated the man she was in love with and left Austin in such a rush, and for what? Over politics? That had led to derailing their marriage plans—probably for good. She was irritated at what Jason had said but more so at herself because she was losing total control of her life. So, for now, she needed to get her life back on track. She would start by heading back to the cabin and getting this running gear off. Then, she'd face the day with her head held high.

As she entered the yard, her mind drifted back to his hand on her shoulder and the way it had caused her body to react so fast. It was downright upsetting to her, and she did not have time for this. That man was a neanderthal, and she had convinced herself that some primeval part of her was responsible for her behavior. *I won't let that happen again,* she told herself with conviction. She was a sophisticated, enlightened female who operated on a different intellectual plane than he did. *Why would he call me ignorant? What was the name of the book he talked about?* As she walked in the front door, she was determined to get back to Austin. She would leave first thing in the morning—no more all-night red-eye drives.

As the next morning dawned, Kayla was up early and ready to head back to her life. She didn't belong here and needed to face the issues she'd left behind. Who needed the problems this Jason guy would bring into her life anyway?

"Kayla, promise me you will stay on interstates and not wander on the back country roads in the middle of the night like you did coming up here." John was trying to use his dad voice, but Kayla was having none of it.

"Have you heard of GPS, Dad? I'll be fine. I'll head straight east to Sioux Falls, then turn south. I'll either stop in Wichita or Oklahoma City for the night. Is that okay with you?" Kayla replied snidely.

Jay interceded. "Just give us a location every once in a while. You know how I worry when you're on the road. Please be careful and let us know where you stop for the night." Jay whispered to Kayla as they hugged, "Please remember to check your smart-ass attitude. It's not an attractive quality for my daughter to have. You know I love you and only want the best for you, sweetie."

As they walked to her car, her mom turned to her. "Kayla, not to change the subject, but did you get to talk to Jason at all? He's quite the package, I must say."

Kayla ignored her mother's observation and reacted sharply. "He is a neanderthal, Mom! He is living in the past. Please, no more discussion about Jason!"

As Kayla got into her car, she looked back up at her mom and dad. They both had a misty look of sadness in their eyes, but she ignored the sudden desire to get out of car and give them another hug. Instead, she turned her attention back to the trip ahead. But as she rotated the key to start the car, all they heard was the clicking of a dead battery. It was dead as a door nail.

"When was the last time you put in a new battery?" John asked, trying to maintain a helpful tone.

"Never, Dad—never."

"I'll have to pull it and take it into town to get it checked out. I suspect you will probably need a new one," John replied, trying to maintain a patient, nonjudgmental tone.

Jason appeared just as John was heading to the barn to get some tools to remove the battery. "John, my guys are almost here. Do you mind if I go unlock the gate for them?"

"Not at all. Just use the key I gave you."

"Thanks, John. After they get here, I'll get them all settled at the RV hookup behind the barn."

"Sounds good."

Before he took off to open the gate, Jason looked straight into Kayla's eyes and repeated, "Remember the book, and then we will talk—okay?"

Kayla gaze softened enough to tell him she would let him know. His eyes were fixed, and the longer he zeroed in on hers, the more she felt that feeling coming back again. *Stop it, Kayla—just stop it*, she admonished herself.

"What book are we talking about here?" Jay asked as her eyes darted between the two.

"*The 5000 Year Leap*, ma'am. I think I saw a copy on your bookshelf in the house, right?" Jason said, knowing he was correct. Kayla rolled her eyes at Jason, but his look was unnerving. At that moment, Jason's phone rang, and he excused himself to answer. As he took off toward the front gate to meet his guys and show them where to park the RV during their stay, his thoughts vacillated between the mission and that spirited woman who, at that very moment, was watching his back as he walked away.

As the girls were observing John pull her battery, Jason's pickup drove by at a slow pace. It was followed by a huge black RV that looked like it was on steroids. The only identifying words on the unit were "EarthRoamer XV HD."

Kayla now turned to her mom in amazement. "What the hell is going on, Mom? Who in the world has something like that? Besides, who would need anything that mammoth? That thing is way above and beyond what is necessary for a man to own. I can't even imagine how much fuel it uses."

Jay had to guard from her daughter the real reason for the RV being at their place. "It's just some of the guys who work in Jason's company coming up to do some camping with him. You have to admit this is a welcome change from Texas."

Jay knew by the astonished look that she was giving her mother that Kayla wasn't buying it.

"Mom, I heard Jason call dad 'Colonel,' and don't tell me he was confusing dad with Uncle Carl or any bullshit like that—I know better."

Kayla's tone told Jay she knew lies were being told—even as a little girl, she'd always known. Thank goodness John had already put Kayla's kit under the back seat in her car. When the time was right, he would contact her and explain the reason and what the contents were for. But the time was not right yet. Not now—not now. As her daughter continued to look at her, waiting for an answer, Jay felt cornered big time.

After Kayla had walked away from God and elected to embrace the progressive movement, there had been an ever-widening crack in their relationship. If Kayla knew what she and John were involved in, she might actually drive away and report what was happening at their ranch. Would she actually betray her parents?

"Mom!" Kayla literally yelled at Jay. "What is going on here?"

Jay braced herself to lie to her daughter, whom she suddenly perceived as a possible enemy informant. In her toughest mom voice, Jay spoke with authority. "First, young lady, do not ever use that tone when you speak to me. Second, Jason simply misspoke when he called your dad 'Colonel.' Jason's company is not just an IT company. They also specialize in cybersecurity and supply bodyguards to people of means, mostly in the Houston area. These bodyguards are all former military Special Forces and are highly trained. They are simply here for a break—a mini vacation, which Uncle Carl arranged with our consent. They do physical training every day and will probably use our shooting range in back to keep their skills sharp...so get over it!"

Jay was somehow excited about her ability to—as John would say—pull a stinky rabbit out of her butt. But did Kayla buy it?

Kayla stared at her mother and finally said, "I'm going in the house to do some reading 'til Dad gets the new battery in my car. Then, I'm outta here."

CHAPTER 22

NSA FORT – HIGH PERFORMANCE COMPUTING CENTER 2 – MEADE, MARYLAND

Luke Anderson sat at his desk with thoughts of going through his daily update list. His intention was to update and follow up on their progress when he came across the hits on John Mogen and Colonel Carl Justine. It had been a week since the first report had caught his attention. Since then, he had asked for further investigation by those further up the chain of command. While the thought was still in his head, he picked up his phone and called his buddy, Nathan Parkinson, at CIA headquarters.

Nathan had nothing new and reminded Luke, "You know, you are still about twelfth on my list, and you really need to call the FBI directly. They have offices in Dallas and Rapid City. Essentially, what I'm saying is, you need to start with them first, Luke. I have to work on the solid stuff before I send people out on hunches, even if they are based on multiple data hits. Sorry, man—call the FBI."

Luke was a tad upset about being put off by Nathan, but on the other hand, it was just a bunch of data hits, and Sam had explained most of them away. Nonetheless, for some reason, it was still nagging at him. So, he decided to give Gloria Baker the okay to request additional investigation from the FBI.

In the past, Sam Hudson would normally get this handed to him, but he had broken protocol by directly contacting Carl Justine. After that,

Luke had placed a written reprimand into his personnel file and removed him from this investigation. In the long run, Sam hadn't been pleased about being pulled in and lectured about any of it.

After being contacted and asked to come to Luke's office, Gloria wondered if he had noticed that she was still quietly looking for hits on John Mogen and Carl Justine. She was nervous as she knocked on his door and then walked into his office after he waved her in. He requested that she close the door behind her, and she complied readily.

To her surprise, Luke began with an apology. "Gloria, I'm sorry about all the mixed signals I've been giving on this Mogen/Justine situation." He hesitated, looking out his office window before he continued. "Something has been nagging at me about the data lineups. I want you to contact the FBI offices in Dallas and Rapid City and request their agents to follow up on these two and this club. Your gut has been a good alert system for us in the past, and I trust your instinct, so let's go with it. Meanwhile, I still want to keep Sam completely out of the loop, which shouldn't be difficult since he thinks we've dropped the whole thing."

The smile on Gloria's face completely betrayed her normally stoic and professional demeanor.

"Okay, now that this decision has been made, get out of here and get back to work!" Luke said teasingly, knowing Gloria couldn't wait to get on this.

Within thirty minutes, she was sending the information on John and Carl as well as the Arlington Colonels' Club to the respective FBI offices.

Even though Luke had wished nothing be revealed to Sam, he knew almost immediately because of the protocol he had set in place but hadn't revealed to Gloria. It was not common knowledge that any request opening a new FBI investigation required the immediate supervisor's approval. It was a backdoor verification meant to ensure NSA researchers couldn't request investigations on their own. As a result, Sam received a call from both the Dallas and Rapid City FBI regional offices to confirm that the request from Gloria had come from Sam Hudson himself. Sam had no choice but to approve the request to keep the water as calm as possible. He was surprised that Luke had forgotten about this protocol—or had he?

Sam's frustration with the whole thing had him on the edge and ready to walk away from the NSA altogether. He had weeks of vacation he could cash out, and he decided right then and there to take some time off starting tomorrow morning. Obviously, Luke had lied to him and had not ended the investigation, and Gloria had been permitted to take the next steps. Overcome with frustration, Sam opened up the computer link necessary to request vacation time so he could head out for Texas tomorrow. He really needed this time off.

After closing out the app, he sat at his desk, letting his mind wander back over the last few weeks. Emotionally, the work had been hard on him, which led him to reflect on how he really missed flying, the feel of serious thrust, of G-force effects on his senses—on his gut. There was nothing like a 3G bank. More and more, he longed to be in the cockpit of a Bone just one more time. With a deep sigh, he realized he would have to settle for an acrobatic biplane he was qualified in. These were fun but nothing like a supersonic bomber.

His thoughts snapped back to the present and on the investigation Luke had decided to go ahead with. Had they gotten more data on Carl Justine or his brother-in-law, John Mogen? How could he contact Carl without a phone call that would be tracked and recorded? Being in the business, he always had access to an encrypted phone, which was very useful for just this situation. On the other hand, he knew Carl's calls were obviously being tracked. He urgently needed to get to Texas—to family—and see if he could contact Carl through them. He knew how urgent a face-to-face meeting was. Not only important but required. He would need two days in his car with his normal overnight stop in Nashville. In his youth, he'd been able to drive nineteen hours straight. Could he still do that? No, he'd better not try it.

Sam Hudson was at a crossroads. He'd been hurt and upset when Carl had called him an asshole for knowing he was in the Rapid City Airport and knowing which flight he and Mary Ann were taking back to

Dallas. He'd been questioning his choice of profession for quite a while now. He thought of himself as a patriot, but his idea of a patriot protecting the God-given rights of his fellow citizens was a whole lot different from the NSA's. It seemed more and more that he was working for an agency that was violating everyone's fourth amendment rights on a continuous basis! They could and did lock onto a U.S. citizen's computer and then start monitoring it if the AI picked up on keywords. They would then watch that computer without the person's knowledge and without any kind of search warrant. This was the government spying on its own people, plain and simple. Totally unconstitutional! Sam was done with the NSA—done.

CHAPTER 23

COLONEL ALLAN NORTH RESIDENCE – DALLAS, TEXAS

Allan had received confirmation that Jason Wilder and his team were in place up in South Dakota. Checking that off his list, he had decided it was time to get updates from the other club members starting with Carl Justine.

During their conversation, Carl had reported that he'd secured four out of the five Bone pilots, who were loyal to their cause and ready to fly. He was in the process of locking down the last one. He had also finalized the plan for taking over and securing Ellsworth Air Force Base. The idea of using the dropdown turret system in the B-1Bs had been resurrected by the Boeing engineers. Thankfully, they had worked the problem, and now, it was a go for use with the mini sub. The rigging to connect and lift wench the subs into place was ready. Securing the WMDs into the subs was still sketchy, but Plan B was already in place just in case the clamping system didn't work.

Allan hadn't resisted grilling Carl on that. "What is Plan B for securing the devices in the sub?"

Carl's reply had stunned Allan, and he was seldom surprised. Carl had explained, "Well, you know that foam insulation that you can buy and spray in between the studs in your house? The stuff that expands a lot? We'll have a man suited up and ready to go in personal protective equipment. He will secure the devices with the foam but only as Plan B. Allan, the clamps should work fine. We have built them to fit all five of the devices. The one for the suitcase-sized device that's going to the CIA is a different design."

Allan had been a little shocked by Plan B and retorted, "That sounds a little redneck to me, Carl, but I guess if you say it will work, I won't worry about how far out in the weeds it is."

Carl had reminded Allan, "It's Plan B, Allan—Plan B! But whatever we do, it needs to be fast and secure, and Plan B is both of those."

Allan had acquiesced and continued down his checklist with Carl. "I know I don't need to remind you but…find that fifth pilot!"

Carl had countered that he was working on it. "Believe you me. I will fly it myself if I have to or get one of the C-17 pilots to train on the Bone. Oh, that reminds me. I have a friend at March who has some C-17s ready at all times and has pilots who are loyal to the cause standing by."

As the call ended, Allan was stressing about that fifth Bone pilot while updating his checklist. He had to just trust Carl and move on with his tasks.

The next call Allan made was to Captain Torger Vigdahl, who was responsible to get the Navy SEAL mini submarines to Ellsworth on time and with pilot/caretakers for all five. Torger also had the responsibility of getting the teams of former SEALs to join Jason's crew in securing Ellsworth Air Force Base with the order of minimal (preferably no) loss of life.

Torger had ordered the larger chutes attached to the subs, and they were ready for testing even though there would be no test before the first and last deployment. In fact, the test protocol was a ruse. The new chutes would allow a soft landing on land with the Kevlar skid attached to the bottom of each mini sub. Ski, the Colonels' Club's active-duty Air Force procurement officer, had arranged for the SEAL sub flyers to be trained on the devices and had set up the dead man switch that would activate the detonation system linking the devices to the flyers' heartbeats. This would be hooked up after the devices were safely on the ground. They had to match the EKG of each individual Navy SEAL attached. The SEALs were, in effect, human detonators. The SEALs were trained on the strict protocol for one man to disconnect while the other stayed hooked up so the device wouldn't detonate!

After Allan connected with Torger and again questioned him on the plan, Torger brashly stated, "We are ready to move the subs to Ellsworth. They're stored three days out, so we need notice. My guys are trained and ready to deliver the packages if the Air Force can do their part."

Allan bristled at Torger's tone but knew he had the best man he could hope for to deliver the devices. "Good work, Torger. Be ready to move at a moment's notice," he said begrudgingly.

Torger couldn't resist. "Remember, Allan, I'm a former Navy SEAL. We live to be ready at a moment's notice!"

"Yeah, yeah, Torger—I remember." Allan was tired of Torger's bravado but glad he was on their team.

Colonel North now moved on to his longtime friend, Colonel Bill Musgrave. Bill was still solid as a rock and as gruff and snarly as one would expect an old Marine to be. Allan liked to talk to Bill since he was a no-nonsense type when it came to the men and women he had served with. They loved Bill, although he didn't even want to hear the word used around him.

"Bill—how are you? Had that knee surgery yet? I called to check on the readiness of your piece of our puzzle," Allan said in greeting.

"Things are just dandy, Allan. My knee surgery has been put on hold. Doctors are trying some bullshit stem cell injections first. The pain has subsided some, but don't you tell anyone that I hurt or am even complaining about it. Speaking about my piece of the puzzle, you didn't exactly give me an easy assignment! Do you know how many teams I've had to put together? I've had to combine some assignments. I've picked up a great kid—computer whiz—who has put together a database of all the names and addresses and has figured out how to combine the captures. I'll be glad to move them out of the country for good! We've also settled on several ways to transport the strays across the border if we can't apprehend them at the rendezvous point."

Allan responded quickly and a little harshly. "Bill, for heaven's sake, do not use certain words please! I know these phones are encrypted, but geez Louise."

Bill came right back. "Allan, I wish you would learn how to cuss instead of using those ridiculous phrases! We are mission ready and will adapt and overcome as needed. I trust the kids I have on the teams. So, how is Carl doing on the logistics?"

"Talked to him a while ago," Allan responded. "There will be two or three chartered 747s waiting for the passengers at Reagan by the time you get them there. After takeoff, they will be briefed that they are being transported to an undisclosed base for their safety. I know it's a big operation and a little scary, but we will make it happen."

"Shit, Allan, I'm not scared—I'm excited. If it were up to me, I would throw their asses out of the airplane so I could listen to them scream like the babies they are!" Bill's tone made Allan a little nervous.

Allan reminded him, "We have a plan, Bill, and we will be sticking to it—no throwing people out of planes. We're talking about a civilized, bloodless restoration of our Constitution, not a French Revolution kind of revolt!"

Bill followed quickly with, "Can I just threaten to—?"

"Don't even think about it! Just stick to the script for crying out loud!" Allan said, frustrated by Bill as usual.

Bill was bothered by Allan's use of another stupid phrase. "Did you just say, 'for crying out loud'? Really…did you just say that?"

Allan had reached his limit now. "Bill, just stop—we'll talk again soon, you ornery old son of a bitch!"

Bill enthusiastically answered, "Now that's more like it!"

Allan rolled his eyes as he ended the call. Next time, he was going to tell Bill how much he loved him just to hear his reaction. He trusted Bill with his life and with the toughest mission of their lives. Bill knew the stakes and would follow their plan. It would be his job to gather every senator and U.S. representative as well as the Supreme Court Justices, get them on those planes, and fly them to North Dakota.

This wasn't going to be an easy task, but he had the teams ready and hoped the announcement to the nation would help the roundup. His people had already been trained and put in place to take control of Ellsworth Air Force Base. Three of the five large Caterpillars he had purchased were ready in Rapid City, and the other two had been sent down to Texas to help with the bogus simulation at Dyess Air Force Base. All the pertinent information on Dyess AFB would be leaked, so all agencies would be following the red herring to Texas, and no mention of Ellsworth would be made—ever.

The next person on his call list was making Allan a little nervous. He knew Jason Wilder. He had spent quite a bit of time with him when he'd set up his home's security. Besides procuring the encrypted phone he was using, he had also provided a two-man detail to protect the Arlington Colonels' Club whenever and wherever they met. This security would be tested at their next golf outing. This call would also include the civilian face of their attempted restoration, John Mogen. Allan had his bio memorized and knew that Colonel Carl Justine was all in for this guy—and not just because he was his brother-in-law. Just the same, Allan needed to get a feel for this new addition to their team. Thank God Jason had already spent some time with him. That would help.

"Colonel North, how are you?" Jason queried. He was glad to hear from the colonel. This meant the go signal would come soon. Jason's heart rate quickened, and that adrenaline rush he lived for washed over him. But he still had some details to go over and some training to do with John and Jaylynn before he was confident they would be ready.

"Hi, Jason. How are things going at your end?"

"Things are shaping up here, Colonel. John and his wife are a great choice. Besides looking great on camera, they are both extremely smart. He is also very articulate, and most important of all, he gets it. In addition, we will be working with both of them to fine-tune their firearms skills. And have you seen his horse? Wow! We have already worked out the plan on how we will approach the gate at Ellsworth and how it will look on their security cameras. Colonel Justine—Carl—is working on getting the Oathtakers at the gate exactly when we show up."

Allan broke in. "Wait, Jason, did you say John's wife? Why are you involving her in the training?"

Jason realized this might be news to the Colonels' Club members. He reluctantly responded, realizing he hadn't needed to mention it. "Well, John and his wife, Jaylynn, have made the decision that it is all or nothing, and whatever happens, they will be in this together. She will be on horseback and traveling with my guys when we get to the gate. She is adamant about her place in this phase and says she will not be denied or wait at home to hear how things play out. They have been through it and through it together—as a couple. They understand the risks and are willing to die for the cause—they just want it to be together. Besides all that, she can shoot an AR really well! They have their own range set up on their property, and they told me they have practiced every week since they got up to South Dakota." Jason hoped Colonel North understood.

"Okay, Jason. Because Carl has complete confidence in you, I'm fully on board as well. In fact, I am trusting you with my life. So, let's talk about the communications. Is everything in place to protect the rest of the Mogen family?" Allan asked, already knowing the answer.

"Yes, sir—we have our teams in place and have already placed the family's kits where they will be readily available to them. We'll call them when the operation is a go!"

"Sounds great, Jason. We'll be in touch—soon." Allan's response told Jason that things were going to get exciting very soon.

CHAPTER 24

MOGEN COMPOUND – THE BLACK HILLS OF SOUTH DAKOTA

John had returned from town and was just finishing up on Kayla's battery changeout. At the same time, Jason was concluding his call with Colonel North. "Okay, Colonel—we'll talk again soon." As he disconnected the call, he was surprised by a hand grabbing his right shoulder. His mind told him that it couldn't be Kayla since she had gone back into the house to look for that book he had told her to read, yet at that instant, his body knew it was her. He already knew the feel of her touch.

This is payback to him for sneaking up behind me in the trees, she thought. "I have pepper spray, you know," she said in a teasing way.

Without thinking, Jason countered, "I have two guns, a knife, and a couple of frags on me!" Why had he said that? Would she think he was joking? He only hoped. He was not his careful self around her, yet he prided himself on keeping his emotions under control during all operations. This was the biggest campaign of his life, and he was blowing it.

Kayla added to his loss of control by immediately saying, "I don't believe you, so I'm going to have to do a body search." She was kidding but immediately reached for him. He felt her hand go down the right side of his torso. When she got to the .45 on his side, his hand grasped her wrist, but it was too late. She had felt the pistol. She was smart and beautiful. Wicked smart, in fact, and distractingly beautiful, and he had to get control of the situation. She stilled when she felt his strong hold on her wrist—firm but careful. It gave her an indication that told her more than his answer to her next question would.

"Who is Colonel North, and why were you talking to him, Jason? I'm really getting nervous about what's going on around here. I feel like I'm being flat-out lied to!" Kayla exclaimed, but her tone betrayed her. It hinted she was fearing something.

The silence between them was broken by John loudly announcing, "Your battery is in, Kayla. You're ready to go."

She did not respond to her father but stepped from behind Jason and fixed her eyes on his. Those deep green eyes were waiting for an answer, and Jason's gaze did not waver.

"I'm doing a security project for Colonel North. He knows your uncle. They play golf together. How far did you get in the book?" Jason asked, trying to divert her attention off of him and onto something else.

"I've finished it, and I learned a lot. I hadn't thought about the other unalienable rights until I came across the list of at least twenty-two on page 125. So, I'm taking the book with me to study more carefully," Kayla admitted.

"I'm impressed you got that far in the short time you had."

By then, they noticed that Jaylynn had walked up to the two of them and was listening in.

"I read the entire book. It's a lot to think about, and I'm going to fact-check it when I get back to Austin."

Jaylynn chimed in, "Kayla speed reads and remembers it all in detail, Jason. She's been able to do that since she was about ten years old."

"Good," said Jason. "Now, we can get together and discuss some of the more important things in detail."

Kayla looked at her mother and then took in Jason. She stepped closer and gave her mom a quick hug, then turned and marched straight up to Jason and hugged him too. Not a one-armed careful hug but a full-body "pulling-him-close" hug. He was sure his legs would buckle at any moment.

Glancing toward her parents, who were standing close to her car, she somehow sensed there was something happening here that was dangerous. So, she turned and whispered in his ear, "Take care of Mom and Dad, okay?"

After he whispered that he would, Kayla marched toward her folks, announcing, "You're both full of shit. I don't know what you're up to, but I *will* find out!" Then, she walked over to hug her dad, and with that statement, got into her car and headed off the property. As she went through the entrance gate, she noticed two security cameras that hadn't been there when she'd come in. She also spotted a figure on a horse that she did not recognize off to her left.

As she turned left out of the gate and headed to Highway 395, Jason got a radio call from one of his guys, Truen Walsh. "D2 has headed out. The GPS tracker we put on her car is working fantastic. Her guardians have been informed and are active."

"Thanks, Truen," responded Jason.

Jason, John, and Jaylynn were still looking down the drive where Kayla's car had disappeared seconds ago. Jason was the first one to break the uneasy silence. "Your daughter is beautiful---very..." he stopped and took an extremely deep breath before continuing, "...smart and intuitive. I don't know if we should have let her leave the property at this point. I'm beginning to worry about her safety."

Jaylynn quickly glanced at her husband as he broke out in a huge smile. Then, Jaylynn followed with her own enormous grin. In confusion, Jason stared at them both, trying to figure out what he was missing.

John responded first. "Jason, what was that hug about anyway? Do you and my daughter have something going on we are not aware of? You really need to trust me when I say that she's a handful and has been since she was three years old. Take it from me, it's better that she's not here... But you have protection on her, right?"

Jason's face instantly turned red. Clearly, John and Jaylynn had noticed the sparks flying every time the two of them were within fifty feet of each other.

"Okay, the truth is that I'm a bit nervous about her blowing this entire operation—and, yes, I am worried about her personal safety. I also couldn't help but notice that we are miles apart when it comes to politics, so I'm positive that things wouldn't work out if we had any kind of long-term relationship, don't you two agree? So, let's just concentrate on carrying out our plan to take over an Air Force base without killing anyone or getting killed ourselves! Time is short!" Jason stopped abruptly, then inhaled deeply as he took off his hat and wiped the sweat from his temple with his sleeve.

As Kayla turned onto Highway 44, she noticed that a horse transport was slowing down to make the turn onto Highway 395. It was a huge commercial-style one that could hold maybe ten horses. The strangest thing about it wasn't its size but what was written on the side of the trailer—"Sons of Issachar" in bold red, white, and blue lettering.

What the heck is that? she wondered. Her curiosity was piqued, and she decided she would do an internet search the next time she stopped. If she remembered right, it was from the Bible. Hadn't she seen this phrase more recently? As she drove on, she never even noticed the white SUV that had pulled out behind her and was following at a discreet distance on Highway 44 toward Rapid City.

Not long after Kayla left, Jason and the Mogens moved into John's study. Jason had already had the room hardened against outside listening as best he could. Even so, they made sure they left all phones across the house out of earshot.

Once settled in the study, Jason continued to explain everything to the Mogens concerning the plan. It had been decided from the beginning that all the strategies would be committed to memory. Nothing would be written down.

Some of the things Jason described to John and Jaylynn came as a bit of a shock to them. "We've been actively recruiting Special Forces and former Special Forces members for several years now. We believe that approximately 75 percent of the active Special Forces are on board and ready for this operation. The percentage really jumped up after the Benghazi debacle. We knew a stand-down was a given and why, but this kind of nonsense has got to stop," Jason declared. "The year before, we lost seventeen SEAL Team members, mostly from SEAL Team 6, when a Chinook was shot down in Afghanistan under strange circumstances, which haven't been explained to this day. That event was really when the questioning started and talk about a major change began. It rumbled through the ranks of patriots and continues to garner support even as we speak. We now believe—we hope—two-thirds of the officers in all branches are with us. The plan is set up exactly like you want, John—no blood, if possible. Of course, the wildcard is still the military officers who think they need to protect the status quo, no matter how screwed up this country is or how far outside of the Constitution it's operating. It's amazing how many swear to preserve, protect, and defend the Constitution and have no idea what it says or what they are supposed to defend!"

Before he could continue, John broke in. "I like your passion, son, but before we go any further, I'd really like to know who's paying for all of this. And how do you know all of this backdoor info?"

Jason's grin grew as he responded to John. "Have you heard of the black project budget the DoD has? Are you aware that the money can be approved and appropriated with only a project name and a one-sentence description? We have people all over the Department of Defense who are true patriots and are willing to keep this on the down low. Besides, only the Colonels' Club are at risk—and now you, of course." Jason paused a beat to see if John and Jaylynn were tracking with him.

As they nodded their understanding, he continued. "All the others who are loyal to our cause have been working within the system to educate and recruit additional assets for this mission. Remember, we have all taken an oath that says, 'I do solemnly swear (or affirm) that I will support and defend the Constitution of the United States against all enemies, foreign and domestic; that I will bear true faith and allegiance to the same; that I take this obligation freely, without any mental reservation or purpose of evasion; and that I will well and faithfully discharge the duties of the office on which I am about to enter, so help me God.' These officers have spent the last two years actually instructing their recruits on the Constitution as it relates to their oath. They've also been emphasizing the failures of the Congress in relation to following the Constitution," Jason explained. He was on a roll!

"John," he went on in a fervent tone, "it would shock you how many servicemen have asked their commanding officers how to defend the Constitution against domestic enemies, and that has become the 'aha' moment for the officers and their men." Jason finished off by saying, "So, we have more than enough funding and more than enough men loyal to the Constitution ready to take this on."

John was dumbfounded by the in-depth answer he'd received from Jason. He opened his mouth to reply, but Jason inhaled and resumed his explanation.

"Our hope is that there are millions of patriots out there who are loyal to the Constitution, but most of all, first and foremost, believers in Jesus Christ. We've been praying they are prepared for this moment and ready to rally around a leader who advances the fight for our republic, our Constitution, and our liberty. That would be you, John. We're just hoping that the militias will present themselves to go out and follow our lead and not do crazy things on their own. This will be a bloodless coup. At least that's our strategy, as you know. We don't want another civil war. With your leadership here in South Dakota and the message you convey, our prayer and hope is that we will be able to deliver to the supporters of this great country and our Constitution the plan and path for this restoration. So, no pressure, John."

Still intent upon sharing the details, Jason finally took an additional breath and rolled his eyes with amusement. "The only problem you might have is the divergent thinking about how to conduct the restoration. And I understand you want the Western Southern Alliance, or WSA, to be a distinct territory, but you really need to be able to articulate exactly what that means and how to do it. I'm on your side in all this. I'm ready to help you set up a distinct Christian nation with a separate government alto-gether, but I gotta tell you, we'll be swimming upstream against a strong current. Lots of people will not be able to envision this kind of separation. I mean, wow, you thought Brexit was hard…"

John and Jaylynn sat there stunned and just stared at one another, both lost in their own thoughts. They had had many conversations about how to do the very thing Jason was discussing. He had articulated all their plans in one succinct strategy. They now understood this endeavor had been in the planning stage for many years, and they were just hopping in at the tail end. They were excited that neither entity wanted a civil war to start between the restorationists, whether there were one or two sepa-rate countries. Would they be admitting defeat if the progressives were given their strongholds, especially New York and California, even though the majority of the people outside of the WSA were so brainwashed and asleep? Would it—could it—work for the whole country?

John and Jaylynn took a moment to contemplate their situation. As Jaylynn's eyes began to glisten, Jason started in again.

"One thing we haven't discussed is the Canada situation. Have you two heard of Wexit?"

John nodded affirmatively at the same time that Jaylynn shook her head no.

"Well," Jason continued for Jaylynn's benefit, "Wexit includes all the Canadian provinces west of Ontario. That is Manitoba, Saskatchewan, Alberta, and British Columbia—at least eastern British Columbia… maybe not Vancouver. We've been in contact with some of the leaders of this movement who are very unhappy with the way they're being treated by the current government of Canada. They are interested in joining the WSA—if we succeed in separating from Washington, D.C., of course. A few of us have been having a separate discussion on their restoration plan. This group really gets it! If this opportunity plays out, that would mean an immediate elimination of the northern border from North Dakota to include Minnesota and over to the eastern slopes of the coastal range in British Columbia."

John had to break in at that point. "Jason, how many people know about all this? How big is this network, and how are we keeping this from getting out to the defenders of the nonsense our country is going through right now? Up to this point, I was a little apprehensive, but now I'm getting really anxious!"

Jason understood where John was coming from, but he remained cool as he continued to lay out the plan. "When you are in the Special Forces, you get to know more teams from countries all over the world, and we know former Special Forces personnel in Canada. We're safe for now. Furthermore, we're prepared to put the plan in motion within days."

Jaylynn's stomach was churning so badly that she had to quickly excuse herself. *What had they done—what had they done?* She was ready to get in her truck and head somewhere—anywhere. Her flight response was taking control of her mind and body. She ran down the hall and made it to the bathroom just in time, as she was crying uncontrollably and throwing up simultaneously. "What have we done?" she kept whispering to herself. "What have we done?" *Snot, tears, and puke—how attractive is that?* Jaylynn thought as she wiped down her face with a cool cloth.

John was very aware of how upset Jaylynn was as he watched her retreat down the hall toward the bathroom. He also knew not to hover at that moment—it would just make things worse for her.

John thought back to the many engineers he had mentored in the oil business. He had stayed calm when things hadn't gone as planned on a project while he'd observed others wringing their hands and sweating about all the issues. John suddenly realized that, although he was sixty years old and Jason was thirty, the roles were reversed. He understood that Jason was trained to keep his emotions in check and be methodical. *Work the problem—adapt and overcome. Wait—that's the Marine motto.* John recognized he was looking to Jason for calm and guidance. Jason was quickly becoming someone John would have to rely on to help him through this. He would be a great son-in-law!

The next morning, as John headed downstairs, he could smell the coffee he always set to brew automatically. He was pouring his first cup when Jason entered the kitchen, stopping in the doorway.

"John, I just got a call from our protection crew following Kayla. We might have a problem. Kayla left yesterday morning and followed the route she said she would. She caught I-90 and headed south on Highway 81 at Mitchell, South Dakota. She then went south to I-135, which turns into I-35. She checked in with Jaylynn last night when she stopped for the night in Oklahoma City. The problem is there was another vehicle following her besides our guys. We're watching both closely, but we think they might be FBI. They haven't approached her yet. They just might be waiting until she comes out to leave this morning. You haven't told her about the kit stashed in her car, right?"

John nervously stirred his coffee. "No, Jason, we haven't told her about her kit—we were waiting for word from you to do that. She does carry a gun of her own though."

Jason looked relieved and let out the breath he had been holding. This was the first time John had seen him on edge, and it was a relief to see that Jason's blood could warm up a little, especially when it concerned Kayla.

Upon feeling his phone vibrate, Jason pulled it out of his pants pocket and put it up to his ear. John detected that Jason was beginning to chew on the inside of his right cheek. This was Jason's tell when he got nervous. As he put the phone back in his pocket, he gave John a look that said trouble was coming.

Jason stood there deep in thought, but John couldn't stand it. "What is it? Is Kayla alright?"

Jason was back to his calm, calculating self. "Yes, Kayla is fine. That call was from our high cover guy, Truen. He let me know we have someone surveilling the property from the road just down from the entrance. Black SUV—probably government. I'll get Truen on his horse to mosey over and get a closer look. We may have to move the timetable up depending on how things go from here on out."

John was reassured by Jason's demeanor and responded, "Okay, we're ready to go when you are." He was ready to get this over with but had no idea who was watching or how Jason was going to handle it. Clearly, Jason was more concerned about the tail on Kayla than what was going on down by the gate. However, he was pleased Jason was as much of a control freak as he was inclined to be.

CHAPTER 25

JUSTINE RESIDENCE – ARLINGTON, TEXAS

Carl and Mary Ann were having coffee outside on the back patio when Carl's phone rang.

"Carl, it's Sam. How are you?"

Carl didn't need to talk to Sam right now. Conversations with NSA personnel were not good—*not* good. "Sam, I will call you right back," he said before hastily ending the call. Then, Carl grabbed his encrypted phone and called Sam back. "Okay, Sam—go."

"Carl, I decided to leave the NSA. I sent in my resignation letter before I left. I was hoping you could have breakfast with me this morning?"

Carl's mind was repeating his family mantra in time of crisis—ho*LY* crap, ho*LY* crap. Carl had to say something, so he blurted out, "So, you say you're in town. That's a surprise."

"I got in last night, and I need to talk to you as soon as you can meet me. Let's just say I needed to talk to you yesterday. It's extremely important, and I'm calling on an encrypted phone. Can we do breakfast—please? I can't stress enough how important this is."

Carl was starting to form a very uncomfortable picture in his head. He realized that Sam wanted to get information to him. But this also opened up the fact that he or Sam must be under surveillance. Alarms started going off in Carl's mind as a beeping sound indicated another call was coming in.

"Okay, Sam, let's meet at Lowery's in fifteen minutes, and I'm bringing Mary Ann with me. See you in fifteen."

Right after hanging up with Sam, Carl answered the other call. It was Jason Wilder.

"Colonel, this is Jason. We have detected surveillance that's not us. Seems that it's on Kayla and on the Mogens' place. We aren't sure who it is, but odds are it's the FBI geeks. I just got a call from your detail as well. You have a black SUV parked on your street as we speak. Just as a precaution, I'm going to alert the other details on the club members that surveillance may have started on their parties. You're the only one I've had a confirmed report on so far. Colonel, we have had a breach somewhere, so we need to either back off and cover or get this mission moving—fast." There was a slight pause. "Hang on, Colonel… Okay, okay. My hacker just ran the plate on the SUV here at the Mogens'—it is FBI."

Carl Justine had to draw on his training from his Air Force days as he took a deep breath to maintain a calm demeanor. He could sense a small change in Jason's voice that was a flag to him. He knew what this all meant. They had to put this project on fast-forward.

Carl started working the problem with his mental checklist. They had to increase the intel ruse pointing to something happening at Dyess Air Force Base to divert attention away from Ellsworth. Jason's men could neutralize the FBI agents in a heartbeat, but that couldn't happen yet— not yet.

Carl heard Jason talking to someone else, so he waited for him to come back on the line. Once he thought Jason had refocused on the call, he spoke, and his tone was composed and very much in charge. "Listen carefully, Jason. We can't take any FBI agents out of the picture yet. Do you understand?"

No reply.

Carl could tell Jason was involved in a very serious conversation with someone, but he needed his undivided attention. "Jason—talk to me!" he said insistently.

"Colonel, FBI just confronted Kayla as she exited her hotel in Oklahoma City. Hang on… My men have their listening device up."

Jason still seemed distracted as Carl boomed out, "No action against the FBI agents unless lives are at stake. Do you understand?"

This time, Jason's response was quick. "Yes, Colonel, we're just monitoring. Kayla hasn't been informed of the placement of her kit, so even though she may be suspicious, she doesn't have intel that would jeopardize the mission."

CHAPTER 26

SPRINGHILL SUITES — MOORE, OKLAHOMA

"**M**s. Mogen? Kayla Mogen?" the FBI agent asked as he approached her car. She had just opened the driver's side door and being addressed by a stranger immediately put Kayla on guard. Her gun was in her purse, which she always carried on her left shoulder. Her right hand was prepared to reach for it.

The young agent was very well dressed and too clean-cut to be some homeless guy, but Kayla was on high alert nonetheless. She turned to face him head on and dropped the small suitcase she was holding in her right hand. As the man reached inside his sport coat, her hand went into the gun pouch of her bag, and she pulled it out discreetly, still hiding it behind her purse.

Meanwhile, a second agent had walked up next to him. Noticing Kayla's demeanor, he quickly identified himself. "FBI, ma'am. Just wanted to ask you a few questions. We mean you no harm."

He realized his younger partner was in danger, but Kayla totally ignored him and continued to watch intently as the first agent carefully pulled his FBI badge out of his sport coat pocket.

She still didn't put her gun back in her purse.

"Ma'am, we..." the second agent started.

Kayla was having none of it. "Don't 'ma'am' me. How dare you come up to me with my hands full of bags unannounced? I should shoot both of you just for pulling this. How do you know my name and…?"

"Ma'am—ma'am, we…"

"Shut the hell up!" Kayla's face was turning red with anger, and her voice kept escalating in volume. "How do you know who I am and that I'm even here? I have no business with you!"

"Ma'am, I'm Agent Jeffries, and this is my partner, Agent Backtow. We have been tasked with checking on a possible threat to our country, so please just hang on. If you are holding a gun in your right hand, could you please put it away so we don't have to arrest you for threatening FBI agents?"

"Well, I would have to know you were FBI agents, wouldn't I?" She was looking at the agent with resolve to stand her ground.

"You do now, ma'am, so please put it away. We need you to step away from the car and answer a few questions. Please walk over here with us." The agent was motioning toward their vehicle.

"Not a chance in hell will I take a walk with you anywhere or get in your vehicle. I know you don't have a warrant since I haven't done anything wrong. But I will walk back into the lobby of this hotel where there are other people, and you may follow me if you would like." Without another glance toward the agents, she picked up her small suitcase and turned to head back into the hotel. As she walked toward the entrance, she slipped her weapon back into her gun pouch.

Exchanging stunned looks, the FBI agents realized they had not handled this well at all. Agent Jeffries whispered to Backtow, "You shut up and let me do the talking."

As the agents walked into the hotel, one of Jason's men, who had gotten into position, followed a few paces behind. Jason's man strolled past them and started looking at his phone, then sat down where he could use his listening device on their conversation.

"Ma'am, please understand, we're just doing our job. We have had a report that your father, John Mogen, may be planning something that would be detrimental to our nation. We know you were at his home yesterday, and we just want to ask you a few questions."

"My father is a patriot and a defender of a Constitution that I think is outdated and needs to be drastically modified. If you knew my father at all, you would know he bleeds red, white, and blue, so what in the hell are you talking about?" Kayla was even more agitated now.

"Ma'am, he's been searching certain things on the internet that are top secret, and his brother-in-law, your uncle, Colonel Carl Justine, just made a special trip to see your father. Not only that, but your uncle is a member of the Arlington Colonels' Club, and every member has been on a watch list since they left the service for one reason or another. But that's something we are not able to discuss at this time."

Kayla actually started to laugh. "I know for a fact that my father has started writing a book about how to restore the Constitution to its original meaning. Written by a bunch of old white slave owners of course! That's all I know."

Jeffries continued, "I suppose you are also aware the men at your father's home are all former Special Forces and work for Jason Wilder's company called IT & P Security out of Houston, Texas? Did you know he is a friend of your uncle's? Why is Jason Wilder and several of his men at your father's home?"

Kayla took a deep breath. "Are we really spending the people's money on this? Jason and his men are helping my parents with the tech they want in their new house. My parents are technologically challenged, even though they think they aren't. The guys are all using it as a little vacation as they help my parents. You should see the eighty-inch television they put up. Super ultra everything—geez! I know nothing about any plan to do anything to threaten the U.S. government other than what might be written in my father's book. Now that I think of it, what would scare you about restoring the Constitution anyway?"

Jeffries looked frustrated. "Again, ma'am, we are just doing our job. Thank you for answering our questions. Good day."

"Stop calling me 'ma'am' for Christ's sake!" Kayla said in a loud voice, shaking her head in disgust as they turned and walked out of the hotel.

Moments later, a very anxious Jason received a text that said only: "She did great—they got a big nothing burger." Jason wanted to order both of those FBI guys to be shot on the spot for scaring Kayla like that. He needed to reign in his emotions before he let his feelings cloud his judgment. God, that woman was his dream girl with one gigantic flaw. He had to be sure any decisions he made always put the mission first—not Kayla Mogen. She had done well and thank God they hadn't requested to search her vehicle. The mission had to go and go quickly—like tomorrow morning!

CHAPTER 27

JUSTINE RESIDENCE — ARLINGTON, TEXAS

"Jason, are you and your guys ready to roll? Are John and Jaylynn prepared to go?"

Jason was on the phone with Carl now that the incident with Kayla had concluded. He was meticulous about organizing missions down to the last detail, even if things had almost gone sideways with Kayla and the FBI geeks.

"Colonel—ah, we have scheduled a final training session with the horses so we can get our formation exact, and we need to get some more rounds off Jaylynn's horse. Buttercup is not quite as calm as I would like when shots are fired around her. Other than that, we are ready. We also have decided to drive two horse trailers so the Mogens can load up and get back home after our little display at the main gate. So, the answer to your question is yes—we could go out tonight if we really had to."

"Thanks, Jason." Carl was in a hurry to end the call. "I'll get back to you as soon as I can. Get that last training session in and reaffirm with me you are a go if I don't get in touch with you first."

Moments later, Carl received a message from the security detail protecting him and Mary Ann. Dammit! FBI agents were sitting down the street from him right now. How did that happen? Crap—he and Mary Ann had to get to Lowery's Restaurant to meet with Sam, whom he really felt like shooting right now!

Carl was quickly on to the next call with Colonel Allan North to see how the rest of the moving parts of the plan were going and how quickly they could initiate their plan. As the phone was ringing, Carl yelled over his shoulder, "Mary Ann—can you get the car out? I'll be right there." Then, as soon as his call was answered, he jumped into his message, not waiting for a greeting. "Allan, we have a problem." Carl didn't have time to mince words since their worst nightmare was coming to fruition. "The FBI is sitting down the street from our home, and they just confronted John Mogen's daughter as she walked out of her hotel in Oklahoma City. But since she knows nothing, there was no issue about her giving them any intel. We have to assume the FBI is watching all of us! I just spoke to Jason, and he is ready to roll with the main gate drama, so I'm checking on how we are doing with the rest of the moving parts?"

Allan was caught off guard by the stream of information coming out of his friend's mouth but was already weighing the urgency of the situation.

"Wow, Carl, I was hoping you were going to take a breath! Why don't we go play some golf this afternoon? In the meantime, I'll poll everyone to see their status. I don't think they can make it today, but I will see. I understand we are compromised, but we need to have all the assets in place before we can go. You do understand that, don't you?"

Carl was extremely frustrated and made that clear as he answered. "Yes, I understand. Could you please let everyone know the timetable needs to be moved up ASAP? One more thing… Sam Hudson called me a few minutes ago. You met him at my house—he's the pilot I used to fly with a lot. He showed up in Arlington and wants to meet. He told me he is quitting the NSA and needs to talk. I'm meeting him in a few minutes for breakfast. He's already heading to the restaurant, and Mary Ann and I are leaving after I get off this call. I'm sure the FBI will be tailing me."

"Okay," Allan said reassuringly. "I'll get us a tee time for this afternoon. Carl, take a deep breath. It's going to be alright. I've really had a feeling of peace about this from the beginning, and I'm sure divine providence is with us, so believe it will all work out. Have faith, Carl—have faith."

"Thanks, Allan, but right now, my hands are sweating as bad as when I was taxiing out for my first combat mission in the C-130. I'm not afraid to die. I—ah, I'm more afraid of failing," Carl said in a calmer voice.

"I realize that, Carl. I'll get back to you after I assess our readiness. I really want to know why Sam is here. So, go to breakfast and find out what he wants. I'm pretty sure he called you about the hit the NSA got on your brother-in-law, so you have a right to be nervous. There also has to be a reason he's leaving the NSA."

"Okay, Allan, I've got to go. Talk to you later today." As he hung up, calling to Mary Ann that he was coming, he couldn't help but wonder what he was about to learn from Sam. Would it be good news or bad news for the plan they were setting into motion?

CHAPTER 28

LOWERY'S RESTAURANT — ARLINGTON, TEXAS

Carl was entering this conversation with Sam with much trepidation. After all, taking a meeting with someone from an intelligence agency was not a smart move given what they were up to. He had to act like nothing was in the wind.

As he and Mary Ann pulled into the parking lot of Lowery's, there was no sign of Sam out front—good. Carl was certain he had a tail. He would be requesting a table at the back of the restaurant so he could watch for the FBI nerds who tended to stick out in a crowd.

Sam was pacing in the waiting area when Carl and Mary Ann walked in. He stopped midstride and hugged both of them, appearing extra eager to see them.

Carl stopped to talk to the hostess. Then, she led them to a half-table, half-booth in the back of the restaurant. Carl sat with his back to the wall so he had a clear view of the front door from where he was sitting. He had left his personal phone in his car in the hands-free holder facing the driver's window and had set it in video mode. It was a crude but effective video surveillance measure that would help him identify who was tailing him.

After the coffee had been served, Sam began the conversation. "It's so good to see you two! You both look great. Carl, maybe a little older, but you, Mary Ann—you're still as beautiful as ever! Are you keeping track of what Carl is up to these days?" He finally stopped talking enough to take in a deep breath, feeling like he had just finished running a half marathon.

Mary Ann looked at Carl for some sort of signal.

"Yes, Sam," Carl jumped in. "She knows all, sees all, and senses all. Anything you want to talk about, she's already aware of unless it has to do with you coming out as gay?"

Mary Ann almost choked on the sip of coffee she'd just taken. Carl was still able to pull her chain after all these years.

At the same time, Sam almost spit his coffee across the table and started laughing. "Geez, Carl, I wanted to tell her in a little gentler way!" he teased.

"Assholes. You are both assholes!" declared Mary Ann.

Carl and Sam looked at her, surprised that she would even use that word. Of course, they both deserved the title for what they had just done to her.

They'd been friends for a long time, and Carl was extremely worried this meeting might seriously jeopardize their friendship—even end it. Carl was in a life-or-death situation, and how this meeting turned out could mean his friendship might be put on ice until their mission was over. But Carl would not make that decision. He had to find out what Sam's plans were, what his thinking was, and how to get him out of the picture. Was he undercover for the NSA? Did they even have such a thing, and if they did, why was the FBI outside watching them all right now?

"So, Sam, you said you're leaving the NSA?" Carl queried.

Sam quickly corrected him. "Left, Carl. I have already left. My resignation letter was sent via email to my immediate supervisor. I've given notice on my leased condo, and I'm in the process of moving back here. I've really had it with the illegal, unconstitutional way all our intelligence agencies are operating. We're truly in a surveillance state. The CIA is operating outside all boundaries with money that comes from God knows where. They decide who gets into power by manipulation. Big Tech has to help them under threats of all kinds. Our fourth amendment right to privacy is gone, my friend—completely gone."

"What made you decide now was the time to leave?" asked Carl.

Sam heaved a sigh. "My boss, behind my back, decided to buy into the whole thing about some kind of plot your brother-in-law is planning because of the hits they got. You know, the book he is writing? I got a blind CC letting me know that my Node lead had contacted the FBI offices in Dallas and Rapid City. Node supervisors get informed when a subordinate contacts other FBI offices as a control. I had to respond that I had approved it, of course. That was the last straw. I was taken out of the loop because I had contacted you, and that is against protocol. Now, all I can think about is how I would just love to get back in the driver's seat of a B-1B and hit the throttles." Finally shaking his head, he said, "I'm so sorry I retired from the Air Force when I did."

Carl was bewildered by all the information Sam had just rattled off. Now, he had to make one of the toughest decisions of his life. *My God,* he thought. *I'm short a Bone driver, and Sam could do that. But can I trust him? In the past, I trusted him with my life when we flew together, but this is different. Can I trust him again with my life and the thousands of lives that have pledged to restore the Constitution of this great country of ours? Or do I turn him over to Jason's guys to sequester?*

"Carl, are you okay?" Mary Ann was concerned with the internal struggle Carl was going through. The stakes were high, and her husband did not look well.

As Carl contemplated what he would say next, she could tell he had made a decision.

"I'm okay, Mary Ann. It sounds like Sam is the one who is not doing okay." After pausing to take a gulp of his coffee, Carl continued. "So, Sam, is this what you needed to tell me? How about that the FBI has us under surveillance and even followed us from our home to this restaurant? I know you called me on an encrypted phone. Was that to protect me—or was it to protect yourself? If you are so upset about how our freedoms— our Constitution—are being violated, what are you going to do about it? Are you the next Edward Snowden? Are you willing to put your life on the line to turn this thing around?"

Carl suddenly remembered they were in a public place and glanced over the faces in the restaurant. He had not been watching the front entrance but determined no one looked like FBI. Then, he went on before Sam could get a word out of his mouth. "Sam, what would you give to get into a B-1B and fly a mission again? What would that be worth to you?"

Sam responded immediately. "My left nut, Carl—my left nut. Sorry, Mary Ann. But you're retired, Carl. Do you still have enough stroke to get me reinstated?"

Carl turned to Mary Ann and asked if she had a pen, which, of course, she did. Borrowing the pen she always had in her purse, he grabbed a napkin and wrote four names on it. Then, he slid it across the table in front of Sam.

"How many of these names do you recognize, Sam?"

"I know two of the four. They fly or flew Bones. What is this all about? What is this list?"

Carl looked at Mary Ann and smiled. Suddenly, she understood what Carl was about to do. This was one big roll of the dice. Mary Ann knew Carl had a sense of peace about it. She could tell by the look on his face, and she so hoped he was right! Carl had to change his communication style now.

"Sam, did you catch the news when that last Navajo code talker died? What a shame—they were truly great heroes. A special language for sure."

Sam smiled. He knew what Carl meant. "I understand what you're saying—a unique language indeed. There have also been studies that twins have their own language only they can understand."

Mary Ann was looking at these two men like they had collectively lost their minds.

Carl knew it was time. "Sam, you need to check out this book that I've been reading. Written by a guy named John. The words are fantastic. Jumps right off the page it seems so real. It's about some unhappy retired military officers building a network to somehow restore the Constitution of the United States of America. They need a civilian to be the face of the…I guess you could call it a coup. A militia colonel leading us back to the original intent of a limited government where its main job is to protect the God-given rights of its citizens. He knows there are patriots all over this country who have been training and are ready to answer the call. The retired colonels are sure that two-thirds to three-quarters of the military will side with this militia colonel and support this cause. The greatest part about this book is that the planned coup is a bloodless one. If I am reading the plot correctly, this is accomplished by using very big sticks to prevent the shooting. The nuclear devices will be delivered by B-1B bombers stolen from Dyess Air Force Base. They will be placed at five predetermined locations around the country. Each will have several human tenders with heart monitors hooked up to them and the detonation system on the devices. The key to this undertaking is to have all the Oathtakers and civilians involved maintain secrecy until the mission is executed. Then, if it's successful, the end of the book reflects a peaceful purge of Congress and the Supreme Court of those who have been purposely subverting—or maybe I should say completely ignoring—the Constitution. At that point in the book, we start over. There are a lot of great plot twists to this story, but the ending is just the best."

Sam eyes were wide open now as he pondered what Carl had just told him. This was the moment… Had Carl made a mistake? Both he and Mary Ann were holding their breath as a smile broke out across Sam's face. He was as sharp as they came and had quickly put it all together. Sam's expression literally lit up. He was so ready for this.

"Carl, this sounds almost too good to be true. I really want to read this book. But there is only one issue that I see. You—I mean, this author, John—is short a name on the list of pilots for the Bones. But I have a suggestion for him—a name he can add to that list!"

Carl and Mary Ann almost passed out from lack of oxygen but slowly began to breathe again. Carl's eyes started to glisten, and a single tear escaped. As Sam looked across the table at him, his eyes betrayed tears as well.

Of course, Mary Ann became a basket case immediately when she saw these brave, longtime friends crying in the middle of the restaurant. All three of them understood that this was a life-or-death decision for Sam as well as themselves if this plan failed. The tension was so palatable that the release of it had caused a flood of emotion that resonated with them all.

CHAPTER 29

JUSTINE RESIDENCE — ARLINGTON, TEXAS

Carl shut himself in his office shortly after they returned home from meeting Sam. He picked up his encrypted phone and put in a call to Colonel Allan North. Sam would stay with them until the mission was a go.

"Allan, we have a problem that was partially created by me. We have an FBI investigation team working on this thing. They've already cornered the Mogens' daughter Kayla and questioned her. They got nothing because she knew nothing but the cover story. They're surveilling me as we speak. I believe we have to move on this now!"

Allan, who was as cool as they came, had a nervous tenor to his voice for the first time that Carl could ever remember.

"I know, Carl—I know. I've already talked to Jason Wilder. He's ready but would like one more day, if possible. Jason and the Mogens are not the problem. Logistically, we are just not there yet. We need one more day to get everything in place outside of Dyess. We're within twenty-four hours, but we just aren't there yet." Carl could hear the frustration in his voice as Allan continued. "We're now aiming for Sunday morning at the earliest. I'm talking 0100 hours."

Carl was not pleased. "Okay, okay, 0100 hours Sunday. The FBI— what if the FBI gets in the way? This is supposed to be bloodless, right?"

Allan's response was reaffirming. "We will...ahhh sequester them until the mission has started. By then, we will have notified all the Sons of Issachar and the Oathtakers. After that, we will be at high risk of someone who's a mole giving us up anyway. Tell John to buy two tickets to Dallas-Fort Worth on the earliest flight out on Sunday. Have him do it online—right now. This will get flagged by the NSA and hopefully move them in that direction. Speaking of the NSA, I hope these phones are as bulletproof as they are advertised and we aren't on someone's radar right now. We may need to code talk from now on. See you Sunday!"

"Lives, fortunes, and sacred honor, Allan!" Carl responded.

Carl now understood the *lives* part only too well—this had to work and work fast.

CHAPTER 30

MOGEN COMPOUND – THE BLACK HILLS OF SOUTH DAKOTA

When John and Jaylynn heard that Kayla had been approached and questioned by FBI agents in Oklahoma City, it became very personal for them very quickly. Though Kayla was tough and capable, she was still their little girl. She had been accosted, and she had to be scared. They knew Jason had people ready to protect her, but they felt awful about putting her in the position to be questioned by authorities in the first place. After this encounter, her suspicions would be even more acute.

They were expecting to hear from her any minute, and they knew that the conversation would include lying to her one more time. She'd become the wildcard, which scared them even more. They'd discussed the situation and decided to wait until the last minute to tell her the truth. After that, she would need to be reassured before Jason's detail took over and whisked her away to a location even John and Jaylynn were not privy too.

Jaylynn literally jumped when her cell phone rang. When she looked down at the screen, her fears were confirmed. It was Kayla. Jaylynn knew she would be extremely upset with them and was not looking forward to this confrontation. She must be halfway to Austin by now.

As Jaylynn answered on the second ring, she could tell Kayla was mad—so livid that she was crying, which was a tell that she was equally frightened. Her mom's demeanor was the opposite, cool as she could be considering the situation, but she acted surprised as Kayla related the details of her encounter with the FBI.

"Mom, I was questioned by the FBI this morning. I didn't know who this guy was walking up to me, but I was ready to shoot him. God, Mom, what are you and Dad doing? What are you doing that the FBI would want to question me?"

Jaylynn had to be the reassuring mother at this point. John was next to her, staring and listening intently.

"Honey, your dad's internet searches for his book about military equipment, Air Force bases, and secret projects alerted the NSA. His search about a black project, which was nothing but a stinky rabbit, has them all in a tizzy just because of a good guess. The fact that Uncle Carl is a retired Air Force colonel showed up and created a *string* that they were trying to put together. The FBI is here and at Uncle Carl's, wasting taxpayer money. You just need to get to Austin and call your fiancé and talk a little more. Maybe you two can work it out." Had Jaylynn pulled it off?

Kayla was agitated but calmer. "Mom, this whole thing just scares me. Did you say that you and Dad are being watched by the FBI? Holy crap! What is this country coming to when they can harass you over some random internet searches?"

Kayla's question caught Jaylynn off guard, but she did not show it when responding. "Well, honey, there are people who just don't believe we need to follow the Constitution. They want it done their way. They say things like 'it's in the best interest of the country' or 'well, if it's not a right, it should be,' and that just doesn't work sometimes. The best one that's repeated over and over again is 'it's for the common good.' Our fourth amendment rights have been violated, and now we're being investigated illegally. The Constitution was written to protect our God-given rights and limit the federal government's reach—but you already know that, don't you?"

Kayla knew she had repeated the words "should be a right" to her mother more than once, and they also had had conversations about it being necessary to amend the Constitution to do things in the right way.

She knew the drill. Her parents thought the Constitution was there to protect God-given rights, and she wanted it to help the people who needed it, not limit what could be done. She thought of all the men in her life…her fiancé, her dad, and now Jason. *Wait, why did I put Jason into this group?* she thought to herself.

Jaylynn continued. "Honey, we love you, and people are looking out for you, so don't worry. I just need you to get home. Think about what you read in that book Jason recommended. We're really not crazy or mean to want to follow the Constitution. We just want the federal government to stop taking money from the producers and then handing out to the nonproducers. It's theft. We want the government to be as small as possible, which will let our citizens have the opportunity to thrive! What you have bought into is more about control than really helping people. Your thinking is destroying our Constitution and tearing our country apart. You have got to wake up, girl!"

Kayla had heard this all before but was now beginning to question what she believed. She had been immersed in progressivism since college and wondered if she had been taught to think the way she did. Her parents had accused her of being brainwashed, and she had insisted she was just thinking for herself. But maybe there was more to what they said than she initially realized.

"Just get back to Austin, Kayla. Are you still there? Did I lose you?"

"I'm here, Mom. I'm just a little bit distracted. I'll call you when I get to Austin like I always do. I know what a worrywart you are! I love you, Mom."

Jaylynn was shaking by the time the call ended. She just hoped when John called and told her about the kit in her car, she wouldn't do something crazy. Jaylynn knew Kayla, as well as their other daughter, Jessica, her husband, and her kids, would be sequestered by Jason's men soon enough. The timing had to be right. Soon, they had to let their daughters know what was about to happen and why. The families had to be reassured that they would all be well taken care of until they were reunited—only if the events went as planned. That final thought put Jaylynn's brain into overdrive. *Stop it, Jay—just stop it. Think positive—think positive!* she told herself.

Jason nervously crossed the yard, heading toward Jaylynn. He needed to hear how the call with Kayla had gone down. As she finished telling Jason that all was good with Kayla, John walked out of the house and approached the two after finalizing the purchase of the airline tickets to Dallas-Fort Worth to get the NSA off their intended target.

Jason took a deep breath and started to lay out the new plan. "We've got a change in the schedule. We are moving the start up to 0100 hours Sunday morning."

As they listened intently to the revised plan, their heart rates noticeably accelerated as a sheen appeared on their individual brows.

"Since it's Friday, that gives us today to get some last-minute training in with the horses," said Jason. "Buttercup is still a little skittish around gunfire, so we need to work on getting her calmer. You also mentioned that you two have some Old West period outfits from cowboy action shooting. Is that right? My guys and I are very active in cowboy action meets. We all love to shoot atop our horses. We even have our own cowboy action posse. At first, we started at the Arlington Club, but they—gently—moved us out of their shoots when we started winning every time. Now, we just compete amongst ourselves. We have over twenty guys who are actively in the posse. Besides period shooting, we also shoot modern three-gun competitions. If I say so myself, we are good. Truen—our high cover guy—was in the top ten in the country last year. It's that kind of good. Anyway, my guys have a request. Since we are going into battle Sunday morning, and it's Friday night, we would like to head into Deadwood to the #10 Saloon—that is, if you'd be willing to take us. Have you two ever been there?"

John looked at Jaylynn and smiled. "We have wandered inside and looked around. We had lunch there when we first started coming up to the Hills. We haven't been back since. You know I don't drink, so we just don't have a reason to go in there, but their food is good, and we would be happy to take you into Deadwood. They might even have the saloon girls there tonight."

Jaylynn chimed in. "Great idea. I'll wear my saloon girl outfit." With a smirk, she looked over to John and teased, "Wear your fancy going-to-town outfit there, Phatty!" She laughed as she started toward the house to dig out her outfit that she hadn't worn in quite a while.

Jason looked puzzled as he turned to ask John about the backstory.

"I'm sure you are wondering why she called me Phatty, aren't you? Well, my Single Action Shooting Society, or SASS, handle is Phatty Thompson—that's Phatty starting with Ph." Jason was intrigued as John continued. "Phatty—his real name was Plateaus Thompson—was a mule skinner. He was sent to Cheyenne by the citizens of Deadwood to collect stray cats and bring them back to Deadwood to take care of the mice that were overrunning the town. The rodents were eating grain, chewing up tents, and just making the local clientele angry. That's where my SASS name originated. We heard his story when we first came to Deadwood years ago. So, just call me Phatty—I'm used to it."

Jason was curious, so he asked, "Can we open carry our revolvers into the saloon?"

John's reply was quick. "You bet we can!"

Jason sauntered away, chuckling at his reply.

Climbing the stairs, John's thoughts moved to Jaylynn's saloon girl ensemble. He was having second thoughts about letting a lot of people see them in town so close to the restoration, and he knew that they would be memorable in their outfits.

When John walked into the master bedroom, he discovered Jaylynn had already changed. Holding her beautiful silver hair atop her head, she asked if she should wear her hair up like that. Her long, slender neck and the off-the-shoulder top of her outfit sent such a tingle down John's body that he was speechless. It literally took his breath away. After all those years, it still did.

"Honey, do you hear me? My hair up or down?"

John began to whisper the answer in her ear and then continued to kiss and nibble on her ear as chills grabbed hold of her entire body.

"Darn it, John, I just put on some fresh panties!" she protested weakly.

John had forgotten how stunning she looked in her outfit. It had a beige blouse that was off her shoulders and a brown bodice leather vest with designs cut into the leather. The skirt was olive green velour. It draped up to her waist in the front and fell all the way to the floor in the back but had a separate beige front section that fell to just above her knees. The long brown lace-up boots finished off her appearance.

Only her silver hair betrayed her fifty-eight years. Her shoulders were as smooth as any twenty-year-old's, and her long legs in those fishnet stockings hadn't lost their shape. John still referred to them as her "Barbie doll" legs. Her updo was highlighting what John called her gazelle neck. What a sight!

John realized he had to get himself ready to go to town when all he wanted to do was take her to bed! It had been a long time since they had played Old West dress-up. He made a note-to-self that they would have to do this more often.

John had all but forgotten his days in cowboy action shooting. He was still in great shape and hadn't put on much weight since retiring. He had barely developed the love handles other men acquired at his age. That could be because he worked out three times a week with weights and did cardio. John still looked like he could be the linebacker he once was. His reflection was a sight in his fancy cowboy clothes. After putting on his long, black leather coattail, he turned, and Jaylynn helped him straighten his red necktie. It was something she always enjoyed doing as she looked into his face. He looked more like George Strait than ever when his was in character—especially when he put on that black cowboy hat.

Jason and his crew had mentioned to him how fast John could still move and how strong he was while doing the tactical training during the last few days. Of course, they all considered sixty to be old since they were almost all under thirty.

John had recommended that Jason gather his crew at the house so they could take some pictures before heading into town. He descended the staircase to see four of the team with Jason dressed as if they had just dismounted at the end of a trail drive. What a great-looking bunch of cowboys!

"Where is Truen?"

"Oh, Truen will be staying behind to watch the place. He captured some great photos of our FBI watcher today with his long lens, and he'll let us know if they follow us into town. Truen prefers to be on his own. Besides, he doesn't function well in polite society if you get my meaning."

"PTSD?" John inquired, and they all nodded in unison.

Jason expounded a little. "Truen—ahh, he functions well in security work not involving personal contact with the clients. He doesn't sleep much, and I'll tell you right now, don't surprise him with your presence. Better he stays here. Best high cover man you will ever hope to have at your six!"

After finishing her makeup, Jaylynn headed down the stairs to join the guys. Of course, Jason's men had ogled over the numerous pics of Kayla that Truen had added for their reconnaissance file. But as Jaylynn approached, their mouths dropped open. There was no doubt where Kayla had acquired her good looks. They'd been around Jaylynn quite a bit but not dressed up like she was tonight.

"Well, boys, are we ready to go to town? You all look like you just stepped out of a John Wayne movie!" she said excitedly. They all had on their dusters and had taken off their hats as she descended the stairs.

John broke the silence. "Okay, gentlemen—let's close our mouths, put on our hats, and head out to the trucks. Whattaya say?"

As they headed out the door, Jason's thoughts unexpectedly turned to Kayla. Was she alright? And how was she going to react to what they were about to do? Shaking his head in an attempt to clear it, he told himself to get his mind on the mission because he couldn't afford distractions when he had a restoration to complete!

Before leaving the house, Jason took John aside and wired him up with the voice-activated radios they would all be wearing again early Sunday morning. Jason thought the #10 Saloon would be a good test run for John. They had completed the sound check for the whole crew and had assigned the call sign Eagle One to John. The rest would be Hawk One through Hawk Five. Jaylynn would be fitted with her radio on Sunday morning, and she would be Ladyhawk. She just wasn't dressed for carrying a radio tonight.

John put his Ruger Vaquero .45 Long Colt into his holster, and everyone else, including Jaylynn, had their cowboy action firearms at their side. All were unloaded, but the Sons of Issachar had all they needed hidden in their dusters.

The team would form up the same from now on. Eric Thompson was point. Jason had nicknamed him their "Belgium." He had the characteristics of the dog—he was aggressive and didn't back down. Jaylynn hadn't understood the description 'til John had explained it to her. Eric was only five-foot-nine but was built like the running back he'd been in high school. He had fantastic situational awareness and saw everything, looking out for the safety of the team. More often than not, his gut feelings were what the team operated on.

Daniel Rodriguez was second. He was the fastest and most accurate shot, especially on the move.

Matt Van Sharrel was on one side of the Mogens, and Zach Overgaard was on the other.

Jason would have John's six until this mission was successfully completed.

CHAPTER 31

THE #10 SALOON – DEADWOOD, SOUTH DAKOTA

The #10 Saloon was crowded for a Friday night, especially for early spring. The tourists seemed to be coming to the Hills earlier than in years past. The hostess with the biggest smile and long curly red hair who was wearing a bustier was quick to meet and greet the group with her bubbly voice. Eric responded to the question about the size of their party, and the hostess replied they would be able to seat them shortly if they wanted to stay in the original section of the bar. Eric nodded, and she acknowledged that it would be ready in five minutes.

The live music hadn't yet started, although the band was setting up. The crowd gradually quieted down as group by group noticed the party waiting to be seated. Someone shouted, "Who are those guys!" hoping someone would remember the line from *Butch Cassidy and the Sundance Kid.*

This got Eric's attention, and he replied, "We're cowboy action shooters, and we heard this was the place to come for a good time!"

A few tables over, a tourist was overheard saying he felt like he was in a real-life western movie. Earlier in the day, he had experienced the reenactment of a shootout on Main Street, and now these guys looked like they'd walked through some sort of time vortex into the twenty-first century.

Eric quietly spoke so he would only be heard by those with earbuds in. "Back corner, two guys—obviously the FBI guys we got pictures of outside the Mogens' place. Man, do they stick out." Eric then took in the rest of the bar. *What an amazing collection of Old West memorabilia*, he thought.

The hostess, who was well endowed and trying to bust out of her bustier, was a treat the guys had needed. First Jaylynn, and now this woman.

As they were being seated, John took the right edge of the table so he could straighten his leg out since it had a tendency to lock up otherwise. Jason was at the end of the table, watching the entire room. Eric, Jason, and, of course, John didn't order a beer, but the rest of the guys were allowed to. They relaxed as much as they could, knowing what was coming in their near future. It wasn't fear they felt but rather the adrenaline they all seemed to need to feel alive.

John and Jaylynn would never completely understand these guys, but the time spent together had brought them closer. The Sons of Issachar were already part of their family. They were good men who loved the Lord and the Constitution, and they were the hope of the WSA that John was eager to form. An alliance of states that would worship God and follow the Constitution. How had they let things get so far away from it?

Driven out of his thoughts, Jaylynn had to yell at him to be heard over the crowd noises. "What are you going to order, John?"

He responded promptly, a little embarrassed at how distracted he was. "I think the twelve-ounce ribeye."

All the others at the table were in agreement about the cut of steak John had selected. However, Jaylynn decided on an eight-ounce fillet with a bacon wrap and a glass of Merlot.

While the orders were being taken, Eric watched the FBI guys as they took photos of the group. Finally, he decided he had had enough. "Hawk One, I'm going to go throttle those FBI guys for taking pictures of us!"

Jason quickly responded, "Hawk Two, you will not go over there. Remember how we're dressed. They'll just claim they are a couple of tourists who wanted to take home some pics for their wives. You stay put!" John smiled at Jason as he verbally pulled Eric's leash a little.

As the band started to play, John excused himself to go to the bathroom. Jason also got up and followed. His job was to shadow John everywhere he went unless they were at the Mogens' compound.

After they left, a very drunk gentleman wandered toward the table where the team was sitting. He looked about John's age and seemed to have his sights on Jaylynn. He weaved toward her and almost tripped, ultimately falling into John's empty chair next to her. Taken off guard, Jaylynn was a bit startled to find a stranger sitting beside her. That was his first mistake. He then put his arm around Jaylynn's shoulders, looked her right in the face, and was asking her to dance when John walked up.

"Get your drunken hands off my wife and get the hell out of my chair—now!" The drunk glanced up at John but dismissed him with a backwards look and proceeded to turn back to say something to Jaylynn. Before the intruder knew what had happened, John had his arm removed from Jaylynn's bare shoulders and had him in a wrist lock. He pushed over his chair, and the man and chair both hit the wood timber floorboards. The whole scene was taken in by everyone at the table, not to mention others in the #10 Saloon. The Sons of Issachar were ready to get up and defend John and Jaylynn, but Jason communicated to everyone to stand down.

As the man regained his stability, he got up and stood almost eye to eye with John, though he was built leaner. At this time, he made his second mistake. He took a wild swing with his right fist. As John blocked the incoming punch, he countered with a strike to the drunk's solar plexus, using a full body turn to get the most out of the punch. The drunk crumpled to the floor, gasping for air.

At that time, his two friends got up from where they had been sitting and started over to the Mogens' table. But Jason stepped between them and John, and the men both stopped and glanced up at the six-foot-four Jason, who dwarfed everyone with his size. Jason, seething, told them, "Pick up your friend and get out of the saloon if you want to stay in one piece."

By that time, a bartender was shouting for the bouncer, who finally ambled over to see what the deal was. All the while, other patrons were yelling, "We have video! We have video!"

Eric was prepared to start taking apart anyone who came close to John or Jaylynn, and then he noticed one of the FBI guys coming toward their table. He advanced to block his path and bumped him a little hard. As Eric pulled him close, he whispered, "Stay out of this, you FBI puke!"

With that, the agent retorted, "I have good video that the bouncer can look at…asshole!"

The only thing that stopped Eric from attacking was the slap of Jason's hand on his shoulder. "We will appreciate it if you can show it to the bouncer," Jason said calmly. "We are leaving—now!"

As they all jumped up and headed for the front entrance, the bouncer blocked their exit. Then, a second bouncer came up behind the first. Their group was formed with Eric at point. Jason brought up the rear with John and Jaylynn circled by the Sons of Issachar, as was now their common practice. By this time, Eric had regained his composure and was talking to the bouncers. He pointed toward the FBI puke who had said he had taken video of the whole encounter.

Finally, one of the bouncers spoke up. "Okay, everybody—nobody leaves until we figure this out. The police are on their way, so just sit tight."

Jason stepped around John and took the bouncer to the side to talk to him. "That drunk assaulted this woman and then attempted to hit the man who put him on the floor. We don't want any trouble and hope you don't either. So, we'll be leaving now, and if you touch any of us, know it will be assault, and believe me, everyone in this place will be using their phones to video what's happening." As Jason began to reach into his front pocket, he stated, "I'm going to write down our contact info so the police can contact us for statements." Jason proceeded to write and then gave him the card with John's name and number on the back.

The bouncer took stock of what he was up against. "Jake is a known troublemaker when he drinks too much. He actually means no harm. I'll look at the video, and in the meantime, you can go—just expect a call from the authorities. I'm sure they will have some questions."

Jason nodded to the bouncer and told the team to get to their vehicles.

Agent Jefferies was livid as he looked over to his partner. "You're a dumbass—no, you're a double dumbass! Why did you involve us in this? We're supposed to be surveilling Mogen! Now you can stay here and show them your stupid video—I'm going to the car to follow them! Hopefully they'll all just go back to the Mogen compound. You can find your way to the hotel, right?"

"I was just trying to get close enough so I could maybe overhear something!" the rookie agent said sheepishly. "They know who we are and what we're doing here anyway, you triple dumbass!"

Jason took control as the group exited Saloon #10. "John, you and Jaylynn head home. Eric and I will follow you. The rest of the team will hang back and see if they can find out where these FBI guys have dug in."

It didn't take long. As Daniel, Matt, and Zach watched, the triple dumbass FBI agent walked down the street a few steps from the #10 Saloon and went into the Holiday Inn right next door. That was tough.

Jason was regretting giving in to his guys' night out request but, then again, was happy to see that John hadn't hesitated to protect Jaylynn (even though she could probably have knocked the guy down without any trouble), and he definitely knew how to throw a punch in the right place without breaking the drunk's face and getting blood all over.

As he and Eric followed the Mogens' car back to the ranch, his thoughts moved to zero dark thirty Sunday morning. Shaking his head, he almost couldn't believe he was involved in the attempt to restore the United States Constitution. Who would have thought...? Bar fights—sort of—and FBI agents weren't the best way to fly under the radar, and Colonel Justine would be really pissed when he found out what had transpired. They all would have to hunker down until they were ready to go early Sunday morning! Nothing was going to get in the way of this restoration. But he would've really liked to have had a taste of that ribeye steak!

NSA FORT – HIGH PERFORMANCE COMPUTING CENTER 2 – MEADE, MARYLAND

Gloria had left instructions in her daily report to call her if anything relevant came up concerning John Mogen and Colonel Carl Justine during her days off. Char had the weekend duty and couldn't help busting out laughing when she told her colleague about the FBI report on John Mogen and the bar fight. They even had photos of John, Jaylynn, and the posse. It was great entertainment for them on an early Saturday morning, but other than that, there was nothing significant to report to Gloria.

They were expecting a report on Sunday morning confirming that John and Jaylynn Mogen had boarded their flight to DFW. All communications concerning Dyess Air Force Base were to be monitored for the rest of the day.

Char did make a note in her report that all the phones that they were surveilling in South Dakota had gone silent. On a whim, Char checked the Arlington Colonels' Club, and they'd also had no activity on any of their phones for going on three days now. No communication at all. Totally dark.

Char put out an advisory on the silence. Maybe some sort of operation was coming up since they'd all gone silent. She thought maybe they could be using burner or encrypted phones, but she didn't attempt to check if there was any out of the ordinary activity or movements coming out of the Mogens or the Colonels' Club that would indicate they had something nefarious planned. She just hadn't bought into it like Gloria had. To Char, it was a job—not a life's mission.

CHAPTER 33

ROLLING HILLS COUNTRY CLUB
— ARLINGTON, TEXAS

Allan North was upset. Torger Vigdahl had said he wasn't available to play golf. He was too busy getting the former SEALs, subs, and special "packages" to the staging areas near Rapid City. Torger had decided on a rural side road east of Newcastle, Wyoming, in the shadow of Elk Mountain, just inside the border on the South Dakota side. The trucks that were hauling all the packages were marked as seismic equipment for oil exploration.

Torger wasn't in Dallas at the moment and wasn't about to disclose that information to Colonel North. Allan assumed he was somewhere in Wyoming or South Dakota. Besides, it was too late for North to stop him now. Earlier, he had relayed to North that Ski had gotten all the packages that were needed. Those packages would be "out for delivery" on time and would not be traceable. They were to arrive on Saturday night at the command center, which had been set up at the communications equipment store just outside Dyess Air Force Base before the operation. This store was owned by a former Air Force communications specialist, and it had been prepped for the command center. If the operation was compromised in any way, it would appear that they were working out of there and not near Ellsworth Air Force Base, which was the actual target.

It was the usual drill when they were at the club—all phones were left in their lockers. Carl Justine's protectors were close by, observing the FBI observing the colonels. Carl had a radio earbud and was listening to his protection team discuss the FBI guys' locations and what kind of listening devices they had.

Since jamming was underway, Colonel Allan North was able to give the current status of the operation to the other colonels. Time was set for 0100 hours Sunday. The black chutes would drop first. The flight line would be secure, and the five hotted up B-1Bs would be ready to go. The bogus high alert status order to get the bombers ready was coming from Air Force personnel loyal to the cause. Three of the huge D11Ts' remotely operated bulldozers were ready, and the man lift to hold the three remote drivers had been rented and was ready to be towed into position.

A propane storage facility nearby would be detonated by former Navy SEALs to start the operation. The bulldozers would then breach the base perimeter fence in three places a few minutes apart. This would distract, confuse, and divide the night guards and overwhelm the officer on watch with inputs.

At this point, Colonel John Mogen and company would appear at the main entrance to the base on horseback and request entry to occupy the four guards stationed there. At that time, they would request an audience with the officer on watch, who would already be overwhelmed with calls.

The third bulldozer's breach would be delayed by seven minutes, and the black UTVs with the B-1B crews would follow the D11T bulldozer in. The UTVs would head straight for the flight line after they received verification it was secure. They'd do this with two-man crews for the Bones. They'd just acquired the fifth Bone pilot that they needed within the past week. This kept them from having to double up on sorties with one of the Bones.

Allan wished Torger was available to give his report. Before he continued, he asked, "Does anybody know where Torger is? His absence is really making me nervous."

Bill and Carl shook their heads in a disgusted "no" gesture.

Allan was visibly upset. "He's in charge of the ordnance and the crews that are manning the subs for God's sake, and he's AWOL. I sure don't doubt his reliability, but what the hell is he thinking? The last time we talked, he said his crews had been training like a NASCAR pit crew, and they had the timing down to within ten minutes for installation and sta-bilization of the ordnance into the subs. He also recruited two of the ten former SEALs that have actually ridden these subs to water landings with the detachable wing system. These two took on the training of the remaining SEALS since this operation was truly a 'learn as you go' enter-prise for most of them. As we know, the GPS guidance system is the key on these flights."

Carl interjected with something they all knew but that hadn't been brought up. "We've never dropped these out of B-1Bs, only C-130s and C-17s. Though both have a lower minimum air speed than the Bone, we believe the mini-sub wing system will hold together. The plan calls for the Bone pilots to take the bombers down to just above stall speed for their drops. The two bombers with the dropdown gun turret attachments will be used for the most critical drops—D.C. and New York. Hopefully those will hold together 'til we get them on the ground."

Allan North and Bill Musgrave were staring at Carl, and all were wondering if any of this would work.

Carl continued, unfazed. "Let's revisit the heart monitoring detona-tion systems. These also haven't ever been used before. But as you know, on each device, one of the two operators assigned has to be connected at all times. If not, the computer software monitoring the heartbeats will detonate. The software has been programmed to recognize enough heart rhythms to keep changing out the human detonators. We just have to be sure this is clearly understood by those who would attempt to send in a broken arrow team to try something."

Bill was not happy about the advanced technology. "What if one of the guys has a scare, and his heartbeat goes wild for a few seconds?"

"Like I said, it's smart software, and it has been taught to recognize a normal, rapid, sleeping, or surprised heart rhythm of all who will be hooked up to it. Heart rhythms are unique, so if these units are compromised and someone tries to hook anybody up that is not in the system, there will be—ahh—complications." As he explained the system, he was trying to convince himself as well as the others.

Bill was still doubtful. "What if they capture some of the guys with the right heartbeats and copy them somehow and feed them to the computer?"

Carl responded by saying, "You're away, Bill. Hit the damn golf ball and stop asking what ifs!"

This made Bill mad. "In my whole damn career, Carl, I've kept myself and my men alive by anticipating 'what ifs'!"

Allan had to put an end to this. "Gentlemen, this is one audacious plan with a lot of technology and a whole bunch of moving parts. We believe we have the technology that will work for us. We have highly skilled and loyal people working on our team and have the plan and timing down. I think our best action at this point is to pray to Almighty God that this will happen without bloodshed and that we restore our nation to the rule of law and to a nation that worships Him instead of the government."

Bill and Carl both took in a deep breath and said simultaneously, "God help us!" A simple but heartfelt prayer.

On the eighteenth hole, Carl let Bill and Allan in on what he planned to do. He then contacted his team and told them to cease jamming the FBI listening devices before speaking the words that would lay the trap. "Okay, gentlemen. Dyess Air Force Base, 0100 hours Sunday."

Together, the group recited, "We pledge our lives, fortunes, and sacred honor to this mission." Hopefully the FBI was listening in to what they said.

Allan was now on a mission to find out where Torger Vigdahl had landed. He was not following the plan, and he needed to be here in Arlington tonight at the command center with the rest of them. *He'd better be on his way back from wherever the hell he was right now!* Allan thought to himself. But he had a bad feeling about Torger being MIA—a really bad feeling.

CHAPTER 34

MOGEN COMPOUND – THE BLACK HILLS OF SOUTH DAKOTA – LATE SATURDAY AFTERNOON

Jason was happy. "John—you and Jaylynn ready to go for spin-up? Well, horse-up, that is. Your riding and shooting skills are great, but we pray that we won't need any of them!"

Jaylynn had a strange feeling in the pit of her stomach. That tended to happen when the "what ifs" were swirling around in her brain. What about her kids—her grandkids? Would they be safe? Would they even talk to them? Would they still have a papa and nana when this was over?

"Thanks, Jason—we are so ready for this. But Jaylynn and I need a little alone time. We're going to drive the Polaris up to watch the sunset and pray for our kids and this country." John was clearly adamant about this, and Jason was obliging.

"Okay, you two, I really don't want either of you out of my sight at this time, but I understand your need to do this. We know the FBI geeks are sitting down from the front gate, so they won't pose a problem. We have planted a—ahh—disrupter on their SUV, so they won't be able to go anywhere when the time comes for us to head out."

Jaylynn was staring at John, and he smiled back at her. "Okay—Jay, let's get the prayer blanket and head up to Flat Rock to watch the sunset," he said with urgency in his voice and a mischievous look in his eyes.

Was he code talking to her right in front of Jason? Again, her mind swirl switched on to other "what ifs," but these quickly left her mind as she realized that this could be the last time for her and John. The emotions she was feeling were about to overwhelm her. Her body was reacting as melancholy mixed with nostalgia tried to take over, but this time, she fought it off.

As they got into the Ranger, she hit him with the blanket in a playful way. They had found what they now called "Flat Rock" after they had already bought the property. It was part of a granite rock formation at the highest point on their land. Flat Rock had popped off the formation after eons of ice expansion and contraction and was sitting at the base. The first time they had decided to give it a try, a rattlesnake had been coiled up in the space between Flat Rock and the main formation and had scared the daylights out of them. After that, John always brought along his Ruger Vaquero .45 Long Colt on his hip with two snake shot rounds lined up to go first out of the wheel.

When they arrived at their destination, John went over first to check it out for critters. The evening sun was still hitting the rocks, and they were warm to the touch, which Jaylynn loved.

Flat Rock looked like a half donut with the half hole just big enough for John to stand in. It was the right height for what they used it for. John took his gun belt off as Jaylynn spread the blanket out on the rock.

Their heightened passion was something that had not hit them in a while. They tried their best to maintain the kiss as boots, pants, and underwear came off. Jaylynn was on her back with her legs up on the rock as John stepped into the half donut hole. As their bodies joined, Jaylynn could not hold back her feelings any longer. Gazing down at her, John understood how she felt as her eyes began to shine and tears started to run down both sides of her face. She wrapped her legs around him and matched his motions with the force of the champion barrel racer she had been so many years ago.

They both knew this might be the moment—the last time they would make love. Jay felt John's tears fall to her stomach as they smiled at each other with glistening eyes. It just didn't get any better, but would they ever get another chance to do this? Would this be it?

Jaylynn closed her eyes and actually let herself just enjoy this moment with the man she had loved both physically and emotionally for thirty-five years. Her endorphins were so strong that she felt as if she were floating above the rock with her entire body a mass of goosebumps. They had become one flesh and could never imagine being separated except by death. She had always declared they would leave this earth together. During this restoration, they would both be carrying a pistol, and they would use them if it came down to that. She just hoped that God would understand.

As they returned to the house, the ride back in the Polaris was different for them. They were taking a good look at their property in the golden light of a spectacular Black Hills sunset. Jaylynn sobbed as John drove, her mind swirl starting again. How would she stay awake tonight? The plan was to take Ellsworth at 0100 hours. Usually, she would already have been asleep for four hours by then for heaven's sake.

"John?" she asked anxiously. "How are we going to stay awake tonight?"

"Jason has some caffeine pills, honey—we will be okay." John was always surprised how her mind worked so differently from his. This was the question that her mind had grabbed onto as things bounced by. Amazing!

That last night, John cooked everyone ribeye steaks that were melt in your mouth and seasoned to perfection—the kind of steaks Texans could rave about. Truen even came in long enough to eat before heading back to his post as overwatch.

Jaylynn excused herself as the cleanup was finishing up. John told her that he and the boys would do the rest. She braced herself as she made her way into the office. Once there, she sat down with a sigh and waited as the computer came to life. She made the first call to Kayla since it might be a short one. At 0100 hours, a timed email that would explain the kit that resided under the backseat of her car would hit her phone. At the same time, another email explaining what was going on would be hitting the encrypted phone in her kit as soon as she powered it up.

Kayla's tone surprised Jaylynn. "Momma? I… Ahhh, I miss you and Daddy. Are you two okay? Is Jason still with you? I've been doing a lot of thinking since I left South Dakota, especially since I finished reading *The 5000 Year Leap* that Jason suggested I read. Well, he pretty much made me read it."

Jaylynn hadn't said more than hello before Kayla had taken off, and she was really winding up now.

"Before I left, Jason suggested to me that I was ignorant of our beginnings as a nation and how special our country is, and that just infuriated me. So, I reread the book and made notes, checking things for accuracy. I have been going through the Constitution and the Federalist Papers. I then read a book about James Madison. Wow! He should be on The Faces—not Teddy Roosevelt. I feel like I have been lied to throughout my whole education. I thought you and Dad were totally unenlightened. I am sorry—so sorry. Is Jason still there? Can I talk to him?"

Jaylynn had to lie to her daughter—hopefully for the last time. "Take a breath, honey—take a breath. Jason is off with his buddies, but I will tell him you need to talk to him. Have you talked to your fiancé since you got back? Are things back to normal again? Is the wedding back on?"

What Kayla said next stunned Jaylynn to the core. "Mom, I realized he is not the one. I haven't stopped thinking about Jason since I drove off the ranch. Please have him call me—please."

Kayla had not listened to them for years. It was as if she had been possessed—no, brainwashed to the point there was no changing her—and their relationship had suffered because of it. Jaylynn was a little shellshocked but finally responded to her daughter. "I'll tell Jason to call you, honey."

Kayla cut in, saying, "Any time, day or night, have him call!"

Jaylynn smiled. "Are you one of those kids who looks at your phone in the middle of the night? Do you look at it if you hear my tone at, say, one in the morning?"

Kayla responded quickly. "Yes, Mom, I never silence my phone at night. But I really need to talk to Jason—I really do. Promise me that you will let him know I need to speak with him. It's important!"

Jaylynn couldn't believe what was coming out of her daughter's mouth. Kayla wasn't one to be impulsive. She had always been made of steel on what she believed in, and it surely wasn't the U.S. Constitution. She'd told them it was just a hindrance and in the way of doing what needed to be done to help people. Jaylynn's heart literally felt warm.

"I'll let Jason know as soon as I can. It might be in the morning though."

"Tonight, Mom—tonight please!" Kayla was adamant about getting in touch with him as soon as possible.

"Okay, honey. I need to call Jessica and talk to the grandkids, but I will let Jason know. Your dad and I love you more than you can understand right now. You aren't messing with me, right? You really have changed your views on how important the Constitution is for this country? Are you really saying that it needs to be restored? Really?"

Kayla shot back, "Yes, Mom—really. Up until now, I just wouldn't let myself read anything that might make me change my mind. Jason said that I lacked intellectual integrity. That I couldn't argue intelligently with him unless I understood what I was talking about. He told me getting loud doesn't win arguments—it just means your mind is closed. I respect Jason and need to tell him—to talk to him."

Jaylynn was eager to relate this conversation to John. "Okay, okay, I'll let Jason know you need to talk. Geez! Let me call your sister, and I'll find Jason! I love you!"

"Love you too, Mom—and Dad. I've been a bitch to both of you, and I am so sorry."

Kayla's response had a ring of true remorse that Jaylynn could literally feel. Ending the call, she was snapped back into reality as John came in the room. She had to tell him right away. "John, I just got off the phone with Kayla. She says she gets it—she reread *The 5000 Year Leap*, the Constitution, the Federalist Papers, and commentaries galore."

"She's a very fast reader, but am I hearing you right? That three-foot-thick brick wall in her head actually came down? Who—wait, Jason actually got to her? She listened to somebody long enough for her to do some research? Of course, she wouldn't listen to us—after all, we are her parents. I know the connection with Jason was immediate, but I thought it was more about bodies than minds. Holy crap—holy crap…"

Jaylynn stopped him. "She needs to talk to him, and she wants to do it right now."

John was standing there in shock. Why now when they might be dead or in prison by tomorrow night? Why? Jaylynn knew John was amazed at this turn of events in his daughter's life.

"John, I have to talk to my grandkids, but I'm going to do a video call. I just need to see them, and I want you next to me. So, I'll get us connected while you go tell Jason that Kayla wants to talk to him as soon as he can get a moment."

John responded as if it were an order. "Will do, and after that, we are doing cigars around the firepit."

Jaylynn knew the guys needed this time and didn't feel left out, especially when cigars were involved. John had planned their time at Flat Rock but now needed some male bonding time. He would be with her again after he took the mandatory after-cigar shower and left his smelly clothes in the mudroom.

Jaylynn smiled wide as the grandkids yelled "Nana!" when she came up on their screen. John, who had just returned to Jaylynn's side, felt a little hurt when they did this, and in the background, their daughter Jessica would always add, "and Papa too!"

After the call, John headed out to the firepit with enough Macanudo Gold Labels for all the guys. These were John's favorite. As he tended the fire, he listened to stories from the former Navy SEALs, former Air Force Special Forces, and former Marine sniper. He felt a little overwhelmed by all the missions these guys had gone on.

He thought back to his time downrange in Cameroon when terrorists had headed toward the medical camps run by missionaries. Jaylynn had been there volunteering, and the camp had been about to be overrun when John showed up with his company's helicopter. The pilot had flown in combat and was good—very good. John had gotten Jaylynn and three children into the chopper before they started to take fire. John had been lifting a fourth child into the chopper when he took a round to his shoulder before one grazed his head. The blood from the head wound had convinced Jaylynn her husband was going to die. Initially, he had been dazed but had come back to reality quickly as he'd told her how much he loved her. As she cried, she'd continued to work on stopping the bleeding.

They'd retreated to an offshore oil platform that was being constructed by John's company. From there, the medic on board the platform had taken over, and John had recovered. He was left with a scar that his hair covered and a nasty scar on his left shoulder.

This had happened over twenty-five years ago, but they both had this event seared into their memories. Later, they found out what had happened to those left in the camp. They felt both relief and remorse mixed with a large dose of guilt because they'd only been able to save a few. He actually did have a story of his own.

Jason was looking at John, who had been very quiet. "John?" he questioned, snapping him out of his trance. "Tell us about Cameroon."

John had come to know Jason in the few days they had trained together. Jason was so wise beyond his thirty years that it amazed John. He was convinced Jason was some sort of empath—maybe an angel sent to protect them. At the very least, he was observant and clever in all situations.

John hadn't even known that Jason knew about Cameroon. He didn't think his story was worthy of retelling to this group of veterans who had seen a lot more combat. However, they were all looking at John, and he realized this was an important moment. Jason had done this with a purpose. John knew he had to tell the story in some detail—explain the setting, why he and Jaylynn had even been there, and what had been happening in the country at the time.

John realized that any story involving gunfire was worthy of this crew—his crew. He was now not just a militia colonel. He was Colonel John Mogen, commander of CREF—the Constitution Restoration Expeditionary Forces. He had to be the man—play the part. He got it, and Jason was helping him become that and hopefully keep him out of trouble.

After John ended the story, everyone remained quiet, waiting for him to continue. He didn't understand that the story wasn't over until he showed everyone the scars. They all got up to take a closer look at the ugly mark on John's shoulder. Jason made eye contact with him and smiled. The only thing left to do now was sniff each other's butts and run wild through the forest and take down a deer.

John wondered what the morning would bring. He didn't care about being shot or killed—he just cared about saving his country. Well, he didn't want to be shot and paralyzed—he'd prefer to just die quickly if he had to. To be in the Lord's presence would be the best outcome! Now, they all had to get what little sleep they could.

—⁓—

"Jaylynn—wake up, hon. It's time," John gently begged.

Jaylynn was startled out of her slumber. She didn't know how she had even fallen asleep at all. Her mind had been going a mile a minute when she had lain down.

"Take this caffeine pill right away and get dressed," John continued. "I'll be out getting the horses loaded up."

Jaylynn glanced at the clock. It was 10:30 p.m. The schedule was tight. They would be arriving just in time to unload Buttercup and Jake, get mounted, and approach the main gate of Ellsworth Air Force Base. Jaylynn was determined that she would not hold up the operation by not being ready.

The cold night chilled her as she stepped out onto her front porch. It was the Black Hills, and depending on the elevation, it could still get pretty cold, even in late spring. She went back inside and grabbed her riding coat. As she stepped out the door for the second time, she saw a frenzy of activity—horses going into trailers, tactical gear being checked and loaded. She would carry an AR just like the rest of them.

Her thoughts were interrupted when Jason approached her. "Okay, let's get this vest on you before we get too far along. It's heavy and hopefully not needed, but we are just being extra careful."

Jaylynn realized she was getting an armored vest, and a shiver went down her spine. "Not exactly a fashion statement, Jason." She was trying to hide her fear.

Jason looked her in the eye and, sensing her state of mind, attempted to reassure her. "Everybody here is afraid of what might happen in battle. Hopefully this is just an appearance to introduce John to the world. Things can go sideways with any operation. Bravery is about overcoming the fear and working through it. No panic…just let your training kick in."

Jaylynn looked straight at Jason, and her eyes started to sparkle. "I'm not worried about myself. I'm worried about John and you and your guys—well, and, of course, my family. I know you talked to Kayla last night…" She was waiting for Jason to say something about the conversation he had had with her.

"Kayla seems to have her head right now. Although, I don't know how she'll react when she receives the email and finds her kit." Jason looked to the sky, took a deep breath, and slowly let it out as he continued. "We have made a tentative date to go out to dinner after this is over—sometime. She is—she is a magnificent woman." Jaylynn could see the sudden change in his demeanor as he focused on the task at hand. "Okay, enough of that. Get your rifle sling ready for your AR. Do you have your—?"

"Yes, Jason, I have my nine-millimeter on and my extra magazine in the sticky." Jaylynn felt like a little girl being dressed for school.

Jason took in Jaylynn as he stepped back. "There you go—extra AR mags. And let's get this helmet strapped to the side." They would ride up to the gate with cowboy hats on for effect, but all of them had helmets with night vision ready to go. "Now you look badass!" Jason exclaimed.

Jaylynn responded with a look that made Jason chuckle. "Holy crap, Jason, all this stuff is heavy. I don't remember it being so heavy when we practiced!" she complained.

Jason was laughing again. "That vest was Kevlar. This one also has a steel plate in it," he explained.

Jaylynn and John would not have anywhere near the kind of kits Jason and his men would have. After doing a little modification to get everything under their dusters, they only had two men with first-aid kits. It had to look like just a bunch of cowboys out for a ride except for John. He was dressed in a distressed replica WWII fighter pilot's leather jacket covered with patches. He would be wearing a ball cap with the CREF insignia on it and some wings to indicate his status as a colonel.

Jason completed the final checks with his team and finally was able to make a phone call to Colonel Carl Justine. "Okay, Carl, one out of four we can handle. Hopefully, he will choose wisely. Time check—okay. We will be at the gate at exactly 0100 hours. The power goes out at 0105 hours."

Jason took John aside and informed him they had a small glitch that they had to overcome at the base. Three out of the four gate sentries on their side were in place, but the fourth one had been reassigned. So, there would be a wildcard at that main gate. John quietly processed the new information, nodded, and tried to hide his concern. He absolutely did not care if he got shot, but he did care if Jaylynn did.

He took in the activity around him, worried that their horses, Jake and Buttercup, looked as tired as Jaylynn. Thankfully, both were great trailer horses and were loaded with no problem. With three days of feed and food packed for Jaylynn and him in the RV part of the trailer, they hoped to be back in forty-eight hours, but they also had to be ready for the unexpected. John just didn't know how the horses would react to being on an airplane for the first time.

John's thoughts were interrupted when he heard Jason's men, the Sons of Issachar, complete the loading of their horses into their slant load nine-horse trailer. He had stepped back next to Jaylynn, and they were waiting by their truck. Beside him, Jaylynn was breathing in the crisp night air. John looked at her with a questioning half smile.

"What, John? I'm just taking in the sights and smells of our place." She was standing beside the trailer, talking to Buttercup and smelling her breath. *Horse poop and pines, leather and oats—drink it all in while you can, Jay,* she was thinking to herself.

Jason's voice startled her; it had a different tone somehow. "Alright, are we all ready for spin-up? John, our horse trailer will lead, you and Jaylynn will go next, and then the EarthRoamer will be last. Truen is staying here to take care of the property—and the dogs. Truen, are you ready with the mini electromagnetic pulse (EMP) weapon?"

Truen answered promptly. "I have the remote in hand. The device has been placed under their SUV, and they will be dead in the water and unable to communicate with anyone as soon as I detonate."

John and Jaylynn hadn't seen much of Truen since he had been their high cover this whole time. He had taken the dogs for walks and gotten to know them well, and now they understood why. Jaylynn looked at him and pleaded, "Please take care of my babies."

Truen quickly responded, "I will, ma'am—I will."

As John handed Truen the keys to Jaylynn's Highlander, she suddenly began to feel a bit jittery. At that moment, Jason turned toward John and Jaylynn, and he could see the stress on their faces. "The pills you took should be taking effect by now, so you may feel a bit wired—especially you, Jaylynn, since you drink very little caffeine. Are you feeling the effects yet?"

John spoke first. "Yeah—feels like I've had a couple cups of strong coffee."

Jaylynn quickly added, "I feel like I'm going to jump out of my skin right now, so I guess it's working! Geez!"

Jason smiled at her. "You were given a third of the dose that John got, and it still might have been too much. Oh well. Better to be super alert than groggy." Looking back to Truen, he gave the order. "Okay, hit the 'go dark' button for the FBI guys."

Truen immediately pressed the detonator on the mini EMP and watched the FBI's SUV go dark.

Agent Jefferies was asleep in the vehicle, and Backtow was watching YouTube videos on his phone. He heard a slight buzz before his phone went dark. Puzzled, he checked the power cord he had attached to his phone even though he knew it had plenty of charge. Then, he reached up and tried the overhead lights, but nothing came on. When he tried starting the SUV, again, nothing happened.

Just as he was waking up Jefferies, he noticed headlights moving down the Mogens' driveway toward the road. All hell was breaking loose in the SUV as Agent Backtow yelled for the now wide-awake Agent Jefferies to check his phone so they could get a call out. When the vehicles reached the Mogens' gate, the FBI agents reached full panic mode.

"What do you mean the flashlight won't work? What the hell happened here?"

Backtow, breaking out in a sweat, tried to start the SUV again. Dead as a doornail. Jefferies stepped out of the SUV at the same moment lightning rolled across the sky. As the big horse hauler pulled onto the main road, he read the words "Sons of Issachar" on the side of the trailer.

CHAPTER 35

JUST OUTSIDE OF ELLSWORTH AIR FORCE BASE – RAPID CITY, SOUTH DAKOTA

Before leaving the Mogen compound, Jason called his group together for last-minute instructions. "Eric will lead in with our truck and trailer. He has the route memorized, but he'll still have GPS up and running. John and Jaylynn will be second in and will stay close to Eric—very close. Eric will wait for you if you get caught in a red light. We do not want any police stops. I'll be behind the Mogens with our EarthRoamer. Truen will hold down the fort here and take care of the dogs. Eric, let's go over the route one more time."

Eric quickly chimed in. "Highway 385 south to Highway 16 to Highway 16 bypass. Jump on Highway 44 to the southeast. Then, it's Longview Road east to Radar Hill Road north. We hit Highway 1416 and then turn north on Ellsworth 'til we turn left into the Loaf N' Jug parking lot. We hug the back end of the parking lot and stop to unload the horses and mount up." This route was longer but kept them at the outskirts of Rapid City.

Jason then surprised John and Jaylynn a little. "After we arrive, we will be met by two of my men, who will take over as drivers on the rigs. Our intended departure will be at 0055 hours, when we will ride to Davis Gate at Ellsworth to make our little show. After that, we will move up Davis Drive along the fence line until we can make a left turn. If all goes according to plan, we should see the rigs waiting for us to reload the horses. We'll wait there until we get directions to proceed to the ramp for loading."

John stepped forward and had to ask one more time, "Jason, how did all this get planned so fast?"

Jason replied with a little smirk on his face. "John, you're only looking at the Arlington Colonels' Club, my guys, and me. What you are seeing is the tip of a very big iceberg. The Oathtakers and the special ops group, the Sons of Issachar, are much bigger than anyone realizes. We've been quietly planning a greater operation involving countless military personnel, past and present. Your plan was on the fringe but is now taking place. It's audacious, I must say!

"We have officers and enlisted men getting things ready for us at Ellsworth. Former special ops black chutes jumped a few hours ago and have already breached the base. Their job is to secure the flight line and have the Bones ready to go. As soon as they are off, we will board a C-17 with our rigs. We will be flying to Minot Air Force Base and unloading there.

"I'm sure I don't need to remind you to be extra alert. Remember, when the officer on watch refuses to hand over the base, the first thing you will see and hear are the propane tanks just off base going up. The Caterpillars will start breaching the fence line at the same time. It will be chaos! The officer on watch should be completely overwhelmed, and you'll only have five minutes to do your thing at the gate. Things will be happening all around us, but no worries—we will be fine. As a side note, that CREF colonel's cap really looks great on you, John!"

Jason was showing emotion like John and Jaylynn had never seen. Jay's eyes had grown wider and wider the more Jason had talked. Her mind was in a swirl again, and she was fighting her intestinal tract big time. She was anxious about her children, her dogs, and especially the wildcard at the gate. "Jason, I am uneasy about the guy who is not in on this whole thing."

"It's three to one," Jason reminded her, "and we'll have them in our sights just in case the other three standing guard don't handle things."

Jaylynn wasn't quite convinced. "I trust you with my life, Jason, I really do, but things could go sideways quickly, and this operation is supposed to be bloodless!"

Jason understood her concerns. "Jaylynn, I have to be honest with you right now. What we are doing is dangerous. Remember the sign above John's computer: lives, fortunes, and sacred honor. This is a war to restore our Constitution—war being the keyword. We have done the best we can to avoid any bloodshed, but we can't completely control every situation—like the weather tonight. We weren't supposed to have thunderstorms, but we do. So, the black chutes jumped four hours early to avoid them. They had to cover ground on foot, which wasn't in the plan, but they did it and are now securing the base as we speak. They are Torger's men, and he was trained as one of the elite of Dick Marcinko's original SEAL Team 6. They did red cell ops that are still legendary. We can trust Torger's crew to get it done."

Jaylynn was glad Jason was riding with them. She was overjoyed his teams were ready to take her family to a safe place when this operation got underway. It would be a morning her girls would never forget! Still, her stomach was churning as they made the left turn onto Ellsworth Street and pulled in behind the Loaf N' Jug store. The store closed at midnight, so they expected no one to be there. This was it.

Jaylynn glanced at John. He looked so ready, focused and poised. He said nothing but smiled at her. However, she was a wreck inside. No fear for herself but for John and her kids and grandkids. She steeled herself, convinced her intestinal tract to behave, and told herself she was ready. God, this body armor with the steel plate inside was heavy! She jumped when the door opened and the guys shot out.

John expected to see two more of Jason's men when they exited his truck. There were five. Jason nodded to John as they had rehearsed, and John took over. "Okay, let's get the horses unloaded and ready to mount. Who are the drivers?" Two young men stepped up and grabbed the keys to the Mogens' rig and Jason's bigger nine-horse unit. Then, two more young men not in uniform jumped into the EarthRoamer with communications equipment that would connect into the satellite dish on the EarthRoamer, which, in turn, would act as a portable command post for John and Jason if necessary.

Lightning flashed across the western sky as John began again. Everyone was now back outside and gathered in a circle. All of them Christians and all about to do something that may not be what Jesus would do, but they hoped the operation would go as planned. No one would get hurt if things went exactly right, and a new country, loyal to the Constitution and especially to God, would get carved out again.

John took a deep breath as they all took their hats off. "Lord, we believe in what we are doing tonight. Keep us safe. Keep all who have to make tough decisions tonight do so with hearts and heads clear. If this is what we are meant to do, guide us and let things fall into place. Let your angel armies fight alongside us as we battle the evil that has a grip on our nation. You are all-powerful, and we will not fear because you are with us always. Thank you—Amen."

Jason broke the momentary silence. "We have eight minutes to be at the Davis Gate, sir."

John quickly responded, "Okay, let's mount up and get started toward that gate. We will adjust our speed on the way so we can reach the gate at 0100 hours."

Jaylynn was at John's side. As he turned to get up on Jake, she stepped in front of him and hugged him for all she was worth. He looked down at her and smiled. Then, they kissed in front of the whole crew without embarrassment.

Lightning flashed again—closer this time. The thunder sounded quickly, and the horses stirred. With grim faces of concentration, the crew got on with their business. John didn't know the young man who had mounted Truen's horse, but he looked like another former special ops guy.

John gave the order: "Let's roll."

At that moment, the back door of the Loaf N' Jug swung open, and the night stocker/cleaner who was carrying trash to the dumpster stopped in his tracks as he looked at the seven people on horseback, fully regaled in cowboy garb including dusters. They were congregated at the south end of the parking lot. As he watched, they headed west toward the pizza place and then turned toward Davis Drive. He just stood there, mouth open, having no idea what they were doing out there in the middle of the night with a thunderstorm rolling in. He also wondered if he should call someone. But what would he tell them if he did? He turned and went back inside.

As they rode out of the parking lot, Jason was receiving updates about the status inside the base. They were a go.

CHAPTER 36

ELLSWORTH AIR FORCE BASE – RAPID CITY, SOUTH DAKOTA

A s the seven rode up to the Davis Gate at Ellsworth Air Force Base, one of the airmen standing guard spotted them first. He stepped forward and shouted, "What the hell have we got here?" This was the wildcard— the airman who had replaced the Oathtaker who had been reassigned late in the game.

The guard in charge of the detail had the rank of sergeant and was Jason's contact. He stepped forward to get a good look. What a sight! It was as if the cowboys from the song "Ghost Riders in the Sky" had just come down to earth for a spell. The lead rider's horse was huge, standing at least sixteen hands with coloring of dapple gray with a long white mane and white feathers. It truly looked like a horse out of a Disney movie.

Jake was a Gypsy Vanner—a smaller draft horse that John had not wanted but that had been given to him by Jaylynn's mom and dad when they had moved to South Dakota. The ranch next to her folks in Texas, which had been in the business of breeding and selling Gypsy Vanners, had gone bankrupt. Because they didn't really know what they were doing, they had lost it all. Jaylynn's folks had purchased Jake, the last horse on the ranch, for eleven hundred dollars (though he should have gone for eleven thousand dollars). Jaylynn's dad thought since John always worried about being too big to sit on a horse, a Gypsy Vanner would make him feel more comfortable to mount and ride. John had literally fallen in love at first sight when he'd seen Jake coming off the trailer. Jake wasn't very fast, of course, but he was strong and gentle. He and Buttercup were buds.

So, this was the sight at the gate. John on Jake with a distressed leather flight jacket covered with WWII patches and a CREF ball cap with colonel wings on it. The other six riders had on the long dusters, leather vests, and cowboy hats.

The wildcard airman again yelled, "Halt!" when they were about one hundred feet from the gate. The sergeant turned and ordered the airman to shut up and stand down. Stopping twenty-five feet away, the riders were in a spread formation with John and Jason in the process of dismounting ahead of them. Jason's contact, the sergeant, turned and whispered something to one of the other guards. Then, he proceeded to walk forward to confront the strange assembly.

"How can I help you gentlemen tonight? Are you lost?"

This was what John was waiting for. "Are you lost?" was the key phrase. John was now on stage. He was at his mark. The cameras would have several angles of him in the lights.

"No, Sergeant, we are not lost. I am Colonel John Mogen of the Constitution Restoration Expeditionary Forces, and we are here to commandeer this base for our use. Please let the officer on watch know that he has been put on notice and has five minutes to turn over the base to us, or we will have to take it by force."

The young sergeant, hiding his smirk behind his raised hand, was shaking his head side to side and shouting to the group of men that he would contact the officer on watch immediately. Depressing his mic button, he conveyed Colonel Mogen's message.

Moments later, the rogue airman was frantically pacing and mumbling to himself as he heard the communication that the officer was busy with a breach and was in the middle of checking it out. Another airman on guard duty was standing next to the one who was in the process of losing it and told him to settle down. They had crazy people coming to the gate all the time.

John looked at his watch. It was 0104 hours. "Sergeant, we have no choice but to proceed to take over the base."

John and Jason were still dismounted when the base went dark at 0105 hours. The battery backup lights at the gate flashed on immediately. Meanwhile, Jason's men had pepper-sprayed the guards. The airman assigned to watch the wildcard lost sight of him in the flash. The crack of gunfire came from the wildcard's gun before the other airman could grab him or his rifle. A report sounded from John's right. Eric had shot the wildcard airman through the neck—too late.

John yelled, "Get that crossing arm up! Let's move!"

As they mounted their horses, Jason reported to John he had been hit with a ricochet and had pain in his leg. Then, he turned to his men and yelled out, "Anybody hit? Everybody okay?"

Jaylynn was shaken by the gunfire. After all, it was only three shots, but one was too many for her.

Eric had finished checking with everyone, and all were okay. "All good, Jason—all good," he reported.

John groaned when he mounted Jake. Jason looked over at him but didn't see anything out of the ordinary. As they started moving through the Davis Gate, Eric came along John's right side. When he looked over, he saw blood streaming down the side of John's face. "Shit, Jason—John's been hit!"

Jason had been on John's left side, so he hadn't noticed the blood. John turned to him and spoke. "It's just a nick—not as bad as it looks. You know how facial cuts bleed. Let's just get to the rendezvous before we do anything." Then, as an afterthought, he stated he'd also been hit in the shoulder. "Might be a problem. At least I'll have a scar to match the one on my left shoulder," he said with a chuckle.

The group rode on while two of Jason's men remained so they could zip tie the hands and feet of the remaining three guards.

The EarthRoamer and horse trailers were still sitting over on Ellsworth Street, waiting for the riders. It was in the process of moving boulders away from the vehicle barrier between them and the street so the horses could have access.

Meanwhile, the riders were advancing along the fence line until they could turn left. Jason was riding beside John so he could keep an eye on him as they made their way. John had never seen Jason so upset before. "I'm so sorry, John—I've let you down. You're my responsibility, and I screwed up."

John grimaced in pain, replying, "It's okay, Jason. We knew we had an unknown at the gate. I'll be okay—take my word for it."

Jaylynn had finally fought her way through the guys and rode up next to John. When she saw the right side of his face, she gasped. He looked terrible, and she started to cry and yell hysterically. "What the hell are we doing, John! Why are we doing this!"

John turned to her and shouted back, "We are saving our country, or we're going to die trying! It's just a flesh wound, Jaylynn—it just looks bad, so pull yourself together! I need your strength, Jaylynn. I need you to stay in control. I won't be able to do this if I'm worrying about you too!"

By that time, they had reached the horse trailers, and Jason was already barking out orders. "Let's get the saddles off and get these horses loaded. Eric, get me a first-aid kit! Let's get your coat off, John."

Jaylynn was confused. "It's cold, Jason... Can't he leave his coat on?"

Jason's response was terse. "Jaylynn, you need to cowboy up right now... Help me get his coat off!"

As they dragged off the garment, John let out an immense groan. Eric was there with a combat first-aid kit, pulling out bandages and blood stoppers. Jaylynn continued biting her lip and trying not to cry as she caught sight of John's shoulder wound. His collarbone was jutting through the skin, and blood was dripping down his chest. A chunk of tissue was gone above that, and a U-shaped crater was left.

"It didn't get an artery, so we are okay," Eric whispered with a sigh of relief. "He'll be okay, ma'am—he will be okay."

Jason grabbed Jaylynn and walked her a few feet away from her husband. She gasped when John yelled in pain as Eric stuffed blood-stopping packing into his shoulder.

"I'm so sorry, Jaylynn—we blew it at the gate. I'm so sorry. He'll be okay—he will."

Jaylynn looked up at Jason, gazing into the face of the son she never had. It was unspoken, but now she understood that Jason assumed he had failed John—and her. She took a deep breath and looked Jason straight on, saying, "We knew the risks, and we know things can go...sideways, as you say. No blame. Let's just move on and pray things are going as planned on the flight line." Then, she embraced Jason as best she could through all the armor and the magazines.

In the background, Jason was hearing chatter through his headgear. The Caterpillars had breached the perimeter fence in three places, overwhelming and confusing the security teams on the air base. The power was cut, communications were compromised, and they had the base personnel secured. The base's patriot personnel were in the process of assisting with the B-1Bs, which were already hotting up the five bombers needed for the mission. They were manipulating the movable bulkheads in the bomb bays, resetting them to accommodate the mini subs.

As he was communicating, the "packages" and personnel came by them down Ellsworth Street and turned onto Kenny Road. They had men out in front of the B-1Bs with signs identifying the units FedEx #1 through FedEx #5.

During all this commotion, one of the trucks pulled off next to John and Jaylynn's horse trailer. As the truck was coming to a stop, a man jumped out. Jaylynn couldn't believe it.

"Carl, what are you doing here? Didn't you tell us you were a decoy?"

Carl looked into the cab and told the driver to head over to the flight line. As the truck moved out, he yelled, "Godspeed, Sam!"

Jaylynn asked again, "What are you doing here, Carl, and was that Sam Hudson?"

Carl was all business. "No time now, Jay. Where is John, and how is he?"

"He's in the RV. Eric, one of Jason's men, is patching him up. He'll live." She couldn't control her lip quiver.

Carl embraced her quickly and then asked, "Is Jason with him?"

"No—just Eric. Jason is over in the field talking to someone about a C-17 I think he said."

Carl went into the RV, followed closely by Jaylynn. John's face had been cleaned up, and Eric was rigging a sling for his shoulder. He looked a little pale, but he had refused any painkillers.

Eric looked up and was shocked to see Carl. "Colonel Justine—sir."

Carl again was all business. "Eric—how are you? And how is your patient doing?"

John smiled up at Carl as he questioned Eric about his condition.

"So, John," said Carl once he'd received an update on everything from Eric. "You went and got your pretty face shot up, huh? Not to worry. We have a full medical team on the C-17, and they'll work on your shoulder when we get you on board."

John just nodded.

With a nod of his own, Carl excused himself. He needed to talk to Jason, but Jason was not looking forward to speaking with him. As Carl joined him outside the RV, Jason noticed he was not upset.

"So, one wounded and one airman dead? Not bad for taking over an entire Air Force base. We can talk about the particulars later. Now, I want to know—is Torger on the base?"

Jason was relieved that Carl was not too disappointed and finally let out the breath he hadn't even realized he had been holding in. "No, sir. Jim Henry is the team leader on the base right now. He is on the flight line. Situation required restraining combatants on base, so we have people detained all over. Radar says the thunderstorm is about fifteen minutes out. Not exactly as smooth as we would've liked, but we're getting things done. We are now waiting to see if those packages were sent out! We are awaiting the arrival of our friendly C-17 out of March."

Carl cut in. "I heard that—but first on the agenda is getting John on board and obtaining medical attention. The FBI raided our decoy command center outside Dyess, so they are already looking for the Colonels' Club. Any chatter from the FBI in Rapid City?"

After being updated, Jason was feeling a little better about things. "No, sir. Those agents at the Mogens' are probably still walking to the highway. They never knew what hit them. So, you Texas guys slipped under the FBI surveillance also?"

Carl was grinning. "We sure did. We have friends with private jets all over Texas. We went to Oklahoma City to file our flight plans. With luck, it will throw them off the trail. Colonel North and Colonel Musgrave are already in Minot, and I landed here at the regional airport. No cameras at the fixed-base operator (FBO) for the NSA or CIA traitors to look at for a while. I still need to touch base with Jim Henry to find out where in the hell Torger is!"

Jason was quick to reply. "Just got word that the flight line asked us to relocate on the back side of a hangar, and they have personnel to guide us. It's going to get real loud when the Bones fire up, so we need to get the horse trailers relocated ASAP. Check that—we're going to be taken into the Pride Hangar, wherever that is."

Carl grinned again. "I know exactly where it is—it's huge and a little off the flight line. No one will be able to detect our little convoy in there."

Jason was yelling out to the drivers to get in the vehicles and get them moving. The EarthRoamer would stay outside next to Pride Hangar to continue with their comms jamming.

Eric radioed to John and Jaylynn that they would be making a short move to another location. Just as the message came across, their horse trailer RV combo lurched forward, and John let out a groan. He was thankful when they stopped moving, and he began to rise from his seat, but Jaylynn was adamant. "John, you sit back down... What on earth are you thinking?"

John leaned over and kissed her softly. "I'm going to walk out of this vehicle by my own power and watch those bombers take off, Jay. That's what I'm going to do."

Jaylynn realized that John needed to do this. "You are so stubborn, John Mogen—I love you!" As they stepped out of the RV, a cold wind was blowing off the Hills. The rain would be coming soon. Lightning crisscrossed the sky.

Jason was standing at the flight line with Carl, so Eric was at John's six now. "Sir, I'll find you two some chairs," Eric said respectfully.

"Thanks, Eric. I need to see the show to believe this is really happening. It's a little surreal for us right now. Any idea how it's going at the flight line?"

Eric responded that he had heard a call for medical. "Sounded like a technician broke an arm while loading one of the mini subs on FedEx #1. I'll be right back with the chairs, sir."

John knew the numbers. FedEx #1 was headed for Langley, Virginia. It was dropping the smallest nuclear device at CIA headquarters. The pilot was Carl's friend, Sam Hudson, who had been employed with the NSA just a week ago. *How surreal is that?* John thought as he heard jet engine noise from one or more of the Bones.

John had agreed to some over-the-counter painkillers but refused morphine. His shoulder was hurting, and the right side of his face was swelling under the compress. Nonetheless, he tried to concentrate on the moment.

Eric was back. "Here you go—two chairs." He helped Jaylynn get John down into his seat. She didn't sit though. She elected to stand behind him as tears rolled down her cheeks. She needed to talk to her children. She needed to know they were safe. She was shaking from the cold wind and then shuddered at the noise as FedEx #1 powered up and started down the runway.

As the last B-1B was taking off, the skies opened up with the torrential rain they had been expecting all morning. Before they could get inside of the hangar, John, Jaylynn, and Eric were soaked.

The rain was going sideways, but John's mind wasn't thinking about the downpour. All he could concentrate on were the big sticks that were finally on their way. He hoped they would prevent the next civil war. Central Park in New York City; The National Mall in Washington, D.C.; CIA headquarters in Langley, Virginia; and San Francisco and Los

Angeles, California. The units deployed to each of these designated areas were waiting for their package to land so they could immediately secure their sectors. There would be no cause for alarm because they were military units hiding in plain sight. The units had to guard the mini subs until the news release explaining their plan was released. John was thrilled the B-1Bs had gotten in the air. Now, he just prayed their C-17 Globemaster could land in this storm.

When Carl and Jason located Jim Henry on the flight line, retired Colonel Carl Justine was in full colonel mode. Jim Henry had never met Carl, but Jason knew Jim and took the opportunity to introduce them.

However, Carl was pissed. "Commander Henry, I need to know where Captain Vigdahl is now!"

Jim Henry had expected the question. "Sir, the captain is not in the country right now. He is at a location somewhere in the Caribbean. I don't know where exactly."

Carl suddenly remembered. "Belize—he has a place in Belize!"

Commander Henry responded a little sheepishly. "I didn't know that, sir. I was just told that he isn't in the country. I can't contact him until our communication jamming is complete. Sorry, sir."

Carl was hot! "Dammit, Commander, you find him and get him on the line ASAP! Do you understand?"

"Yes, sir—yes, sir. I'll get right on it, sir," the commander stuttered, backing away from the colonel as swiftly as his legs could move him out of the area.

Carl, holding his temper in check, stopped the rapidly retreating commander and calmly addressed him. "Commander Henry, you and your men did a great job tonight—thank you. Any casualties?"

"Only one, sir—a broken ankle on the parachute drop. I sent two men in the UTV to pick him up. We had to drop them a few clicks away. The C-17 needs to get on the ground!"

Jim Henry had been under Torger's command before Torger had retired. Jim was now in charge of TRADET for SEAL training and was still active Navy. He felt he could relay additional information about

Vigdahl. "Sir, the captain did ask me to communicate to the Colonels' Club that he was doing this for Dick Marcinko and SEAL Team 6. I didn't understand what he meant."

"Thanks, Commander. I really don't understand what he meant by that either, but thanks. Any word on the C-17?" Carl asked with a little anxiety in his voice.

Grabbing the radio, Commander Henry made the call, and they both waited for a response. As the time passed, Commander Henry became edgy. When the radio finally chirped, the commander visibly jumped but recovered quickly so he could pass the information to the colonel. "Sir, the C-17 diverted west, so they will come in behind the storm. The thunderstorm cell should be past us in about ten minutes. It seems to be moving through rapidly."

Carl turned to Jason, who had been quietly listening to the conversation. "What are we hearing from Minot, Jason?" Minot Air Force Base was their final destination tonight. The base commander was an old friend of Carl's and a great patriot. He was set up to receive their flight and all the rest of the flights scheduled within the thirty-six-hour window. "And what about the F-16s out of Sioux Falls?"

Jason was ready with updated information. "Sir, Minot is ready to welcome us, and Sioux Falls Air National Guard has six fighters ready to scramble if needed."

Carl felt good about the reports. The snafu at the Davis Gate had left his brother-in-law shot and an airman dead. Not the plan, but things go sideways sometimes.

CHAPTER 37

OUTSIDE THE MOGEN COMPOUND AND RAPID CITY, SOUTH DAKOTA

The two FBI agents left stranded near the Mogen compound thought they would go inside and try to locate a phone. As they headed down the driveway toward the house, a warning shot rang out and ricocheted uncomfortably close to them. Immediately, they turned tail and ran back to the main gate, veering onto the highway at a dead run. They caught a ride back into Rapid City after a state trooper came across them.

When they finally arrived back at their office, Jefferies was still ranting and running his mouth off, more to himself than his partner. He had a terrible feeling in his gut. They were supposed to make sure the Mogens got on that flight to DFW in the morning. He was sure he'd seen at least John in one of the trucks pulling a horse trailer and leaving the compound.

Meanwhile, Backtow had picked up the landline and was calling their immediate supervisor to report in on the current situation. Not a fun thing to do at two in the morning.

As that call was going on, the senior agent checked the scanner for anything that might relate to the Mogens. There was a radio call from a Pennington County sheriff's deputy. "Unit 10 to dispatch. We have a problem at the Davis Gate, Ellsworth's south gate... Ellsworth is dark. Three of the guards have been bound with zip ties, and the fourth guard is deceased. No sign of riders on horseback per the report from

211

the Loaf N' Jug employee. Wait, one airman is telling me the riders came through here and disappeared into the base. Not sure what's happening on the base."

Dispatch responded, "10-4, Unit 10. Do you need backup?"

The deputy was uncertain what to do at this point. "Dispatch, I have tried calling the base—could you try to see if you can get through? I don't want to enter the base unless I need to."

"Stand by, 10." Moments later, dispatch was back. "Okay, Unit 10. I'm not able to get through to Ellsworth. I'm sending two additional units to meet you at Davis Gate."

"I copy, dispatch. Unit 10 will hold at Davis Gate."

Agent Jefferies started screaming at his younger colleague, who was still on the phone with their supervisor, Molly O'Keefe. "Tell her we have a major problem at Ellsworth. Tell her there has been a breach at Ellsworth, and they are totally dark! We need to get in touch with the Pentagon!"

Agent Backtow hung up without saying a word to Agent O'Keefe. His partner lost it and grabbed him, ready to smack him until his brain registered what he was yelling, but Backtow spoke up first. "She heard you—she heard you… She's coming down!"

"We don't have time for that! I'm calling the Pentagon and the CIA—now!"

CHAPTER 38

ELLSWORTH AIR FORCE BASE TARMAC — RAPID CITY, SOUTH DAKOTA

Jason was relieved when he saw the C-17 from March Air Force Base on final approach. The rain had finally stopped, but a cool wind was still blowing, and the smell of wet blacktop after a heavy rain was pungent. He was on the radio informing all personnel to get ready to board.

John and Jaylynn returned to their sleeping quarters in their RV. Their truck and trailer, driven by one of Jason's men, was first in the C-17; Jason's Featherlite pulled in second; and the EarthRoamer came third. Several Polaris side-by-sides entered next.

After being secured, John stepped out of the RV and watched men dressed in black stream into the cargo bay. He suddenly understood how big of an operation this was and how many patriots this beautiful country had. These patriots were willing to lay their lives on the line to pull off his crazy, audacious plan to restore the rule of law to the country they all loved. As the magnitude of this impressed upon him, he felt his eyes start to water.

John didn't notice Jason or Carl walking up next to him. Carl spoke first. "John, we have everyone on board except the Polaris bringing an injured man in. They are just a couple of clicks out. We need to get you into the medical pod up front."

John had flinched when Carl had begun to speak and then groaned in pain from his shoulder. "Carl, I'm staying here until that last Polaris drives in," John said in a voice that made the other two suddenly realize that he had been the best choice as leader of the restoration movement.

They didn't argue with John as Jason took Carl by the arm. "Just got a report that the last Polaris is on base. They've taken some fire but are still on the move."

Carl looked over at John. "This bird is ready to start taxiing as soon as the ramp is up."

By then, Jaylynn had joined the group. Seeing no one coming into the cargo bay, she questioned, "Are we ready? Can we get outta here?"

"We are waiting on one more Polaris—the last of our men," John replied.

Jason moved quickly toward the end of the plane, and as the three of them watched, he and about ten men headed down the ramp with guns up. They heard distant gunfire, and Jason and his men swiftly opened up.

A Polaris came roaring up the ramp into the cargo bay and slammed to a stop. The driver was yelling for a medic as he jumped out of the UTV. Another soldier fell out of the passenger's side onto the grating, bleeding from more than one gunshot. Men swarmed the Polaris to assist him and the soldier with the broken ankle as Jason and his men continued firing even as the cargo ramp was rising. One of Jason's men went down. The rest of his men gave heavy cover as Jason shouldered the injured man and carried him farther into the C-17. It was Zachariah Overgaard. Jason became bloody from Zach's extensive wounds. The injured man was in bad shape after taking a round through the neck.

At that moment, John was moving from the ramp area and being escorted to the medical pod. He and his escort heard yelling to move aside as Jason rushed by with Eric right behind him. Eric was holding Zach's neck with a bloody scarf.

Jaylynn watched all this with a furrowed brow and a heavy heart. She had hoped all this was over, and they were all safe. However, it wasn't to be. Jason and his men had provided cover for the men in the Polaris.

Military police (MPs) had come from another part of the base. It seemed not all of the barracks had been neutralized by the gas bombs shot to put out the remaining personnel. More casualties kept coming by from the Polaris that had driven in at the last second. The C-17 lurched forward as the brakes released. It had been at full power and was lined up on the runway ready to roll.

"Okay, John—let's get you to medical," Carl reminded him.

"Carl, I think the other injuries should go first." John wasn't feeling well at all, and Carl knew it, so he explained that there was room in medical for several casualties at once and he needed to let it go. John complied, and Carl and Jaylynn made sure he got to the medical pod.

The C-17 lifted off without additional incidents and headed north to Minot Air Force Base. The base commander there was Colonel Bob Richards, who was a hardcore restorationist and a friend of Carl Justine. He had spent the last year getting an officer staff who reflected his mindset transferred to Minot. The base was theirs without firing a shot and would be their headquarters for the next thirty hours at least.

After settling John in medical, Carl went to search out Commander Jim Henry, who had led the special ops raid on Ellsworth. He still didn't buy it that the commander wasn't in the know on where Captain Vigdahl was and wanted to get some answers.

CHAPTER 39

MINOT AIR FORCE BASE — NORTH DAKOTA

Forty-five minutes after takeoff, the C-17 was descending into Minot Air Force Base. John Mogen would need an operation to repair his collarbone. A military orthopedist at Minot was ready to do that surgery at 0700 hours.

John was in the medical pod when they stopped working on Zachariah and called out his time of death. The loss was hard on everyone, especially John who had smoked cigars and told stories with Zach the night before. Outside the medical pod, he heard a distraught scream from Jason as he was told the news. This bloodless coup had seen a very bloody night in South Dakota. John hoped that this battle at Ellsworth would be the worst of it!

Everyone in the C-17 soon heard about Zach. Jaylynn, concerned about Jason, found him alone, sitting in a jump seat with his head in his blood-stained hands. She sat down next to him, silently put her arm around him, and began to cry with him, giving comfort that would not be enough to bring his friend back.

John had refused any major painkilling drugs. The landing at Minot was smooth, but he still winced with pain. As the C-17 Globemaster finished taxiing and the engines wound down, he reflected on how they had successfully taken over Ellsworth long enough for them to *steal* five B-1B bombers, along with several Air Force personnel who believed in their cause.

All were getting up and preparing to disembark at Minot as Carl Justine stood and initiated the speaker system in the cargo bay. John Mogen was standing at his side. Carl needed to brief this group on the plan taking place. They deserved to know what was happening with the nuclear devices specifically. Up until this moment, only a few people had been privy to this information.

Ladies and gentlemen, I am Colonel Carl Justine, Air Force, retired. I would like to thank each and every one of you for what you accomplished tonight. Our fate lies with the success of the pilots and crews delivering the big sticks and depends on the people in power at this moment recognizing they need to listen and not initiate any plan against the men guarding them. I can now tell you that the Navy SEALs embedded with the devices are the actual detonators. The detonation systems are physically hooked up to the heartbeats of the men tending them. This has never been done before. Each device has two men connected at all times. Three teams of two men each are assigned to each of these devices with a technician available to do the changeout of links. At least one 'learned' heartbeat must be hooked to the detonation system at all times to keep the device from going off. Pray for those SEALs please."

With this new information, Carl had everyone's attention. John and Jaylynn were also hearing this for the first time. Human detonators—wow!

"The man standing next to me is Colonel John Mogen. Next to him is his wife, Jaylynn. This crazy, audacious idea we are bringing to life as we stand here right now came from John. He will lead the Constitution Restoration Expeditionary Forces as needed to take our country back to the rule of law!"

John was a little shocked as Carl handed him the microphone. He took a deep breath, collecting his thoughts. At that moment, a literal roar came up from the crowd in the cargo bay. John was proud of all these patriots but still a little unstable from his wounds as he stood there. He looked at Jaylynn. She had tears in her eyes as she held his good arm tight. John got a rush of adrenaline when he realized the cheers were for him. He had gotten himself shot, an airman killed, at least three others wounded, and Zachariah killed. He didn't know what the rest of the night would bring, so he pulled out the most authoritative voice he could muster as he fought back the tears. "Pro Deo et Patria!" is what came out first. John was surprised at that and quickly explained, "For God and Country! For God and Country!"

Another roar came up from the patriots in that cargo bay. This one was louder than the first and sounded as if it came from deep in their souls, as if a burden had been lifted and they could express the joy of the moment. John had to go on. "This night—your names, your deeds, this hour—will be written in history. You will be known as those who chose to risk your lives, and one who gave his life, to restore our republic. God bless you and Godspeed as we attempt this restoration without the bloodshed of all-out civil war! God bless you! Jaylynn and I thank you from the very bottom of our hearts. God bless you all!" Yet another resounding roar came up from within the C-17.

Carl was in awe of John. A short but inspiring speech in his condition was remarkable.

Jaylynn felt more of John's weight shifting toward her. As the cargo bay opened up, John was led to a wheelchair waiting to transport him to the base clinic. He stopped them and said, "I want to watch them leave the cargo bay."

Commander Jim Henry was the first to turn toward John. He stepped in front of him and saluted. As the rest of the crew filed past, they stopped and saluted as well. John didn't really care that they saw the tears streaming down his face. These were the men and women who really understood what was at stake and would give their lives for their great country.

As the last soul walked down the ramp and out of the back of the C-17, John said to no one in particular, "May God have mercy on our souls. May He give us victory if it is His will. Now I'm ready for some serious painkillers."

Carl and Jaylynn were both in tears but started laughing when John asked for help with his pain. Jaylynn was a big mess. That damn pill Jason had given her still had her wide awake. She'd been crying half the night and felt like she was still coming apart.

Carl knew how she felt. "Jay, I know you need to get some rest. Let's get you all out of here and into the guest quarters the base commander set up for you and John. I want both of you to get some sleep before his surgery, which is scheduled for 0700 hours."

She hugged Carl and said, "I can't believe this is really happening, can you? Where is my bag? Boy, do I need some water and an extra hormone pill! Let's get settled into those quarters you're talking about."

As they walked off the C-17, arms locked, Base Commander Bob Richards greeted them. There was a vehicle waiting to take them to their quarters.

After getting his much-needed pain meds, John Mogen was in happy land, but before they left, he still told the doctors tending him to wrap up his surgery in a timely manner. After all, he had work to do.

CHAPTER 40

NSA FORT – HIGH PERFORMANCE COMPUTING CENTER 2 – MEADE, MARYLAND

"**S**low down, Gloria." Luke Anderson glanced at his clock. "It's 0530 for God's sake. Run that by me again."

Gloria was frantic. "Okay—Ellsworth Air Force Base was breached early this morning. Five B-1Bs were loaded with cargo that, I'm told, looked like little submarines. They're all still in the air as we speak. Our night watch has been trying to verify any operation or red cell but can't. And guess what else, Luke? Guess what?"

Luke had no time for this crap. "Gloria, please stop with the nonsense!"

Gloria felt a little ashamed of the kid games. "Sorry, sir. Six riders showed up on horseback at the lower entry gate of Ellsworth. At 0300 hours our time, two men dismounted their horses."

Luke was now out of bed and trying to make himself some coffee. He had to break in. "Gloria, stop—just stop. You're telling me six people on horseback took over one of our Air Force bases? I thought we were watching Dyess Air Force Base for something like this?"

"Luke—listen to me!" Gloria was shouting now. "Not the six horsemen at the gate but the Caterpillars that breached the fence lines at three different places. They had people, some sort of special forces, neutralizing the base's security personnel. Then, they brought in vehicles with these little submarines and loaded them on the B-1s. They did all of this in thirty minutes. One report says the two men who got off their horses at the gate demanded that the security detail notify the officer on watch. The two guys calmly told security they needed to surrender the base within five minutes or they would take Ellsworth by force. Facial recognition has already identified the two men as Jason Wilder and—by golly—John Mogen. *The* John Mogen. The guy we have on our radar! The guy just writing a book…my ass, Luke!"

Luke Anderson was in major shock, and Gloria was on a roll. "The next report says a C-17 landed and picked up the special forces and all vehicles involved, including trucks pulling horse trailers. The Pentagon has nothing on this mission or where the C-17 was out of. There was no flight plan filed as far as we can track. Hang on—got to go. Getting a call from the office… I'll call you back." With that, Gloria was gone.

Luke immediately placed a call to Nathan Parkinson, who was his contact at the CIA. Nathan was up—but barely. He hardly had a chance to answer. "Nathan, are you there?" Luke was in a state of agitation.

"Yes. Who is this?"

"It's Luke—NSA. Luke Anderson. We have a problem—a big problem. That guy in South Dakota I asked you to investigate—remember that?"

Nathan pondered the question. "You mean the guy who's writing a book who you thought might be actually planning some real crap? That's about tenth on my list. Did you call the FBI about it?"

Luke was pissed now. "Yes, Nathan, we did, but it's way too late to talk about that at this point. A man on horseback with five other men showed up at the south gate at Ellsworth Air Force Base last night and took over the base. One of them was John Mogen—that guy writing the book. Dammit, Nathan!"

"Hang on, Luke. Got to take this call from my boss—gotta call you back."

Nathan didn't get a chance to say hello before his boss started yelling, "Get your ass down here immediately. We have a big problem, and it involves something you should've followed up on. Joint Special Operations

Command (JSOC) is spinning up, and I need some answers—*now*! They don't even have a destination for crying out loud! We've had an Air Force base breached—five B-1B bombers gone and a ghost C-17 we're still looking for. Get down here, do you hear me? The Pentagon wants to know what we have on this!"

Nathan had never heard his boss this incensed. He dropped everything, including the phone, and dressed faster than he had ever done in his life.

FBI FIELD OFFICE – RAPID CITY, SOUTH DAKOTA

"Yes, ma'am... No, we don't know what it was. We just know the vehicle and all our electronics went dead. After we finally caught a ride to the office, we heard something was going down at Ellsworth. Somebody got in. Report of bombers taking off and a cargo plane that landed. The base power is out—that we know."

The senior FBI agent was sweating as he talked to his supervisor, Molly O'Keefe. "Jefferies, you're our most experienced agent. Okay, let's start working the situation... You called the Pentagon and the CIA already. Is that right?"

"Yes, ma'am. The Pentagon had already received a call from someone at Ellsworth. They reported that all their comms had been jammed during the breach. Whoever is doing this—running this—has serious technology. Tech that put us dead in the water."

Molly's other phone rang. "Yes, sir. No, sir, we don't know where John Mogen is at this time. Yes, sir, we'll get right out there and find him, sir."

After hanging up her second line, she switched back to the call where she'd left Jefferies hanging. "Okay, I want you two to get another vehicle and drive out to the Mogen place. Find John Mogen or find out where he might be. We are last to the party on this one and looking bad, so get going. Now! I'm in the process of calling in more agents. What time were they supposed to take off for DFW?"

Jefferies quickly replied, "0715 hours on a United flight with a stop in Denver. We expected them to leave their home around 0530 hours or so, but they may have left at midnight—driving out with their truck and horse trailer. We aren't sure it was them in the truck. Could have been a decoy or something like that."

Molly was incensed. "Well, get another SUV and get your asses out to the Mogen compound to see if they are there. I'll send other agents to cover the airport and Ellsworth. Now, get going!"

"Yes, ma'am!" Jefferies was upset and embarrassed as he threw down the phone. "We are so on our way!"

CHAPTER 41

FEDEX #1 B-1B BOMBER NEARING DROP ZONE FOR CIA HEADQUARTERS — LANGLEY, VIRGINIA

Sam Hudson was loving life right now. The takeoff and top speed run was the most exhilarating thing he had done in years. His copilot was also acting as his combat systems officer, and the two former Navy SEALs in the back were preparing for their stealth mini submarine drop. Their mission necessitated the use of a separate frequency for all five FedEx B-1Bs for their communication in the event any of the other rogue B-1Bs tried to break into their transmission.

So, Sam was shocked and confused to hear a voice come in over their frequency. "FedEx #1, this is FedEx #6. Do you copy? Over."

Sam's heart rate instantly climbed up fifty beats. Who was this, and what the hell were they up to? Sam had to be careful. "Say again, please— did you say FedEx #6?"

The response came quickly and professionally. "Roger, FedEx #1. This is FedEx #6 on final for Langley. You are to divert to secondary target at NSA Fort Meade. Please respond in the affirmative."

"FedEx #6, please identify yourself."

With alarm bells going off in his head and his mind going a mile a minute, he realized he had to find out who this unidentified plane was.

Had the CIA gotten wind of their operation? How could they add a target without notifying the other pilots? He knew his secondary target, the Fort Meade location, was his old stomping ground—the NSA.

"Sir, we are ready to drop the package—we are in the window. Over." Sam was frozen in time. What the hell was going on?

"FedEx #1, this is FedEx #6. Please reply. Divert to secondary. We have dropped on Langley. You are to divert." Sam had to do something!

"Sir? We are ready to drop..."

"Sam, do you copy? Are we a go for the drop?"

Sam saw a bright flash ahead. It was below them at ground level. Was that Langley? Who the hell was FedEx #6? Then, another much bigger flash erupted right ahead of him.

Sam quickly gave an order. "Do not drop—I repeat, do not drop. We are diverting to secondary! Reset your GPS for secondary. I repeat, reset for secondary! Tell the SEALs to reset their GPS now! Cory, get up here now!" Cory moved into the cockpit per Sam's order. "Look at that, Cory—look!" Sam had veered slightly north to reset for Fort Meade just as the shock wave hit their aircraft.

"What is that, Sam? That is huge. Is that nuclear?"

Sam's hands and brow were sweating profusely now. "FedEx #6, did you just drop on Langley—did you—what are you doing?"

FedEx #6 responded quickly. "FedEx #1, divert to secondary. We have dropped on Langley per orders from Captain Vigdahl. He said to relay to you this was for Dick Marcinko and SEAL Team 6."

Sam was frantic. "Was it nuclear? Was it nuclear? We were not supposed to detonate—just drop, dammit. Was it nuclear? FedEx #6, do you copy?"

"FedEx #1, please copy that you are diverting. FedEx #6 needs to verify you are diverting. Over."

"FedEx #6, we are diverting! Tell me you didn't just nuke Langley!"

"FedEx #1—FedEx #6 dropped a bunker buster and then a MOAB after the GBU-43B. Not nuclear—I repeat, not nuclear."

Sam's body was totally shaking now. Had he been set up?

Cory had moved back into the bomb bay again. "Sam, we're ready to drop on the secondary. Do you copy?"

Sam had forgotten how fast the B-1 covered ground. Even with the wings swept forward, the gear down, and the flaps deployed, the slowest he could go was 150 knots, which was still over 170 miles per hour. He had the B-1B on course for the secondary drop zone as fast as possible with a slight course adjustment to the northeast.

"Proceed with drop—proceed with drop." Sam had to complete their mission and get this plane on the ground. He switched frequencies and broke his silence. He had to notify command.

"CREF Command D.C.—this is FedEx #1. Do you copy?"

"Command D.C. copies, FedEx #1. Is your mission complete? Why are you breaking silence?"

"We just dropped on our secondary—Fort Meade, NSA. I repeat, we dropped on our secondary target, Command. Someone who called himself FedEx #6 dropped live on our primary. Dropped very large conventional on Langley! Please let ground know that their people outside Langley might be compromised—unable to move. Get the ground units ready at our secondary please."

CREF MOBILE HEADQUARTERS – MINOT AIR FORCE BASE – NORTH DAKOTA

Colonel Allan North was in shock. He had just received a call from their command in D.C. about the radio transmission from FedEx #1. "That son of a bitch! That son. Of. A. Bitch!"

North had been notified that Langley had been hit, and he just knew Torger was somewhere on a beach in Belize! "Get me Colonel Justine! Where is Colonel Justine right now?"

"Sir, they are on the ground here at Minot."

Colonel Allan North was on his encrypted phone. When Carl saw Allan's number flash on his screen, he quickly answered. "Allan, how's the mission going?"

Carl had not heard Allan in such a rage like he was in right now. "That son of a bitch Torger just took out Langley with a MOAB, and

227

people will be reporting it as nuclear for sure! Besides that, FedEx #1 was ordered to divert to secondary and dropped on the NSA. They might not listen to us now that this damn thing went hot with what Torger pulled!"

———⋙⋘———

FedEx #1 had just made their turn north when Cory spotted the fighters on their tail and yelled, "I'm hitting countermeasures. Fighters—multiple fighters!"

Sam had just gotten the wings swept back on his B-1 when he had to slam his throttles forward and pull back full on the controls. The B-1 was a lot bigger than the fighters, but Sam was still going to go into evasive maneuvers. He decided to go straight up as fast as possible with afterburners on for as long as he could. Ejecting at this altitude was something Sam didn't even want to contemplate! Even with this maneuver, the fighters were following but not firing. He had people waiting for him at a former AFB in Loring, Maine. He just had to make it there.

One fighter was riding alongside him now as he climbed. Damn, those F-22s were good airplanes. They were trying to hail him, but he purposely did not respond. Passing through forty thousand feet, he started to level off as he headed north. He didn't understand why they weren't firing at him. Maybe it was because he was heading away from the D.C. area? They were still calling on him to respond, but he told Cory to absolutely not answer the calls.

Cory let out a huge exhale and sounded relieved as he mumbled to Sam, "They are still on our radar and have turned back to the south. I don't know why... Maybe they're after FedEx #2? I'm hearing FedEx #2 telling someone to go—ah, screw themselves. Different fighters, I guess. Neither one of us got that close to D.C. airspace before we dropped. Maybe because we aren't transponding?"

Sam was dropping altitude as fast as his B-1B could handle without coming apart. He would drop down to ground and start following the terrain.

Cory reminded him, "Sir, we are not supposed to low-level Bones anymore."

Sam snapped back, "They're still capable, aren't they?"

"Yes, sir—sorry, sir. They are still set up to do that!"

As they approached Maine, the morning light was beautiful through the cloud cover, golden rays giving way to a new day. FedEx #1 rattled a few windows and nerves as they headed for Loring. Waiting for them there was a private jet they would be transferring into for their return trip to Minot. Sam had shut off his radio audios when the fighters had started hailing them, so Cory had to tap him on the shoulder to get his attention. Loring was now a civilian airport. They would make news by landing there.

"Sir, FedEx #2 was shot down over the Atlantic after they made their turn south. We've lost FedEx #2, sir." Sam didn't understand why FedEx #2 had been shot down, but he wasn't going to let Cory see the concern in his eyes.

"Well, I guess today we're the lucky ones. What Captain Vigdahl pulled at Langley has put us all in a 'shoot on sight' directive... We are truly in a war. I can't think what might be waiting for us at Loring now."

As Sam murmured on, Cory was again getting chatter in his ear. "Sir, we are getting a transmission via military satellite communications." Colonel North, prior to the day's activities, had acquired access to MILSAT. In the preflight briefing, all the B-1Bs had been informed this might happen.

"To all FedEx pilots: Great job! All packages were delivered on target. Local news stations are starting to report about activity in their cities. A press conference has been called by a general at the Pentagon. This will commence in fifteen minutes. Please pray for the families of the crew of FedEx #2. They were successful in delivering their package but were engaged and shot down over the Atlantic Ocean before they could make it to their rendezvous point. All other Bones must immediately get to their appointed locations for pickup.

"Things have changed for us. Captain Vigdahl went rogue, and his men took out the CIA headquarters with very large conventional weapons. This action of Captain Vigdahl has changed our peaceful restoration attempt into something very different.

"JSOC has their people heading to Ellsworth at this moment. We are still jamming Ellsworth from all communications. We're still going forward with our operation. Our objective has not changed. We'll continue to go big as fast as we can to stop any additional bloodshed on either side. What happened at CIA headquarters may cause the deep state to go crazy, so we must be prepared and anticipate any retribution. Thanks again to all. See you at the rendezvous point in Green River."

Sam couldn't believe Colonel North was broadcasting this information over the MILSAT. Did he mean to?

HANGAR AT MINOT AIR FORCE BASE – NORTH DAKOTA

As the C-17 completed the unloading, Carl found Jason. "So sorry about Zach, Jason—so sorry."

Jason just nodded, trying to maintain his professional demeanor. "I will have to inform his parents."

"Is John already in surgery?" Carl inquired. Jason thought Carl had been briefed on this. However, as Jason continued to stare at him, he noticed a peculiar look in his eye, and Carl continued without an answer to his question.

"Captain Vigdahl went rogue on us, Jason. He had a separate bombing run planned for CIA headquarters. They hit HQ with a bunker buster—a big one—and a MOAB, and to my understanding, it's leveled. We'll all be considered part of this unless the general can persuade the country otherwise."

As the two of them conversed, Jaylynn walked up, gave a tired smile to Carl, and handed Jason her phone. She stated Kayla needed to talk to him. Carl nodded, and Jason took the call.

As expected, Kayla jumped all over him. "How could you? You asshole—how could you involve my parents in something like this? Have you seen the news? Have you seen the CIA headquarters? Good God, Jason, how…?" He realized she could no longer talk and was crying.

"I'm sorry. I am so sorry… We couldn't tell you. We are trying to take our country back peacefully and quickly. Someone in the operation went rogue. The CIA wasn't supposed to happen—that was *not* supposed to happen! Where are you? Are you with my guys? Just tell me you are safe!"

Kayla was so upset, she could barely talk. "Yes, Jason. Mom just told me about the plan and that it was for my safety that I not know, but I don't know if I can even believe that. You didn't tell me—you didn't warn me. Why, Jason—why?"

This was gut wrenching for Jason—all of it. "We couldn't trust you not to give us away. We almost sequestered you in South Dakota. Even though I care about you, I couldn't trust you."

Kayla shot back, "How am I supposed to trust you, Jason? How? I was actually beginning to like you—to care about what happens to you. Now I don't care if you get shot. Mom told me that Dad got shot twice. You asshole… How…?" Kayla vapor locked again. "If you actually give a damn about me, how could you do this?"

Even though he wanted nothing more than to continue this conversation with Kayla, he was being called to go. "Kayla—I think I actually have fallen in love with you, and someday, you might understand what we were trying to do. It's bigger than you and me. Hate me for eternity but try to understand and try to look at the larger picture!"

"Screw you, Jason Wilder. Screw you! You got my father shot!"

Jason was suffering significantly in the face of his loss. Everything seemed to be going south on them during this op. Not only had this operation cost him one of his teammates, but he had also betrayed the only woman who had really rocked his world. He took a deep breath and kept repeating "for God and Country" over and over in his head before he spoke.

"Kayla, listen to me, please. In a few minutes, there will be a press conference from the Pentagon. Could you please listen to what the general has to say? Just listen…for me, please?"

Kayla was still in a mindset she couldn't get out of. "Why should I listen Jason—why?"

Jason reiterated, "Just do it for your mom and dad—for your family. For once, just think of someone else other than yourself! I have to go—I'll call you back as soon as I can."

In the silence, Jason realized his heart and mind had to move on from Kayla Mogen and back to the restoration.

Eric yelled, "It's starting, Jason—it's starting!"

Jason joined his men as they grouped around the TV monitor with many others from the flight, including Jaylynn. She was nervously pacing the room as she waited for John's shoulder operation to be over—she couldn't just sit.

The *Liberty in America (LIA)* anchor stopped in mid-sentence. "Okay, ladies and gentlemen. We're going to the Pentagon for a briefing on the explosion at CIA headquarters in Virginia this morning. General Greg Morris, head of military intelligence, is going to be… Okay, here he is."

As the general stepped to the podium, viewers could sense how visibly shaken he was as he began to speak. He looked extremely weary, and the sight of his wild gray eyebrows and full face made him look like the old football coach John Madden. He drew in a deep breath and began to address the gathering. "Ladies and gentlemen, we have received a statement from a group calling themselves the 'Western Southern Alliance of States.' They have communicated in this statement that their military arm is called the 'Constitution Restoration Expeditionary Forces,' or CREF. Their commanding officer, Colonel John Mogen, put out the following…"

Jaylynn's head popped up, and she looked uncertainly at Jason, for she knew that John was in surgery and hadn't written anything.

General Morris continued. "And I quote… This morning at 0100 hours, CREF executed a plan to restore the United States Constitution. We've made every attempt to do this peacefully. Unfortunately, and ashamedly, we have failed in our original endeavor due to a rogue member of our group. This member elected to act upon a personal vendetta against the CIA. You may think of us as a terrorist group and monsters from this time forward, and I'll not put any effort in to change your minds.

"During our operation, we placed nuclear devices in five locations, starting with the cities of San Francisco, Los Angeles, New York, and Washington, D.C. There is also one in front of the NSA headquarters in Ft. Meade, Maryland. I'm giving fair warning... Please do not try to neutralize the men tending these or try to disarm them. The detonators connected to these devices are tuned to the heartbeats of the men managing them. If they are disconnected or if their hearts stop beating, the devices will detonate. We have done this to assure the people of the United States we want to avoid a civil war that would kill millions of Americans, a lot more than the first civil war did.

"The president, his family, and the cabinet members are safe. The president is not the problem. The problem is the 535 congressmen and -women and U.S. senators plus all nine Supreme Court Justices. We are demanding all to evacuate Washington on aircraft we have provided at Reagan Airport. We have enlisted the Secret Service and Capitol Police to help with this evacuation. As you are reading this, units from Joint Base Andrews have secured Ronald Reagan Airport. I know you will question me on this, but I assure you, all members of Congress, the Senate, and the Supreme Court will not be harmed.

"The citizens of the United States sympathetic to our cause are done trying to stop those in Washington who are attempting to turn our country into a socialist hellhole. We intend to form our own separate nation—under God. Any decision to detonate the nuclear devices will now be made by the actions of others—not us. Please let us separate in peace. We have no intention of interfering with any commerce. We are and will remain capitalists. We have published our initial territorial boundaries. It will be up to the populations in certain counties how they want to go.

"Citizens of the United States of America, now is the time. You must choose between the USA and the WSA. Please take no actions against us, and this will be a peaceful separation. Those who believe in God and the rule of law are urged to migrate to WSA territory. A new map with the defined WSA territory has been sent to the news agencies and can be disseminated now. We will not set our borders in place immediately. All travel and commerce will continue unabated for now. God bless the WSA."

Jaylynn's mouth was agape as the general finished reading the statement. Who wrote this? Since it wasn't her husband, it had to be her brother. Carl was standing next to her, and she glanced up at him the way she had when they were growing up as their parents were questioning them... She shot him the "Did you do this?" look, and he just smiled back at her. Then, he nodded in the affirmative without her saying a word. Jaylynn was exhilarated but still terrified. For now, they were still alive and not taken into custody—yet.

Jason approached Carl and Jaylynn. "Sir—we have the rest of the Mogen family sequestered and are transporting them to their designated safe house as we speak. Colonel Musgrave reports that they have 497 of the 544 from Washington accounted for, and the balance of the roundup is continuing. Some senators and congressmen are out of the country. He wants to know what to do about them. He has some flight information and..."

At that point, Carl broke in. "Tell him to keep them out of the country, if possible. Otherwise, have our teams waiting for them when they arrive. I'm sure they will see our live stream when we do it. Remind Colonel Musgrave to treat them with respect when they get them in custody!"

At that moment, Carl's cell phone rang. He looked down at the caller ID and signaled to Jason that he needed him to be in on the call. As he answered, Carl interrupted Colonel North on the other end. "Hang on, Allan. Could you start over please? Jason is here, and he needs to hear this. Okay, go ahead."

Colonel North resumed speaking. "Okay, Carl. JSOC has a team headed for Ellsworth. Two Reapers just took off from Creech, and two Global Hawks took off from Grand Forks. I'm not sure yet if they are headed for Ellsworth or Minot. We do have confirmation that the

Reapers headed north-northeast could take them to either of those bases. The Reapers are still six hours out. I'm sure this was ordered by the CIA and not the military."

It was clear to both Carl and Allan that all the three letter agencies were on to them and doing everything they could to intervene. The colonels just hoped they had enough of a head start to complete the mission.

CHAPTER 42

CIA UNDERGROUND SATELLITE OPERATIONS CENTER OUTSIDE WASHINGTON, D.C.

Nathan Parkinson was still shaken up from the blast that had vaulted his car almost off the highway as he was heading to work at Langley. After receiving a call as he was in transit, he'd diverted to the alternative site, where he'd witnessed the remaining fallout of that detonation. He was convinced it was a small nuclear explosion. The ops center was set up as a duplicate site mimicking what was found at CIA headquarters in Langley. He was met at the entrance and briefed on the ride down the elevator to the Situation Room.

He hit the ground running. "Okay, people—I'm Section Chief Nathan Parkinson. I need to know what we know about the location of John Mogen and the members of Arlington Colonels' Club, and I need to know now!"

"Sir—Jamie Collins, sir. Have you seen the press release by General Morris, sir?"

"No, I haven't. Do I need to?"

Jamie had to cover this base. "Yes, sir, you really need to take a moment and watch this."

As Nathan watched the video, he became even more convinced that his decision to back-burner this whole thing had been the wrong one. He had let the nation down.

Jamie then began giving the location status to his section chief. "We believe John Mogen may still be at Ellsworth. He was on camera at an entry gate. The footage shows he may have been wounded by an airman guarding the gate. It also appears that at least one guard stationed at the gate was down. In addition, we know that the FBI teams assigned to follow the Arlington Colonels' Club members to what was supposed to be their command center outside Dyess were fooled by imposters wearing professionally made face masks. When the agents entered the communications center, they found four men playing poker. Those men were taken into custody, and after a quick search, the discarded masks were found."

Nathan broke in. "What a surprise—the FBI got fooled…again! Do we know where anyone is? Any other camera footage?"

"Sir, we're checking. South Dakota—not many cameras in that part of the country. We do have retired Marine Colonel William Musgrave on camera at Ronald Reagan…we believe. He got off a private jet at the FBO terminal. Face recognition picked him up."

Nathan was not happy with this additional information. "Anything else? Do we have anything?"

Jamie continued with a shaky voice. "It's been confirmed after the B-1Bs took off from Ellsworth, a C-17 followed about thirty minutes later. We don't know where it went, but at this moment, we are trying to get civilian radar information on its flight path. The takedown of Ellsworth was done by professionals who knew the base well. Ellsworth went dark—no main power or emergency power. Some kind of jamming is still being done to all of Ellsworth comms it would appear. Personnel have to get off the base and out of jamming range to make contact. The FBI has also dispatched their people out there to make contact. Right now, JSOC has a team enroute to Ellsworth. Unfortunately, they are coming out of California. In addition, General Morris ordered two Reapers and two Global Hawks in the air. They are inflight toward Ellsworth as we speak."

Nathan was assembling all the related details in his head. "Okay, people—this is what I want. Number one, forget Dyess—that was a ruse. Two, get the FBI chief in Rapid City on the line. Three, find that damn

C-17! Four, get a team to Reagan now! Find Colonel Musgrave. Five, I need to know where this John Mogen is. For all we know, he could be back at his residence—where is that? In the Black Hills somewhere?"

A young woman at a control console broke in. "Sir, I have the FBI office head in Rapid City on line one."

"Put the call on speaker!" Nathan said tersely. Those present could almost see the steam rising, he was so hot.

"Ms. O'Keefe, do you understand how far behind we are on this thing? What the hell are your agents doing out there? You couldn't keep track of one guy? Holy shit!"

Molly was having none of this. "Our job was to establish that Mogen and his wife got on that flight. We didn't expect a mini EMP to disable our agents during watch. Whoever is behind this has assets and personnel that we weren't aware of, and obviously you weren't either, I take it? We have dispatched agents to the Mogen compound. They should be arriving within minutes. We also have agents interviewing people at Ellsworth. We'll have updated reports shortly. I'll call you back as soon as we've received them and bring you up to date. Stay off my ass, and I will stay off yours!" With that, the line went dead. She was gone.

Nathan's face was redder than before. The young woman at the control console was smiling as she turned her back, making sure Section Chief Parkinson didn't see her.

This had been a precise and ferocious attack on the CIA itself. Nathan had to keep himself in control, which was difficult because he wanted revenge on those responsible. He didn't know how many people had died in the attack at Langley, but he knew he could have been one of them. "Okay—bring up a map of the Ellsworth area. How far is Mogen's compound from Ellsworth? Pinpoint both for me." As the map came up, Nathan smiled. "Okay, okay. I want a Global Hawk diverted to the Mogen compound. I also want one of the Reapers on station at the Mogen compound. We are going to take it out."

Jamie interjected. "Sir, we are talking about American soil here—we can't..."

Nathan cut in. "Shut up and do as I say. We are talking about enemies of the State. I don't care if they are domestic—we are going to take it out!"

Jamie didn't flinch. "Sir, we have FBI agents who will be on site soon. We…"

"Dammit, we have time to get them out of there!" Nathan retorted. "How far out are the Reapers?"

"They are five hours out, sir," Jamie replied in disgust.

Nathan addressed the room. "Ladies and gentlemen, these people have bombed our headquarters. They have placed nuclear devices in our cities. This is war, and we are taking the gloves off! Is that clear to everyone in this room? If you can't handle it, get out, and I'll be accepting your resignation. From now on, everyone will follow my orders without question. Is that understood?"

There was a nodding of heads and murmuring throughout the room.

"Get me JSOC! We have to get a team to Reagan ASAP! Let's order a shutdown of all traffic in and out of Reagan now! Lock down Reagan to all ground traffic also!"

At that minute, a shout came from another part of the room. "Sir! Sir, Fox News just replayed the live statement from General Morris about the situation."

Again, Nathan Parkinson listened intently to the WSA news release. After it was completed, he revised some of his orders. "Okay—I still want to find Colonel Musgrave but forget the rest about Reagan. Bring up the satellite images of the Mogen residence. Notify those drone pilots to push as hard as they can to get on station."

The satellite image of John and Jaylynn's home popped up on the center screen in the room. Nathan stepped up and studied it carefully. The outbuildings were on the edge of the forest but in view. "What are those three white tanks on the left?"

Someone broke in. "Sir, they appear to be propane tanks. They look like they could be about one thousand gallons each. I'll do some checking to confirm the size and let you know."

Nathan's eyes lit up with this new information. "Let's target those tanks first!"

"Sir, the Global Hawks will be there way before the Reapers."

Nathan was steaming again. "Why can't we put a couple of rockets on those Hawks? Geez!"

CHAPTER 43

MOGEN COMPOUND – THE BLACK HILLS OF SOUTH DAKOTA

Truen Walsh was hanging out at his camp in the trees. He had finally gotten some shuteye, but he never slept soundly anymore. He jumped a little when his phone vibrated in his pocket. It was Jason.

"Truen, we need to get you and the dogs out of there. Get things ready to go. How long will it take you to get to the trailhead for pickup?"

"What's going on that I need to get out of here?"

Jason wasn't in the mood for long explanations. "The CIA has two Reapers and two Global Hawks in the air heading your way, and if we can't knock them down, they may get to you. The Reapers are coming from Creech, and they're probably going to Ellsworth, but their flight path takes them right over you. How long will it take you to get to the Pilot Knob Trailhead?"

Truen's mind was already in motion. Since he had the mission in his head, he didn't need notes. Truen was the one Jason had always depended on to remember every detail, down to the floorplans of buildings and exit strategies, during missions.

Truen came right back. "In the dark, it will take me forty-nine minutes. I can go faster if I take the power line right of way, but I won't be in the trees at that point. I can put on night vision, but that won't shield me from infrared detection."

Jason had a gut feeling about this, and his gut seldom failed him. "Okay, Truen—pack up and get ready to go with the Ranger. I know the dogs will love a Ranger ride. I'll get back to you."

"Copy that, Jason. I'll get the dogs loaded and head to the top of the ridge behind the house and wait for a call. Got to go—I see vehicle lights and flashlight activity down at the entry gate. I think the FBI has gotten back already. See ya!"

With that, Truen rushed to get his bugout bag. The Ranger was behind the barn, so the start-up would be dampened by the building.

He yelled for Sadie and Lilly to come. They were a little groggy but perked up quickly as he grabbed water and food for them. Then, he lifted them into the Ranger's dump bed equipped with a rubber mat so they could grip with their claws. He had to keep an eye on Sadie since she loved to peek around with her paws on the side of the dump bed and her ears flapping in the wind.

Truen kept glancing back at them with his night vision goggles on. Lilly, not recognizing him, growled before she identified his smell. Then, they were off in the dark, headed for the top of the ridge with the dogs' tails wagging for joy about the UTV ride.

Before leaving the compound, he activated the electrification for the front gate and fencing they had installed after first arriving. Anyone would have fun trying to get in.

The two FBI agents at the gate were in a quandary, trying to override the system. "Opening automatic gates was not covered at the academy!" yelled Backtow, the younger agent.

"Okay, whiz kid. Get the shotgun out of the SUV. Let's climb over this gate and get up there!" The experienced Jefferies was still fuming and holding his less qualified partner accountable as he replayed the botched events of earlier in the morning. The gate looked easier to get over than the six-strand barbed wire.

"Get the night vision goggles too! I'm going to climb over the gate, and then you can hand me stuff." Because the wrought iron gate was six feet tall and had vertical bars, the agent was going to have to pull himself up by grabbing the top rail… "Son of a bitch! Son of a biiiitch!" Jefferies yelled as his arms flew over his head and he fell backward onto the ground.

Backtow dropped what he had in his hands and ran over to his partner. "Are you okay?" he asked without thinking.

"No! I am not okay! What a dumbass question!"

Charging ahead without thinking, the younger agent continued with his asinine questions. "Do you want me to go over first? Did you lose your grip? Can I give you a boost?"

This sent Jefferies into a moral dilemma that he had to fight his way out of. It had been an extremely trying night, but he reminded himself they had a job to do. However, he was so close to telling his partner to give it a try—so close.

"No—it's electrified, and the same thing will happen to you. I just don't know if it's contained to the gate or includes the fence too."

Backtow immediately walked over to the barbed wire fence coming off the gate and gingerly reached out to barely tap it before his partner could tell him no. His hand snapped back so fast it just about pinwheeled his arm off at the shoulder.

Jefferies just stood there, shaking his head as his associate profoundly announced the fence was also electrified. Rolling his eyes, he regarded his coworker with disbelief, unsure how much more he could take. Needing a deep breath, he calmly gave an order. "In the back of the SUV, there is a bag marked 'tow cable.' Could you bring it to me?"

As Backtow headed to get the tow cable, Jefferies turned on his flashlight and started looking for something in the barrow pit next to the main road. He finally found what he was looking for. After Backtow returned with the cable, he gave his younger partner more orders. "Okay—this is what we're going to do. See, this tow cable is coated with plastic. We'll strip some of the plastic covering off the tow cable, spreading it apart enough to be able to wrap it around our grounding rod."

His colleague really wasn't a good learner. "Excuse me, but do we have a grounding rod?"

His superior, who by then was looking around for their thick cold-weather gloves, yelled for him to just strip some cable and shut up. Jefferies then jammed his shotgun into the mud. As Backtow completed the cable stripping, his partner grabbed the cable, wrapped the stripped section around the shotgun barrel, put the large gloves on, and dropped the metal hook over a strand of the barbed wire.

The green Backtow said matter-of-factly, "We really should have had our gloves on earlier when we tried to climb over that fence."

Quickly, the senior agent's right fist made contact with his partner's solar plexus. In turn, his body hit the ground, knocking the breath out of him.

Out of patience, Jefferies hissed at his less experienced counterpart, "Get up and get your ass over that fence so I can hand you our gear. We need to find this John Mogen guy—now!"

CHAPTER 44

HOME OF RETIRED MASTER SERGEANT JACK ELLIS — RAPID CITY, SOUTH DAKOTA

Jack Ellis was sound asleep, but he always kept his gun and phone within reach. Although he was eighty-one years old, he was still in exceptional shape. He'd lived alone since his wife had died years earlier. He had not wanted to live after her death, but a good friend had convinced him God still had a purpose for him and that was to help sponsor more AA babies. Many nights, Jack would sit outside with his .45 auto ready to do the deed, but every time he tried, the phone would ring, and it would be one of those babies he sponsored through AA. It got to be silly. He finally acquiesced to God's "interventions" and stopped contemplating taking his own life.

Waking suddenly, he reached for the buzzing phone, knowing it was likely one of his babies needing help. It was 0330 hours.

"Jack, this is Jaylynn Mogen. We need your help. Remember that plan John discussed with you? You know, the one he was going to write about? Well, it's in progress right now. John and I are in another state, and John has been wounded. He's in surgery right now."

Jack's head was a little foggy from sleep, and he wasn't processing the words coming out of Jay's mouth all too well. "Hang on, Jay—are you talking about the plan to take back our republic?"

Jaylynn had her phone on speaker so Jason could listen in, even though Jack's phone wasn't encrypted. By this time, it probably didn't matter—he hoped. Jaylynn gritted her teeth when she realized what Jack had said. She realized she should have given him time to wake up a little more. Maybe it was a little too late, but she tried her hand at code talking. "John needs help, Jack. We need you to run an errand for him." Jack sensed tension and pleading in Jaylynn's voice. "You know John would come and help, no matter what and no matter when, right?" she continued desperately.

Jack was wide awake now. If what Jaylynn said was true, then the plan to restore his beloved republic was in progress, and it sounded like he might have a chance to be involved. His adrenaline was building like crazy. Suddenly, he realized he shouldn't have mentioned the plan specifically. "Okay, Jay, what exactly do you need me to do?" he queried.

Jaylynn was quick to respond and relieved that Jack was clued in now. Jaylynn knew it was time. "I'm handing the phone over to someone John and I trust with our lives. He will let you know what to do."

After a brief pause, Jason began talking to him. "Good morning, sir. I understand you were in the military."

"Yes, I was, son. I was a drill sergeant when we were feared by all who knew us. I also played football for an Army team. Broke opponents' bones for fun."

"Sir, we need your help, and I've been told we can trust you. I have a man we left in the Hills who needs to get out. I have evacuated all but him and the Mogens' dogs. We need to get them to a location to the south of your location. Quite a ways south. Do you know the Pilot Knob Trailhead parking area?"

There was a pause that made Jason uncomfortable. Finally, Jack came back. "Got it on my phone's GPS. I can be there in thirty minutes."

Jason was immediately reassured. "Okay—great. You need to pack a bag because it's a long trip up here. I understand you have a trailer that could haul a Polaris Ranger. Is that right?"

Jack was getting dressed as he listened. "Yes, I do, son. I assume you need it also?"

Jason was reassured again. "Yes, sir, we need it, if you could hook it up?"

"Can do. Let me get going. Let's say a forty-five-minute ETA for the bag and trailer."

"Got it, sir. I'll let my man know. Thank you, sir—thank you!"

Jason was ecstatic he could get Truen and the dogs out rapidly. He'd lost one member of his team and didn't want to lose another during this operation. His intuition that trouble was coming to the compound was stronger than ever, and he didn't want to leave another behind, especially since he had decided to pull out the protection detail at the place. That had probably been a mistake. If a Reaper drone was headed to the Black Hills area, he didn't know what the CIA might pull—especially now that that idiot Vigdahl had succeeded in leveling their headquarters!

Jason had to trust the message that was sent out to the Sons of Issachar and the Oathtakers throughout the country had been received favorably. It was essential that the majority of the Armed Forces personnel sided with the WSA. Their estimation was that 66 percent to 75 percent would side with them. With so much at stake, Jason was praying these numbers were accurate.

CHAPTER 45

MOGEN DAUGHTERS — TEXAS

Kayla was up and getting dressed. Her stomach was upset—hell, her life was upset! She had to be ready to go in thirty minutes.

Outside her condominium complex, the FBI was still watching her. The two agents were drowsy, as would be expected at 0330 hours. They had a clear view of where she garaged her car, but her condo was inside the courtyard, so they had to occasionally get out and check for movement and maybe any lights on in her condo.

The agent whose turn it was to make rounds opened his door, exited the SUV, and started to walk the breezeway and check for any movement in or around her place. She was the best assignment they had had in a long time. The girl was absolutely stunning.

His partner watched from the SUV while he turned the corner, heading into the breezeway. As he waited for his partner to reappear, he was startled by his phone vibrating by his side. He promptly answered the call but didn't even get a "Hello" out before the caller was relaying new orders. What was he being told? Pick her up now? He sat listening to his instructions with his mouth agape and his heart rate accelerating rapidly. This had stopped being a routine stakeout, and the order to take her into custody in the middle of the night alerted him to the urgency of the situation.

After being hung up on, he hit his radio mic and called to his partner but got no response. A second call went unanswered.

"Do you copy?" he repeated into the mic. They always did a radio check before one of them left the SUV. Why now—why stop working? He'd received orders to get the girl into custody and escort her to the Dallas FBI office ASAP. He tried the radio one more time—still no answer.

He got out of the SUV, not very happy at all. He had to find his partner and secure Kayla Mogen so they could head to the Dallas office. His only hope was that Kayla would be in some sort of nightie when they made their entrance. However, his night ended quickly as he felt hands grab him and a needle enter his neck. His lack of situational awareness got him, and all went black.

As Jason's men knocked on Kayla's door, she trusted this was really them. She hesitantly opened the door to the secondary chain lock—nine-millimeter in hand.

"Cowboy up, ma'am. We gotta go."

Kayla was still edgy and asked only one question: "Who sent you?"

"Jason Wilder, ma'am. Are you ready to roll?"

As she holstered her gun and opened the door, she reminded him, "There are some FBI nerds watching me."

The young man, who stood as tall as Jason, responded, "Yes, ma'am. They're asleep—for a while, in fact—and won't be bothering us. Trust me on this."

Kayla understood and responded, "Got it, and if you don't mind, would you please call me Kayla? What's your name?"

"Mark Buckley, ma'am—ahh Kayla. Sorry. We need to get going."

Mark had a photo of Kayla on his phone but was still flustered as she stepped out of her condo. She was more dazzling in person. He had to remind himself he was in the middle of an extremely dangerous mission, and he had to keep his wits about him. Now was not the time to be distracted by a gorgeous woman.

As they walked to the waiting vehicle, her questions began. "What is the plan for me? Where are we going, and what exactly is going on?" She hardly took a breath as she peppered Mark with rapid-fire inquiries.

Mark was swift to respond. "We are taking you to Austin-Bergstrom International. There is a private jet waiting for you. It will fly to DFW and pick up your sister and her family. Y'all will then be flown to Sky Harbor in Phoenix, Arizona. You will disembark and be taken to a secure location to wait for your parents to join y'all.

"Now to answer your second question, your father and your uncle's plan to restore our republic—phase one—has been carried out successfully. I'm not at liberty to divulge more than that at this time. There's only been one major glitch in the operation, which caused us to accelerate your recovery and relocation. So, let's get going!"

This, of course, made Kayla want to ask a hundred more questions, but she recognized she needed to comply with Mark's instructions. She knew enough for now. Where did Jason find all these hunks—smart hunks—to work with him? She just couldn't resist one more question as they entered the waiting SUV. "Mark, can you tell me where my folks are right now? Are they still in South Dakota?"

Mark was hesitant to answer. "Kayla—I just can't talk about that right now. They are safe but not in South Dakota. Their horses and dogs are being taken care of and are secure. You will see them in maybe twenty-four hours."

When Kayla had received her instructions via email, she had retrieved the kit planted in her car. The instructions were very specific. She was to leave her phone behind in her condo, but doing this had been much harder than she'd thought it would be. She wanted to get on the internet and figure out what her parents and Jason were involved in. She hated not knowing.

When she was growing up, her folks had gone to great lengths to hide her Christmas gifts. At the age of seven years old, she had figured out Santa was a hoax and would make it her mission to discover where her parents had hidden her gifts. She would sneak into their bedroom and thoroughly probe all areas they might consider hiding them. Her parents finally had to stash them with her grandparents or friends because she had become such a little detective. She just couldn't help herself. She didn't like to be surprised.

She understood that this obsession had robbed her of a lot of joy, and she was finally recognizing that some things were out of her control. She also realized that she couldn't control everything in her life all the time. Her more or less uncontrollable attraction to Jason and what she was doing right now had her feeling completely out of her comfort zone. She had to calm her mind and just wait and wonder. She longed to see her parents. She yearned to see Jason again and wrap her arms around him and then tell him—tell him what? She didn't even know what she would say to him. She couldn't be in love with him already—could she? *Stop being ridiculous, girl!* But she took this chance to find out something about him.

"Mark, how long have you known Jason?"

"Since the Air Force, ma'am—excuse me…Kayla." Mark knew she wanted to know more about Jason just like every woman he seemed to come in contact with. "We were in the Air Force Special Forces group. Air Force Pararescue, that is. We specialized in communications. We saw our share of combat but not like the SEAL Teams. At different times, we worked with both the SEALs and Delta Force. Jason is the coolest dude I have ever been around. He concentrates on the job at hand, even when we were downrange taking fire—it didn't matter. He could keep up with the Navy SEALs, and they noticed. That's also how he is in business. I've been with him since he started. He has been devoted to getting his business up and running, and we've been very successful. A lot of very well-off people in Texas are our clients. The private jet you will be taking out of Austin-Bergstrom International belongs to one of them. It allows us to transport you without leaving a trail for the NSA or CIA deep state dudes. Because of all his hard work, Jason has gotten to the point where he can take some time off. Maybe find a girl and start a family. Then, he ahhh…" Mark hesitated and stopped talking.

Kayla prodded, "Then what, Mark—what?"

"Well, then he got the call from your Uncle Carl. We knew about a year ago that the Arlington Colonels' Club had been mulling over plans to overthrow the deep state and get the country back on track and…"

"Whoa, Mark—just whoa! The deep state is a conspiracy theory and..."

"With all due respect, Kayla, Jason and the rest of the team have seen things, witnessed what the deep state is capable of, when we were in the service fighting for our country. Things America shouldn't be involved in. Shouldn't be doing toward or in foreign countries. Trust me when I tell you the deep state is real and, by now, already knows we are in the middle of an operation to stop them. This is why we are moving you and your sister off the grid. Believe me when I tell you people from within the United States do disappear never to be seen again. That doesn't just happen on foreign soil. The people behind this are definitely cold and ruthless. Your uncle and father are in the middle of an operation to end the deep state and literally get our country back to the constitutional republic it's supposed to be."

Taking in all of what Mark was saying, Kayla was in complete shock but finally understood her life at this very moment would be changing. She didn't know if it would be for the good though. At that point, she interrupted, saying, "So, I'm just another mission to Jason? I mean, for all of you?"

Mark was quiet as he pondered how much to convey to Kayla. There was talk amongst the troops about a girl that had thrown Jason off mission. In all the time they had worked together, they had never seen this happen. This was her—this had to be her. Mark and his crew had ogled her photo from the time they'd acquired it for their recon, but she was absolutely more magnificent in person—even at zero dark thirty.

"Mark? Earth to Mark. Are you there?"

What the hell? He thought. *They were all in serious danger, so would it hurt to tell her?*

Shaking his head in an attempt to clear his thoughts, Mark spoke up. "Ah yes... I mean no—you and your family are, let me say, a special part of this operation." Taking a deep breath, he went on with his explanation. "Jason spent more time than was needed on this plan to keep you and your family safe. He told us all in no uncertain terms that if we did nothing else but get you—ah, and your family—to a safe place, we would have a successful mission. He also asked me to pass on to you that as soon as he has completed his other assignments, he will be joining up with us. I want to assure you that you are more than just a part of this mission. But I really can't say any more than that."

Switching gears back to the issue at hand, Mark continued with the rundown on the upcoming operation. "Now, when we get to the FBO, we will drive directly onto the ramp, straight to the private jet. It should already be hotted up and ready to move after we board. For additional protection, I have to ask you to cover your head with a scarf until you get into the aircraft—got it?"

She nodded as Mark looked away. Kayla couldn't seem to hold back her grin. Why she smiled at a time like this, she just couldn't figure out, but she was smiling. It had been a long time since she had felt butterflies floating through her. She couldn't wait to see Jason.

She sat back and was quiet as they made the turn into the private FBO area of Austin-Bergstrom. She recognized the private jet. It was a Gulfstream—a top-of-the-line private jet. One of the men handed her a scarf, which she wrapped around her head. Then, Mark got out of the SUV as another team member got into the driver's seat. Mark quickly escorted Kayla to the jet and followed her up the stairs.

After entering the jet, Kayla took off the scarf and turned to see Mark talking to one of the pilots. The other one had already closed the side door, and Kayla realized then that Mark would be traveling with her. "So, Mark, you are going with me? Are you some kind of handler?"

Mark turned to her with a serious look. "My assignment is to get you safely to your destination. I'm your bodyguard and will defend you and the rest of your family with my life."

The Gulfstream was already on the move before Kayla had a chance to take her seat. Reality was setting in, and she now realized this was not a game. She took in her situation as a wave of fear overtook her. For some reason, she heard the voice of her mother quietly talking to her when she was a little girl. "Remember, Kayla, always turn to Jesus when you're scared, and He will be there with you, even if your dad and I can't be."

She hadn't thought about Jesus in years. She tried to turn away from Mark as the tears she had held back for hours—hell, maybe for years—started to stream down her face.

Noticing her emotional state, Mark seemed to understand her tears, which soon turned into sobs, as he gently placed a box of tissues in front of her. All Mark could say was, "We'll be on the ground at DFW in just a few minutes to pick up your sister and her family."

Kayla nodded through her tears and gave a thumbs up. She felt completely out of control—completely. She started whispering a prayer, something she hadn't done in a very long time. *Jesus, take the wheel!*

It seemed like they had just finished their climb out when they started descending again. Before she knew it, they were on the ground and taxiing. They had barely come to a stop when the door flew open. Kayla peeked out the window to see Mark at the bottom of the stairs talking to Jessica Jo and Dave, Kayla's sister and brother-in-law.

Jesse was the first up the stairs. As soon as she entered the plane, her eyes met Kayla's. Jesse could see Kayla had been crying and now watched her eyes well up again as she approached. Her younger sibling had become a hardcore feminist progressive, which had strained their relationship at best.

As they hugged, Kayla lost it again, her chest heaving with sobs. Jesse held her tight and realized her sister literally felt softer to the touch—less tense than she had felt in years. Jesse spoke first. "Mark is giving us a couple of minutes before Dave and the kids come in. I guess he knew you needed it. Our lives are never going to be the same. You know that, right?"

Kayla knew only too well that things would not return to normal, but she had come to terms with that. "I wish Mom and Dad would have prepared me a little bit. I knew something was up—I just knew it!"

Kayla was attempting to pull herself together when her sister found the courage to speak up, even though it was going to be hard for Kayla to hear. "Kayla, they—ah—they could not trust you with the information because of your political bent. You know that, don't you? They truly love you, no matter what…no matter how you treated them or thought of them. Their love for you has never wavered. To be clear, Dave and I did not know either but for different reasons."

Kayla was again on the verge of tears as Mark broke things up. He was concerned that the CIA might go around the president and ground all air traffic. "Ladies, we really need to get off the ground! Are we ready?"

Kayla stopped her lower lip from quivering and responded, "Thanks, Mark, for understanding. Yes, yes—let's go!"

As Dave and her niece and nephew entered, her brother-in-law could see that Kayla had been crying. He went straight to her and hugged her in spite of all their past arguments and conversations where she'd called him a neanderthal—many times over. She had accused them both of living in the past and not understanding how the world had to change.

Kayla now was beginning to realize what unconditional love looked and felt like. When her fiancé had told her he just couldn't marry her because he couldn't accept her as she was without trying to change her, Kayla simply could not understand it. Everything had to be on her terms. She was a strong woman, but the refusal to bend had cost her one more relationship. Was she having an epiphany? She'd been completely thrown off guard by Jason. He was his own man, and although she could tell they had an immediate connection, he wouldn't consider a relationship with her on her terms. He was a conservative Christian man, like Dave, her brother-in-law, whom she had despised—but he had still loved her anyway.

Mark's voice snapped her out of her own private thoughts and jolted everyone into action. "Seatbelts, everyone! Let's get rolling." He looked at Kayla. Her deep green eyes had already become legend among Jason's men. He completely understood how Jason could be taken with her, even if she was his complete opposite. This was the daughter of the guy who was the impetus for this restoration movement. Globalists versus nationalists, patriots versus traitors, Christians versus Satanists. She was still a spectacular woman.

"Are we all squared away here?" With a hint of humor in his voice, Mark continued by saying, "We have to get you to your vacation destination!"

Kayla smiled at him, understanding that the kids must have been told a different story about what was going on. Looking at her niece and nephew, she exclaimed, "We are so ready, Mark—this is going to be a great adventure!"

She suddenly remembered how her father had always planned countless adventures for them growing up. He would say, "Life is an adventure, so let's get out there and find it!" She didn't recall how many, "Oh, Dads" she had given him. She had been a wet blanket before every adventure and refused to admit she was having the time of her life. Now, she was recognizing how blessed she was and how ungrateful and contrary she had been—and, through all of it, loved. Truly loved.

"Are you alright, Aunt Kayla?" her niece asked.

The tears were streaming down her face again. "I'm so happy, Libby—so happy. Sometimes, I'm so happy I cry because I don't want the moment to end!"

Kayla was actually telling the truth. She felt happy. She felt safe. She felt as though she had been under some sort of spell and had just woken up. Maybe—just maybe—all the brainwashing had been erased. If people all over the country were risking their lives to save the republic, maybe she should ask the "why" question. Were they all really crazy?

She had a big decision to make. She now realized what she had believed in was wrong. She had been convinced the United States was evil and needed to turn away from the founders. She now questioned all she had been taught and why she had not been taught the nation's true history. Was it wrong to try to get the world all together on the same page? Was America greedy and selfish, or was it really that city on a hill? Could it be a combination of the two? She knew the history. She knew she had set out to "bend the arc of history" and now wondered what that really even insinuated. When she and her colleagues would all yell "let's go bend it," did they really know what that meant?

She remembered the fierce argument she and her father had had over the gay issue in the Church and why that had been the last straw for her. He'd kept saying their job was to build up and edify the Church here on earth, and the decision to accept sin into the Church as godly behavior was tearing it down—tearing congregations and denominations apart. He'd explained, "We still love all people as children of God, but we still have to hold onto certain truths." She remembered him saying, "Kayla, truth is not a moving target. Some truth is literally set in stone."

At that point, she recalled trying to convince him that truth was what each person believed it was. "My truth may not be what other people believe," she had argued.

He'd then said something she would never forget: "Kayla—that is Satan talking, and that's why we have chaos in the world and especially in our country. You and your thoughts are creating chaos. We hold fast to the truth as we know it. Unchanging truth inspired by the Creator."

She'd lashed out at him for being so unloving and so last century. It had not been a pretty ending. It had hurt their relationship—deeply.

This rift was fracturing families all over America. She now recognized it was what had driven her father to do what he was doing right now: risking his life and her mother's life for what they thought was right—was truth.

Unbuckling herself, Kayla reached over and hugged her sister and then her brother-in-law. Both of them understood and believed just like her dad. She gave them a real hug this time, giving it her all, hoping to relay her ability to change and her new path. Then, she hugged Caleb, who was ten, and Libby, who was seven but already the family empath. In all her life, she had never been so exhausted with no words to share, so she returned to her seat and buckled back up as her gaze met her sister's again.

"Kayla, we were all kept in the dark about this operation. I know it was to protect us. We found out when we got the email and opened our kit. Dad and Mom knew it was for the best. It was for our protection."

Kayla's tears started again. This time, she fell asleep with her face still wet. A while later, Kayla snapped awake. Libby's head was resting on her lap. She was sound asleep. Caleb was also sleeping.

Mark said quietly, "We are descending into Phoenix Sky Harbor. We'll be getting into a couple of SUVs and heading north after we land. What does everyone want for breakfast?"

Kayla was astonished at how well everything was planned for them. She also was surprised at the resources at their disposal. There were a lot of people stepping up for the cause—the restoration of the Constitution. Kayla wondered how many people really understood all this.

She still had the copy of *The 5000 Year Leap* in her backpack. She was frustrated by how her public education had caused her to detest the founders, to think the Constitution was no longer valid. She felt played. She felt so ignorant about her country's history—true history.

Now, she was reading through the Federalist Papers. *Madison was an absolute genius!* she thought to herself. *Why don't we teach this? Why does academia marginalize, and downright ignore, what a grand experiment America was and still is?*

CHAPTER 46

CIA UNDERGROUND SATELLITE OPERATIONS CENTER OUTSIDE WASHINGTON, D.C.

Nathan Parkinson was frustrated. "Where's my Reaper? Where is that damn Reaper?" he asked no one in particular. He was just talking to the wind.

"Sir, last location was over Warren Air Force Base in southern Wyoming. Do you still want to hit the Black Hills location first?" Jamie was the only one brave enough to respond to Nathan's inquisition because the rest of the staff were terrified to even open their mouths. Parkinson's mood was getting darker by the moment.

Nathan snapped back, "Yes, dammit—hit Mogen's place. Propane storage first and then the main residence! Level the damn thing!"

"Sir, the FBI has several people there doing a search for evidence," Jamie replied.

"Well, I'll get them out of there! I want that place gone as soon as the Reaper is on station! It's just a little late for evidence now, isn't it?"

Switching gears quickly, Nathan's attention went off to another tactic. "Do we have any additional data on the Western Southern Alliance system the general talked about—this John Mogen group? Have we identified who can set up a detonation system tuned to human heartbeats and how this could be done? Is this even possible? Has anyone researched for any studies or papers on this thing—this technology? Find the company or the techie who built this system—right now! Let's find something!"

Jamie spoke up. "Sir, we do have some intel on the B-1Bs that dropped the devices. Two of them landed at Loring AFB in Maine. They left their aircraft parked on the runway, and then the pilots were picked up immediately by unidentified units right there on the runway. Two more have landed at Mojave Airport in California. We are verifying that an immediate pickup was made of the personnel also. You know the outcome of the fifth bomber, which was shot down before orders were given to monitor them and only fire upon them if their bomb bays opened up. I guess the B-1s are expensive assets."

"No shit, Sherlock! I still would have smoked all of them! Get your people researching this detonation system with the heartbeats! Find that programmer!"

CHAPTER 47

MINOT AIR FORCE BASE — NORTH DAKOTA

"Colonel Justine, we have confirmation that the four remaining B-1Bs have reached their rendezvous locations and the personnel have been retrieved," reported Jason. "The FedEx #2 crew appears to be lost but still no confirmation on that. The convoys have arrived as ordered and have established their perimeters around the five big stick sites. The alternate drop at NSA in Maryland has ground support of ten men, all Sons of Issachar, in that detail. The full convoy should arrive within thirty minutes. I'm still a little nervous about whether they will be able to hold until reinforcements arrive."

"Thanks, Jason. What's the status of the drones?"

"The Global Hawks have made it to Ellsworth. Word is they think we are still at Ellsworth. The C-17 we flew with the transponder off and at low altitude hasn't been found as far as we can detect—still a mystery to them. Also, our sources put the Reapers passing the southern border of Wyoming about five minutes ago. Foss in Sioux Falls is becoming tricky. They have been briefed on the strike Torger let loose on CIA headquarters. I don't know if they will help now."

With this added update, Carl got a terrible feeling in the pit of his stomach. They needed those six F-16s out of Foss Field as air support for the overwatch duties in the operation. "Let me make a call."

Carl quickly picked up his phone. "Hi, Phil. Yes, I know what happened at the CIA. Yes, it was Torger. But did you watch the press conference? I understand, Phil. Could you call your pilots into the room and then put me on speaker?"

When all were settled in the room, Carl did his best to convince the South Dakota National Guard pilots to complete the mission and get in the air. It was a split down the middle. He had persuaded three of the six to get airborne. For God's sake, they were already supposed to be headed to Minot. Carl briefed the remaining three pilots on what the revised operation would entail. Two of them would proceed to the Black Hills, and one would head for Minot.

It was now a sprint to see whether the F-16s would make it before the Reapers reached their target. Maybe he was worried for nothing, but Carl wouldn't put it past the CIA to divert those Reapers. F-16 insurance was definitely needed.

CHAPTER 48

MOGEN COMPOUND — THE BLACK HILLS OF SOUTH DAKOTA

Dawn was breaking over the Hills. The most incredible sunrises tended to follow turbulent weather, and after the massive thunderstorm the Hills had experienced earlier in the morning, this sunrise was not a disappointment.

At the compound, the FBI was breaking all the rules. They ordered everyone from the Rapid City office to converge on the Mogens' place. No warrant—nothing. This was the biggest incident since 9/11, so they were wasting no time delving into all things Mogen. But the lead agent was getting frustrated at the lack of evidence. The laptop with all John Mogen's writings was gone. Other than books about the founders and the Constitution, there wasn't much evidence at all. They did find some rough draft maps of the United States with states in red and some not. Some of the states had checkmarks in them while others had question marks.

After running frantically up the outside steps and into the house, the panicked lead agent began rushing around the Mogen residence, shouting, "Get out! Get out! All of you, get out—now! Load up the SUVs and get out of here as fast as you can!"

When he was sure everyone was gone, he ran for his vehicle. He heard the sound of a small turboprop before he saw it—the Reaper in a sharp bank circling the compound. He was headed toward the gate as the first missile hit the row of three one-thousand-gallon propane bullet tanks. He pulled off after he turned onto Highway 395 to watch the light show.

The Reaper was going into another sharp turn. As it leveled off, two missiles let loose and headed straight for the main residence they had just vacated. The whole sky lit up while he watched John and Jaylynn's dream home splinter into pieces and ignite instantly.

As the Reaper turned and flew in the opposite direction, going away from him, a missile shot directly over his head. In an instant, the Reaper had disintegrated in midair. The agent dropped to his knees at the sound of the F-16 flying over him. He was confused at what he had just witnessed. Why would anyone want to blow the place up, and why did an F-16 just smoke the Reaper?

As the agent stood there, watching in utter amazement, the F-16 turned to the northeast, heading toward Minot AFB.

IN THE SKIES ABOVE SOUTH DAKOTA

Just as the F-16 turned northeast, heading for Minot, the pilot of the second F-16 heard his radio squawk. "Shadow 2, copy?"

"Copy, CREF—go ahead."

"Shadow 2, we have a possible drone sighting heading toward Ellsworth or at Ellsworth—over."

"Copy that, CREF. Shadow 2 will adjust course to Ellsworth. Estimate two minutes."

"Roger, Shadow 2. Hunt fast!"

Hunt fast, the F-16 pilot was thinking. *No kidding.* Minot might not be attainable fuel wise if he engaged again.

As he observed what was left of his fuel supply, he received two radar hits on his screen. He slowed and dropped altitude as he passed a C-17 on final. JSOC was landing. Okay, one identified—now the other one. At that second, he picked up a visual on the other radar hit—a drone. He slowed down more as he made a turn to line up on it.

"Get a tone—get a tone, dammit!" He didn't realize he was talking out loud. As he fired, his missile caught up with it in seconds. Just as the drone went up, he caught a glimpse of his target and realized it might not be a Reaper. "CREF, I engaged and smoked a drone, but it was not—I repeat, it was not—a Reaper!"

CREF was quick to respond. "Roger that, Shadow 2. Let me confirm that—we believe it was a Global Hawk on station over Ellsworth. Shadow 1 is arriving on station at Ellsworth. You need to head to Minot, Shadow 2. Copy?"

"Roger that! I may not have the fuel to make Minot, CREF. Definitely cannot make it back to Foss."

"Stand by, Shadow 2—checking contingencies."

Shadow 2 decided to climb. It would use more fuel but would dramatically increase his glide time if needed.

"Shadow 2, vector to Bismarck Airport. There is an Army aviation support base at the southeastern end of the runway. We have friends there who will refuel you and ask no questions. Contact happening right now. They have been informed about an F-16 from South Dakota Air Guard coming in low on fuel. Copy?"

"Roger that, CREF—Bismarck Airport. Thanks. I can make that—barely."

"Shadow 2, this is Shadow 1. What am I hunting for?"

"Shadow 1, I'm guessing they put up two Reapers and two G-Hawks. Look for the second Reaper and Hawk in the Ellsworth area. Copy?"

"Shadow 1 copies—thanks." Shadow 1 was carrying an aux fuel tank that was slowing him down and changing his performance slightly.

"Shadow 1, this is CREF. Break off and vector to Minot. Copy?"

"CREF, copy that." Shadow 1 didn't agree with or understand the order but turned north for Minot.

CHAPTER 49

CIA UNDERGROUND SATELLITE OPERATIONS CENTER OUTSIDE WASHINGTON, D.C.

"Sir, we just heard from Creech. One of their Reapers, the one that just released two hits on the Mogen compound, appears to have been destroyed. We lost our feed a moment ago. Not only did we lose the Reaper's signal, but we also lost the one from the Global Hawk at Ellsworth. Grand Forks says it appears to have been eliminated also."

Another tech jumped in. "Sir, we have a call from FBI Rapid City on line two."

Nathan bristled as he responded, "Bring it up on speaker!"

The Rapid City bureau chief came in hot. "You son of a bitch! How could you? My people had all of five minutes to get off the Mogen property before you had the whole place up in flames! I've called my director, and he's talking to your director, and this is not just for a chitchat, let me tell you! I hope he fries your ass! If he doesn't, I'll call the president!"

Immediately, Nathan gave the order to shut down the audio on the call. He hadn't given an order to notify Rapid City FBI in his rush to take care of the problem. He was red-faced as he looked around the room, but everyone chose to look away at that moment.

Jamie stood up, knocking over his chair in the process, and looked straight at Nathan. "Have you completely lost your mind? Thank God we got a dispatch out to them in time to save their people. You were going to let them all get blown up, weren't you? Weren't you?"

Before Nathan could answer, the command center door opened. A security team entered the room and approached Nathan. "You need to come with us, sir. We have been ordered to relieve you of duty."

Nathan stared at Jamie as one of the security team handcuffed him and led him toward the door. As the door closed behind Nathan Parkinson, the whole command center erupted with cheering and clapping. This crew had to be able to sleep at night, and Jamie knew it.

"Okay," Jamie announced, "let's concentrate on finding anyone in this world who is working on a nuclear detonation system that learns heartbeats for cripes' sake. Let's work the problem, people! If this is real, it puts us in a very delicate position. All Broken Arrow teams have been ordered to stand down. What scares me is another 'Parkinson' handing down irrational orders. Does anybody have any new information on what's going on at Reagan?"

A young woman started to read from her screen. "Yes, sir—troops all over the airport. Reporting four Kalitta Air 747s lined up. They have been loading congressmen, senators, and possibly Supreme Court Justices for evacuation out of D.C. No confirmation of whose orders are being followed. The president is assumed to be with his Secret Service detail underground in the nuclear safe bunker for now. No confirmation of this. They can get him to other places in the tunnels too."

Jamie was puzzled at some of the information reported. "I don't remember a contingency plan to evacuate the government this way. I thought the underground via the tunnel system in Maryland was the contingency site. Find the general who gave the briefing on all this and get him up on audio."

Jamie had a funny feeling in the pit of his stomach. A phantom C-17… Someone shooting down drones… Troops at the nuclear device landing locations within minutes… And now prestaged airliners at Reagan? This seemed way bigger than a retired engineer from South Dakota. "Get me all the information you can on the Arlington Colonels' Club. This has to be the tip of a really big iceberg. Let's dive down and find the rest!"

CHAPTER 50

MINOT AIR FORCE BASE — NORTH DAKOTA

Colonel Carl Justine had received confirmation John and Jaylynn's place had been lit up by a Reaper drone. Those damn F-16 pilots' hesitations had cost them the Mogens' dream. First John was shot, and now their house was gone. How was he going to tell his sister?

The surgery had gone well, all things considered, and John had come out of the anesthesia. He was talking but still groggy. The surgeon described to Jaylynn that John's clavicle was pinned and screwed back together. All the muscle tissue and tendons were still there and had been reattached to where they should be. John would have to be in a sling for eight weeks minimum, probably more. The damage from the round that grazed his head would need a plastic surgeon, but it was glued and Steri-Stripped up as cleanly as possible for now. Jaylynn was just overjoyed he was alive.

Carl walked into the room just as the doctor was finishing. Jaylynn looked up at him and started relaying what the doctor had told her. He already had the information but listened quietly to Jaylynn's rundown.

"That's good news," Carl said, trying to take his mind off what he had to tell her. "Can I have you for a few minutes while he gets some rest? Let's go outside to talk." By the time they left the room, John had already drifted back to sleep, totally drained from the whole ordeal.

"Jay, we've decided you two will spend more time at the backup site in Arizona when we're done here. We…ahh, we—" he stuttered.

Jaylynn knew her brother all too well and recognized something was not right. "Carl, what is it? Are you talking about the safe house for the kids and grandkids? Is Truen bringing the dogs to Arizona? Just tell me what's going on, Carl!" Jaylynn had cried so much in the last twenty-four hours, she thought she had no more tears.

Carl took a deep breath. He had to tell her about the house, even if he dreaded it. "Jay, the CIA bastards sent a Reaper drone and took out your house in the Hills. We were able to get the dogs and Truen out in time, thanks to Jack Ellis. Jack and Truen are driving the dogs to the Arizona site. The last report I had on their location was that they are turning off I-70 and heading south on Highway 191.

Jaylynn did not start crying this time. "So, Truen and the dogs are okay? That's all I care about right now. We can always rebuild. Those CIA bastards! Those bastards! They had no reason to blow our place up—none!" Jaylynn was yelling now. Stress was taking over, and her anger was spilling out. Now, she really knew the evil living in this country, her beloved republic. The corruption had to be pulled out by the roots, and they would start with the CIA!

Carl was hugging Jaylynn when they heard a large airplane landing. They looked up to see a C-130 Hercules throttling back with flaps down as it prepared to make the turn at the end of the runway. This would be the first of many coming in from all over the country. Special and regular forces had been waiting for the word to come to Minot to defend the provisional government that would soon be organized there before being moved to Arlington, Texas. This site had been chosen to be the eventual capital of the Western Southern Alliance. But for now, they had to protect Minot AFB and secure the border crossing into Canada, north of Antler, North Dakota, on Highway 256. Some of their Canadian partners had been tasked with preparing the building in Pierson, Manitoba. At the same time, their staff at Minot AFB was preparing the quarters and fixing meals so all would be ready for the guests coming in from Washington, D.C.

Jason Wilder had been occupied all day with preparations for the ceremony to take place the next morning. So, when he came across Jaylynn sitting outside the base's hospital, he could tell by her demeanor that she had been informed about the drone strike. He needed to say something.

"Your family is safe in Arizona, Jaylynn. You have a true friend in Jack Ellis. He responded quickly when we needed him the most."

Jaylynn stepped over to Jason and hugged him. It was an embrace that felt like she was seeking to hold onto what was left of the life she knew—anything that she was familiar with. He had become like a son to her in such a short time. Jason was surprised at her show of affection, but he welcomed the hug.

Carl walked up as Jason began to inquire about John's condition. He glanced at Carl before continuing. "How's John doing? Should we call on someone else to deliver the speech tomorrow?"

Jaylynn interrupted. "John will do it. You may have to prop him up a little, but trust me, he will deliver that speech. You both know how important it is that he does this. In the past, he's recovered from going under anesthesia quite quickly and without much of a hangover. They're going to keep the nerve block to his shoulder until after his speech."

Carl nodded to Jason, which told him to have someone ready, just in case, but to expect John to deliver. Carl recognized how much John believed in the restoration, and his face really needed to be seen by the entire country at this moment.

Martial law had been declared already, and the chaos in the cities where the devices had been dropped was out of control. Traffic jams were occurring by citizens fleeing, causing miles of congestion. The local authorities had been slow to repurpose lanes to outbound status, and because of this, people had taken to abandoning their vehicles and walking or running from the cities. The San Francisco Bay Area was the worst with people walking across bridges by the thousands. As a result, the bridges were clogged by abandoned vehicles. In desperation, the local authorities had called in large cranes that had been working to clear the Bay Bridge and

Golden Gate by dropping deserted vehicles over the side one by one. The only emergency vehicles able to operate were helicopters.

The bombing of the CIA headquarters in Langley, Virginia, had been reported by most of the major news outlets as a possible nuclear device. It was corrected later, but the first report stuck in the mind of the public, and it was almost impossible to turn the herd. People were in a panic to get out of the cities where the devices were dropped any way they could. It was chaos turned to self-induced carnage.

CIA UNDERGROUND SATELLITE OPERATIONS CENTER OUTSIDE WASHINGTON, D.C.

By default, Jamie was now in charge of the investigation and the response to the attack on the country. They had to move to a much larger room as they swelled with more technicians and screens.

The NSA headquarters were now completely abandoned. Gloria and two assistants from the NSA had been ordered to go to the CIA site. As they settled in, Gloria filled Jamie in on all the information they'd uncovered on John Mogen and the Arlington Colonels' Club. She also had additional info on the flights leaving Washington, D.C., from Reagan.

"Okay, the Kalitta 747s leaving Reagan filed flight plans to DFW. Their ETA should be about four to five hours from now. The Congress and Supreme Court have basically been evacuated, but we have no information on who ordered this evacuation. We do know Colonel Bill Musgrave—former Marine—has been overseeing this. It has been confirmed he was on the last plane out of Reagan. Kalitta says the request for the charters came through normal Pentagon channels. Seems they don't ask a lot of questions—they just supply the aircraft and crews. That is why we use them. We—"

"Sir—sir," a young woman broke in.

Jamie gave her an annoyed glance. "Yes? This had better be important!" His temper was on a short fuse.

"Sir, you asked us to immediately notify you if we found a connection to the heartbeat detonation system for the nuclear devices. We think we have!"

Gloria jumped in, asking, "What is she talking about?"

"Hang on, Gloria!" Jamie wanted to hear this. "Go on. What have you got?"

"Okay sir, this is a long shot, but we've been checking connections to Jason Wilder and his company—or companies, I should say. We came across a great deal of communications with Pipeline Guardian. This company supplies leak detection systems for pipelines—like oil pipelines. These systems are required by the government. This company supplies the type of smart system we are looking for."

Jamie interrupted. "Cut to the chase, Cindy. How does this relate?"

Cindy looked flustered. "It's—they are smart systems and can monitor wave or intermittent flows. They learn variations in flow patterns. So, they could—maybe with some tweaking of the system—learn how to detect the normal blood flow of a person. The website says smart systems learn the differences of when the flow is in startup mode and can learn anomalies in that flow. They can identify what is normal for a certain system, so—"

Gloria looked baffled while Jamie had an aha moment. He exclaimed, "Blood flow! Normal flow, flow when taking a run, flow when excited or scared. It could learn what a human being's blood wave flow looks like under different conditions!"

Cindy was pleased Jamie had caught on. "Their website says that, over time, the smart system learns the ever-changing pipeline parameters, so it determines a pattern between everything that occurs in normal operation versus off-normal operation. Their website also states, 'This prevents unnecessary shutdowns and alarms on the system because it detects if operations are still within acceptable parameters.'"

Gloria had never heard of this technology but still asked the question. "Don't you think someone could hook this up to a person and it could learn their heart flow rates and blood pressure?"

With this new information, Jamie was getting more energized. "Cindy, get in touch with this Pipeline Guardian company and see what you can find out about this particular system! We need to better understand the workings on this. Maybe we could use it to defeat those systems at the nukes! Better yet, get their techie people to the nuke sites, and after that, round up all their employees who are in the know. Let's get down to the particulars—we need to figure out that heartbeat technology ASAP. Also, dig into any other companies that might be into this kind of technology. With any luck, we might be able to get ahead of this whole thing!"

Within ten minutes, Cindy had reviewed another pipeline leak detection company, and they had some simple examples. "Sir, the more I investigate this, the more I think it's doable. The heart is a pump that starts and stops about seventy times a minute. The software wouldn't care if it's mechanical or human flow and pressure. They could just change the parameters and make it fit within the numbers in the program. It's a pump with flows and pressure. I definitely know they can pull this off!"

CHAPTER 52

MINOT AIR FORCE BASE – NORTH DAKOTA

1400 HRS

Colonel Carl Justine watched as the first Kalitta 747 touched down. The flight plans that had been filed had been for DFW airport, not Minot Air Force Base, as a ruse. Lunch was almost ready for the Washington chuckleheads. The temporary living quarters were prepared with cell phone jamming activated in all the units.

Colonel Allan North was in charge of the management of the Congress and Supreme Court personnel. He was obviously well educated. He was a smooth talker and had a voice that just oozed confidence and authority. He would convince the group that they were all safe.

Bill Musgrave had been conducting private talks with certain congressmen and senators while flying to Minot. These particular men and women would be the seeds for the provisional government that was being set up until the Western Southern Alliance was fully defined and up and running as a separate constitutional republic.

Senator Paul Carbajal of Texas and Congressman Ted Gosnor of Arizona had been singled out to be the point men for the new republic. Both of these men were part of a back-channel system the Colonels' Club had set up. The colonels had spent considerable time and effort making sure these two patriots could be trusted. These elected officials hadn't known the when, where, or how of the restoration—just that it was in the planning stage.

Musgrave had informed them of the situation, and hopefully they understood the role they'd be playing. Since they would have the full backing of the military—well, at least most of the military—they had to understand this was supposed to be a peaceful transition, if not for Torger Vigdahl's betrayal. They had made sure of both men's protection and ensured they had "plausible deniability" that could stand up to any investigation.

Colonel Bill Musgrave was walking toward Colonel North and Colonel Justine. He caught the attention of the senator and congressman who were standing nearby. "Gentlemen, let me introduce you to Colonel Allan North, retired Army and graduate of West Point," said Bill. Ted Gosnor took note of the ring on Colonel North's finger as Bill continued with his introduction. "This gentleman is Colonel Carl Justine, retired Air Force."

After handshakes were exchanged, Senator Carbajal spoke up. "Gentlemen, Congressman Gosnor and I have been very outspoken about the course our country has taken—let me say, the wrong course our government is moving toward when it comes to the continuous, pernicious, and very calculated violations of our Constitution and the purposeful erosion of the very rights our Constitution was adopted to protect. However, you've put us in quite a precarious position by what transpired earlier today at CIA headquarters. This was under your watch. We understand that you obviously didn't intend for that attack to happen, but—damn, it's tough to explain."

The senator stood there, shaking his head, before continuing. "It's very hard to explain and get past. About half of America won't understand or believe that a shadow government exists in our country, and in my opinion, because of your actions, it is now almost eradicated. Not only that, they think that the New World Order is some kind of grand conspiracy even though it has totally been out in the open since 1979 with the installation of the Georgia Guidestones, which clearly states what their endgame is. I just hope that part of the country will support our undocking from those lost states and get past what happened at CIA headquarters. Our hearts are heavy, and our spirits are troubled right now, as you can understand."

Congressman Gosnor spoke next. "We get what you…*we* are trying to do. We just pray the military will have our six as we work through this idea. I, for one, am excited about the whole direction. Our citizenry has been moving farther apart for years now, and we've become two separate countries even though we know we would be stronger united. But there is one thing I want to bring up. I don't know if the public spirit of the United States will embrace WSA overtly calling this new country a Christian nation."

Colonel North listened carefully before replying to the concerns of Carbajal and Gosnor. He took in not only their words but, more importantly, their tone and inflection. "So, gentlemen, let me address the CIA headquarters first. We were absolutely mortified by what took place in Langley. In our run-up to this grand restoration, we spent an unusual amount of time ferreting out the traitors to our republic, but we, admittedly, got blindsided by what happened today.

"The Arlington Colonels' Club has been working on numerous plans to turn our country around for quite a few years. Circumstances such as runaway debt, rigged elections, and the assault on our rights to free speech, to freely worship, and to keep and bear arms accelerated to the point that something had to be done quickly. By golly, you're right—ours was a risky plan, and it had to be done without bloodshed.

"Believe me when I say our hearts are troubled by what went down, but we must move forward. We can't exactly say 'my bad' and give up on what we're trying to do. You two gentlemen and those additional men and women, whose names you have brought forth and whom you say must be part of the new republic's government, are absolutely free to inform the American people that you all knew nothing about this plan and didn't agree with how it was carried out. It's all on our back.

"Colonel John Mogen, who's in charge of the Constitution Restoration Expeditionary Forces, will—hopefully—be giving a speech spelling out the why, what, where, and when of this whole thing. You have a choice in this matter. You can boldly be part of this or decline any involvement. If you decline, we'll find someone else to take up the cause. History will judge all of us based on the decisions we make now and the actions we take from this time forward."

Colonel North took a breath as he finished speaking and looked in the face of each of the gentlemen standing before him. He had placed his whole life on the line with this restoration plan because he completely believed it was the correct thing to do for his country. Hopefully that showed through his words.

Everyone in the circle just stood there in silence. Jason was now a part of the group and had found himself near tears as he'd listened to Colonel North speak. The reality of the situation had finally hit him hard. Jason had only slept two out of the last thirty-six hours and was running out of adrenaline quickly. However, being present at this moment—this seminal moment—in the history of the American experiment in self-government had him wide awake.

Senator Carbajal looked at Congressman Gosnor and smiled. "'Lives, fortunes, and sacred honor.' As Benjamin Franklin said, 'We hang together, or we will hang separately!' This is something we both want to be a part of, and we will do everything in our power to see that this new Christian republic is successful. God be with us all in this endeavor!"

There was silence again. They all seemed to understand that it was a solemn moment in the history of the Western Southern Alliance. Even the big, strong Special Forces guy, Jason, let a tear roll down his cheek. He saw hope in this grand vision of a city on a hill and what it could look like. This city would touch all inhabitants of the world, and because of that, they would see what was possible when people loved freedom and loved the Lord God Almighty. He was proud to be even a small part of all this.

Congressman Gosnor broke the silence this time. "Paul and I have already made a list of who we think should remain as part of the new provisional government. All representatives will have to take a course on the Constitution and understand it completely and then prove they are believers in God and God-given rights! We agree that a single body of two representatives from each state is the way to go to begin with. Figuring out how to separate the states into two different countries and do it without bloodshed and overwhelming fear again will be a monumental task, but we are up for it. The economy worries me the most. The states' borders need to be left open to interstate commerce for at least a year, I think."

Colonel Allan North interrupted at this point. "Okay, gentlemen, now that lunch is over, let's get you to your quarters. You'll be housed in a different area from the rest of the group. Get your heads together and start putting your ideas down on paper.

"Here is a copy of the address our leader, John Mogen, will present tomorrow morning. He has some very specific things we need to accomplish within the first thirty days and then by the end of the first year. We also received great news from the military. We've been informed the high-ranking officers are giving standdown orders throughout the country. We have units touching down from all over the republic with the help of the Air Force. We'll be well protected at Minot until we can move to the new site of the provisional government in Arlington, Texas."

Just as Colonel North finished speaking, another C-130 touched down. The tent city was growing quickly in the field off Bomber Boulevard as well as in another field to the south of that site. It appeared the intelligence that had been gathered and the work the Oathtakers had done over the last two years was paying off big time. Generals and colonels, both active and retired, had received the message that this was their last chance to maintain a republic in North America. The big unknown was how challenging it would be to get the New World Order believers to stand down. Many were embedded in every government agency, and they would not go quietly.

CHAPTER 53

John Mogen amazed the medical personnel with how fast he was recovering. As expected, he suffered very little hangover from the drugs. Perhaps that was what had made him a functional alcoholic during his drinking days. He asked that he be given no morphine or any other narcotic drugs. Over-the-counter Ibuprofen was all he would take to manage his pain.

His right arm was in a sling from the repair of his shoulder. The right side of his face was swollen and displayed a bluish purple and red line from his right eye to just past his right ear, which had been stitched together. The rest of the wound had been glued and was being held by multiple Steri-Strips. He was truly a sight to behold, but he was alive. The team would be setting up the cameras for his address to the country so that the picture angle would rest on his left side.

John knew he was supposed to record a press release. Earlier, he had given his notes to his brother-in-law, Colonel Carl Justine. He knew he had to get up and get going, but as he started to leave the bed, Jaylynn asked him what he thought he was doing.

"I'm going to the bathroom!" John announced.

Jay smiled at her handsome man. "You have a catheter in, John. You can whizz away."

John realized what he really needed was to reevaluate how mentally ready he was to give this address. "Jay, I really need to get up and sit in the chair. It will help me if I'm vertical."

Jaylynn knew John was serious, so she told him to wait until she called a nurse. If they could remove his catheter, then maybe he could get up.

John was fast becoming himself as he pleaded with Jay. "I would prefer that you just pull out this darn tube… I want to make sure they don't break anything."

Jay just shook her head as she walked out the door. Although she was acting coy in his presence, she was excited that John was feeling well enough to lead with his penis instead of his brain—typical male. She loved it.

As the nurse left the room after being convinced to remove the catheter, John was thankful for this one thing getting him closer to normal. Sitting in the chair next to his bed, at first, he was a little lightheaded, but that sensation was quickly going away. He asked Jay if she could scout out some coffee to quell the slight nausea he felt now. Jay beamed at him, glad that she had her man back, and headed out the door on her assigned mission. He was a colonel after all.

Colonel Carl Justine had sent a runner to check on John Mogen's status. The runner had returned with the news that John was sitting up and drinking coffee. Carl turned to look and nod at Colonel North and Colonel Musgrave. Jason Wilder would join them later.

Sighing, Carl said, "Well, gentlemen, let's get this over with. John needs to know what has transpired since he went in for surgery. I will get Jason to get the Mogens to join us."

Jason quietly entered John's room. Jaylynn's face lit up with a smile as he joined them, but John couldn't smile without experiencing pain. Jason was a little stunned at how black and blue John's face was. It might have been just a flesh wound, but it looked nasty.

"Hey, you two, if you're up to it, we need to meet the club members in the conference room down the hall." Jason stood there a moment in the quiet, waiting for an answer. John adjusted his body as he sat up a little straighter, exchanged looks with Jay, and then nodded yes. Jason and Jaylynn were at John's side to help him, but John did not use their support and pushed up on his own power. As he moved, he felt the bullet-created groove in his right cheek more than the shoulder injury, but the pain was manageable for now. As they walked down the hall and around the corner, John saw three of the four Colonels' Club members outside the conference room.

As he reached them, he asked, "Where's Captain Vigdahl? Did we find him yet? Did we get all the packages delivered safely? Did we get the D.C. evacuees here yet?"

Colonel North glanced over to Carl, who already knew it was up to him to inform John what had happened since he'd been put under. At the same time, the colonels were more impressed than ever with the questions John had just asked after his ordeal. They all would have asked the same questions.

"Sorry for the barrage," apologized John. "Hello, gentlemen—it's great to meet you all face to face. It's also admirable to know we still have patriots who understand their oath!"

John glanced toward Carl, who motioned the group toward the conference room. "Let's go in and sit down."

John noticed Jaylynn had tears in her eyes, but she quickly turned away as they entered the conference room.

Sitting down directly across from John, Carl slid him the speech he had also given to General Morris. Carl said a little sheepishly, "That message was released to the press, John. I hope it's close to what you would have said since you were stated to be the author."

John looked up from the papers resting in front of him on the table, a little shocked and confused. "So, that's why Torger isn't here? Do we know where he is?"

Allan North now spoke up. "We think he's in Belize, John. He has a place down there. We'll take care of him. We won't kill him, but he will be banished from the United States and the WSA. What he dropped on the CIA headquarters was conventional, but some of the mainstream press has been reporting it as a small nuclear device. The MOAB can give the appearance of a nuke. As you can imagine, D.C. is a mess right now, as are the rest of the cities. Evacuation by panic doesn't go well, as you might envision."

Allan looked to Carl to take over again. "John, we have all five nukes in place. Most of Congress and all of the Supreme Court Justices are here and ready for your speech tomorrow morning. The Air Force shot down one of the B-1Bs that dropped to New York City before the military issued a no shootdown order. FedEx #1—Sam Hudson in command—diverted and dropped at the NSA headquarters and got to their rendezvous site in Maine.

"Vigdahl taking out CIA headquarters was more than a big malfunction in communication. It will be hard to overcome, but it's happened. We must take responsibility for the good and the bad of it, and then we have to go on. If I put myself in Torger's shoes, I understand that he wanted to take out some of the deep state and send them a message at the same time—those that are left at least.

"The CIA has sent out Global Hawks and Reapers, but they don't know our location yet. However, I'm sure they will soon. Right now, we have F-16 air cover from the Air Guard out of Sioux Falls. On other matters, Jack Ellis is on his way to Arizona with Truen Walsh and your dogs."

After hesitating for a moment, Carl delivered the next bit of news to John. "Your—ah—your house in the Hills was hit by a Reaper drone, and it's gone. I'm so sorry, John."

John looked at Carl in disbelief. He and Jaylynn had loaded important papers, passports, and some real photos they hadn't scanned yet as an afterthought. Jaylynn had sent the girls a timed email to be delivered three days after this crazy thing was in progress, telling them these items were in the living quarters in the RV—just in case. He never thought this might be significant.

He suddenly pictured his library in the loft of their home. He had over a thousand books on the shelves there. Not just any books. Some were antique history books about the republic. A lifetime of collecting was gone. John was one of those dinosaurs who had to have a tactile experience of real ink on paper. Many of his books were covered with highlighting. When looking for a specific book, he had no problem heading straight to the library shelf and pulling it out from its position from memory. This wasn't just stuff to John.

Suddenly, he remembered how Thomas Jefferson had given his entire library to restock the Library of Congress that had been destroyed by the British in the War of 1812. John could rebuild his library. Carl had been quiet while John pondered what he had told him. "All gone, Carl—all gone? I thought you said those Reapers only had a single kill missile that did little collateral damage. Why are you saying all gone?"

Carl explained further. "John, the new Reapers are bigger and can carry more. You might have been thinking of the Hellfires, but they also have what are called GBU-12s. These are guided but have a five-hundred-pound bomb on them. They most likely hit your house with two of these. We have people on the way to your place to see what can be recovered. I'm so sorry, John."

John took an extra deep breath, then winced with pain. "I guess that's not as bad as what happened to our founders, who made the same pledge we have." As he took another pause, he requested, "Just see if they can find any of my books. Any other updates, Carl?"

"The CIA is operating from an alternate site, so we are heading there with our troops to shut it down right now. We've also heard that a JSOC team has dropped into Ellsworth and is gathering intel and looking for you, I presume. We have troops pouring in at this moment, and we will have a significant force here. We have shot down the two Global Hawks and Reapers sent out, but we expect the CIA to send more Global Hawks from Grand Forks to keep an eye on us, especially when they zero in on us. We are planning to take over Grand Forks AFB as soon as we can.

"After your speech tomorrow, you and Jaylynn will be heading to Arizona. The rest of us will head down to Texas to complete our timetable for our reform of this government. After you heal up, you can join us in Arlington. We know you have some agenda ideas for the Constitutional Convention, and we'll need your input."

Everyone was waiting for a reaction from John. As he looked around the room and then back at Carl, he calmly asked the group, "How could all of you not know Torger was planning something other than the bloodless plan we had?"

Carl was quick to answer. "We're so sorry, John. The man attended a Bible study with us for years and is a believer—or we think he is. We were deceived, and so was Ski. She supplied the weapons for him, thinking it was for our operation. Even as we speak, we're searching for him in Belize. We should've put in place more controls and cross-reporting systems. Unfortunately, we were blindsided."

Colonel Allan North was reading a message on his phone while Carl was finishing up. He was next to speak. Looking up, he addressed the assembly. "Gentlemen, I've received an email from Captain Vigdahl. Let me read what he wrote... 'My friends, I'm solely responsible for what took place at the CIA headquarters. Please do not punish anyone involved. I have my reasons to despise the CIA that you just couldn't understand. As a Christian, I know the concept of not answering evil or violence in kind, but since I know what they are capable of, I took matters into my own hands. They are people without a conscience. They will not hesitate to kill all of you by any means necessary. They do understand what I did will uncover them. The deep state will be scurrying around like the exposed rats they are. They operate outside the Constitution with impunity, and they assumed immunity. You have to deal with what I did, and I'm sorry for that. I have to live with what I have done also. I couldn't overcome what they did to SEAL Team Six. I stooped to their level because I knew none of you could or would do so. There is a time to kill, so if you send someone to find me, make sure it's a clean kill. I still love each one of you, and I love our republic.'" North looked up from his phone with conflicted emotions.

John got up and left the room. Everyone let him go. He had to get out into the fresh air. As he walked out of the building, he was amazed at the activity going on. C-130s being unloaded. Humvees, Polarises, and bigger stuff driving off aircraft. Troops with piles of gear on the ramp, waiting to be taken to their assigned area where tents were set up. A busy place!

Jaylynn and Jason were sitting in the shade behind John as they kept an eye on him. The latter caught John's attention.

"Good news, John. We're hearing from Oathtakers all over the country. The military is behind us. We're hearing most of the military has standdown orders. We were right about the numbers. The Joint Chiefs of Staff have issued a statement for all branches to remain calm but stay on full alert. Broken Arrow units have set up in the vicinity of all five nukes but have orders to take no action at this time. If they move on the sites, we will take appropriate action to protect the nukes. The CIA has their special units, and I don't know their status. One of our friends at Ellsworth made contact with the JSOC team leader. They're not cooperating with the CIA, and they are listening."

John broke in. "That's all good news, Jason. How many people were killed at the CIA headquarters? Do we know?"

Jason knew the news of what Torger had done had shaken John to the core. "I'm guessing at least one thousand—maybe more. The above-ground building is pretty well flattened, but we don't know how much of the underground facilities were affected. None of us are happy about the hit. I was sick to my stomach when I heard about it."

John had a pensive look on his face. "I'm beginning to wonder what evil is and who's really evil in this situation." John paused as Jason acknowledged his comment.

"John, I have firsthand knowledge of what the CIA has done and is doing. Evil lives there. I know there were people killed who didn't know and would never have agreed with what the Company was involved in. Machiavellians rule there. They have no conscience. They only have goals and objectives to be accomplished any way they can. Trust me, it is pure evil—more than you know or I would discuss in front of Jaylynn. It's done, John. We have to move on," Jason said reassuringly.

John was rapidly becoming drained of energy and feeling uncomfortable as he faced those at the table. "I need to lay down. I need to go over my speech. I need..."

Jaylynn cut him off. "Let's get you to our quarters so you can rest—okay, hon?"

Jason still had his six. John and Jaylynn had become very special to him in the short time he'd known them. Now, all he could think about were all his failures when it came to his interactions with their family. He had gotten John shot and would never forgive himself for that. He had been responsible for the failed mission at the Ellsworth gate. That was all on him. He had lost his buddy and team member, Zach Overgaard, to a bullet through his neck. He had also made a mortal enemy of the Mogens' daughter. But he was still on a mission, and he would see that John and Jay made it through safely to be united with their family in Arizona, where they all could heal before making the trip to Arlington.

John's face would be broadcast to the entire world tomorrow morning. He had to be protected, no matter what Jason's own role might be from this point forward. John would forever be the face of the constitutional restoration. He would be loved and hated by millions of Americans. The hope was that the millions who still believed in God and God-given rights would rally to their cause. Hopefully, John could alleviate the fear.

Any paradigm shifts from what people knew as "normal" would be terrifying. A normalcy bias was just built into most people. Evil people could and had changed the definition of what was normal. The deep state had slowly and methodically changed the country's thinking to the point that people believed anything said by them was the truth.

This restoration would be a "shock and awe" sort of change. When the public found out what the deep state had really been up to for decades, a percentage would never believe it. It was just the nature of the human mind. A revelation that what one believed one's entire life to be true had now become totally false—it could be too much. To find out the government really kept secrets might be a big surprise to the general population.

A restoration of what the founders had intended would be a lot for most to absorb. Most really didn't understand how far they'd been led astray. The younger people had been purposely taught to despise the founding fathers and view the Constitution as an outdated document, which the nation didn't have to follow anymore. This would change! It would change with one speech from one patriot who could articulate their status and their destination back to their roots, their values, their morals, and their Creator, who had given them rights as free men and women.

This had to happen before another generation was brought up through the usurped school system. That was why public educators fought private schools and homeschooling so much. The indoctrination of young people was taking place in public schools. Socialism and communism weren't viable and inevitably resulted in tyranny. That was the endgame. The complete control. *We stop this now—in its tracks!*

Just as he was arriving at the Mogens' living quarters, Jason's phone vibrated, alerting him to a new text message. He took a deep breath and slowed his mind back down.

Jaylynn said a second time, "Jason, are you alright? Jason?"

He looked down at her and smiled. "I'm just fine, Jaylynn. It's all coming together."

"I can take it from here," Jaylynn said. "You do what you need to do."

Before Jason left, Eric arrived to stand guard outside their quarters. John was already asleep with Jaylynn's hand ever-present on his leg. She needed to maintain physical contact with him for her own peace of mind. Just a hand on his bare leg. Something only couples really in love over time could understand.

As the tear ran down her cheek and landed on a page of her Bible, she started reading. "*I will say of the Lord, He is my refuge and my fortress; My God in Him I will trust.*" Psalm 91. The Warrior's Psalm is what she was reading as she would be told later. She stopped at verse fifteen and reread it. "*He shall call upon Me and I will answer Him. I will be with Him in trouble; I will deliver Him and honor Him.*" Another tear hit the page as she looked for a tissue—again.

CHAPTER 54

The text Jason had received was from an employee at Pipeline Guardian who was communicating through an encrypted phone. The FBI had just shown up, and they wanted to question every single employee. They were also inquiring whether anyone was familiar with or knew Jason Wilder and his relationship, working or personal, with Pipeline Guardian. The FBI had sequestered all employees so they couldn't leave or talk to anyone on the outside. However, the employee who'd texted Jason had quickly detoured into the bathroom when he'd overheard what the FBI was demanding.

After reading the message, Jason quickly made another call. He had men and women on their way to Pipeline Guardian posing as lawyers, with the appropriate credentials, within thirty minutes. These people were actually Special Forces and were under orders to stop any interrogations. If the situation escalated, they were authorized to stop the FBI by other means.

Jason had already moved the two Pipeline Guardian employees involved with the software developed for the heartbeat detonation system to a mountain retreat out of cell phone range before the restoration had begun, and no one at Pipeline Guardian knew of their whereabouts. How in the hell had the CIA or NSA figured things out so quickly? Thank God his intellectual assets were safe and secure and would soon be better protected than they were now. It was fortunate the other employees had no knowledge of the project.

Jason turned his attention to John and the address he would be delivering tomorrow. It was only known to him and the Colonels' Club that he was slated to stand in for John if he was unable to give his speech. Since he was so massive and looked like he'd just walked off a magazine cover, the club had deemed Jason was their guy. He would have to shave off what he called his special ops beard, which he dreaded, and find a 4X or 5X shirt and coat to hide his build so he didn't come across as special ops.

For now, he hoped and prayed John would be able to rally and make it to the podium. He was their spokesman and leader, and the nation would truly relate to him. He flourished in this position—more so than any of them could have ever dreamed. For such a time as this, God raised up John Mogen to do this.

Jason was grateful just to be his protector... His attention was drawn inward as he added the conclusion of the statement in his mind: ...*and his son-in-law*. No matter what he did, Kayla Mogen would simply not vacate his brain and especially his heart. Jason sighed heavily, sat down, and began to read the speech John was going to deliver tomorrow. The speech was fantastic!

CHAPTER 55

Sam Hudson was in the right seat of a C-130 Hercules again. They were on final approach into Minot Air Force Base. He couldn't believe how fast he had gone from being an NSA pod supervisor to being involved, even in a small way, with this restoration. He thanked God that his mentor, Colonel Carl Justine, had bravely invited him in.

He had gone from a B-1B sortie to a comfortable right seat of a C-130. He would soon be joining Carl and the rest of the patriots involved in this enterprise. He was hoping all had gone well since the drop he had made at NSA headquarters. He still had a lot of questions floating around in his head for Carl about the unexpected explosions at Langley. It had definitely not been part of the plan. The only thing communicated to him was it hadn't been nuclear but had been a very large conventional ordnance. Unfortunately, it would leave a permanent mark on their cause. It would definitely present the Company with a huge setback, which he presumed was the whole idea.

As the C-130 touched down, he was excited to be at the heart of the restoration, to see Carl again, and to get some answers. After he'd completed his assignment, the F-35s had chased them part of the way to Maine. He had lost ten pounds of water weight just knowing at any moment they could be shot down. What a rush!

Carl hadn't been informed Sam was arriving on the C-130. Their cargo bay was full of current and former Navy SEALs from the East Coast. Many of them were accustomed to the room and comfort of the larger C-17 and were complaining in a lighthearted way. SEALs thrived on hardship and were known for being able to sleep anywhere, noise or no noise. In Sam's opinion, these were the greatest warriors to ever walk the face of the earth. Having them on their side was critical.

As he prepared to disembark, he let his mind travel back to the mission so long ago when he and Carl had dropped the SEALs off California's coast riding the winged mini subs. He sat shaking his head in amazement. Today, he had actually dropped former SEALs out of his B-1B to a soft landing at NSA headquarters. Sam was excited but scared as he thought of this current mission. They'd pulled it off, but where did they go from here? He wanted to meet this John Mogen guy who was the face of the restoration. He was wondering how a civilian could handle all this pressure. He had to be a very special guy.

Sam stayed put as the Navy SEALs exited the aircraft. Then, he left the cockpit and walked down the cargo ramp in the rear. *How did he find out?* he thought to himself.

Carl, flanked by two Air Force MPs, was standing at the back of the plane. He declared in a loud voice, "That's him—he's NSA. Arrest him now." The two MPs came forward and started to grab Sam's arms. However, Carl couldn't hang. He started to laugh uncontrollably.

Sam shook his head and replied to the prank. "Not funny, Carl, not funny at all." Carl was in a full laugh now and ordered the MPs to let him go.

"Carl, fill me in. How are we doing? What's going on? You know me—I hate not being in the know. It drives me crazy. I thought they were going to smoke us in the Bone—you know that, right?"

Carl responded, "Easy, Sam, easy. We're doing terrific! The CIA mess is something we'll have to overcome, but we're in control. The Joint Chiefs of Staff have ordered a full standdown. We have the Congress and Supreme Court sequestered here on site. Their fate will be announced in the morning. I do believe we've pulled it off!"

Sam was thrilled to hear all this, but the scene at CIA headquarters still haunted him. Carl sensed this, so he went into detail about the whole saga of Torger Vigdahl's rogue move, which had cost them a mostly bloodless coup. They had planned on engaging a different strategy to root out the deep state. Unfortunately, the collateral damage from the bombing at the CIA included personnel who had been clueless about the deep state. It was also hard to explain to the country that they were the good guys when tagged with something like that. Nonetheless, they had to move on with the plan.

Sam was still concerned after hearing what Carl had to say. "Damn, how could you not realize one of your own was planning something?"

Carl understood where Sam was coming from. "No excuses, Sam. We all got blindsided by this. I didn't think a watcher was needed for the Colonels' Club to be sure we stayed on track. We had a lot of failures on this one. Our procurement person didn't follow protocol and notify us when a change was made in the original—ah—order for ordnance. Let's call her Ski. She was as upset as the rest of us…we think. Can't assume about anyone anymore, can we? On another note, we're extremely glad Colonel Musgrave didn't shoot half the Congress on the air flight with him! I was worried about him a little.

"Our goal must be the same as we go forward. Form a new republic based on actually following the Constitution and the Lord. We have to separate the blue states out of the new republic. We've already heard some scuttlebutt about some very high-level military officers intending to undertake keeping the country together. We have to prevent that move as fast as we can. Tomorrow morning can't come soon enough. We'll let the world know our plan for the restart with a remnant of Congress. We'll call a Constitutional Convention for the WSA states immediately. I'm glad you are here, Sam. We need help in intelligence for sure."

Sam was beaming. "Boy howdy, you need help! It will be ugly at first. So, are you offering me a job, Carl?"

"Yes, I am, Sam. You know what the enemy is up to, right? You were smart to walk away from the NSA. The job of chief intelligence officer is yours if you want it. We actually have money to pay people from the get-go."

Sam shot back, "I accept with pleasure!"

Carl was pleased. "Let's get you up to speed with our operation. We'll tour our command here at Minot and then find you someplace to sleep. It's good to have you here, Sam. I'm really happy you didn't get shot out of the sky!"

Sam was exhausted. He had been able to get a little shuteye during the last flight but not enough. As they walked, Sam emotionally collapsed right in front of Carl. Overwhelmed by the moment, Carl broke down as well, so he turned and gave him a huge bear hug.

Sam whispered, "You don't know how close I came to chickening out about leaving the NSA…so close."

Carl understood how life decisions could turn on a dime. He also recognized God's plan. "Sam, God has put you here with me for such a time as this. Let's get you some sleep—you traitor!" he joked as they headed off to find Sam a bed.

CHAPTER 56

CIA UNDERGROUND SATELLITE OPERATIONS CENTER OUTSIDE WASHINGTON, D.C.

"**S**ir! Sir, we have a problem at Pipeline Guardian—sir!"

But all Jamie could concentrate on was video from Reagan Airport. They now recognized what had transpired there was part of a rogue mission. They had also established through additional radar data that there was extraordinary activity taking place in North Dakota with multiple inbound flights arriving from all over the States into Minot Air Force Base.

The agent was now screaming at Jamie. "Sir! Please! Sir!" Jamie quickly turned his attention to the shouting agent. "Sir, the three FBI agents sent to Pipeline Guardian have been forced out of the company's office building in Dallas. Sir, ten people in suits marched into the office, claiming to be lawyers. By their actions, we think they are either active or former special ops. Bottom line—we're out in the cold on that investigation for now. The lawyers conveyed to our agents to come back with a warrant with sufficient specificity or to not come back."

Jamie was astounded by this bit of news. How in the hell had they gotten there so fast? It was an understatement to say Jamie was not happy! "Did the agents get anything that might help us before leaving? Anything?"

"No, sir," is all the agent at the console could say.

Jamie turned back to the screen showing the influx of air flights into North Dakota. "When will our Global Hawk be on station at Minot? Didn't it just come out of Grand Forks?" It sounded like more of a statement than a question.

The agent responsible for communications with Grand Forks responded, "Sir, we should be coming online with video in fifteen clicks. I'm putting it up on screen three. Okay—here we go. Now, the Air Force base is straight ahead—see it? We're bringing up two-way audio with the remote pilot so you can communicate with him."

Before Jamie could say or ask anything, the audio from the drone pilot came over the comm. He was occupied with the task at hand. "Okay—evasive action and countermeasures. They have a lock. Breaking hard right—missile is on me."

Another voice came in from Grand Forks. "You knew they smoked the last one we sent!"

The pilot snapped back, "I know, I know—I came in ten feet off the ground but had to make a climb so the surveillance view was better!"

At that point, screen three went to snow. Jamie didn't need to ask what had happened. The Hawk had been shot out of the air. Moving on, he asked when the satellite adjustments would be completed.

"Sir, I—aaah, Buckley Field wants to talk to you," the agent in charge of satellite acquisition stuttered.

Jamie had to keep his cool and not let this rebellion outmaneuver them, so he calmly responded, "Okay, okay, bring up the audio. This is Ops Lead Jamie Collins. We're working the nuclear terrorist attack situation. Who am I talking to?"

The Space Warning Squadron at Buckley Field, west of Denver, had control of surveillance satellites. "This is Colonel Mason Johnson, Mr. Collins. We have a standdown order concerning that situation. We specifically have orders not to respond to requests from your agency at this time. You might want to limit your losses for now. We understand you have lost five very expensive drones. The WSA has fighters in the air continuously and has control of the airspace around Minot. If you'd been watching the news, you would have seen the announcement. They are broadcasting their intentions live tomorrow morning at 0900 hours Mountain Time. You know their nuclear devices are real, right? Or do you even have a clue?"

Jamie had just been pushed over the line—the line one reaches when one has not slept in too many hours and has been under intense stress for way too long. He suddenly realized he was at the point Nathan Parkinson had been at when they'd removed him from duty. He shook his head and took a super deep breath. "Cut off the audio now! Now! Let's get low-tech, people! Get me some boots on the ground. Let's get a look at the damn Air Force base. Get me some eyes on it *now!*"

With that, Jamie walked out of the room to compose himself. Five minutes later, he was back. An agent let him know that two FBI agents out of Minot were headed from town to the Air Force base. But an hour later, Jamie was advised that Highway 83 North had been shut down, and a military checkpoint had been set up ten miles from the Air Force base. The FBI agents had left the area and were heading back toward Minot but detouring onto every back road they came across. However, they found all roads closed off by military personnel. The plan now was to use ATVs in an attempt to see if they could get closer to the base.

Jamie sat slumped in his chair. They had nothing. This whole thing was well planned and had included a lot of active-duty military personnel to pull it off. Jamie still didn't understand the magnitude of the oath taken by the military. This oath meant something to them. They were people concerned about the failure to follow the Constitution and the attack on their God-given rights guaranteed by the Bill of Rights.

The Arlington Colonels' Club had been formed because the time had come to stop all this treason in its tracks. Officers in the military had taken it upon themselves to make sure all their personnel were trained on the Constitution, which most no longer studied in American schools, and it had worked. Furthermore, most of them were all in with the restoration taking place. The renewal of the Constitution was a big win for the country because the restoration would reverse the information war that was being waged against the current culture hostile to freedom!

The last gasps of the deep state were being heard, being played out, in this CIA Situation Room. The Colonels' Club had quietly infiltrated all branches of the military. Because of this, there was a revival going on. God's spirit had moved amongst the troops. The CIA had lost the battle. Minot North Dakota had become the center of restoration for now.

As more and more planes landed at Minot, the colonels became overwhelmed by the country's response. Not only colonels but generals and enlisted personnel from all branches were getting out of aircraft to report for duty and to pledge their loyalty to the Western Southern Alliance. They wanted to meet this Colonel Mogen guy. They wanted to shake his hand for stepping up. Over six hundred former and active flag officers were in this group.

CHAPTER 57

LAKE MARY ROAD — MOGOLLON RIM — CENTRAL ARIZONA

Kayla and Jessica's family had landed in Phoenix at Sky Harbor Airport. At the FBO, they were transferred into a smaller Beechcraft King Air twin-engine turboprop. The transfer was quick, and they were airborne within minutes. They didn't know it at the time, but they were heading north to Payson, Arizona. They were not familiar with the area, but when coming in on final approach, they could see for miles, and the vistas were so majestic. The sunrise was glorious with pinks, yellows, and purples as they taxied in.

As they got their first look at the Mogollon Rim, they spotted a Blackhawk helicopter parked off the runway in an area used for wildfire suppression aircraft. The Cessna taxied up next to the Blackhawk. One more swift transfer, and they were in the helicopter. The crew issued hearing protection to the family. Again, they were in the air within minutes, flying over the beautiful mountains covered in the various greens of the pines. They figured they were in the middle of Arizona, but they weren't really sure where.

The flight was over quickly, and they touched down in an open field surrounded by a pine forest. As the Blackhawk was spinning down, the family's attention focused on two six-passenger Polaris Rangers driving

307

out to meet the chopper. Two uniformed men riding in the UTVs exited the Rangers and walked over to collect their bags.

Curious as to where they were, Kayla inquired about their location once she was out of earshot of the kids. One of the men replied to her, "Ma'am, you're in the middle of Arizona, up on the Mogollon Rim near a place called Happy Jack. This is your safe house 'til things are—ah—stabilized. It should be just a few days, and then we'll have you back in Texas. This area was offered to us by a supporter of the cause—the WSA. So, let's get you and your family settled in your vacation home."

Since Kayla was not one to let others plan her life, she pursued the Marine for more information. "Do you know what's going on—what this is all about?"

The young Marine smiled. He had been well briefed by Jason to expect this from Kayla. "Ma'am, we're in the process of restoring the Constitution of the United States of America! It's our honor to protect the family of Colonel John Mogen, who is leading this restoration. Your father is our civilian commander in chief. He's also commander of the Constitution Restoration Expeditionary Forces, who have militia units located all over the United States. Our new nation will be called the Western Southern Alliance, and the capital will be located in Arlington, Texas. As we speak, there is a sorting out going on, deciding which states or parts of states will join the WSA."

Kayla could not contain her shock. In all her imagination, she had never thought this was what was going on. This whole undertaking was so surreal—just surreal.

As they headed away from the chopper, they spied a log home through the pines. When they cleared the trees, the family spotted a corral to the left side of the glorious cabin. Well, some might call it a cabin, but it was truly a grand lodge, tucked into the pines at the edge of an open meadow. Armed troops were stationed around the perimeter, about one hundred feet from the home itself. The family noticed there was another chopper landing zone on the other side of the main road as a large two-rotor

Chinook helicopter came in. There was quite an operation going on across the main road with a serious but temporary-looking encampment set up.

Mark, who had been escorting them on this trip, approached the family and motioned for them to follow him into the accommodations set up for them. "Let's get you settled in the house, and you all can figure out who goes where. Of course, one of the master suites needs to be reserved for your folks, who should be here in a couple of days. The guys will bring in your bags in a few minutes after you have settled on which rooms everyone will occupy."

Caleb let out an enormous whoop! "Dad—I knew we were going on a surprise vacation, but this is so radical! First, jets and helicopters, and now, this awesome place in the mountains! And you didn't tell us Papa and Nana are going to be here too! Wahoo!"

Caleb and Libby had been kept clear of the quick briefing the adults had received earlier. Before they'd left that morning, their mom had told them about the adventure they were going on. If needed, their dad would explain things later, at least to Caleb. He was a very smart and perceptive young man at the age of ten.

After finishing a simple dinner, Caleb came running in from the deck, which wrapped around three sides of the home, shouting to the family to hurry and come outside. Several Rocky Mountain elk were grazing amongst the trees. They looked shaggy, like they had a light tan winter coat on. Since it was late April, they were in the process of losing their winter coats. They would be calving in a month or so.

While the group was watching the majestic animals, a couple of yellow labs came running around the house, barking as they headed for the elk.

Kayla took off after them, yelling, "Sadie! Lilly! Leave it! Leave it!" The dogs stopped at the command and turned toward the family as the elk trotted off. Instantly, Sadie and Lilly swarmed Kayla, glad to find family. She endured them licking her face—at least a little. "Where did you two come from?"

Suddenly, Truen Walsh was behind her. She hadn't heard his approach. It was the Truen way. "I brought them from the Hills. Your dad's friend Jack Ellis gave me a ride."

Kayla was still trying to catch her breath from being surprised by Truen. She stepped away from the dogs and headed over to give him a huge hug. Truen's PTSD seemed to abate momentarily as he carefully hugged her back.

She whispered to him, "Thanks for bringing the dogs, Truen, and thank you for protecting my family—my folks."

He responded in a way that surprised her. "Ma'am, this is the very first time since arriving back from Afghanistan I've felt like I belonged to something. I—ah." He actually started to tear up, something he hadn't done for a long time. He'd been in robot mode for far too long as far as emotions went, just going through the motions and doing his job. It had kept him sane and stopped the suicidal thoughts. The guys were great—they were family—but something about this Mogen family was special.

Soon after, Caleb and Libby came running up to pet and hug the dogs with their parents right behind them. Kayla introduced everyone to Truen, explaining he had brought the dogs all the way from South Dakota. She continued to describe how she met him. "I heard about Truen last time I was up at the ranch. Before this all started, he was the overwatch at Mom and Dad's." She had noticed Truen above the ranch, moving through the trees, and had asked Jason about him. She knew more about him than he realized. "Truen," she questioned, "who's watching our folks' place right now?"

Truen observed all of them and paused before continuing. "Ma'am, the CIA took out your folks' place with a drone strike. It went up in flames a couple of hours after I got the dogs out of there. It will be rebuilt for them when it's safe to do so. There's evil in the deep state, and that's why we need to completely wipe out the faction. That's happening as we speak—I hope. You won't hear about that operation on the news."

Kayla didn't realize Dave, Jesse, and the kids were standing right behind her. She had held back her tears as Truen choked up, but now, she lost it again. Jesse started to cry too.

Caleb asked his mom, "Why are you crying? What did he mean, Mom? I know what a drone is. Who shot a missile at Papa and Nana's house? Why would they do that, Mom? Why?" Now, Caleb was crying as well.

Dave was livid as he gestured to Truen with a head nod to the right and started walking off. Truen followed immediately. "How much danger are we in exactly?" Dave demanded once they were out of earshot.

Truen hesitated longer than Dave felt comfortable with. He didn't really know him, so he was troubled by his prolonged silence. But when Truen answered, he spoke with authority. "Jason Wilder and the Colonels' Club have many friends in high places. This restoration has been in the planning stages for at least three years that I'm aware of. It's clear by the amount of backing from the rest of the military and private sectors that we have the support needed. I can't tell you we will be 100 percent safe here, but let's call it 99.6 percent. This contingency was planned quickly but effectively. We have your six, Dave. More people than you could possibly imagine are ready to give their lives for the family of John Mogen. He has already become a legend because of what happened at Ellsworth. He will be giving a speech later this morning, and then you will understand more."

Truen didn't bring up the fact that John had been injured at Ellsworth. He just didn't think the family needed to worry about that right now. "We're working on getting the deep state players out of the game," he continued. "Jason tells me the military has responded in numbers every true American would be proud of. But we thought this would be the case. Only a few teams think the Company still has the power to order them around, and I'm sure we're getting word out to the drone commanders and pilots to stand down."

Kayla and Jesse were occupying the kids as Dave and Truen spoke quite a few yards away. Caleb and Libby were entertaining themselves and the dogs by tossing sticks they found off the back deck. As the two sisters watched the action, Jesse said, "I have noticed, thanks to Jason, you might be having a change of heart when it comes to your political ideology."

Kayla was speechless, recognizing Jesse was right. Suddenly, she realized she had been convinced the country that she had grown up in needed to abandon the old, musty document and the despicable founders and take a new direction. After reading *The 5000 Year Leap*, she understood how offensive this was to her family and how patient they'd been with her, even when she'd called them names like, say, unenlightened. Now she had to face the fact that it had made her an outsider in her own family—the one person her family could not trust.

She looked at Jesse with red, swollen eyes. All she could utter was, "I'm so sorry for the way I've treated y'all." Jesse quickly grabbed her sister and engulfed her in a huge bear hug, which got both of them crying again. Would the sobbing ever stop? Moments later, the tears turned to laughter.

CHAPTER 58

MINOT AIR FORCE BASE — NORTH DAKOTA

Even in her sleep, she knew something was out of place. As Jaylynn reached over to touch John, she realized he wasn't in bed. John knew she couldn't sleep without him by her side. She glanced at the bedside clock and saw it was 3:33 a.m. Looking around the room, she focused on John hunched over the small desk, which sat against the opposite wall of their quarters. He had his arm in the sling like he was supposed to.

"John—John, what are you doing up? You need to rest."

He turned toward his beautiful wife. Even if her hair was a tangle, he could still recall those many years ago when his gorgeous bride had walked toward him. The only light in the room was coming from the small desk lamp he had on. John smiled at her and responded, "I'm working on my speech. Making a few changes. I want it to be just right."

Jay, who was more awake now, responded, "John—it is what it is. You need to come back to bed."

He smiled again. "I can't sleep—the shoulder hurts too much, and I will not take any more of that stuff they are giving me. I need to be completely lucid by 0900 hours. This has to be done right! Everyone is counting on me, and I need to have a clear head."

At that instant, Jay realized there was no going back to sleep. In six hours, her husband, who had made love to her on that flat rock in the sun before they'd left the Black Hills, the man she was just glad to have alive, would be the man delivering a speech that would be heard all over the world. She guessed he had a right to be concerned about every jot and tittle.

His voice broke into her thoughts. "Jay, I'm trying to think of the word that is worse than malicious. You know, planned maliciousness? That word."

Jay beamed at him. They had always been a good team. "I believe you're thinking of 'pernicious.' It's a step beyond malicious."

"Thanks, sweetie—that's it!"

Jaylynn was concerned about his discomfort; she hated it when he was hurting. Suddenly, she remembered the nurse giving her an envelope of prescription strength pain meds before leaving the base hospital. "John—I just remembered, I have some 800mg Ibuprofen that you can take." As she dug the package of pain reliever from the bottom of her purse, she got up and poured John a glass of water. These would help take the edge off the pain for a while.

CHAPTER 59

Jason Wilder and Colonel Bill Musgrave had everything ready to go. They had received word Colonel John Mogen was prepared to do his thing. His face was a red and purple mess on the right side where the bullet had grazed and split his ear in half, but his left side looked okay. He was adamant he wouldn't wear an arm sling during his ride on Jake or during his speech. The buses stood ready to transport some congressmen and senators away from the base.

Liberty in America would be covering the speech. They'd been instructed to place their cameras at three specific locations. John had been fitted with a radio earpiece so he could receive instructions or be notified of any problems that might arise. Jaylynn would be astride Buttercup, riding by John's side. Jason and his men would be mounted and stationed in a semi-circle around the Mogens as they entered the crowd. Daniel Rodriguez, one of Jason's team, would be waiting to take Jake and Buttercup when the couple dismounted at the edge of the stage.

The C-17 was up and running and would taxi up behind the assembly of Congress members and Supreme Court Justices. The strategy was to turn the C-17 at a safe distance from the crowd, but the blast from the engines would still ruffle the group and certainly get their attention. This display would signal the arrival of someone with power.

John was carefully fine-tuning the speech he'd written word by word. The world would be watching—he had to get it right. At the same time, he was testing his right arm by moving it around but was flinching and moaning as he did so.

315

Jay was stunned. "John, what on earth are you doing? Stop doing that—you're going to mess up what the surgeon repaired!"

John turned and managed a slight smile. "I'm trying to figure out what positions I can put my arm in and have the least amount of pain. I need to know this before I jump on Jake and give my speech." Now, he was gesturing with his left arm as he held his right arm in a neutral position.

Jaylynn was shaking her head. How did John think of these things? She knew how bad he must be hurting. She recognized how crazy the last fifteen hours had been, and now her husband was addressing the citizens of the U.S. It would mark a new chapter in their history, a new beginning, and her husband was the face of this first chapter. She was astonished his plan had worked.

Jaylynn's head was spinning. So much had changed in a matter of weeks. She had no house to go back to, but at least her family was safe. Their lives had been thrown up in the air, and she still wasn't sure where they would land. Would they ever be safe again?

It amazed her, as she looked over in his direction, that he was up and on task. She watched him with wonder and love. They both had committed to this crazy idea, not knowing if they would end up in charge, in prison, or in heaven. Now, they were at the biggest pivot point in American history since the Civil War. She still couldn't get her mind around it! They had found out what one man with an idea could do! With help, of course.

John was calling her name, and he was getting louder. "Jay! Earth to Jay!"

She was startled out of her train of thought. "John—yes. What do you need?" she responded as she came back into the moment.

"I need your help getting my clothes on. The uniform they brought last night—I have to get it on. But first, could you put some deodorant in my left armpit?" he asked in a frustrated tone.

Jaylynn smiled at him as she got up to get his uniform. She was wearing only a pair of panties, and his body tingled as he took in her scantily clad body gracefully exiting the bed.

"What, John? Why the look— Oh, good God, John…always the man! Get over it!" she exclaimed. At that instant, she knew he was going to be fine. She still had it. She still took his breath away, and she did love it and loved him.

With little effort and only a few moans, they got him into his uniform. Now, he looked like a real military man. He was dressed in fatigues as he'd requested—desert camo. The cap he wore sported the CREF acronym on its face. It also had the wings designating his rank of colonel. John had specially designed the CREF cap. It was dark brown with bright gold lettering. In the future, these caps would become the thing to wear in all the red states. They wouldn't be able to make them fast enough.

Tears filled Jaylynn's eyes as she stepped back to take in the complete picture. She quickly moved forward and carefully enveloped him with a full hug. John's left hand slid down her back, settled on her left butt cheek, and gently massaged as they kissed. For that moment, they were home in the Black Hills on their balcony, slow dancing to a fifties tune as the sun set.

John broke the silence first. "It's your turn now. Let's get you into your outfit!"

She knew John had picked it out and was a very interested spectator as she put on her bra and then the beige riding top and pants. The brown leather riding boots stopped just below her knees. Her fitted brown leather jacket was perfect. She stared at the matching brown riding crop, which was laying on the end of the bed, and said, "I'm not taking that riding crop. It will make me look like a Nazi, and that's definitely not the look I want!"

John was quick to reply, "Good call. I hadn't thought about the message it would send."

With his mouth wide open, he stood there gazing at his wife, speechless. Jay looked amazing.

His adrenaline was flowing nicely. He didn't even feel his shoulder injury but still felt some tightness around the stitches on the right side of his face as he grinned. He would see a plastic surgeon as soon as this all quieted down. Jaylynn had done her best to put some makeup on his face wound. John placed his cap on and adjusted it so tight that he could barely get it on his head. This was just for the ride. He didn't want to lose his hat during their entrance.

Jaylynn complained, but John insisted she not wear a hat. He wanted her striking silver hair, which reached to the middle of her back, flowing and flying in the wind as they rode in. The biggest question was whether she could keep Buttercup from racing ahead of Jake because she always won the races they had at their ranch. Tonight, they needed to highlight John on Jake—with any luck, slowly galloping in. Jake was amazing to look at, a Gypsy Vanner with the contrasting gray coat, a white mane, and feathers. He was an extremely handsome and formidable horse.

That was the picture CREF was presenting, and since only LIA was allowed on the base to cover this address, they had complete control. Cameras were in place, and staff were advised to cover the event as they saw fit. They knew the right side of John's face was still swollen and bruised but covered with makeup.

CHAPTER 60

Colonel Allan North pushed his chair back and stood up before the assembly started eating breakfast. He began by blessing the food, the fellowship, and the future success of their mission. Then, he said, "Ladies and gentlemen..." He paused, starting to vapor lock before launching back into his message. "Ladies and gentlemen—we've spent years working on this endeavor with blood, sweat, and many tears. This restoration of our beloved republic would not have been necessary if we had had servant leaders who were true to the Constitution and to our Creator. From the beginning, we failed to understand the long game the socialists and communists were playing. They invaded our institutions and got a foothold because we were asleep at the wheel. It's up to God and the historians to judge our past actions—or maybe I should say...our nonaction.

"Unfortunately, we had to do something extreme. We knew something audacious had to be prepared to turn this country back to God and the rule of law. That plan...this plan, which was one of many we had been considering and planning for, came to fruition when Colonel Mogen independently arrived at the same game plan. When he and his wife, Jaylynn, agreed to be our civilian leadership on this, it was on. We went fast, and we went big, and by God's mercy, it worked.

"So, here we are, facing the monumental task of building a Christian nation known as the Western Southern Alliance of States. We already have a faction in place, fighting back to keep all the states together and not separated into two countries. We know there will be challenges to face even as we are speaking to you today. A year of hard work is ahead of us. We thank and honor all of you for your bravery. We know just as our founders pledged at the beginning of this great union, you have pledged your lives, fortunes, and sacred honor to accomplish this.

"We'll hear from John Mogen in an hour or so. The Mogens' sacrifices are considerable. They lost their home during the takeover, and I'd personally like to thank John for putting his life on the line for all of us as our leader and our spokesman. He's no figurehead, and we place our complete trust in him going forward as we put this new nation together. Let's all roll up our sleeves and help him complete what we set out to do."

With that, Colonel North sat down, and the room burst into applause. All John could think about was the "going forward" part. He hadn't had much time to think about the next steps. He had written some things down, but he realized now they might actually be implemented. He would really have to look at everything. This had to be done right so the new nation didn't end up abandoning their Constitution again due to purposeful undermining of the principles, especially by the judicial branch, which had truly exceeded their powers.

John was poring over his notes as he sat at the table. He knew his written speech so well that he might not even need it on the dais as he addressed the assembly, but it would be placed on the podium waiting for him just in case.

He felt a hand gently nudge his left shoulder, but it wasn't Jay's. It was Jason Wilder, who'd quickly become the son he never had. "John, it's time to get to the plane. Your notes will go with Carl to the stage."

John had been so engrossed in attaining one last look, he didn't realize the entire congregation of the officer's dining room had gathered around him, along with Jason's men. He noticed a camera aimed at him. Scanning all the faces focused on him, he realized this was history in the making and got an overwhelming sensation again. *No crying, John,* he thought to himself. *Not this time.*

Jason and Eric helped John up from his chair. He accepted the assistance without complaint. Over to his left, he noticed Jay was observing him and giving him her "go get 'em" smile, along with a very subtle affirmative nod. She looked amazing!

With his feet firmly planted beneath him, John again looked over the assembly and observed everyone had removed their hats.

Jason moved to the center of the group. He was definitely a presence. "Ladies and gentlemen, let's pray… All-knowing, all-seeing, and all-powerful God, God of our founding fathers—bless us this day. We seek to restore not only our country but also our nation's devotion to you, our deliverer. You have blessed us with success in this restoration. We humbly ask that you continue to do so. Please forgive us for our failures. Our failure to speak out as the evil one slowly turned many in this nation against you. Let us go forth the way our forefathers did when the British were defeated. No killing but forgiveness. Let those who turned their backs on our Constitution and you, Lord, never gain power again as long as we have breath and faith in you. Let this day be remembered as the day truth prevailed and the liars were exposed by your light. In all we do, let your son, Jesus Christ, be glorified. God bless the WSA. Amen!"

As soon as Jason finished, a resounding chant of "WSA" started in the room and grew louder and louder until everyone was shouting at the top of their lungs. Jaylynn's tears were messing up her makeup—again.

Jake was calm even though there was commotion all around him in the C-17 cargo bay. The horses had been training with Jason's men to alleviate their nervousness in the bay. They knew the sound and feel of the jet and had been up and down the ramp several times. Even so, Buttercup was still restless.

As John approached Jake, he put his hand on him, and Jake instantly calmed to his touch, giving his familiar snort. Gypsy Vanners were such special horses. Jake sniffed John's right shoulder and then lowered his head down on that shoulder. John winced, but he still brought his right hand up to stroke Jake's cheek. Even though Jake had only been with him for a year, an instant bond had linked them together—a bond only understood by people who had had not just any horse but that special horse. A once-in-a-lifetime horse.

Jaylynn walked up and stood by John's side, carefully hugging him. John couldn't resist. "I see you fixed your makeup—you look amazing!"

Jay knew John was messing with her. "Leave me alone about my makeup! You know how I am!"

John continued to tease his wife, knowing she would be shedding more tears. "Just stay hydrated, honey."

Jay softly poked him in the ribs, and he released a groan. "Oh, God… John, I'm so sorry—so sorry!"

John started laughing and grimacing at the same time, and again, she gently smacked him as his moan grew louder.

As the C-17 was making its last turn, the jet blast hit the crowd of the Washington elites. The crew shut down the two engines as fast as they could so only the auxiliary power unit turbine was running. Jason and Eric would lead the contingency down the cargo ramp on their horses with John and Jaylynn following close behind. They would break into a loping gallop before they got to the crowd. The troops had separated the crowd in the center so they could ride through the middle. The ramp was down. It was time.

Jason and John heard the radio call in their earpieces. It was their go signal. Jason looked back at John and Jaylynn, smiled, and turned his head back to the front. John gave Jake their signal to move forward. As soon as they hit terra firma, the horse's speed increased from a walk to a loping gallop. What a sight!

It was obvious John and Jaylynn were the two to watch in the group. John was a sight to behold on Jake. He sat with power, confidence, and presence. At the same time, Jaylynn's silver hair was blowing in the wind. The spectacle of power and beauty had come to fruition. The crowd was transfixed. The murmuring got louder as they flew through the crowd.

Of course, Buttercup decided that it must be a race between her and Jake. Jaylynn had her hands full holding her back, soothing her with a gentle touch. Meanwhile, the pain in John's shoulder was talking to him, and the right side of his face was extra tight from the stitches.

Jason and Eric respectfully broke right and left as they approached the stage. The *LIA* had their cameras following John and Jaylynn as they rode through the center of the crowd. Jaylynn could not hold Buttercup back any longer, and on John's nod, Jay let her go. Jaylynn was a sight, riding off to the left ahead of John, her hair flying, a look of confidence on her face. She was in complete control of her ride, as people would comment later. One of the cameras followed her off, and another picked her up as she came to the right side of the stage. For a moment, she had inadvertently stolen the show, but now, the focus was back on John. He trotted up and dismounted Jake directly onto the stage, which stood three feet off the ground.

John was astonished as he stepped up to the podium and took his first look out into the gathering. He knew military personnel had been streaming in for the last twenty-four hours, but he was still stunned by the number of them surrounding the much smaller Washington crowd. They had closed ranks behind the C-17, so all were hemmed in. It was very moving to see the throng of military joining them in this fight from across the country. All flight operations would be stopped during his speech, and fighters were already in the air, patrolling the airspace around the Minot Air Force Base.

He turned full circle, taking in the total picture, and caught sight of the big screen behind him. He had to chuckle as he stood there looking at himself...looking at himself...

At that point, he received communication through his earpiece. Comms was calling. "Colonel Mogen, we have one of our F-16s chasing another Reaper about ten miles out. Be ready to clear the stage on our call." He looked over to Jay, who had dismounted and was standing on the edge of the stage to his left.

As she listened to the comms report through her earpiece, she swiftly glanced over at her husband. He smiled at her—a big smile! What the heck? She got it and smiled back. If they went out this way, it would be together. She completed her journey from the edge of the stage to John's side. A roar went up from the crowd of service people surrounding the

Washington elites as she put her arm around John's waist and waved. John waved too, and the crowd thundered again. What a weird and wonderful feeling.

The comms radio came to life again. "Sir, we got the Reaper. Get ready to hear the rumble." About three seconds later, the reverberation hit Minot AFB. John and Jay did not recoil.

After another five seconds, all involved were notified the music would be starting. John held onto Jay as she attempted to leave the stage. He whispered, "Stay with me for the song."

Shortly after the music started, lyrics flashed onto the screen. The song had become an anthem of sorts for believers in the military. The Washington crowd, especially the clueless democrats, didn't know what was happening. Clapping started up in sync with the music. It grew louder as over seven thousand servicemembers clapped in unison. Meanwhile, many in the Washington group were growing more anxious.

By the time the singing started, John and Jay were fighting back tears. To hear "Days of Elijah" sung with this much passion was overwhelming. Then, all broke into the chorus: *Here He comes, riding on the clouds...* The sound was incredible—the very ground was shaking.

John held tight to the podium as tears fell onto his speech. He could feel the presence of God here—in this place, at this historic moment. He glanced over at his wife; her mascara was streaming down her cheeks. John smiled down at her, and as he released his grip on her hand, he thanked God for the woman who stood by his side. She gave him one last hug, whispered, "I love you, Colonel Mogen," and then stepped behind him and walked off stage right.

Comms came on and asked John to confirm his mic was hot. He gave them a thumbs up. Comms responded, "Okay, you're live. Be careful what you say from now on." John gave them another thumbs up. Then, he turned off the mic, reached for the Kleenex on the podium, wiped his eyes, and blew his nose. After that, he turned his mic back on.

The last chorus of "Days of Elijah" reverberated through the air, ending with a roar that was absolutely deafening. John bit his bottom lip as he fought back more tears. Jay was a hot mess just offstage. He began to pray silently. *Lord, help me to do this. May it bring nothing but glory to you and your son. Let me feel the presence of the Helper right now! Thank you, Lord—thank you.*

"Okay, John—give us one more thumbs up if you're ready to go." Then, all waited for John to give them the signal.

CHAPTER 61

LAKE MARY ROAD – MOGOLLON RIM – CENTRAL ARIZONA

Dave had been working alongside the communications guys setting up the monitors. They would be watching the *Liberty in America* network feed and also the WSA feed, which took in different camera angles. He was so excited that he couldn't sit down. Jesse and Kayla were already down in front of the largest flat screen. Dave brought his laptop and set it up on the coffee table in front of them.

Somehow, all the other news stations' programming had been shut down. Only one national feed was showing up from the satellites. An emergency broadcast message came on, announcing an impending address to the nation by a spokesman for the Western Southern Alliance of States. Panic had the nation in its grip. Almost every American that could, would be watching to see what was going on. The standdown of the regular Armed Forces of the United States was almost complete. Even though the deep state was still working behind the scenes to fight the WSA initiatives, it was sorely losing.

Kayla was still a bit perplexed while Dave and Jesse seemed to be in the know and all in. Kayla was a person who liked to control all situations; however, at this time, she had never felt so out of control, personally and professionally, in all her life. Her emotions were bubbling up in unexpected ways, and most of all, she had alienated Jason Wilder to the point of no return. What exactly would they be seeing on the screen? She didn't have long to wait.

The *LIA* feed came up with a pan across a large crowd. Then, it focused on the cargo ramp of a C-17. The feed switched to a split screen with the news anchor on the right side announcing the civilian commander of the Constitution Restoration Expeditionary Forces had arrived. The screen reverted to full picture as the announcer continued his commentary.

"Let's watch his arrival. We're told his name is John Mogen, and he serves as commander of the civilian militia that formed up all over this country. He will be... Wait a minute... Okay, here he... It's my understanding he is the one with the ball cap on, and his wife is riding next to him. Yes, they are on horseback. We've been informed the crowd of civilians they are riding through consists of all members of the Congress, both the House of Representatives and the Senate, as well as the U.S. Supreme Court Justices. As you can see, the rest of the crowd surrounding them are men and women in the regular forces of the United States military."

Kayla's mouth dropped open as she saw her parents riding through the crowd. She recoiled as Dave and Jesse joined in yelling and clapping with the military personnel already cheering. The family now caught a glimpse of their mom standing offstage. They had watched her ride in on Buttercup moments before, and she'd looked amazing. Now, she was striding on stage to stand by their dad's side, wrapping her arm around his waist as a roar went up from the crowd. Kayla actually shook her head and refocused. The scene was so surreal to her. The whole world was watching her parents right now.

When the music started, Jesse and Dave started clapping along. They hopped up and joined arms just as the singing of "Days of Elijah" started. Kayla sat in amazement as she watched many of the military people on the screen do the same. When the chorus came, her sister and brother-in-law started swaying back and forth as most of the military personnel were doing on screen. They were singing at the top of their lungs and knew every word of the song.

Kayla had never heard of it and felt completely left out since she had put God out of her life years ago. What in the world was going on? When the song ended, Dave and Jesse screamed, applauded, and jumped up and down. They must be possessed by something. Not the devil—there was no devil.

Jesse turned and noticed Kayla still sitting on the couch. She had tears in her eyes as she looked at her lost sister who didn't have a clue.

The camera was now on their father, who was at the podium. The closeup on the computer feed showed him wiping his eyes and giving a thumbs up. Dave exclaimed, "Look at the right side of his face. It looks like a wound of some kind. I think I see stitches—yes, look, stitches and swelling." The *LIA* feed was set up on the left side of the stage and was just enough off-center to hide his injuries on his right side.

Unreal… As she was trying to digest the scene on the screen, Kayla caught a glimpse of Jason below the stage in front. He had a helmet and sunglasses on, but she could tell from his stance and build that it was Jason. Her body reacted immediately. Her face flushed a deep shade of pink. Thank God Dave and Jesse's eyes were glued to the screen, and they didn't notice her body's reaction to just seeing Jason. God, that man had an incredible effect on her—no other guy even came close.

What have I done? she thought to herself. *And how can I fix it?* Apologizing wasn't something she was good at, but she would do it if that was what it took to get him to forgive her. She wanted this man in her life—bad. His intellect, his will, and his physical strength were all something she had never experienced before in a man. She admonished herself again about always having it her way. She didn't need to control everything in her life at every moment but needed to let life just flow. She began to understand what her mom and sister had been trying to explain to her all along. A relationship, a true love relationship, was compromise—meeting in the middle. Both individuals giving of themselves 150 percent to the other. Being strong together.

Kayla had been through two relationships, both of which had ended with the man telling her they were tired of her attempts to dominate everything. They'd had no room to be themselves. She'd stifled them, and the thought of a life like that had driven them away. She was unbending. But marriage was bending toward one another, not away.

"Kayla!" Jesse had almost screamed it. "Dad is getting ready to speak—pay attention!"

Kayla shook herself out of her self-pity and refocused her attention on the large screen.

MINOT AIR FORCE BASE – NORTH DAKOTA
APRIL 29TH—0900 HOURS – 18 HOURS INTO THE RESTORATION

John gave a thumbs up and was ready to address the throngs of patriots and those watching on air. His mic was hot, and the stage director responded with a thumbs up to start anytime. John took a deep breath, cleared his throat, and began.

"First, we pray to God Almighty. Father God. God of Abraham, Isaac, and Jacob. God of this nation's founding fathers. The Uncreated One. It was only by your divine providence we were allowed to exist as a nation. Your hand was upon us, leading us, helping us form a government. For the first time in five thousand years of human history, you gave the power to the people. You led us to form a government that was meant to protect our rights and ensure maximum freedom to pursue happiness. We've become the greatest nation on the face of the earth because of you. We founded this nation on your principles. We thrive and help others thrive because of our reliance on you and what you have taught us. Forgive those who have diverted this nation from you and attempted to make us a godless nation. Today, April 29th , will from this day forward be known as the day our nation reasserted to all the world that you are our God, and we are your people, and we will again live by your principles and restore our Constitution. Our founders said they knew your finger was on that document when pen was put to paper. We will again be called a Christian nation. We ask forgiveness if what we have done has caused harm. Our intent was to prevent bloodshed and avoid the disaster of a second civil war. We dedicate this new nation in your name. Those of us who still believe in you and abide by the rule of law will move forward with great anticipation as we follow your lead to reform this nation... One nation under you, God. Bless us in this endeavor, and dear God, may you bless the WSA! Amen."

As John ended the prayer, a roar went up from the crowd, and it was deafening. The chant of "WSA" began again. John waited patiently for the cacophony to die down enough to start his address.

"I take full responsibility for any loss of life at Ellsworth Air Force Base and CIA headquarters as well as those who have lost their lives evacuating the targeted cities. While the rogue action was created by one of our members, the destruction of the CIA headquarters still drops on me. We can do nothing to reverse this action but can only deeply regret what happened.

"Many of you may not realize how close we were to a bloody civil war. Our last civil war had at least 620,000 war causalities and an unknown number of civilian losses. Our actions have prevented great loss of life overall. We seek a peaceful separation of states. Those who honor God and the rule of law, which is the Constitution, see no way to reconcile with those who would usher in socialism and tyranny as a package. This mindset will only bring misery as it has every time it's been tried anywhere in the world. We will not swallow that pill!"

Another resounding uproar from the crowd forced John to stop speaking for a time. After the assembly quieted to a rumble, John finished his declaration. "This stops here and now!"

As John proclaimed this last statement, two columns of soldiers formed a human corridor from the assembly to the waiting buses. John continued with contempt in his voice as he directly addressed the Congress.

"All members of the Democratic Party—you have disregarded the Constitution. You've purposely brought this nation into bankruptcy with unsustainable debt. You've passed laws directly in conflict with God's moral law. You have persistently failed to protect our national borders and continued to create chaos, causing crime and death to vulnerable women and children. You've tried to put an end to our energy independence and weaken our military. You have attacked our right to free speech and our right to worship as we see fit—being led by our conscience. You've attempted to deny our right to self-defense. You've attempted to make wrong right and right wrong. You have purposefully ignored the Constitution of the nation after taking an oath asserting true faith and allegiance to it. You are evil liars. You're no longer part of us. By my authority, I charge you all with treason against this nation and our Constitution, which each of you swore to uphold, I might add. The penalty for treason against the United States is death!"

A terrifying outcry rose from the crowd, but John continued with disdain in his voice. "But no one is going to be executed here today. We the people are removing you from our midst. You are all hereby sentenced to a lifetime banishment from our land starting immediately. Now, follow the instructions from the Armed Forces personnel as you load the buses. You are being taken to Emerson, Alberta, Canada. You shall never set foot on this soil again. If you attempt to return, any and all citizens of the USA or WSA may summarily execute you on the spot. You are ordered to surrender your United States passport before you leave. You're no longer a citizen of the United States of America, and you're not welcome within our borders. We will provide transportation to your family members if they wish to join you in Canada."

The congressmen and senators, who had just been told they were to be expelled from the United States, started loudly protesting, saying they'd been lied to about why they were being brought to Minot. However, because they were completely surrounded by the troops, they didn't have a choice but to proceed to the buses. The troops had placed fifty-five-gallon drums at the entrances to the buses. The banished individuals' passports were tossed into the open fire and burst quickly into flames before they even boarded.

They screamed, "This will not stand!" and "We'll be back, and you will all hang!" as they were forced onto the buses.

John resumed his address after the loud whining and threatening had died down. "For you republicans, we have generated a list, which will be read by Senator Paul Carbajal and Congressman Ted Gosnor at this time. For those of you whose names are read aloud, please come forward into the roped-off area in front of the stage. Supreme Court Justice Calvin Thomas will also read the names of the Justices that are to remain on the high court. All names not listed are immediately removed from Congress or the high court. We are providing 747s to fly you back to Washington, D.C. Thank you for your service. You'll never be allowed to hold an office of trust in either the USA or WSA again."

John stepped back from the podium and waited while the names were called. As the three gentlemen reached the end of their lists, John stepped up and stated to the crowd, "The buses to my right will transfer you to your planes."

John paused for a moment as the remaining degraded members were ushered out. "Now, let me speak to the people of the United States. Business and government will continue to operate without disruption while we transition into two autonomous countries: the USA and the WSA. The free market will flourish, and regulation of businesses by the government will purposefully be dismantled as much as possible. We believe it will take one year or less to peacefully separate.

"The proposed map of the WSA states and boundaries is available on the WSA's official website. Individual counties within certain states will have to decide which way they want to go. The WSA must be contiguous, so those of you who wish to live in the Christian nation, which will be the Western Southern Alliance, may have to relocate.

"If you are a county sheriff in the Western Southern Alliance of States, listen carefully. We will maintain order—as peacefully as possible. We're depending on you to follow the Constitution within your own jurisdictions. More information can be found on our website.

"Now, let me speak to all who have been training for the war to regain our republic. You are now members of the Constitution Restoration Expeditionary Forces. Your actions must remain peaceful if at all possible. You are charged with assisting your local sheriff as he or she needs. Within the borders of the WSA, you are safe to make yourself known. Again, this directive is spelled out on our website.

"Thanks to all for standing down long enough for us to accomplish this with minimum bloodshed. We all recognize how close we were to an all-out civil war. We would also like to thank the Armed Forces for standing down and supporting our goal to peacefully restore the Constitution. We'll be working extremely hard to put in place a limited government that will properly protect our God-given rights.

"In one month's time, on May 30th, we will be gathering in Arlington, Texas. All states within the Western Southern Alliance territory will send two representatives. They must believe in God and be knowledgeable about our Constitution. We'll be discussing how to make adjustments to the Constitution to ensure this corruption will never be allowed to happen again. Only men and women of high moral and religious character need be sent.

"We also would like to thank the many private citizens who have given time, money, and resources to the cause of restoring freedom. Just like our founding fathers did, many pledged their lives, fortunes, and sacred honor to this restoration.

"This is our new beginning; we must let peace and freedom reign across this land as we renew our allegiance to the Lord and to our founding principles of freedom! Don't get me wrong—we have a lot of work to do and many questions to answer. Remember this Restoration Day. Remember, by the grace of God, we saved hundreds of thousands, possibly millions, of lives by avoiding a bloody civil war. Our Armed Forces faced a dilemma of who to support. They understand the oath they swore to preserve, protect, and defend the Constitution, and we also have the same goal.

"Remember this: During this short transition, the U.S. federal government will operate as it has in the past, though it's sloppy and top heavy. Commerce will continue normally; only government will change—at least in the Western Southern Alliance territory. The WSA's government footprint will become much, much, *much* smaller. The government will protect your God-given rights and not attempt to take them away.

"Tomorrow at 0800 hours Mountain Time, we'll have a news conference with several cable networks participating. You all need to get on board with what we have just accomplished. Simply stated, we have saved the American republic. Business will thrive, and regulations and taxes will be absolutely minimized! God bless the WSA!"

The remaining multitude at Minot erupted with shouts and applause. Now, John was done—not just with his speech but done physically. He received word through his earpiece that the cameras from *LIA* had finished transmitting. At that point, he leaned forward on the podium and, with no strength left, barely held himself up with his left arm.

Jason jumped up onto the stage with Jaylynn by his side. He whispered, "Let's get you offstage, John. Are you hearing me, John? You did a great job—great job."

Jaylynn was crying again as she and Jason assisted John off the stage and into a Polaris Ranger. He was spent, and they had to get him back to his quarters before he collapsed.

LAKE MARY ROAD – MOGOLLON RIM – CENTRAL ARIZONA

Kayla was absolutely in shock over what she had just witnessed. Dave, Jesse, Truen, and Jack had shouted their approval throughout the speech—so much so that Kayla had had to keep turning up the volume.

They were watching the military feed now; the *LIA* cameras had signed off. Kayla watched in disbelief as Jason and her mother helped her father off the stage. She could see the black and blue bruising coming out on his beat-up face as the makeup ran down in his sweat, and his shoulder was sitting at a strange angle even after the surgery that had put his body back together a few hours before. She and Jesse started to cry as they saw their mother weeping and gingerly helping their dad offstage. John had hung in until the end.

Kayla was still trying to come to terms with what had transpired on screen. It was hard to wrap her mind around the fact her parents, along with her uncle, were at ground zero—the key players in this whole thing. It also appeared they had actually pulled it off!

Jesse grabbed her and pulled her out of her thoughts, literally yelling in her face. "They did it! They actually saved the republic—our rights! Kayla! Do you understand what happened? They did it, and now, there won't be another civil war. Thank the Lord!"

Kayla could not find the words to respond to Jesse.

It didn't even feel real as she watched Jason at her dad's side. He had his helmet off now. She knew Jason and her mom would take care of her father. Reality sucked, and hers was coming at her full force. Would Jason ever speak to her again? She'd spoken to him with such anger the last time on the phone. She knew if anyone talked to her like that, she wouldn't give them another thought. Would he ever even acknowledge her again? Even with all the uncertainty about their relationship, she couldn't keep her body from experiencing a tingle every time she got a glimpse of him on camera.

Stop thinking about yourself, Kayla, she chastised herself. *You should be thinking about Dad and Mom right now.* She shot out of her seat abruptly and realized her parents would be either seen as heroes or traitors, depending on who the question was posed to. But in her heart, she knew they were heroes.

Kayla was startled out of her thoughts by Jesse, who again was in her space. "Kayla, who was that gorgeous guy helping Mom get Dad off the stage? He looks so much like Chris Kyle—you know, the Navy SEAL sniper who was murdered. They did a movie on his life. I can't believe how stunning the guy is!"

Kayla's face started to flush. "That's Jason Wilder. He's former Air Force Special Forces. He owns a computer and security—I mean, his company does computer systems and people security out of Houston."

Jesse's eyes opened a little wider. "That's the guy Mom was telling me about—she said sparks flew between the two of you from the moment you met. Is that the same guy, Kayla? Is it?" Jesse read the look on her baby sister's face and knew the answer. Kayla's expression said it all.

"Jesse, I've never had such a strong reaction to a man like I've had with Jason. Since the first time our eyes met in South Dakota. You know how much of a control freak I am, but I lose it all when I'm in his presence or even when I see him on screen. I can't stop myself and it's—it's…uncomfortable for me."

Jesse put her hands on her hips, looked her sister in the eye, and let her have it. "Bull crap, Kayla! Those kinds of feelings should be nothing but exciting to you—not 'uncomfortable'! Let it happen. Let go for once in your life, for God's sake! Get out of control, or you just might lose him!"

Kayla stood there, staring at her sister. Through the years, she'd observed Jesse and Dave, who had the same type of relationship as their mom and dad. Both marriages reflected an easygoing, fun-loving bond with the blessing of being together. They played off each other, competed with each other in all facets of their marriage.

Kayla had never felt that with any of her boyfriends. She had to ask her sis, "What is the secret, Jesse? How do you do it—you and Dave?"

Just as she asked the question, Dave came over and grabbed her sister. He lifted her in the air, set her back down, and bit her neck—geez. Jesse was giggling like a schoolgirl and loving every second.

Dave realized he had stepped into a girls' heart-to-heart when he witnessed the look Kayla gave him. He planted a serious kiss on Jesse and then turned to the kids. "Come on—let's go for a ride in the Ranger! Truen will drive for us. Let's find some elk!"

Kayla was staring at her sister with that "okay, tell me" look that begged to be answered. Jesse collected herself and began the story. "It all started when I asked Mom, 'How will I know when I meet the man of my dreams? The one I want to spend the rest of my life with?' She told me this story about when she met Dad. It was lust at first sight, and within a week, after two dates, she knew he was the one. There was no question in her mind, but then it got weird. You know how this family has a thing for chocolate peanut butter cups? Do you know why that is?"

Kayla was deep in thought about the smiles and laughter over peanut butter cups. The crazy *in-love* looks delivered between Mom and Dad and then Jesse and her husband had always perplexed her, and she felt like she wasn't in on some inside joke. Kayla finally replied, "I always wondered what the big deal was and why we used them for s'mores instead of just plain chocolate. Okay, sis—tell me. What's the big deal?"

"Okay, but you need to ignore the yuck factor when I tell you this because it's our parents—got it?" Jesse waited for her to respond. When Kayla nodded in the affirmative, Jesse continued. "Okay, okay—this is how I remember Mom telling it to me. They were on their second date. They had left work and were having a picnic together in a park. Mom had packed some peanut butter cups. As they were finishing lunch, Mom slipped one into her mouth without Dad knowing it. Okay—okay—they had already kissed by this time. Dad and Mom's eyes met, and he leaned in and started to kiss her. I mean—oh God—French kiss her. She was trying to return the kiss and swallow the dang peanut butter cup at the same time, but it was too late—Dad got the full taste of the chocolate and peanut butter. He pulled back with eyes wide and then broke into a huge smile. Mom said she started to apologize and was seriously embarrassed, but in the meantime, Dad asked if she had any more of them. She said yes and then questioned why, still not quite catching on as his grin grew even wider. Then, he took the cup she offered and popped it into his mouth. He chewed a little and then started kissing her again—yes, French kissing. Tongues, peanut butter, and chocolate all mixed together."

Kayla could not handle it. "Stop, Jesse—just stop. You have to be making this up, so just stop it."

Jesse smiled, holding her hands up as she crossed her heart. "Now, the first time Dave and I went camping, he brought the ingredients to make s'mores. I didn't tell him what to bring, and guess what he brought for the chocolate? Peanut butter cups! I already knew he was the one, but—boy—did that seal the deal. A life together with peanut butter cup kisses."

Wow! Kayla just started laughing. Her whole life, she'd seen this unspoken bond in her mom and sister's relationships with their spouses, but she had never truly noticed. "Is this a real thing, Jesse—really?"

Jesse went to the kitchen, then came back with some peanut butter cups and set them on the end table. They waited at least twenty minutes before Dave, the kids, and Truen returned. Truen normally didn't come in the house at all, but Caleb had forgotten his ball cap in the Ranger, so he walked into the great room to drop it off.

Dave looked at his wife, wondering how the talk had gone as he glanced between the two sisters. Without hesitation, Jesse picked up a peanut butter cup from the table, opened it, and began to eat it with "yums" and a little moan. Dave's response was immediate. He grabbed a cup and popped it into his mouth.

Kayla was about to gag as Dave and Jesse headed off to their bedroom. She yelled after them, "I'll watch the kids. Remember…you have kids!"

As she turned back to Truen, she noticed he was staring down at a peanut butter cup. Kayla smiled and declared, "Go ahead, Truen. You can have one. Be my guest. Take two or three if you want."

"Thanks, Kayla—these are like heroin to the team. Jason makes sure we have a stash of them all the time. He packs them for all our assignments. They make great s'mores when we're on camping trips."

As Truen turned and walked away, Kayla's body erupted in chills, and then she was swept up in a physical longing even she could no longer suppress. She picked up a peanut butter cup and imagined French kissing with one in her mouth. Would Jason ever talk to her again? Would he ever look at her again? She was crying softly as she popped the peanut butter cup in her mouth. Jason loved these—of course, he did. Ridiculous—just ridiculous.

MINOT AIR FORCE BASE – NORTH DAKOTA

It was 0500 hours when Jaylynn's eyes slowly opened and focused on John sitting at the small desk in their room. He was diligently writing. Shaking her head, she noticed he at least had his right arm in his sling. He had had a good night except for the two times he had turned to his right side. As she drifted back to sleep, she noticed there was some dried blood on his pillow, which must have been from the wound on his face. She didn't see the streak of dried blood that had gathered at his chin.

Jaylynn stirred again at 0600 hours. The previous day had exhausted them both, and as she lay there, she realized she had slept solid for ten hours. When she got up to pee, John lifted his head from his task and followed her journey across the room. She only had panties on, and John never got tired of seeing her mostly naked. It never got old—never.

Her sleepy eyes met his. "What, John? What's with the big, goofy grin on your face?"

"I love you—what a body!"

Jaylynn didn't feel hot. "I'm a complete mess! I have to take a shower." Suddenly realizing he was up and dressed, she asked, "What are you doing up so early?"

The look on John's face instantly turned somber. "Don't you remember the press conference with the media is today? I'm writing down some questions I imagine I'll be asked. I want to be ready. I don't know how many questions I'll actually get, and I expect the three colonels will get most of them, but I need to be prepared. We have a briefing scheduled at 0900 hours, and the interview has been changed to 1300 hours."

"John, did you forget you are also a colonel?" As Jaylynn reminded him, she got a glimpse of the right side of his face with the dried blood line down to his chin. "Put the pen down, John. Get up and get in the shower with me. You need help getting cleaned up."

John was quick to take her up on her offer. The shower wasn't the biggest, but they would make do, and he needed another Ibuprofen anyway. *No friskiness this morning,* he thought, but Jaylynn didn't look like a mess. She never looked like a mess to him.

As they all sat around at breakfast, Colonel Bill Musgrave appeared nervous—much more stressed than normal. Colonel Allan North picked up on his edginess and asked him if he was ready to answer questions.

"Hell yes, I'm ready. If one of those reporters gets smart with me, I may have to give them a good slap to the face!" Allan just stared as Bill carried on. "Don't give me that ring knock on the table, Allan. I'll really try hard to control myself."

Colonel Carl Justine sat there and just smiled. "Bill, we've communicated to them they can ask anything they want, so they may try to push our buttons. Hopefully, they will ask us what the people really want to know. All we can do is answer truthfully—simple as that."

Musgrave literally growled as he put another bite of pancake in his mouth. That set them all off laughing.

The interview stage was set up so the four colonels were sitting behind a long table at the front of the crowd. John sat at the far right with Carl next to him. Carl leaned over to John and whispered, "Can you believe it's been thirty-six hours since we started this operation? Exactly thirty-six hours…" John looked at him and just smiled. God was surely protecting them.

Jason was standing at John's six, and Jaylynn, sitting off to the right of the stage, admired him in his full dress uniform. She wished for just a moment that Kayla would wake up and see what was possible with Jason. He was wicked smart and looked like he had just walked off the cover of a romance novel. However, it didn't bode well that they had kept things from Kayla, and it had hurt her. Kayla had never handled being excluded from the plan well.

The small audience of a little over a hundred included the Minot AFB officers and their wives as well as some enlisted who had been picked by lottery for the remaining seats. All in attendance were asked to remain silent during the interview. No clapping or cheering. The three different cable news networks that were represented had sent their best military experts. Sitting with their backs to the crowd were Pete Heidleman, an Army officer, and Greg Kellerman and Lea Gabella, both former fighter pilots.

Lea was first to direct a question to the colonel of her choice. "Colonel Mogen, you have been called by some, and I quote, 'the biggest monster of a terrorist in world history.' How would you respond to that description?"

Jaylynn was absolutely mortified, but John was ready for this question.

"Thanks for not sugarcoating it, Lea. I take full responsibility for what has taken place. Three airmen were killed at Ellsworth AFB, one at the main gate and two during the firefight when we were trying to get into the C-17, and we've been informed over one thousand people were killed at Langley. This restoration of our republic was designed as a bloodless rebirth of our country, for our citizens and for our Constitution. I offer no excuses, but I do take exception to the description in your statement.

"I believe we were within months of a second civil war in this country. Our first Civil War resulted in 620,000 American soldiers dead and 476,000 wounded. This second civil war would've been much worse. If you check with the *Civil War Center*, you will see the number of people who died in the conflict is estimated at 750,000 if you combine both military and civilian deaths. In 1860, there were thirty-one million people in the United States. That means that 2.5 percent of the population died in the first Civil War. With today's population, that would mean 8.25 million people would possibly be dead if we had continued on the path to a second civil war. Chairman Mao and Joseph Stalin, along with Adolph Hitler, killed an estimated one hundred million people in the last century. My question to you is how do you measure monsters?"

The room went silent after the question was posed. Sitting on the left end of the table, Colonel Allan North was smiling. He then interjected. "Remember, Lea—Colonel Mogen didn't cause the deaths at the CIA headquarters. That was orchestrated and carried out by Naval Captain Torger Vigdahl. However, we take the blame for not recognizing what he was planning."

Pete Heidleman asked the next question. "Colonel Mogen, you say the WSA will be a Christian nation. How do you plan to handle the abortion question? Are you a womb to tomb guy?"

Jaylynn, now standing with her arms wrapped around her body, was so proud of the way John had answered his first question but was again holding her breath as John contemplated this next one.

"Well, Pete, I think science and theology are not enemies in this case. It's clear at the point of conception—that spark of life—a unique human being is there. The form doesn't matter—the substance does. That being said, I'm not a womb to tomb guy. The term womb is too vague. I'm a conception to coffin guy. The WSA will defend the rights given to us by God, and one of those is life. The WSA will defend life from conception—no exceptions."

A shout followed by full-on cheering came out from the crowd. Colonel North rose from his seat and reminded everyone there were to be no outbursts during the rest of the interview. Those in the gathering immediately grew silent.

The next question was directed to Colonel North by Greg Kellerman. "Colonel North, how did you get the military to back this—this, ah… coup?"

Colonel North hesitated. "I guess I can divulge that now. We have spent the last five years actually teaching and explaining the Constitution to all the officers and enlisted men and women we could. Since the Constitution is mentioned in the oath we all take when we enter service, and our public schools are not instructing our youth on it, we knew we had to educate our country's military…

"If you take an oath to support and defend the Constitution against all enemies, foreign and domestic, you need to know the Constitution and how we have 'God-given' rights. I can tell you now, our military personnel take this oath seriously, and they now recognize how 'domestic' enemies were trying to destroy this country. By the way, we would like to thank David Barton and the Wallbuilders for all their help with this training. Okay, Lea—next question."

By now, Jaylynn was barely breathing. Each question was a constructive one, and she was elated at how prepared the colonels were. There was no discussion about subjects being out of bounds.

"Colonel Mogen—what now? Are you really going to build a separate country? Can you fill us in on what your plan is?"

Things had moved forward so quickly that Jaylynn was also concerned John might stumble over this question. Together, they had drawn up a map of what area they hoped the WSA would contain, but they really hadn't talked about any details.

John looked down at his notes and pulled out a sheet of paper. "First, let me say the U.S. government in Washington, D.C., will continue to operate for a period of one year. Your benefits such as Social Security and Medicare will continue. We will immediately eliminate many government departments' authorities in the WSA states, such as the Departments of Education, Energy, and Interior.

"Any state or part of a state that wants to join the WSA and isn't on our preliminary map is free to hold elections and present the results to the WSA. We, the WSA, will be having a Constitutional Convention in Arlington thirty days or so from now. You'll be given the details soon.

"We will be eliminating the sixteenth amendment and going to a national sales tax. We will run on a balanced budget. We will set term limits on representatives in an amendment. If we have a Senate, we'll eliminate the seventeenth amendment, and the state legislatures will choose senators. The fourteenth amendment will be clarified so that anchor babies are gone. We will require any law passed by our Congress to justify the proposed law by legal brief tying it to an enumerated power.

"All representatives elected by the states must take a course on the Constitution and pass a test to prove their understanding of it. Our new Supreme Court nominees must do the same. They will also be required to have full knowledge of the Federalist Papers, and they must understand what our founding fathers meant in the various articles and sections of the Constitution. Original meanings will be understood and followed.

"Military personnel will be given the opportunity to stay with the outlands or join WSA forces. The WSA will retain control of all nuclear capability as well as Space Force personnel and assets. The WSA will ensure we have energy independence. We will match any tariffs other countries attach to our exports. If you want free trade with the WSA, drop your tariffs to zero. I'd recommend the patriots in the outlands migrate to the WSA states. I would also recommend that anyone who is a Satan worshipper or who belongs to an intolerant religion seeking to dominate or destroy those who don't believe as they do migrate out of the WSA states within six months.

"To those who are now part of the Constitution Restoration Expeditionary Forces, we know you have been training for this moment—some of you, for years. We have sent out a notice to all county sheriffs in the WSA states. We have informed them many trained patriots are available to help them in any way they need. We ask that no vigilante actions be taken against anyone. Remember, this is a non-violent restoration. We do have at least two rogue officers with troops who have chosen not to accept the peaceful separation. We ask all of you in those areas to report to your sheriff ASAP and offer your help. We're sending regular troops to help with these issues. Colonel North can give more details on this.

"The WSA states—especially the western states—need to prepare to take control over all of the national parks, national monuments, national forests, and Bureau of Land Management lands. You, as a state, will decide what to do with these lands. The federal government has no enumerated power in our current Constitution to hold bare land. If you choose, by vote of the people in your state, to keep them as parks, understand that the WSA will not be responsible for the upkeep or operation of these parks. If the convention of WSA states chooses to change this decision, it will be done at the convention.

"The governors of the WSA states have already been invited to a meeting in Arlington, Texas, fifteen days from now. Please understand the WSA government will move fast and decisively. Our current Congress has become a self-serving, overspending nightmare. This stops now. The culprits who are downright traitors are gone. As you saw, they have been banished from this country for the rest of their lives. It's going to be a bumpy ride for a while, but the outcome will be an unbelievable blessing for all law-abiding and God-fearing persons. I think I have spoken enough for now. Rest assured, we have a plan."

The room was in awe of what had just been articulated. If anyone was in doubt about what was going to happen going forward, it was clear the colonels—especially John—had a clear blueprint, a vibrant vision going forward.

Jaylynn observed the fatigue in John's face and knew he was feeling his injuries. Carl noticed her as she shifted her head sideways toward John. Jason—who noticed everything—saw Jaylynn's head bob motion as well.

In an instant, Carl spoke up. "Thanks, John! That was a lot of great information. I believe Colonel Mogen needs to take a break after that. Let me give some more detail on the governors' meeting coming up."

Jason bent down and whispered in John's left ear. John slowly got up with Jason standing directly behind him. No one in the crowd perceived Jason had a hold of John's belt as he attempted to rise. Through the battle, Jason always had John's six.

Jason pulled John's chair back as he stood up. Though John was lightheaded, he nodded to the gathering. Those assembled ignored the directive to stay quiet. Almost in unison, they rose from their places and started cheering. Carl stopped mid-sentence, rose with the other colonels, and joined the standing ovation John was receiving. Jason deftly switched his right hand into John's belt and came along his left side, which shielded John from the crowd as they walked off the stage to their right. Eric was there to assist Jason with John, who was getting paler with every step. The injuries and lack of decent sleep had caught up with him.

Greg Kellerman shouted to John, asking for just one more question. "Colonel Mogen, Machiavelli said that 'the end justifies the means.' Is that what happened here? Whatever it took or takes?"

John turned back around and stared at Kellerman. The room got very quiet. John had some adrenaline left after all. "Mr. Kellerman, do your homework! Machiavelli never said that in those words. He did say, 'For although the act condemns the doer, the end may justify him.' God and history will judge me, not any of you." Jason then made sure John headed out of the assembly and to his quarters.

The room erupted with cheers and applause again. Some of what John had said even surprised the other colonels, who had not discussed all the details of their plan. This thing had moved so fast! Carl reached over to look at the paper John had pulled out. The title at the top of the page was "How to Build a New Nation Under God," but the page was only full of bullet points without additional detail. Wow! John had 90 percent of it in his head. They needed a transcript of what he'd said pronto.

Lea spoke up. "Colonel Justine, I believe you were going to talk about the governors' meeting that is to take place in fifteen days."

"Yes—yes," Carl replied, even though his mind was still replaying the points John had just revealed. "We—the Air Force, that is—will be supplying transportation and lodging to the governors if they request it."

As Carl continued the interview, Jaylynn left her seat and headed backstage. She was stopped by an MP, who soon realized she was John's wife and let her continue. As she met Jason and Eric, she insisted, "Enough! He has done enough!"

Jason gently put his hand on her shoulder and said, "This is it, Jaylynn. He's done. We're taking him back to your room, and then tomorrow, we are traveling to the secure site so you can join your family. You'll both be able to rest and enjoy family for at least a week."

Of course, Jalynn lost it and started crying—yet again. John was seated in the front of the Polaris, and Jaylynn jumped in the back behind him. She noticed a trickle of blood had made its way down the right side of his face again. The Steri-Strips, which they were using instead of stitches, were holding and supposed to limit a scar, but the wound kept popping open and resealing as the blood coagulated.

As they were exiting the Polaris, wanting to get John settled in their quarters, an airman came running up to Jason. Out of breath, he panted, "Captain Wilder—we have a problem! We have Reaper launches from Creech. Five Reapers! We received intel from Buckley Space Command. We have fighters intercepting out of Luke. Four are headed our way, and one is headed southeast!"

Jason was incensed. "Creech was supposed to be in standdown!"

The airman replied, "We understand they received a presidential directive via the CIA to launch!"

"The president needed to stay out of this—he's toast now!" Jason yelled.

John stopped mid-step as he was nearing their door and knew they were not going to their quarters. He instantly realized they wouldn't be staying at Minot.

Jason quickly grasped the situation and was on his radio. "This is Captain Wilder. Do you copy?"

There was a quick reply from Daniel Rodriguez. Jason was barking orders over his radio. "Spin up the C-17 and get the rest of the men and the horses loaded in. I'll bring the colonels and the wives to you." Clicking off, he turned to the airman, who was awaiting further instructions. "Airman Jones—we need vehicles to the auditorium. We need to get the colonels and their wives to the C-17 stat!"

"Yes, sir!" Immediately, the airman began clicking on his radio. The evacuation plan was in action.

Jason turned to Jaylynn. "Gather your bags now and get back here! Eric will help you! Go!"

John looked up at Jason and, with tension showing in his face, asked, "Where is the Reaper going that is headed southeast, Jason? Is that…?"

Jason cut John off. "They couldn't have found the secure location—how could they have found it? Holy crap!"

Jason pulled out his SAT phone and punched in the number of the commander of the forces on the Mogollon Rim in Arizona. He ordered him to contact Truen Walsh at the Mogen house and activate the evacuation plan—immediately! The commander assured him he would activate the anti-missile battery protocol as well as the Phalanx Weapon System.

LAKE MARY ROAD – MOGOLLON RIM – CENTRAL ARIZONA

Truen Walsh was driving away from the Mogen family cabin in Arizona when he got the call. He spun the Polaris around so fast, the Marine in the right front seat nearly fell out of the UTV. As he drove up to the cabin, he was shouting at the young Marines who were on watch to get everyone out of the house immediately! As Truen slid the Polaris to a stop in front of the cabin, his mind went flying back to his time spent in Afghanistan, and his body went to a strange place. He couldn't fail this time!

Upon their initial arrival, the family had been briefed on the evacuation plan in case of invasion but had gotten very comfortable with the peace and quiet of the area. Dave was the first to react. Kayla and Jesse were having a conversation, and the kids were playing a video game with headsets on. Dave jumped up and started yelling at whoever would listen to him. "Get the kids now! Move! Move!"

Jack Ellis, who was camping next to the house and sleeping in the back of his pickup, had been sitting in a chair reading, but Truen had already grabbed him up. Now, he was in the bed of the Polaris with a "hang on tight!" order. Of course, Jack didn't sit down in the back but stood up.

MINOT AIR FORCE BASE – NORTH DAKOTA

Back at Minot, Jason was exchanging information with Colonel Justine. Carl was already on the SAT phone with a friendly at Luke AFB. His friend agreed to scramble two F-16s to find and intercept the Reaper headed for central Arizona.

After Colonel Justine's call, Luke AFB could not pick the Reapers up on radar but contacted Creech, wondering why they had not notified Luke AFB of a training mission to see what they would say. They responded it was classified.

Receiving a call back three minutes later, Carl was informed that his contact at Foss Field, where the F-16s were based, didn't know whether the F-16s would intercept in time. The South Dakota National Guard's F-16s were already heading south to cut off the four Reapers heading toward Minot, along with the four F-22s out of Luke. These aircraft had been given the CREF squawk code.

LAKE MARY ROAD – MOGOLLON RIM – CENTRAL ARIZONA

In Arizona, Kayla was running with Libby and jumped into the front seat of the Ranger, putting her niece in the middle between her and Truen. She had her evacuation bag with water, food, and a nine-millimeter pistol with extra ammo on the floor between her legs. She quickly asked Truen what happened.

"Attack by air—Reaper drone headed our way. Are you buckled in?" Not turning around, he yelled over his shoulder, "Dave, are the three of you buckled in?"

Dave responded with an affirmative, shouting, "Go, go, go!"

Truen slammed the accelerator to the floor and headed to the rock outcropping a mile into the forest. The outcropping concealed a small cave big enough for ten people and was perfect cover from an air attack. Kayla was comforting Libby, who had started to cry in the chaos. The two labs were following close behind the Ranger as the family went over a rise so fast that the Polaris took off airborne, and they all went zero G's as it dropped back to solid ground. Caleb squealed with delight as they took a sharp corner. Meanwhile, Libby was screaming louder and louder. Kayla was extremely impressed with Truen's driving skills. He could definitely maneuver this thing!

Truen was relieved once they reached the outcropping, and he began yelling before coming to a full stop. "Out! Out!" Jack Ellis jumped out of the back and immediately got back into the front right passenger seat and buckled up. Truen just shook his head and was ready to take off as one of the young Marines was trying to get buckled up in the back seat. Truen ordered the young Marine to get out and stay with the family. He floored the Polaris as soon as the Marine's feet hit the ground. Truen slid to a stop and picked up the dogs who had stopped in the middle of the road.

As he headed back to the cabin, Truen was shouting at Jack, "You're my responsibility, Jack—dammit!"

Jack did not hesitate to yell back. "I'm an old warrior. Young man, I'm eighty-two years old. Let me die fighting—dammit!"

Truen was almost back to the cabin to see if he could get some of the family's things out when he got a radio call.

Their radar operator had a target.

CHAPTER 62

CREECH AIR FORCE BASE
— COMMAND CENTER — NEVADA

The discussion amongst the Reaper pilots was ongoing as they flew to their individual targets. The officer in charge picked up on their discussion and told them to stop talking and stay on mission. But one of the pilots had had enough. He was piloting the drone that was heading for the Mogen safe house on the Mogollon Rim in Arizona. "Sir, I don't think we should be targeting a residence in our own country again. That's just not what we do."

The officer in charge was conflicted about the order himself. He understood it was a presidential directive, but he had been watching the colonels' press conference with interest.

The pilot broke into his thoughts. "With all due respect, sir, I would like to be relieved of duty."

The officer was rubbing his chin and pondering the situation but was snapped back into reality when the pilot reported, "Sir! Permission to abort mission. I'm on final now!" As the pilot shouted his request, a missile was spotted on his on-board radar.

As the pilot took evasive action and launched countermeasures, the officer in charge made a decision. "Break off—break off! Return to base!"

But it was too late; missiles were fired. The Reaper pilot went into a climbing turn as the countermeasures he had launched threw the missiles off course. He had nothing left as he had launched everything he had available. He had taken some hits from the Phalanx weapons when the Reaper had come into its range during his turn. He had damage but was still flying and on course to return to Creech. He was in the clear and almost to altitude when he detected another radar signature. "Sir—should I attempt to defend myself?"

The officer in charge shook his head. The Luke AFB F-16 was closing in, and as it made a high-speed turn and locked on its missile, the Reaper, with a full capacity of ordnance, exploded in a spectacular manner.

The officer in charge remarked, "You didn't have a chance against that F-16… Good job anyway."

One of the remaining Reaper pilots queried the officer in charge for any modification in their orders. The officer in charge silently grabbed one of them by the shoulders and turned her around to face him. The remaining three looked to him for instructions as he did this. The officer was shaking his head "no" as he gave the verbal order. "Okay, Gomez and Lewis. Go into engagement mode. Roden and Kappel, take evasive action and attempt to continue with the mission."

The four F-16 pilots immediately went into full dogfight mode. They'd never had an air combat mission against aircraft as slow as the Reapers before, but they made adjustments quickly. The threat from the Reaper drones was now neutralized. The commander at Creech AFB announced that they would no longer launch sorties against any targets within the borders of the United States.

CATTLE RANCH OUTSIDE GILLETTE, WYOMING

They were in the middle of a roundup when they heard the first deafening explosion. They had heard the resonance of jet aircraft before and hadn't thought much about it. They watched as the mass of what had once been an aircraft impacted the ground with another booming crash. The rancher and his son quickly left the roundup to the others and headed to the crash site in their side-by-side. They heard more explosions on their way.

The son, having served in Afghanistan, felt some angst bubble up. He had pulled the lever action 30-30 out of the scabbard that was mounted in the side-by-side and looked ready to shoot something—anything.

His dad immediately knew he was caught up in one of his PTSD episodes. "Randy—we're in Wyoming. We're not taking any enemy fire. It's alright, son."

At first, Randy looked at his dad with a blank stare, having no recollection of where he was or who was speaking to him. However, after a moment, life returned to his features. He blinked his eyes, shook his head, and took a deep breath. "It's the sounds, Dad—it's the sounds. Those jet fighters brought it all back. I know the sounds."

Randy's dad replied, "After we check this out, I'll drive to the top of the ridge and see if I can get any cell service. I'll call 911, and maybe we can get someone out here to check this out."

As they reached the crash site, a small grass fire was burning. So, they pulled out the shovels and began to put out the flames. As Randy went to the upwind side of the wreckage, he immediately recognized what had crashed. "Dad, this was a drone. A big drone—not a fighter."

MINOT AIR FORCE BASE – NORTH DAKOTA

Jason had just signed off the call where he'd received an updated sitrep on the four drones headed for Minot AFB. They had been cleanly blown out of the sky and were no longer a threat.

In the interim, Carl Justine had contacted the commander of Luke AFB, who had agreed with the assessment that Creech AFB, north of Las Vegas, had to be dealt with immediately. The commander understood the deep state was very much alive and continuing to carry out their objectives. It was time to stand down or be taken out. Five F-35s from Luke would be in the air within fifteen minutes.

Carl had finally gotten through to Creech and was in the process of making the commander understand the seriousness of the situation. "No, we're going to destroy all your hangars and anything that sits on the tarmac. No, we don't care if you want to stand down now. Get your people out of the hangars and into their bunkers. You have failed to honor the standdown order! No—just get your people out. You have fifteen minutes!"

Colonel Justine was done talking and slammed the receiver down with a bang. Just then, Jason rushed into the communication room to join him, and he was hot.

"Colonel—we have a leak! I already have my guys on it… We will find out where it's coming from. I have a gut feeling it might be someone here at Minot. Tell me, how well have we been screening those who are being briefed?"

Carl had a pained look on his face. "Not well enough—probably. We might have been infiltrated by a deep state mole. Or maybe the activity on the Mogollon Rim was noticed by someone?" Carl wasn't certain now. Looking around, he thought it might even be someone currently present.

"Carl, do you know everyone in this room?" Jason was pushing him now. "I don't want to get fooled again. Once was enough. Just like Torger—it might be someone we know."

Carl was deep in thought, but suddenly, his face lit up with relief. "The sign-in sheets, Jason—the sign-in sheets." He unobtrusively spoke so others could not overhear their conversation. "Let's look at them. The sentry has everyone sign in to enter the building."

Jason went over to the sentry on duty and asked to see the sign-in sheet. He had him identify everyone in the room, but there was one person missing: an Army captain whom Colonel Allan North had vouched for. Where was he?

The guard said he was outside taking a break. Jason noticed the captain had signed in and out twice that morning. Taking the log over to Carl, he pointed to the captain's name and then silently headed outside. They had stopped jamming cell phones since none of the Washington folk had cell phones now.

Jason observed the Army captain talking on his cell across the quad and stealthily walked up behind him. He listened in on the conversation the captain was having as he advanced toward him.

"No, sir, I didn't know they could react that quickly, and now they're going to take out Creech with F-35s coming out of Luke. Maybe we can get a company team loyal to our side into Arizona and approach on the ground?"

Jason had heard enough and was just about to explode. Dread radiated through him as he realized Kayla was in Arizona. He wouldn't let any injury come to her or her family, even if she hated him. Jason quickly ripped the captain's phone out of his grip with his left hand, spinning the captain around, and drew his .45 with his right hand. The last thing the captain saw this side of hell was the barrel of Jason's .45 staring him in the face.

After he called the MPs and explained what had transpired, no one questioned him further, knowing who he was. Jason's thoughts went to the phone grasped in his hand. Who was this traitor reporting to? This was one piece of information they needed to find out. He knew the phone was likely encrypted, but if they could attain the last number called, they would go forward from there.

Grabbing the captain's identification badge and wallet from his pants pocket, Jason headed out to find Colonel Allan North. First Torger, and now this Captain Crowder. *This whole thing is starting to smell,* Jason thought as he stormed back into the building, leaving the MPs to take care of the body.

Colonels North and Musgrave were settled in an enclosed room off to the right of the main communication area, making phone calls to military bases all over the country. They were updating all on the plan of action going forward.

Just during the short walk into the building, Jason's thinking had become clearer. He realized if North was involved in this, an attack at this site would take him out along with the rest of them. Taking a deep inhale, he decided not to confront him at this time.

The comms room was insulated and shielded, so the shot wouldn't have been heard inside. But the situation required him to inform his superiors about what had happened outside the building.

Carl Justine and Jason interrupted Colonel North mid-conversation. At Jason's urging, the colonel signed off his call and gave the men all of his attention. Jason reported what had occurred outside the building and, by the look on Colonel North's face, Jason gathered he'd had no idea there was a traitor operating in their midst.

"Sir, I had my phone in my top shirt pocket, and I decided to record the conversation before confronting the captain in case he said something incriminating. Would you like to hear it?"

Colonel North just stood before the men in shock and stared blankly at Jason. Time stood still as all remained motionless. Finally, North regained his speech and answered in the affirmative. At that time, Jason queued up the recording on his phone and played it for the colonels. Jason's recording didn't stop just at the conversation; it continued to play all the way through the blast of the shot.

If there had been any color left in Allan North's face before hearing the recording, it was almost now nonexistent. Carl Justine had known him for over ten years, and he knew something was amiss. "What is it, Allan? Why are you so shocked? Torger pulled another one on us, so don't blame yourself."

Allan looked at both of them, visibly shaken, and dropped his head in defeat. Finally, he spoke. "Captain Crowder is my niece's husband—her husband! What am I going to tell my niece? What the hell am I going to tell her?"

Carl placed his hand on Allan's shoulder and replied, "We're going to tell her that he was a casualty of the restoration. How he died and what he was doing will be classified."

Allan shook his head, excused himself, and escaped outside. Carl and Jason were left in silence.

Carl's attention turned back to Jason, and he could see how upset he was. Quietly, he said to the young warrior, "You did the right thing, Jason. Think about what would have happened. A court-martial and years in prison. A disgrace to his family for all time. You did the right thing."

Jason knew Carl was right, but he had to confess to Carl. "I did it out of rage, and that's unacceptable. I just can't let myself get out of control like that again."

"Jason, your instincts and actions were necessary. I have your back—just remember that." Carl was trying to be reassuring. "We have to move on. This restoration is relying on us. I have your next assignment, and I know you need a change of scenery also. I need you to get on the C-17 and escort John and Jaylynn to their next destination. Luke AFB aircraft are going to level Creech—it's probably happening right now. I think the Mogen family is safe in Arizona, but we're going to move them out of there just in case. The Blackhawks stationed at their location will transport them to Luke, where you will pick them up. You will refuel at Luke and then fly on to Dyess AFB, which is under our control now. John needs to be in Arlington next week anyway. You will have fighter support all the way. Got it?"

Jason smiled just a little. "Yes, sir. I'll get right on it! The C-17 is already spun up and mostly loaded."

When Jason entered the C-17, he saw all his men except Truen. The horses were in the trailers. John Mogen was in the front section, settled in a hospital bed where Jaylynn was attending to her man. He put in a call to Truen, who was all over it.

"Yes, sir," Truen said. "We are loading, and the Blackhawks are spinning up. The Apaches will be at our six. We hear the fighters out of Luke will be delivering high cover for us. We should be at Luke in an hour or less."

Jason was not happy about transporting John all over the place, but he had no choice. Before he ended his call, he thanked Truen and then headed up front to brief John and Jaylynn about their travel plans.

John was awake and alert, and he had some questions for Jason. "What happened back there? I understand we had an informant."

Jason relayed what had transpired and the information that the traitor was part of Colonel North's family. John and Jaylynn's eyes went wide open! Jason continued, "Thank God we got fighters in the air in time to intercept those drones. We still have some deep state operatives out there who might cause us trouble, but we're on our way to uncovering them. You'll be seeing your family in about three hours, so get some rest, you two."

Jaylynn grabbed Jason's arm. "Thanks for taking care of us and our family. I know you're upset with the shooting, but this is not your fault. We realized this was going to be a messy business. We love you, Jason—thank you."

Jason's eyes began to glisten. "You two have become very special to me also. Now, get some rest."

Jason had been focused on the task for so long, he felt he might not be able to move to the next level with Kayla. It wasn't that he didn't want to push ahead, but he was afraid he would miss something. He might not anticipate a threat to her or her family. He knew the FBI and CIA possessed teams that were extremely dangerous. His thoughts drifted to his future, and he wondered whether Kayla would be a part of this new, exciting time in his life and the life of the country. He was anxious about seeing Kayla again. He speculated about how hard a punch she could throw. Well, he would find out soon enough.

To pass the time as the C-17 rushed toward his destiny, Jason began reading through dispatches that had come in earlier in the day. The Joint Chiefs of Staff had released a statement stating the military of the United States was on alert but continued to stand down while they assessed the threat to the five cities. They had confirmed the devices were real, so Jason knew that meant the military was stuck for now, especially since one device was sitting in the middle of D.C. and the other was resting in front of the NSA building.

Shuffling through the stack, he picked up another dispatch that surprised him. Militias were traveling to the Dallas-Fort Worth area. Camps were being set up in parks and open spaces, especially in the Arlington area.

The next post covered the continuing exodus out of Los Angeles and San Francisco, both of which were still gridlocked with thousands of abandoned vehicles. While Jason had no respect for those in California who had let their state destroy their lives by a thousand little cuts, he still felt the fear that must be at its peak right now. Families with children were trying to get to safety and hating all of those involved in this restoration operation. for putting them in this position. There were reports of people being shot and others being run over by vehicles driving on the road's shoulder while passing stopped traffic. Emergency vehicles couldn't get to the injured. Jason could truly imagine the chaos.

Despite hearing the announcement they were descending into Luke AFB, Jason didn't sit down and buckle up but instead went over to where the horse trailers were stationed. The horses had already been through a lot and had to be stressed. Maybe he could give them a little comfort and calm them during the landing.

A contingent of Special Forces had been handpicked to travel with the colonels, who were taking up most of the jump seats as they taxied in. With their first officer, Jason was setting up the detail to guard the ramp area. Everyone in the aircraft acknowledged Jason was the one who was calling the shots. He had Eric and Daniel, two of his own team, guarding him at all times. Jason's man who'd been shot in the neck at Ellsworth, Zachariah Overgaard, was in a body bag in the medical pod morgue section. Guards were already stationed toward the front of the plane where the colonels were with their wives and where John and Jaylynn waited in the medical pod so John's wounds could be checked . The ramp was lowered. The fuel trucks were positioned so the C-17 could take on more fuel. They had to maintain a full fuel load in case they had to divert for any reason.

The rest of the Mogen family, along with Truen, would board soon. Meanwhile, Jack Ellis was heading back to Deadwood in his pickup. He wouldn't accept help or a detail to protect him.

Jason was calmly stroking his horse's nose and mentally going over the last day and a half of regrets. He had failed to keep John Mogen safe at the Ellsworth gate. He had summarily executed a traitor in anger with his .45, and he had held a dressing against Zach Overgaard's neck trying to keep him from bleeding to death. How was he going to tell Zach's family?

He snapped out of replaying the events as the Mogen family boarded. They were led by the two yellow labs, who were catching strokes from the troops as they ran past. Jason's heart rate jumped as he saw Lilly and Sadie dashing up to him with tails wagging, sniffing all the new smells. Then, he saw her. She was garnering a lot of attention from the men. As the family was boarding, he noticed she popped a peanut butter cup into her mouth and was holding another in her hand. When she spotted him, she took off running through the crowd toward him but was suddenly met by an unmovable wall of two former Navy SEALs, who stepped between her and Jason.

She was flustered. "Jason, don't they remember who I am? Please tell them to let me through."

Jason was chuckling as she fought to get past them. "Let her through, guys—it's alright. If she hits me, I deserve it, so stand down."

She ran the last ten feet toward Jason, leaping up as she wrapped her long, slender but powerful legs around him, and started to passionately kiss him. It was instant. He tasted the peanut butter and chocolate and got a high, but that wasn't the only thing that got high as they kissed. That moment in time was grander than they had hoped it would be. Nothing they could have possibly imagined compared.

Kayla oozed back to earth, ending the kiss—for now. She gazed up at Jason, her face shining with a joy he had never witnessed in her. Beaming, she said, "Hey, soldier—you want a peanut butter cup?"

He adored her playfulness. "You know I do, little girl!"

By now, the occupants still on the plane were trying to get a look at the two as the catcalls and hoorahs filled the fuselage. A first kiss usually didn't happen in the presence of over one hundred Special Forces personnel!

Jason was consuming the second peanut butter cup as Kayla cuddled up and began French kissing him again. Chocolate, peanut butter, and two tongues. It just didn't get any better than this, even though he was extremely lightheaded and thought he was going to lose it before it really started. How did she realize he'd love all of this?

She stopped long enough to whisper in his ear, "Is there a bathroom on this plane? I'm a little wet." She again continued to lick bits of chocolate off his chin.

Jason's body tingled all over as she uttered her need. He then noted, "I can tell you were a barrel racer!"

Kayla giggled.

The moment was interrupted by a thundering of applause. Virtually everyone on the plane was clapping and cheering. Even Jaylynn, who had come out of the medical pod to greet her family, witnessed the scene and broke into an immense smile. She was elated to see the two of them kissing!

Sadie and Lilly were the first to find Jay and nearly wiggled out of their bodies. She had missed the playfulness of the two four-legged members of her family.

When the rest of the family caught up with her, Jaylynn began hugging and crying and laughing all over again. John was now up and joined the reunion as well. He was feeling better, even though his shoulder had a lot of healing to do. But for now, the last of his adrenaline was kicking in. The swelling on the right side of his face had receded a little, but the purple along with several shades of red looked dreadful. His face just felt tight, but he beamed with a happiness he hadn't felt for quite a while.

Of course, a trickle of blood traveled down his right cheek because of that smile. Noticing the blood, John's granddaughter, Libby, became very upset. "Papa—what happened to your face? You're bleeding, Papa!"

Jessica bent down so she could look her daughter directly in her eyes and started to explain things. Caleb quietly came up to his papa and grabbed ahold of his hand. John leaned over to hug him, and Caleb's eyes were glistening. Softly, he spoke. "I'm glad you're okay, Papa. We were very worried about you, and I prayed for you all the time because Mom said I should."

"I'm fine now, Caleb. Thank you for praying for me and Nana. Nana and I are going to live near you for a while."

Caleb was starting to cry a little now. "Papa, you lost your house, but you can stay with us 'til you get a new one!"

Now, John was tearing up and hugging his grandson as he replied, "We'll do that, Cabe. We'll stay with you for a while."

Of course, Jaylynn started to cry. Finally, some happy tears were coming. Her family was all together once again, and they all were safe for the moment. Plus, John's folks were both gone, but Jaylynn's parents had been picked up and were being transported to Arlington to join the family.

Dave observed John as he stood back up and took in the moan as it quietly escaped from his father-in-law. "What now, John?" Dave inquired. "What are your plans?"

Everyone around the circle silently waited as John wiped away his own tears.

Jason immediately broke in. "Maybe the entire plane needs to hear this, John. If you'd like, we can put it over the loudspeaker so we can all hear." Jason nodded to John as if to say, "It's your show."

"Jason, I've given enough speeches—these guys don't need to hear me again." But Jason's look told John he needed to do this one more time. With a sigh, he walked slowly over to a mic so he could talk to the assembly.

Jason clicked on the mic. "Ladies and gentlemen—attention please. Colonel John Mogen would like to address all of you for just a moment."

John rolled his eyes as someone in the C-17 yelled out "Mogen for president!" as loud as they could. That started the chant, "Mogen for president—Mogen for president!" The colonels and their wives were taken by surprise by this impromptu demonstration of support for John. So, they listened intently to what the first president of the Western Southern Alliance of States would say. The people had spoken.

John looked at Jaylynn and finally smiled, then winced as the wound on his face reminded him it was still there. John didn't need to ponder what to say, and of course, it would be from the heart.

"Let's pray... All-powerful and all-knowing Heavenly Father, it's only by Your divine providence we are here, now, in this place—to rebuild Your shining city on a hill. Your hand was upon us as we endeavored to right this ship. To turn back to You. To create a nation *under God* again. Please continue to bless us as we move forward. Thank you for all the brave men and women who were…who…" John started to vapor lock as he did every time he thought of all those who had believed and helped to make the restoration a reality. "…who were gladly willing to sacrifice their lives for our beloved republic. Lord, be with us as we carry on. In Your Son's name we pray—Amen.

"Again, I thank all of you who stand shoulder to shoulder with us, come what may. You must remember… You are not traitors or terrorists—you are patriots. History will remember us as those who restored this nation—who turned it away from those who would take this nation down a path to socialist and communist destruction. We will rise as a nation under God! A nation whose government protects individual rights, protects our national security including borders, and provides a place for business to thrive—for dreams to come true for those willing to work for those dreams.

"When we land in Texas, we will begin the process of forming a new nation. We'll put together a government as small as possible and with constraints that will never allow a Fedzilla to be spawned ever again. John Adams said our government will only work for moral and religious people, and this is what we will teach our children, and this is how we will pick our representatives. We will teach the children the Bible and the founding documents. We'll make sure our children know we are unique in world history, and we are *exceptional!* We will succeed! Let's make our founding fathers proud! Let's go build our Western Southern Alliance of States as free men and free women!"

A shout went up in the cargo bay—so deafening, it was shocking. Jaylynn was so proud of her man as tears rolled down her cheeks. It seemed her tears had bubbled up easily since they'd hit the Ellsworth gate! Build a nation? Wow!

Jay's attention was drawn back to her husband. She could see him wincing as he was being congratulated vigorously and shaking hands with the crowd around him, although he was still smiling. "Okay, everybody," Jaylynn called out. "John needs to rest up before we land in Dallas. Please excuse us and thank you for your support."

As they stepped back into the medical pod, she turned to her husband of thirty-five years and quietly asked, "John, do you know how to build a nation from scratch?"

He smiled at his beautiful wife and tried to hide the pain he was in. "We don't have to do it from scratch. We already have a fantastic template; we just need to tighten it up in places. The new borders will be a challenge. But remember the Scripture we had on our wall at home? *Psalm 1:3: He shall be like a tree. Planted by the rivers of water, that brings forth its fruit in season, whose leaf shall not wither. And whatever He does shall prosper.* Remember what the fourth verse says? *But the ungodly are not so, but are like the chaff which the wind drives away.* We'll take it one day at a time. We have that time. Don't they have to rebuild our place in the Black Hills?"

As he studied Jaylynn, he wasn't convinced she was as sure.

"John," she said. "You know that the deep state won't go down easy. We're still in danger, and you know it."

John knew she was right. He pulled her close as best he could. "God is on our side, Jay. He will lead us and protect us for as long as He wills."

She responded, "I pray it's God's will we grow old together after this is all over. Now rest, my love. We have a nation to build. Rest."

CAPITAL OF THE WESTERN SOUTHERN ALLIANCE OF STATES – ARLINGTON, TEXAS

"**M**r. President, your first appointment is here. Are you ready for them?"

"Sure, Eric—send them in." Acting Western Southern Alliance president John Mogen had never worked harder in his life. God had challenged him and Jaylynn in amazing ways during the last three months. He had agreed to be *acting* president until their home in the Black Hills was rebuilt so they could retire again, and an election could be set up in a way that was secure from fraud.

The governors of East Oregon and East California, as well as the acting governor of the state of Jefferson, were ushered in. John had stopped using the sling on his right arm, even though his shoulder was still extremely sore. He observed the exchanged glances between his guests as they noticed the discoloration on the right side of his face from the round that had plowed its way through his face and right ear.

"Welcome, ladies and gentlemen. Please, please sit down." John was already standing at the eighty-five-inch interactive screen installed in his office for just this purpose. He had a map of the state of Jefferson pulled up and divided into the counties voted on by the residents. The election results had been forwarded to the capital here in Arlington. The numbers had been an overwhelming win for the state of Jefferson. John touched the screen in the lower right, and the voting results populated inside the boundaries of each county.

"Okay—the people have spoken. The state of Jefferson was overwhelmingly approved by the citizens of the counties involved. As the governors of East California and East Oregon, you have the responsibility to run your states in a way so more counties will not want to leave you for the state of Jefferson. I realize you will be losing land and tax base, but you just have to accept it.

"The state of Jefferson has had an existence of sorts since 1941, so we are talking about two or three generations working toward this moment. Lives have already been lost in this fight. I have sent a clear message to the governors of the states of Coastal California and Coastal Oregon that, if we have to, we will move in with troops if they attempt to use state troopers or rogue National Guard units to defend old borders. I'm proud of the state of Jefferson's militia for defending their borders, even if it was a bit premature.

"While I'm the commander in chief of the Armed Forces, I will not do things by executive order. As you know, a vote in the WSA Congress will take place tomorrow. The votes from the counties are there for approval of the state of Jefferson, but each one of you will be allowed to state your case before Congress. If it is approved, I will sign it. Any questions?"

The acting governor of the state of Jefferson, Katie McFarland, was smiling so widely that her face was about to break. "Thank you so much, Mr. President. My grandfather was one of the founding members. They first met to discuss the state of Jefferson in 1941, and my family has never given up on the dream of our own state. Thank you—thank you!"

John was a little taken aback. "You're welcome." Then, he moved on to the next subject. "Now, Governor Tucker, you're aware more counties in East California are seeking to join the state of Jefferson? You need to go back and visit each county and convince them East California will be nothing like the last messed-up state you had."

Governor Tucker was quick with his response. "I understand that, Mr. President—I've already scheduled meetings with those counties.

They need to hear that our desires and goals for our state match those of the state of Jefferson." They shook hands, and Eric ushered them out.

As John was looking at his calendar on his tablet, Jason Wilder entered the room. "John, we received a copy of a letter from the Social Security Administration to someone in Idaho." Jason handed the letter to John. It stated all payments to citizens in the WSA would be ending by month's end!

John was livid. "We made an agreement to maintain the status quo for one year while we transitioned! What department sent this? Who signed it? Who sent this? Here it is…Stockton. Give me a minute to think."

At that moment, Jaylynn Mogen walked into John's office. They had a date for lunch in just a few minutes.

"Give me a minute, Jay," said John distractedly. "We have a big problem with a bureaucrat in D.C. He's trying to shut off Social Security payments before we're ready to make the switch to the WSA funding!"

Jaylynn was now pondering the issue along with John and Jason. She was first to break the silence. "John, don't we have control of the Navy?"

"Yes, Jay, but we can't exactly attack them."

"No, John—I understand that. But we can prevent delivery of any crude oil to the blue state refineries. Can we shut down the diesel and gasoline shipments to all those states? Shut down the pipelines. We can probably grind this to a stop if we do that, can't we?"

John was gazing at Jay with pride and then glanced at Jason, who was smiling. "I love you, Jay! Come here!" As John embraced her, he asked Jason to tell Kayla (the WSA press secretary) to draft a statement that would be released. "Give this Stockton guy twenty-four hours to rescind his directive or face the wrath of the citizens of the blue states when they have no fuel to heat their homes or fill their vehicles and they have to walk everywhere. Tell Kayla her mother will help with the specifics of crude embargoes and pipeline shutdowns. We control the energy system, and the WSA will be energy independent for sure!" Taking his wife by the hand and giving it a quick squeeze, John asked, "Where are we going to lunch?"

"We're going to Saltgrass Steakhouse—meeting Carl and Mary Ann!" John was so ready to be out of the office for a while. "Let's go, John—the detail is waiting for us!" Jay was so pushy.

"I miss the Black Hills, Jay—the smell of the pines."

"Yes, John—we just have to wait for the house to get rebuilt. I miss it too. Maybe you can sneak out early so we can go ride the horses?"

John laughed. "You know I can't sneak anywhere these days. As soon as I get done with my last meeting about the proposed state of Absaroka, I'll try to get away."

"What on earth is the state of Absaroka?" Jay was lost on this one.

John had heard of it as a boy growing up in northeast Wyoming. "It's a collection of counties from northern Wyoming, western South Dakota, and southeastern Montana. The Wyoming group wants Sheridan as the capital, and the South Dakota group wants Rapid City as the capital. I say they don't need to do this at all because the WSA will protect their interests, but I still need to listen to them. Some of the ranching families involved in this go back to the 1880s."

He had decided to honor all requests for realignments for the people's sake. The map of the WSA was still in a state of flux, but they had to finalize the preliminary borders as quickly as possible.

Before taking lunch with his loving wife, John glanced at his afternoon appointments. It looked like the first one was with representatives from the Wexit group out of Canada. The western provinces were desperate to become part of the WSA. John had already agreed in principle to this, and the western Canadians had already held elections. The only thing left to do was shut down the border points of entry. If that union happened, they already had a problem brewing because some of the banished representatives and senators now lived in their territory. People would want to shoot them for sure.

Another issue popping up daily was from the two delegations from China (the PRC) and Taiwan and one from Russia, who continually asked for an audience. For some reason, they didn't understand the word "no." Even though the new State Department was still forming, this fell on their doorstep. Since the new State Department wouldn't be like what they'd left back in Washington, D.C., John would have to talk to these delegations, but only after some special intel had been completed.

John's main concern was keeping track of the election preparation and making sure it stayed on track. He was looking forward to stepping down as acting president of the WSA. Communications he received from all over the new country continually begged him to run for the position. However, he was covertly preparing to endorse Jason Wilder as the candidate for the Patriot Party, even if he wasn't old enough. He and Kayla would make a great first couple.

As their wedding date drew nearer, Jaylynn was in full swing as their wedding planner. John loved her detailed mind, which allowed him to not worry about the particulars and enjoy the union of his daughter and Jason (whom he had become very close to these past months).

As they headed out of the building for lunch, another group of protestors with signs reading *"REMOVE THE NUKES"* were stationed at the entrance of the building, and they began shouting at them. John couldn't tell them they planned on doing just that within the week.

Jaylynn studied John's face as he began praying before lunch. He had aged quickly in the last few months—adding some gray hairs. He looked weary. She silently thanked God for allowing her to traverse this speck of time on earth with this great man, this strong man, this amazing husband, father, and acting president. As he finished praying, he looked at her—at the tears streaming down her face—and asked, "What, Jay? What is it?"

"I just love you, John—I just love you." As he gazed at her across the table, he saw a smile break through her tears. Their lives would never be the same, but—the Lord willing—they would again sit on their porch in the Black Hills, dogs at their feet, watching amazing sunsets as the wind whispered to them through the pine trees. They would then say, "This is where we belong—this is home."

There was no word in the Hebrew language for retirement. John and Jaylynn would come to understand this. No one had ever attempted to build a true Christian nation. Isn't that what they'd started out as? What did it really look like? How did one do it and stay within Biblical principles? Was it even possible? They were already getting blowback. Could they hold it together? Was their vision…God's vision? Their republic had been destroyed by those led by the Evil One. Could they somehow implement a government and follow John Adams's advice that "our Constitution was made only for religious and moral people"? The original founders knew they needed to write a document with an understanding of *Jeremiah 17:9*: *"The heart is deceitful above all things and desperately wicked; who can know it?"* How could they reintegrate religious studies successfully? How would they require elected officials to be moral and religious? How would they get out of this continuous campaign cycle?

John had studied the British system, which didn't limit contributions but limited how much could be spent on a campaign and didn't allow campaign ads on television but gave candidates timeslots of a few minutes per day. Their campaigning period was twenty-five working days or about five weeks. He was leaning toward this defined system. Also, if they wanted moral and religious representatives, how would they test them? John was studying a book by Fergus M. Bordewich called *The First Congress*. If they were going to shut down the nation and reboot it with a new name, he had to get a plan together to figure out how they would do it. Looking back to go forward.

Congress had been completely corrupted and infiltrated. He was looking at ways to build in some integrity, starting with who got elected and then putting rules in place to prevent a Congress that was awash in money. He was working on how to combat professional lobbyists, which would just move their shops to Texas. John knew he would get some flak, but he decided to put forth a proposal to provide housing for the legislators and pay significantly higher salaries to help them be less tempted. Pragmatism over idealism might work.

The future was bringing John and Jaylynn a challenge in building a nation that would be held up as the model moving forward—or maybe it would fall flat on its face and deteriorate as the hounds of Satan tore it apart before it even got started. *God help us as we figure out how to build a strong Christian nation!*

ACKNOWLEDGMENTS

M y beautiful wife, Susan, who listened to my complaints about our country's failure to follow the United States Constitution and encouraged me to put pen to paper. She spent hours straightening out my stream of consciousness and convoluted syntax of a story.

My friend Gary Burris, an Air Force veteran and coworker, who helped me coalesce my ideas and was a beta reader for me.

My friends Don and B.J. Voakes and Dan Tucker who gave me great feedback.

My old fellow linebacker friend who is no longer with us—Jack Elbert. His life was a story of redemption, as he helped so many as a sponsor in AA. He was a bigger-than-life character and became a character in this book.

The men in the Tuesday morning Bible study who have followed and encouraged me through this process.

Andy Symonds and the entire staff of Ballast Books who led this novice through the publishing process with professionalism, patience, and positive reinforcement.

For all the God-fearing patriots out there who love this country, love the Lord, and hope for restoration every day. We all thank God for this nation.